THE IMMORTAL MARK

THE COMPLETE SERIES

AMY SPARLING

THE IMMORTAL MARK

BOOK ONE

Copyright © 2019 by Amy Sparling

All rights reserved.

First Edition January 31, 2017

Cover image from Deposit Photos

Typography from FontSquirrel.com

No part of this book may be reproduced in any form or by any electronic or mechanical means, including information storage and retrieval systems, without written permission from the author, except for the use of brief quotations in a book review.

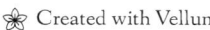 Created with Vellum

ONE

THE NAME *CARA* IS SCRIBBLED ON THE SIDE OF MY GRANDE ICED COFFEE with milk and whipped cream. I reach for it on the pickup counter, unable to hide the little smile that spears on my lips because they finally spelled my name right. Starbucks isn't a luxury a girl like me can afford very often, and I probably only came here four times in the last year, but they've never spelled my name right until now.

I've seen Care-a and Kara and Karra, but never Cara before now. Which is weird because my name isn't all that unusual. Maybe the baristas can tell I'm a boring person with a boring life, so their misspelling of my name is a way to invite me out of my shell, to turn into someone worthy of a name with a hyphen in it.

Or maybe they're just lazy.

I turn away from the crowd of teenage girls who have just huddled up next to me while they wait for their drink orders. They're probably sixteen or so, but I already feel disconnected from them, despite knowing we were probably both in Sterling High School just a few weeks ago. I'm not like them; I guess I never have been. Mrs. Youngblood used to tell me I was an *old soul*. The kind of kid who seemed much older than her real age because I was quiet and kept to myself and bothered to think about life in ways that my peers didn't. She'd mention it almost once a day, and it really annoyed me. I was just quiet. I wasn't old. I wasn't channeling the spirit of a wise elderly monk. Luckily, that foster parent didn't last long.

I take a sip of my coffee and send a text to my best friend, Riley.

Ready?

I stand next to a shelf displaying stainless steel coffee mugs while I wait for her reply.

No! I need another hour!

My thumbs ache to fly across the phone screen, telling her it's been three hours since she originally told me it'd only take forty-five minutes. This is boring. I'm spending the entire day collecting free stuff by myself. What's fun about that?

Riley must be able to read my thoughts because my phone lights up with another text.

Sorry! I'm hurrying! Xoxo

With a sigh, I sink into a chair at the back corner of the coffee shop. I take a long sip from my drink and my stomach begins to hurt. It had seemed like a good idea when I thought of it months ago. Sign up for every store loyalty card that gives free stuff on your birthday, then collect all the awesomeness as a free present to yourself on the one glorious day a year you get to claim as your own.

Today I am eighteen.

I've had a free strawberry banana smoothie, a free turkey and swiss sandwich on wheat bread at my favorite sandwich shop, a free cup of frozen yogurt, and now this free coffee. Seeing as how I don't eat that much in an entire day on most days, I probably shouldn't have had it all in the last two hours.

I push the coffee aside and stare out the window. This Starbucks is right on the boardwalk in Sterling. We're a coastal Texas town with a beautiful view of the Gulf of Mexico, which is to say, not a very beautiful view at all. Our ocean water is brown and salty, overflowing with nasty bits of seaweed that they occasionally bulldoze into piles on the beach. Our beaches are littered with broken shells and old cigarette butts, and our lifeguards, when they bother to show up, aren't even attractive, which pretty much shatters every stereotype ever of beach lifeguards.

But this scrappy little town is my home. I was born here, and I'll probably die here, and now I'm turning eighteen here. Unfortunately, my best friend isn't at my side, and now I have a stomachache, so this birthday sucks.

Okay, maybe that's a little dramatic. Riley *will* be at my side, just after she's done doing whatever she's doing to celebrate my birthday. When she turned eighteen two months ago, we snuck into the movie theaters to watch her favorite actor walk around shirtless in one of those stupid college life comedies that are mostly trashy humor and not exactly real comedy. After, we celebrated her legality by buying some scratch off lottery tickets, which only won two dollars. Then we went back to my Uncle Will's house and ate the cake I'd baked for her and binged Netflix until dawn. I'd love to see if Mrs. Youngblood would still call me an old soul after watching me eat half an entire sheet cake and then fall asleep on the floor in front of the TV.

A few minutes go by and I'm feeling stupid sitting here alone. Everyone else here is alone too, but they have laptops as companions and they all seem heavily focused on their work. I have nothing but a cheap prepaid cell phone and this half empty coffee that's making my stomach hurt. I toss it in the trash and head back outside, the salty air filling my lungs as I turn north and start walking back to Uncle Will's house.

It's a nice day outside. Hot and a little humid, but the sun shines brightly overhead, sparkling down on the ocean. Our waves are never surfing quality, but surfers are out there anyhow, trying to catch something that's so small it collapses back into the ocean the second it begins to look like a real wave.

I watch the summer tourists hanging out, enjoying their vacation in their brightly colored beach towels, brand new ice chests and umbrellas stabbed into the sand. I close my eyes and breathe in the smell of the ocean, tinted with the coconut scent of sunscreen and a hint of freshly baked bread at the bakery down the boardwalk.

Sterling is a good place to live. Maybe not the best, but it's good. I am a legal adult now, and although I have no desire to buy a cigar and gamble and any other things I'm legally allowed to do, I am old enough to think about my future. With the noose of high school behind me, everything is in front of me. Sometimes it doesn't feel like that. Sometimes the crushing weight of reality claws its way into my mind, telling me that I'll never get into college because I'm broke, I'll never be loved because I never have been, and I'll never amount to anything but some loser's second wife, and that's only if I get lucky.

But right now, in this very moment, I'm breathing in salty air and the wind is whipping my hair all around, and the ocean is so huge and impossibly vast, and I just have a good feeling about things. I'll get a better job than the part time joke that I currently have at the Surf n' Shop. I'll get a place of my own with Riley and we'll make something of our lives. Everything isn't hopeless. Not on a day like today.

UNCLE WILL's house is a one bedroom brick bungalow that was painted lime green in the seventies and hasn't been updated since then. He lives two blocks from the sea, in what used to be an old neighborhood filled with old people, but now more and more houses are being sold and then remodeled into something marvelous. Some of them are even demolished to the ground and rebuilt. But Uncle Will's house is still here, the same as always.

I skip up the four stairs to the front door and grab the pink envelopes stuck in the mail slot on my way inside. There's a weird stench of burnt sausage in the house. I don't know why Uncle Will even bothers cooking when he's so terrible at it.

"I'm home," I call out as I set the mail on the coffee table and turn to head to my room. *Home* is a relative term, as is my bedroom. I've lived here six years, but the room I sleep in hardly looks any different than it did when I arrived. It's technically a formal living room, with two doors. One leads to the kitchen and is closed off with a folding accordion door, and the other is an archway that leads into the hallway. You can't close it off because there's no real door, but after the one time my uncle accidentally walked in on me in my underwear when I was thirteen, we've had a sheet thumbtacked into the wall to give me some privacy.

I sleep on a fold out couch that I'm too lazy to fold out, and my clothes are kept in a dresser we picked up at a garage sale. I would kill for my own closet so my clothes don't get so wrinkly, but when I remember that some people like Riley don't even get a dresser, I shut up and count my blessings.

"Cara, is that you?" Uncle Will's voice is booming and deep, like a lumberjack or maybe a professional wrestler. Unfortunately for him, he's actually kind of short, is balding, and has a beer gut that could put him in the running for best Santa Claus impersonator.

I hear the screen door slam closed as Uncle Will enters in through the back yard. "Yes, I'm here," I call back.

"Can you come in here for a second?"

I drop my purse on the couch bed and push open the accordion door that leads to the kitchen.

"What's up?"

Uncle Will smiles at me from his place at the kitchen table. He's wearing a crisp new button up shirt, navy blue to match his eyes. It's a drastic change from the worn out T-shirts he usually wears, but getting a new girlfriend will do that to you I guess. This isn't the first thing Rachael has changed about him. He's also wearing contacts instead of his old wire frame glasses.

"Happy birthday," he says, his lips creasing into a hesitant but caring smile. He holds out a pale yellow envelope, the kind shaped like a greeting card.

I smile and take the card. "Thank you."

"I haven't seen Riley yet," he says, clearing his throat. "I thought you two were doing something for your birthday?"

"We are, but she's not ready." I give him this look that says *you know how Riley is,* and he nods because he does know. I open the envelope and read the birthday wish on the card he selected for me. It has butterflies on the cover, flocked with glitter and a sweet message about how I am a niece he is proud of.

Inside is a twenty dollar bill. "Thank you," I say closing the card. "You didn't have to do this, you know."

Uncle Will's painting business has been struggling lately, so I feel immensely guilty about him giving me money. He shrugs away my words and extends a hand toward the chair across from him. "Can you sit down for a minute?"

My stomach tightens, feeling ten times worse than it did when I ate too much food and chased it down with coffee. Uncle Will usually keeps to himself. He doesn't ever ask me to sit with him unless there's food on the table and he's offering to share it with me. The twitch in his brow and the crease above his lips tells me this isn't a fun chat about having a happy birthday.

The chair groans as I drag it across the floor and I slowly sit down, nausea rising in my stomach.

"I have some—uh—bad news, Cara." Uncle Will stares at his hands, which are intertwined on the kitchen table, his knuckles white with worry.

A lump rises in my throat as I realize this is the kind of moment where people tell you they're dying of cancer. "What is it?"

"I'm going bankrupt." He says it all matter-of-factly, like maybe it took him a while to admit it to himself but now that he has, he can admit it to anyone. My eyes dart to the birthday card in my hands, the twenty bucks he needs more than me.

"No—" he says, holding out his hand. "That money is yours. I can spare it," he says with a chuckle. "But I can't keep my business going any longer. No one wants their house painted by the little guy anymore. It's all corporations with dozens of guys who can paint anything in an hour instead of one guy taking two days." He shakes his head, the disgust over big corporations clear on his face. "I just can't sustain it anymore. Rachael is helping me file for bankruptcy."

"I'm so sorry," I say. "That's...awful."

He nods, and the worry lines in his forehead deepen. "Cara, I'm losing the house."

Maybe I'm just an idiot, but the words don't really hit me at first, probably because my brain has realized the reality of this situation long before I have. "What do you mean?" I say, looking around. The house seems fine to me.

"I can't pay the mortgage anymore. I'm behind two months." He sighs, a heavy drawn out confession. "They're foreclosing on me, and I'm losing it. I'm going to move in with Rachael, but she has a two bedroom apartment and a son she gets every other week so—" He swallows, and I watch his Adam's apple bob, feel the waves of regret rolling off him. He doesn't want to say it, he doesn't want to tell me this unbelievably bad news.

So I say it for him. "I can't go with you."

His lips flatten. "Uh, no you can't, Cara. I'm sorry."

"I understand." That lump in my throat is threatening to cut off my airway. Riley and I are already planning to move out, but we're nowhere close to being able to afford our own place. I look up at my uncle. "When?"

"A month. Maybe less, but, Cara, I'm not going to leave you on the streets or anything. We can stay in this house as long as we can. I've been reading about squatter's rights and a lot of times if you just refuse to leave, they can't evict you for some time, so—"

"It's okay," I say, cutting him off. There's a thin line of sweat on his forehead and I suddenly feel like I should be comforting him even though he's the one with the girlfriend to live with and I have nothing. "You've given me a home as long as you could," I say, forcing a smile. "I'll figure something out."

"I'm here for you in any way I can," he says. His shoulders don't seem as tight anymore, but I can tell he still feels horrible. "I'm going to sell off all this furniture since we don't need it at Rachel's and I'll give you some of the money, okay? I'll help you find a place. Maybe renting a room with some college kids or something."

I nod, even though sharing a house with people I don't know sounds like a freaking nightmare. "Thanks."

My smile is tight, but I stand up, pressing my birthday card to my chest. "I'll be fine, Uncle Will."

And I almost mean it when I say, "Don't worry about me. I'll figure it out."

TWO

I don't remember much of my mom. That's kind of a lie...I remember things. But I don't allow myself to remember them. I don't actively reminisce over those days when I was a daughter and she was a mother. Some people are supposed to be there for you and they let you down. That's all there is to it. Thinking back to the past just seems so pointless. It's gone, it's over. It happened before and remembering it now won't do a damn thing.

As I sit on my couch bed in the room that's not really a bedroom but has been all I've had for the last six years, I find my thoughts drifting to the woman with sunken in cheeks and wrinkles around her eyes. My mother had white blonde hair like mine that she kept tied into a tight bun on the top of her head because she never had time to fix it between working at the gas station, hooking up with men she'd bring home for one or two nights, and scouring the town for drugs.

Her name is Jenny Blackwell and she's Uncle Will's younger sister. But just like how she's not really my mom anymore, she's not really his sister anymore, either. I was five years old when a police officer approached me at the McDonald's on forty-second street and asked if he could sit down. He was a cop and I was scared of cops. I had seen men in uniforms like his take my mom's friends away in the back of their cop cars and then we'd never see them again. I'd seen Mom's eyes widen in fear when we'd see a cop on a street corner, and she'd make us turn the other way even if we weren't going that way. I was scared of this cop, but I also knew they could arrest me, so I said yes, he could sit with me. I didn't want to disappear and never come back like the drug addicts who lived in our cheap apartments, but in a way that's kind of what I did. I talked to the officer and then I disappeared and I never went back that McDonald's again.

He asked me about my mom and why I was alone. I told him I was always alone here at the McDonald's, but it turned out he already knew all about it. The manager had called the police on me because they felt that my mom leaving me there eight hours a day wasn't very good parenting. I thought it was okay. She gave me money for food and there was a playground with slides and a ball pit and usually there were some other kids I could play with until their parents took them home. No one else stayed as long as I did.

The cop did not think that was okay.

I was taken away and placed into the foster care system with other kids who spent most of their days screaming and throwing tantrums because they wanted to go back home to their parents. I wasn't like them. I didn't really care if I went back with my mom. Here, I had food all the time and hot showers and a bed that had clean sheets to sleep on. A few years into it though, and I could see why the other kids yelled. I had grown to hate foster care. I wanted out. I traveled from foster home to foster home, always being treated fairly nicely but never like a real family member. One time I'd spent six months with this family who had three kids of their own and two foster kids including me. They were all nice and we all got along really well. No one ever fought or yelled. And then their grandparents came over to visit and my foster parents were taking photos of everyone. My foster mom, Shelly, held out her camera and said, "Okay, now let's get a picture of the real kids with Grandma and Grandpa."

She didn't say it in a mean way, but it cut me to the core. I wasn't her real kid. I wasn't worthy of a photo because they last forever. And I wasn't forever.

I met Riley at a counselor meeting at school one day. The counselor had called us in because we were both foster kids and she wanted to give us one of those feel-good talks about how we're welcome to talk to her anytime we wanted. But we never wanted to.

Riley and I became instant best friends. We met other kids at school and soon realized that their versions of Christmas and birthdays were not at all like our versions. From the age of nine to twelve, I stayed at Good Grace Shelter, a group home for kids like me. Riley was there, too. Here, we plotted our future together. How we'd break out of poverty and marry nice men with fancy cars and parents who would like us. We'd get good jobs (I'd be a pastry chef and Riley would be a kindergarten teacher) and we'd have money to buy our kids lots of presents and brand name clothing. Our husbands would love us and they would have big extended families who loved us too. It would be perfect.

Things changed a little bit when my mom went to prison for drugs and writing hot checks and stealing a car with her boyfriend. I hadn't heard from her in years so I didn't care, but somehow my uncle found out that I was in a group home instead of living with my mom. I didn't really remember him but he said we had met a few times when I was a toddler before Mom's drug habit got really bad and she stopped coming around. He said she must have been ashamed of her addiction because she hid us from the rest of the family. He felt compelled to rescue me from the group home and when he said I could have

THE IMMORTAL MARK

my own room at his house, I felt compelled to let him even though he was a stranger to me.

Riley had to stay behind. She doesn't have parents at all; they're both dead. But we still went to school together and the Good Grace Shepard people were really nice and let me come visit her and even have sleepovers sometimes. Once Riley turned sixteen, she was allowed to sleep over at my house so long as her grades were passing and she hadn't gotten into trouble at the home. When she turned eighteen two months ago, they gave her six months to get out. She has a stack of papers to fill out to sign up for government benefits, but Riley doesn't want that. I don't want it either. We want to take care of ourselves.

Over the years, our dreams haven't changed. We're going to get out of this. I believe it with all that I have, because I can't bear the idea of failing. I won't become like my mother. I won't have kids unless I can afford them. I won't dive into drugs and never resurface. I will be better than that.

Unfortunately, now my plans are all screwed up. Riley and I had a six month timeline to get our own apartment. We've plotted and calculated and were fairly confident that we could afford our own apartment at the complex on west beach, so long as we saved up four thousand dollars by then. Cristal Cove Apartments are the cheapest around, and it shows. They're run down and occupied by seedy individuals, but the rent is cheap. It's a stepping stone until you can afford something better. Once we saved up four thousand dollars, it would be just enough for the deposit, first month's rent, and some cheap furniture like a couch, silverware, towels and shower curtains, that kind of stuff.

So getting kicked out of Uncle Will's house isn't the worst thing ever. I have a plan.

It just happens to be four months too soon for my plan to work.

I grab the spiral notebook off my dresser and flip it open. Riley and I have two thousand one hundred and four dollars saved. That's enough for the deposit but not quite enough for the first month of rent. My heart sinks.

Riley and I both work at Surf n' Shop, a combination surf shop and convenient store on the boardwalk. The pay is okay but they refuse to give us any more than twenty hours a week, despite how often we beg for more. I take over any extra shifts I can, especially now that I've finally graduated high school, but it's still not enough. And every business within walking or biking distance has our applications on file. Too bad no one ever calls to set up an interview.

Just like Uncle Will's business, the economy in Sterling, Texas has gone to hell. No one is hiring and everyone seems to be one paycheck away from homelessness. Despair is in the air, in every inch of town except the beaches where people come in from out of town.

I flip to the back of the notebook and pull out the cloth makeup bag with the word *fabulous* stitched across it in gold sequins. Riley got it from her secret Santa in dance class our junior year. There was a five dollar limit for the gifts, and I've always suspected this bag costs more than that. I unzip it and shove the twenty dollars I got from my uncle inside, tucking it away with the rest of our money. On the notebook, I cross out the number and write $2124.

Using the old laptop Uncle Will gave me, I get online and go to the Cristal Cove Apartments website, hoping that maybe fate has heard my dilemma and decided to make all apartments half off this month.

Hey, weirder things have happened.

The website is state of the art, elegantly designed and including features that let you pay your rent online. It's kind of misleading, since the apartments themselves don't look very nice from the outside, but Riley and I have never been inside of one so I'm hoping for the best. I check their availability section and find that they have two apartments available for rent. The cheapest is $1250 a month. The deposit is one month's rent, so it'd cost $2500 to move in today. My heart flutters around in my chest.

We're so close. We wouldn't have any furniture or any savings at all, but if Riley and I could snag an apartment before I'm homeless, then we can make it work. We can pile blankets on the floor instead of a couch. I have this laptop that we can use as a TV if there's any free Wi-Fi around. Together, with our Surf n' Shop jobs, Riley and I bring in about two thousand a month, so we'd barely have enough for rent and food. It would suck, but we could make this work. One of these days we'll find better jobs and we'll get nicer things.

I look up at my room, at the dresser against the wall, the couch bed I've slept on for six years. Uncle Will said he was going to sell it all, but maybe he'll let me keep some. I scramble up and run to ask if I can have some stuff for my new apartment, but he's already left, probably gone to Racheal's house.

Instead, I call Riley.

"Allllmost ready," she says instead of a hello. The sound of wind in the background makes her voice all staticy. She must be outside, near the boardwalk. Probably walking over here now.

"That's not why I'm calling," I say. My heart is thundering in my chest and I'm not sure if it's because I'm terrified or excited that we have to move out earlier than expected. "Uncle Will is losing the house to foreclosure and moving in with his girlfriend. I have to get out, like, soon."

"Seriously? We're not even close to four thousand," she says, her voice losing some of its happiness.

"I know, but I think Uncle Will will give me some of his furniture. Like my couch and dresser, and maybe even the dishes and stuff since he'll be moving in with his girlfriend. It'll be tight, but Cristal Cove has two apartments available right now. We should go apply."

Riley sighs. "We've already done this math. With our paychecks now, we'll have like six hundred dollars for food, the electric bill, and everything else. It'll be impossible to make ends meet. We need full time jobs."

Anxiety starts to take over my optimism. "We need a place to live," I say. "You know Margret is risking her job letting you stay there that long. You're supposed to leave the home when you turn eighteen. You'd feel like shit if you got Margret fired."

Margret is the manager of the group home. She's always been really nice to us, probably because we're two of the only group home kids who aren't constantly in trouble with the law.

"Yeah, I know," Riley says with a sigh. "We really need better jobs, though. I've been talking with her and she tells me about all these unexpected bullshit bills that happen when you don't think about it. Like if you get sick and go to the doctor and it's two hundred dollars for antibiotics, or you need some expensive suit for a job interview."

"We'll figure it out," I say. "We'll babysit or walk dogs or something. Let's spend the rest of the day going around and seeing if anyone is hiring."

"We know nobody is hiring, Cara. We check all the time."

"Maybe someone quit today," I say, smiling in an attempt to make myself feel better. "Maybe two full time employees just up and walked out of Garlands Grocery. Let's go check."

She laughs. "Fine, we'll swing by and ask if they're hiring. But that's all. One place, and then we have to forget about it for the rest of the day. We have better things to do."

"There is nothing better than looking for a job," I argue.

"Yes there is. We can worry about our futures tomorrow. But today, it's your birthday and we're going to celebrate. Now open your front door because I'm here."

The line goes dead just as there's an impatient knock on the door. I take a deep breath and imagine locking all of my worries up in a safe to open later. She's right, after all. It's my birthday. I should have some fun, even if it feels impossible.

THREE

Riley Winters was given the unfortunate nickname of Mickey Winters when we were in seventh grade. As a twelve year old, she was only five feet tall with brown scraggly hair and a tiny little mouse-like face. Not that I would ever admit it to her, but Riley is kind of mouse-ish. She's soft spoken and petite. The assholes at school called her Mickey for Mickey Mouse, and made fun of her relentlessly. Margret told her it was because they were flirting with her, but even now I'm not so sure that was the case.

At the start of eighth grade, Riley dawned a pair of black combat boots she found at the army surplus store and threatened to kick anyone's ass if they called her anything but her real name from then on. She was still picked on a few times, but not nearly as much. That year we learned that bullies stop bulling people who stand up for themselves.

Now, she's a legal adult and still looks like that tiny girl from junior high. Riley's hair has gotten a little better, though. Today she's swept it up into a messy ponytail, with little fringes hanging down to frame her face. She's wearing those same combat boots, paired with a black mini skirt and a long flowy tank top she pulled from the clearance bin at the Shop n' Surf.

The only thing missing from my best friend's face are her signature high-arched eyebrows.

"Give me a sec," she says, holding up her purse. She turns to the right where a little mirror hangs above the key rack next to the front door. She leans forward, then drags her eye pencil across her brows, expertly making sharp lines around the neatly plucked hairs that still remain. When she's done, she nods once into the mirror, caps her pencil and then turns to me. Her lips split into a devious grin.

"Happy birthday, Cara!"

I roll my eyes because this is not some fancy event to celebrate, but Riley crushes me into a hug anyway. I'm taller than she is (I mean who isn't?) but I hug her back.

"You are going to be so psyched for what I have planned," she says, wiggling her newly drawn on eyebrows at me.

"Riley," I say, giving her a look. "You can't spend any money. I meant it when I said it last week but I *really* mean it now. We need every dime we have, so no spending anything on me."

She makes this long drown out sigh, sticking her tongue out like I've bored he life out of her. "You done? Because I'd like you to know what I haven't spent a dime, okay?" She puts her hands on her hips. "And this is still the best gift ever. Even more so because it's free."

I eye her skeptically. "So what is it?"

She gives me a once over, dragging her lips to the side of her mouth. "Are you ready to go?"

I glance down at my cut off shorts, flip flops with little rhinestones on them, and the simple black shirt I've chosen because it's a V-neck and fits me well. It makes me feel feminine, unlike those baggy polo shirts we wear to work. "Yes?" I say, hoping she won't make me change.

"Good," she says, hooking her arm through mine. "Let's go."

We walk the two blocks to the boardwalk and then Riley turns left. "There's not much down this way," I say, staring out at the vast stretch of beach, hindered only by a pier amusement park. Most of the places to go in this town are to the right, along the boardwalk and the busy part of the beach.

"There's one thing," she says in a sing song.

My brows pull together. The only thing down here is massive. The Sterling Pier, a family fun permanent carnival built out on a pier that overlooks the ocean. It's massive, lit up and sparkly, the lights on the carnival rides glittering out onto the water below.

It's also very expensive.

"We can't afford the pier," I say, rolling my eyes. I come to a stop on the boardwalk. Ahead of us, people are excitedly walking toward the mammoth of a pier, which Riley and I know from experience charges ten dollars a person just to go inside. One time a couple of years ago, we thought we'd just walk around and pretend to be like normal people who could pay for those things, but we couldn't even get inside. They make you pay an entry fee, and then all the food and rides cost extra.

Riley's eyes widen and she stares at me with this expression that tells me she'll be a terrifying mother someday. "I told you I didn't spend anything and I meant it. Now trust me. I'm your best friend, after all. I wouldn't screw you over."

Hesitating, I start walking again, wondering what the hell she's up to as she leads us right to the entrance of the pier. It's been decorated like it's an old circus, with big plastic awnings decorated like orange and red circus tents, with lines of white lights blinking in a row.

I get nervous as we step forward in line, all the people in front of us handing over their cash and credit cards, when Riley and I don't have either one of those. When we reach the front, a middle-aged woman with thick black glasses smiles at us.

"Welcome to Sterling Pier," she says as if she's said it a million times today. "How many in your party?"

"Two of us," Riley says, standing confidently. I'm beginning to worry where she's going to take this, when she says, "I'm Riley Winters. I have two tickets at will call."

"Sure thing," the woman says, turning to look under her desk in the ticket booth. She retrieves an envelope with Riley's name on it, which she slides under the plexiglass to her.

She stamps our hands with a big seashell stamp and then opens the gate for us. "Have a Sterling-tastic day!"

And then we're inside.

I turn to my best friend once we're a little way away from the entrance and that woman can't overhear us, because surely there's some mistake here. "What the hell was that?" I say, poking her in the arm. "Did you buy these tickets in advance?"

Riley gives me a sneaky smile. "No, ma'am. I meant it when I said free." She opens the envelope and pulls out the contents. There are two wristbands, red ones that mean you get unlimited rides for the night, and two food vouchers, each valued at fifty dollars.

My eyes bug so hard, they almost fall out of my head. "What is this?" I say, whispering.

"I have a hook up. And I used it for your birthday," she says, fastening the unlimited rides bracelet around my wrist, and then holding out her arm so I can do the same to hers. "This was all free, I swear."

"How?"

A small blush rises in her cheeks, making her look vulnerable for the first time in, well, since seventh grade. She glances around and then leans in close to me. "I did a little flirting with this guy who came into the store the other day. His name is Chase. Tall, red hair? You remember him from school?"

I think back but shake my head. "Not really."

"No one does," she says with a shrug. "He's kind of quiet, and keeps to himself. Well, I got to talking to him and he was wearing a nametag from here, and I told him how I wished we could go but had no money and the next thing I know, he's offering to give me a recoup package."

"A *what*?"

"It's for when someone has bad customer service, or like, their food order is wrong or something. The manager is allowed to give out a free pass and stuff to recoup their losses and beg them to come back to the pier again. He got one for me." Her eyes flash conspiratorially. "So if you talk to anyone, make sure to say they're really improving on their service since the last time you were here." She winks.

I realize I'm smiling like a huge idiot. Spending the evening at a carnival, riding rides and playing games and eating junk food is kind of childish. But that's what makes it so great. Riley and I never had that kind of childhood. Warm tears sting the back of my eyes. This is the nicest thing anyone's ever done for me.

"I can't think of a better way to spend my birthday," I say, blinking back tears. "You are seriously the best friend ever."

Riley grins and tosses her ponytail over her shoulder. "I know it."

For the next hour, we explore the pier and take in everything it has to offer. It's narrow but long, stretching out way over the water, where people fish off the end of it. There's a Ferris wheel, a small roller coaster, and tons of rides, all colorful and blinking with hundreds of lights that spin around and change color as the rides move. In the middle is a large swing set, where all the swings are in a circle and once the thing gets going, it pushes you way out and nearly sideways, where you're literally swinging over the ocean.

I probably won't be trying out that one.

The arcade games are included in our free wristbands, so we play some skee ball and ping pong and discover that we're really bad at air hockey. After a while of having more fun than I've probably ever had, we head for the food area, the smell of deep fried goodness making our mouths water. There's a line of carnival games to the right, and I watch a little boy try his hardest to knock over a pyramid of bottles with a baseball. Beside him, his dad cheers him on, while his mom claps at his attempts. A sharp pain flitters through my chest at the sight of this happy little family. I wonder what it would have been like to grow up with that kind of life. But then I shake the thoughts away and focus my attention straight ahead.

"I can't even decide what I want first," Riley says, tapping her food voucher card against her nails. "It all looks so good."

"I'm thinking something small for now, otherwise we'll puke on the rides," I say, gazing up at the yellow marquee in front of a funnel cake stand.

"Hot dog?" she says.

I shake my head, because someone has just walked by me holding the most glorious looking snack food ever. "Soft pretzel."

She laughs. "You get a pretzel, I'll get a hot dog."

The pretzel is huge, and warm and the softest thing I've ever bitten into. I take a bite while scanning the area to find where Riley went, since the hot dog stand was a few stands down from mine. I know it's stupid, but in this moment, if a meteor hits me and kills me, I can die happy having experienced a fun night on the Sterling Pier.

"Hey!" Riley says, somehow appearing next to me, which makes me jump, nearly scaring the pretzel right out my hands. "This hot dog is so much better than the shit they serve at Good Grace." She makes flirty eyes at the food in her hands and then takes a bite.

We find an empty bench and sit so we can finish our food, and even though it's carnival food that has a reputation for being crappy and overpriced, it's still amazing.

"Okay, so I've never been on a ride ever," Riley confesses as we make our way back to the busiest part of the pier. "What should we do first?"

"Ferris wheel," I say, nodding up at the huge wheel in front of us. "It looks easy enough."

I've never been on a carnival ride either, but I've heard stories from people at school, about how certain rides are known to make you puke. The Ferris wheel isn't one of them. It's big and slow and perfect for old ladies, so it seems like a great first ride to me.

"Oh hey, there's Chase!" Riley's face lights up and she waves at someone to our right. I scan the crowd and find a guy dressed as an employee, his bright red hair shaggy and blowing all over his face from the breeze. He's holding a broom and one of those scooper things that go with it. When he sees Riley waving at him, he smiles bashfully. She turns to me. "I'm going to go say hi and thank him again for the tickets. You want to wait in line for us?"

"Sure thing," I say. Talking to strangers is awkward for me, and I'd only feel like a third wheel if I went with her. While she rushes over there, I step into line behind four other people. The Ferris wheel has only just started, so we've probably got a while to wait.

The two kids in front of me are clearly siblings, both with prominent brows, small noses, and the same golden hair. I watch them argue over who gets to sit in the spot closest to the ocean, and I feel like telling them to cherish the fact that they have a family who takes them out to do fun things instead of arguing over petty stuff. One of them stomps his foot and the other goes to hit him. He launches backward to avoid the hit. I step back, too, just to get out of the way.

And then I crush into some guy's chest. I freeze, feeling the chill of his leather jacket on my bare shoulders.

"Crap, I'm sorry!" I say, turning around with apologetic eyes, hoping he's not one of those douchebags who will yell at me in front of everyone. I mean, he *is* wearing a leather jacket in the middle of July.

"It's not a problem." His voice is like honey, smooth but with a deep rumble that makes my toes tingle.

I meet his gaze. And swallow.

His lips twist into a grin, a contrast from the sharp line of his jaw, which has just a hint of stubble. This guy is hot and he knows it. Dark brown hair, messy up top but swept back in a way that looks like it was meant to be messy.

His amber eyes meet mine, thick eyebrows pulling together. "You okay?"

Snap out of it, Cara!

I blink and gasp for air. Heat rushes to my cheeks as I mentally yell at myself for being so stupidly obvious that I was checking him out.

I nod, again, *stupidly*, and then inch backward to put some distance between me and this perfect, perfect man. Even in all of the romantic movies I've watched with Riley, I've never in my life seen anyone so gorgeous. There's a hint of mystery in his features and that only makes him hotter. And now I can't look away.

"I'm fine," I say quickly, my voice so high they might as well call *me* Mickey Mouse, and then I spin back around, my heart pounding louder than the melodies from the carnival rides.

Right when I catch my breath, the delicious woodsy scent of his cologne brushes past my shoulder. A shadow falls over my right.

"You don't seem okay," he whispers, that voice of his sending a chill up my spine. And then he straightens, and I'm suddenly missing having him hover next to my ear.

I turn around on shaky knees and look him dead in the eyes with as much confidence as I can summon up.

"I'm sorry again that I bumped into you," I say, offering him a smile but I'm not sure if it looks right because I'm suddenly so nervous. "If I don't seem okay it's probably because I hate the idea of bothering random people."

"Like I said, not a problem." He gazes at me thoughtfully. "Is that really why you're nervous?"

"I'm not nervous," I stammer. I take a deep breath—hoping to convince him and myself—and say it again. "I'm not."

His lips are the perfect shade of dark pink as they stretch into a grin. "Liar."

FOUR

"Wha—I'm not—" I put a hand on my hip, but he just smiles. There are hundreds of people around us but he's only looking at me. "Are you always this easy to mess with?"

Exhaling, I glance over and see Riley standing with Chase. They're both staring at me. I'd blush if I wasn't already pinker than cotton candy. Riley's eyes widen and she gives me a thumbs up. I turn back to the guy.

"I'm not nervous. And you're not messing with me. I'm totally normal."

"Mmhmm," he says, scratching his neck. I'm not used to standing next to someone so much taller than I am. Uncle Will is short for a guy, and Riley is positively tiny and they're the only two people I see besides customers who are on the other side of the counter at work. So the way he has to look down at me does make me a little nervous. "I'm Theo, by the way."

"Cara."

He doesn't make any motion to shake my hand, which is good because my palms are sweaty.

"Next up!" The voice sounds a little annoyed, or maybe overworked. We glance at the ride, where an older man wearing a faded Sterling Pier shirt is letting people off the carriages one by one. The first two people step into a carriage, and then he moves the wheel slightly so the two bratty kids in front of me can get on the next one.

Theo steps up beside me. "Looks like we're next."

"Oh, um, I'm riding with my friend," I say, turning back to Riley, waving to get her attention. She gives me this demure look and then turns back to Chase with a renewed look of interest in whatever he's saying.

"Looks like she abandoned you," Theo says, his voice low.

I let out a huff. "Riley!" I call out, cupping my hands to my mouth.

"You gettin' on or what?" the ride operator says.

Riley blows me a kiss and then shoos me away with the back of her hand. "Go!" she calls back. There's a subtlety in her eyes, something only I would understand.

Ride with the hot guy.

My heart slams around in my chest. "Ready?" Theo says, and it really bothers me how calm and relaxed he is at the idea of riding next to a total stranger for five minutes.

"Sure," I say, if only to spite Riley. She probably thinks I'm too chicken, and I am. Which is exactly why I need to prove her wrong.

"After you," Theo says, extending his hand toward the carriage.

I walk up the rickety metal steps onto the platform. The ride operator holds open the chain that goes across the carriage. "First one in gets the ocean view," he says.

I turn to Theo, lifting an eyebrow questioningly. "You first," he says. I climb in, grabbing onto the railing as the carriage rocks under my weight. Theo's cologne hits me in a whoosh as he slides in next to me, his body taking up more than half of the carriage. My heart pounds, and I keep my knees together, my hands in my lap, trying to stay as small and unbothersome as possible.

The ride lurches forward for a few seconds and then stops abruptly for the next people to get on. I look around wildly, amazed at how high we are and we've only just moved a little bit. Soon, everyone is loaded and the ride begins.

This thing is supposed to be fun and not scary, but here I am, a little terrified. "Whoa," I say, looking out over the ocean as we reach the very top of the wheel. I hold onto the railing in front of me. We're so high it's getting a little unsettling.

"You seem a little scared," Theo says. I turn to him, just as we swoop back down and begin another trip around the wheel. The lights of the surrounding rides bounce off his chiseled face, making shadows and rainbows of color spill over his hair.

"It is a little scary," I admit, gazing back out at the ocean. "It's beautiful, but scary. I've never been on a Ferris wheel before."

"Really?" There's a surprise in his voice, and when I look over I find him studying me, confusion knitted in his eyebrows. "Are you not from around here?"

"I was born and raised here," I say with a sarcastic chuckle.

"And you've never been on the Ferris wheel?"

I shrug. "It's a long story."

"I have time."

I look over at him. Growing up in foster care isn't exactly a long story. I could say it in two sentences, maybe even one, but I have no desire to let this stranger into that part of my life. My phone buzzes from my front pocket. I lean back to pull it out and I hold on tightly out of fear of losing it at the top of this thing. There is definitely no money to buy a new phone right now.

I have a text from Riley.

Chase is showing me the hilarious security footage of this drunk guy from earlier. Take your time with the Ferris wheel hottie.

There's a winking emoji at the end of it. I want to reply, but I can't risk letting Theo see her text, so I shove the phone back in my pocket.

"Looks like my best friend has ditched me," I say, frowning.

"That seems a little weird," Theo says, his gaze focused on the ocean. "Especially since she didn't like that guy."

"What makes you think that?" I ask.

His shoulders lift. "I could just tell. Seems like she was talking to him out of obligation."

I gnaw on the inside of my lip. If he could tell that much from a few seconds of looking at Riley, what can he tell about me?

"She probably won't be long," I say. "He gave us free tickets tonight, so she's just being nice."

"I'm happy to be your companion until she's back," Theo says.

I narrow my eyes at him. This guy is probably in his early twenties, and he's entirely too hot for someone like me. "Why?"

There's a twinkle in his eyes and I'm not sure if it's from the lights anymore. "Why not?"

When the ride is over, I expect Theo to go his own way, but he stays at my side. "So, if you've never been on a Ferris wheel before, have you been on anything else?"

I shake my head. "I've never been here before. It took me eighteen years to get to a kid place," I say with a snort.

"You're eighteen?" I don't know why it sounds weird when he says it, like maybe he's surprised in a bad way.

"As of today," I say, looking at my feet.

He stops right in the middle of a group of people who are all trying to get to the next ride. "Well then," he says, grinning at me until my knees go weak. "Happy Birthday, Cara."

"Thank you," I say in this silly way.

"What's next?" Theo gazes around. "The swing?"

"No way in hell am I getting on that thing."

He laughs and motions for us to walk again. I follow along next to him, my whole right side hot from being so close. "What's your favorite animal?"

"Umm, elephants," I say after a moment of thought.

He frowns. "That's not very cuddly."

"You didn't ask me my favorite cuddly animal."

"What's your favorite cuddly animal?"

"Puppies."

He looks at me, not like he's trying to figure me out, but more like he already knows. And in a way, I know this is crazy, but it almost feels like maybe he *does* know me. Maybe we were friends in a past life. Maybe I'm just delusional from all the fun in the air.

Before I realize it, we've walked clear across the pier. We're right in the middle of the games area that Riley and I avoided earlier because it costs money for these games. Carnies heckle to the crowds of people trying to win prizes. Little kids try and fail at winning a goldfish by tossing a ring over a bottle. Two teenage girls flirt with a younger carnie who has abandoned his dart throwing game for their attention.

"Let's see..." Theo says, gazing around at the selections. "There we go!"

He leads me to a game booth just like Riley and I saw earlier. You have to throw a baseball at a stack of bottles in order to win.

Theo hands some cash to the guy, who hands over three baseballs. "You want to play?" Theo asks me.

I shake my head. "I'll cheer you on instead."

Theo doesn't need all three baseballs. After one throw, the entire stack of bottles collapses. The carnie lets out a low whistle.

"Damn, son," he says, rubbing a hand across his forehead, a lit cigarette dangling from his lips. "That's never happened before. Any prize you want, it's yours."

"The elephant," Theo says, pointing up at the very top of the booth. My stomach flips over and twists inside out, leaving me feeling like I'm floating. Is this really happening?

Apparently, it is. Because soon Theo hands me the elephant, a soft well-crafted plush toy that's clearly better than all of the other cheaper toys. It came from the highest shelf, the best prizes for the best scores.

"Thank you," I mumble, smiling at the elephant's adorable face, with its long trunk made of grey fuzzy fabric. Panic rises up in my chest as I hold the prize in my hands. A cool breeze blows over the pier, but it does nothing to cool down the fire in my cheeks. The truth is, no one's ever won me a prize before. No guy has ever given me anything. I don't know how to act, what to say, what to do.

"You should probably get back to your friends," I find myself saying instead of all the things I want to say. "They probably miss you."

"No friends to get back to," he says, shoving his hands in his jean pockets. "I'm all yours until you tell me to leave."

My toes tingle. *All mine?*

I blink. I have to get out of here, away from this guy. The more time I spend with him, the more I'll let myself daydream about the kind of life I'll never have. Girls like me don't get guys like him.

"I'm sure you have better things to do than win strange girls stuffed elephants."

"You aren't that strange," he says, bumping into me with his shoulder. "And I can't think of anything else I'd rather be doing."

FIVE

My skin still tingles from where Theo's arm brushed against mine. The tension in my shoulders seems to lessen a little with each minute that passes. I try to tell myself it's no big deal to casually hang out with some guy you just met. It's not like I'm going to get drunk and sleep with him or anything.

My stomach does a flip flop at the idea.

"You're a little strange yourself," I say, recalling what he'd just said a moment ago. I fold my arms over my chest and peer at him. "It's July, and you're wearing a leather jacket."

He chuckles. "And I'm hot as hell in it."

"Yes, yes you are."

The words are out before my common decency can kick in and tell me to keep that thought to myself. Theo's grin turns flirty, his amber eyes crinkling at the corners.

I roll my eyes, pretending like that smirk of his isn't totally doing it for me. Then, because all the sweat from my palms is going to ruin my elephant, I open my purse and shove him inside. "So why the jacket? If you're trying to pull off some handsome mysterious dark stranger vibe, you're doing a killer job."

He smooths his hands over the leather. "I rode a motorcycle here. The wind from the beach stings like hell, so the jacket is necessary. Although now it just makes me look like a douche."

If I were bold, I'd ask him for a motorcycle ride. I've never been on one before and tonight seems like a night of firsts. But I am decidedly *not* bold, so instead I say, "You don't look like a douche."

We reach the end of the pier and Theo puts a hand on the railing that looks out at the Gulf of Mexico. Waves crash against the concrete pillars below us, bringing the salty smell of the ocean with them. "What do I look like?"

"Like the kind of crazy hot guy girls check out from afar."

His head inclines toward me. "Why from afar?"

I shrug. "Because they'd be intimidated to talk to you."

"But you aren't?"

His words are an invitation into something deeper. I've all but declared how sexy I think he is, and now he's calling me on it. It'd be easy to turn and run away and pretend this never happened, but it's my birthday, dammit. I'm going to have some fun. I put both hands on the railing and lean up on my toes, looking down at the ocean. It's at least twenty feet below us, maybe more.

"I'm on an adventure," I say. "New places, new people, new experiences. And I guess that includes talking to you."

"I haven't really given you much of a choice," Theo says.

"No you have not." The wind is harsh out here over the water, and it whips the coiffed perfection right out of his hair. Somehow, this makes him more attractive.

"I apologize for following you around all night." He turns, leaning on the railing while he faces me. "But it's kind of your fault." He reaches out and sweeps the hair off my face in one quick movement. My breath catches in my throat, surprise over the gentle gesture freezing me in place.

"Why is it my fault?" I say once the feeling returns to my face.

"You've mesmerized me." His hand lingers in the air a second, and then he must change his mind about what he just did because he shoves both hands in his pockets. "I can't seem to leave."

I swallow. "If you still have that problem when this places closes for the night, you might be in trouble."

"Do you always joke about serious things?"

I'm about to smart off with another sarcastic comment, but his question makes me stop and consider it. "No," I admit after a moment. My gaze turns to the ocean. "I'm not usually sarcastic at all."

"So why now?"

I shrug. "It's a night of firsts."

What I really want to say is that my jokes are coming from a place of insecurity. Because there's no way he's flirting with me, there's just no way. Even though all evidence would suggest that he is, I know I can't believe it. I'm simply not worth this guy's attention.

"So why are you here alone?" I ask. As it turns out, I'm not quite ready to leave, either.

"Business trip." He turns slightly, so that his back is against the railing. I'm still leaning my elbows over it, looking out at the ocean. "I had a few hours to kill before tomorrow, and I was drawn to all the sparkly lights and fair food."

"Fair food is the best," I agree. Wind pushes my hair in my face again and I leave it there a minute, hoping Theo will be compelled to brush it away. When he doesn't, I just feel silly, and push it behind my ears myself. A silence settles over us, and all it does is make me imagine what it'd be like to take a step forward, wrap my arms around his waist and lean into him, my lips brushing against his.

Whoa.

"A business trip?" I stammer. The silence is broken, but Theo's gaze on me is not.

"Yes."

"In Sterling? This place is kind of a…dump," I say with a laugh.

"That's um, exactly why we do business here, actually."

"Where are you from?"

He turns to me, the shadows on his face giving him a mysterious and slightly frightening look. "Everywhere."

"But not here," I say softly.

"But not here."

Something changes in the air between us. It's as if we both have the same thought at the same time. I am not a bold person. I don't take risks and I never volunteer to be the first to do something. But something beyond my realm of understanding takes over me. I step forward, my fingers and toes tingling as I do exactly what I'd been imagining for the last few minutes. My feet slip into the space between his, white flipflops between black Converse. His arms extend, hands taking my hips. His touch sends a warm shiver down to my toes.

It all happens so fast and so slowly at the same time. My hands slide inside his jacket, fingers moving over the ridges of his abs, stopping on his chest. His heartbeat is steady beneath his shirt. I experience everything in slow motion. Warm hands pulling me a little closer. A scruffy jaw dipping down…Theo's lips pressing on mine.

I close my eyes, reeling in the scent of his cologne, the feel of his lips on mine, softly moving to deepen the kiss. I don't think I'm breathing, I don't think my heart is beating. I am wrapped in his strong embrace, warmed to the core by the heat between us. His lips part and his tongue slides across my bottom lip in an experienced way that tells me Theo is not like the guys I messed around with in high school.

I gasp for a breath, then lean up on my toes and press myself closer to him, my hands sliding up around his neck. His fingers make a strong grip on my sides, not willing to let me go, even though the very idea of stepping away from him is pure agony.

I kiss him back with everything I have. A soft groan escapes his lips and I run my tongue across them. His breath tastes like Cherry Coke. Suddenly I can't think of a single better taste in the world. Theo tightens his embrace and my feet lift off the concrete.

He is definitely not like the guys from high school.

I don't know how much time passes, but by the time his lips pull away from mine, I am a puddle of ecstasy. My breathing is labored, my lips swollen in the best way.

He smirks, slowly setting me back on my feet. A chill fills the space where our bodies had been pressed up against each other. My stomach twists with a newfound ache. He's only a few inches away but it feels like miles.

His thumbs hook into the belt loops in my shorts, and he stands there holding me in place. We're still too far apart in my opinion, but the look he gives me says he's just as enamored as I am, and for some reason, I'm too high on his kiss to even allow myself to think otherwise. Theo is totally into me, and I am totally into him. I don't even understand it, but there's a connection here.

"Happy birthday to me," I whisper.

"You are so beautiful," he says back.

I'd probably blush if I weren't already flushed from head to toe. "I'm nothing special."

He shakes his head. His left thumb unhooks from my shorts and he brushes his knuckles across my cheek, never taking his eyes off mine. "You're one of the special ones."

"Special ones?" I ask, tilting my head.

He nods slowly. "Very few people in this world deserve everything it has to offer. You are one of them."

A sudden buzzing sound appears to the left. It's a black box with a screen and a little blinking red light at the bottom. It buzzes and floats through the air. And it's coming straight at me faster than any seagull could fly.

I shriek, throwing up my arms to block my face. Theo pushes me to the side, putting himself between me and the thing. At the corner of the pier, two teenage boys are laughing, one of them holding a controller with a long antenna.

I realize it's a drone, and they've been filming our very private moment. The drone swoops around Theo and hovers in front of my chest. I turn and scramble around the pier, trying to get away from the stupid thing.

My foot runs straight into the leg of a concrete bench next to the railing. Sharp pain soars up my ankle. I cry out in pain as I watch Theo grab the thing right out of the air and throw it over the pier into the ocean below.

"Get the fuck out of here," he says to the kids with the controller. His voice is a low growl, the most frightening thing I've ever heard. Chills prickle across my arms. The boys run away.

When Theo turns back to me, all of the rage in his expression is gone. I reach for the railing to lean on, since my ankle is hurting worse by the second, but an evening dew has settled on the metal and my hand slips off. I fall to the right, and my hurt ankle gives out, making me tumble straight on top of the bench.

Sharp concrete edges collide with flesh. My cheek hits the ground. Pain radiates everywhere.

"Cara." Theo kneels over me, his hand on my shoulder.

"I'm sorry," I mutter, wincing from the pain in my ankle, hands, knees—everywhere.

Theo's concerned expression turns quizzical. "You're sorry?"

"We were having a perfect moment and I ruined it," I explain. I am in far too much pain right now to even allow myself to be embarrassed. But I'm sure that'll come later when I relive this moment for the rest of eternity.

"It's far from ruined," he says, a coy grin tugging at his lips. "You've just set me up to be a hero." With gentle movements, Theo scoops his arms underneath me and picks me up. He places a soft kiss on my forehead. "Let's go."

SIX

I'M PRETTY SURE I DIDN'T HIT MY HEAD DURING MY FALL, BUT I FEEL like I'm in a daze as I'm carried across the carnival and toward the hotel in the center of the pier. It's a small building in comparison to the vast carnival out here, and I'd forgotten there were hotel rooms here. When the pier was renovated a few years back, they remodeled the old indoors conference rooms and included twenty hotel rooms. They're so popular it usually takes months in advance to book one.

"Where exactly are we going?" I ask as Theo carries me across the hotel lobby and toward the elevator.

"I'm going to use my magical powers to heal you," he says without a hint of joking in his voice.

"You're what...?"

He gives me this devilish grin. "I am taking you to a first aid kit."

I smile even though I'm still in pain. Theo doesn't let me down until we're standing in front of room 301.

"How's the ankle?" he asks, taking out a key card from the inside of his leather jacket.

I put some weight on it, holding onto the wall for support. "Not so bad anymore."

"Good. You and Riley walked here, right?"

My heart stops. The hotel room door clicks open softly. Chills prickle over my arms. "How did you know that?"

Theo runs a hand through his hair, the first sign of weakness he's shown all night. "I saw you walk up," he says, a little bashfully. "I was eating nachos near the Ferris wheel and saw you and Riley walking up the boardwalk. You just had this unique excitement in your eyes and I thought it was sweet."

He steps into the room, turning to see if I'll follow him in.

"That's..." I say, not sure what to think.

"Creepy?" he says with a chuckle. He puts a hand on his heart. "I wasn't stalking you."

"That sounds like something a stalker would say." But I can't help the smile that stretches across my face. Margret always said I had the best intuition, and it was because of my keen instincts that she made me go everywhere with Riley, who doesn't exactly have the same reservations when it comes to making good choices. Of course, here I am alone in a hotel with a hot stranger from out of town, so maybe Margret doesn't know what the hell she's talking about.

I swallow and study Theo's features. My intuition isn't telling me anything bad right now. I step into the hotel room and his expression softens. The room is small, but elaborate. The king sized bed is so tall and plush, I'd probably have to jump to get on it. There's the biggest TV I've ever seen on the wall, a small bar with black granite counter tops, and a beautiful balcony view of the ocean. The place is spotless and it smells like Theo.

I clutch my elephant to my chest, hoping he'll take away some of the pain. Shorts and a tank top are probably the worst clothing choices when you're going to take a spill into a concrete bench. My knees are skinned, my elbows raw and bloody. There's bruises up my legs and my left toenail is broken from bashing it into that bench leg. I ache all over, but luckily nothing is broken or otherwise permanently hurt, except of course, for my pride.

Theo uses the hotel room's first aid kit to clean all my wounds, but he says they shouldn't be bandaged for now because they aren't too bad. Instead, he smooths some antibacterial ointment across the scrapes, then leans in and blows softly until the stinging sensation goes away. Watching a guy blow on your knee shouldn't be erotic, but damn if my mind isn't taking that image of his lips and going places with it.

"Doesn't look like your ankle is sprained," Theo says, his fingers holding onto my foot.

Good. I can still walk home with Riley.

"Shit," I say, as I reach for my phone from my pocket. "I haven't talked to Riley in forever."

She's only sent me one text in the last hour I've been alone with Theo.

Having fun? :-)

Heat rises through my belly when I think of exactly how much fun I had been having before that stupid drone. I send her a quick reply.

Where are you? Sorry I've been gone so long. And yes, yes I am. ;)

I'm biting the inside of my lip while I send the text. I only realize it when I put the phone down and see Theo staring at me. I'm sitting in a chair and he's kneeling on the floor, first aid kit at his feet. From here, we're eye level.

"Everything okay?" he asks, referring to my text.

I nod. He is so handsome it takes my breath away. My throat is dry, my hands clammy. It doesn't even make sense. We were making out earlier and I was fine with that, but now that he's gently cleaned my wounds, I'm more nervous around him than I've ever been.

"You're one of the good guys," I say, my voice soft.

Something dark flits across his features. He reaches for my hand, running his thumb across my knuckles. "Thank you for tonight."

As I gaze into his eyes, I'm overcome with the desire to be back in his arms. "The night's not over," I whisper.

Leaning forward, I take hold of his shoulders and pull him toward me. Our lips find each other like they've been doing it forever. Soon I'm lifted out of the chair, my legs wrapping around Theo's waist. He carries me over to the bed, sets me down gently.

His eyes roam my body, sending a shiver down my spine. And then he lowers himself on top me, his hands tangling in my hair, his lips kissing me with more passion than I'd thought possible.

My heart pounds with delight. What a wonderfully perfect eighteenth birthday. I thought I'd be bored and miserable thinking about my future tonight, but instead I'm spending it with the most amazing guy I've ever met.

And then it hits me.

Like a freight train of reality, I'm hit with clarity. This is stupid. It's wrong, and pointless, and will only lead to me getting hurt in the end.

I push Theo's hard chest, urging him to get off me. He backs away, concern knitting his brows.

"We're not going to see each other again, are we?" I ask.

He runs his hand down his face, leaning back on his knees. "No."

Tears sting my eyes. As much I want to pull him back down and slide into his arms and slip into a fantasy world for just a little longer, I know I can't.

"I have to go," I say, scrambling off the king sized bed.

"Cara," Theo calls.

I grab my phone and purse off the table and shove my elephant under my elbow even though I kind of want to leave it here. Tears sting my eyes at the same time my cuts and bruises cry out in pain from walking.

I reach the door and pull it open, wishing I had the willpower to walk right out of here, not looking back. But I can't, and I turn around, finding myself face to face with him again.

"Thank you for tonight," I say, my voice barely a whisper.

"Thank you," he says, brushing his fingers down my cheek. I lean into his touch and my skin tingles when his fingers fall away. "You've reminded me what I should be fighting for."

I'm not sure what that means. But I can't stick around to find out. I have to go. I need to put as much distance as possible between me and this night because this kind of thing will never happen again.

My flipflops splat across the concrete of the pier as I rush around, meandering through the carnival games, past the food stands. I call Riley, and press the phone to my ear, desperate to hear her voice.

"Hello?" she says after a few rings.

"Where are you?"

"Enjoying some cotton candy. This stuff is amazing when it's freshly made. Where are you?"

I gaze around and find the cotton candy stand. There's Riley, picking off a piece of pink cotton candy, her phone tucked between her ear and shoulder.

I hang up and rush over to her. "Can we go home now?"

Her eyes widen. "Are you okay? Did that asshole do something to you?"

I shake my head, willing the tears away even though they're trying to break through. "No. He was great. But he's from out of town and he's leaving tomorrow and there's just really no reason for me to get carried away talking to some guy."

She frowns and leans her head against my arm. "I'm sorry, Cara. We can go if you want to."

"Yes," I say. "Please."

"Hey, you're the birthday girl," Riley says, a smile forming on her lips. "Your wish is my command."

We make the walk back to my uncle's house in silence. Riley's the kind of best friend who knows when to talk and when to just be there for me. Eventually I will tell her more about the mysteriously wonderful guy I met, but it's too raw to talk about now.

My key is barely in the lock of Uncle Will's front door when I hear it. The sounds of lovemaking. I turn to Riley.

"Ew!" she whispers.

Rachael's blue Mazda is parked in the driveway, but it's only nine at night and I figured they'd still be watching a movie or something.

But as clear as day, I can hear the moans and gasps of two people getting it on in the other room. I take a step back and pull the front door closed.

"I refuse to go inside that house right now," I say, twisting the lock back.

Riley giggles. "I mean... good for him, I guess? He's found love and all that..."

We share a laugh. "We can go back to Good Grace," Riley offers. Technically lights out is at ten, when all the residents of the group home have to be back and in bed. It's a two mile walk from my house, but we could make it.

"Might as well," I say. "If anything can take my mind off Theo, it'll be the stench of those dorm rooms."

"Theo," Riley says in a sing-song voice while we walk. "That's a really sexy name."

"I know, right?" I find myself smiling even though my heart aches. I stare at my stuffed elephant as feelings of longing clutch at my heart. "He was so...regal."

"Regal?" Riley squishes her nose. "That's a weird adjective."

I shrug and kick at a loose piece of gravel on the road. "I'm not sure how else to describe him. He was a gentleman. Caring and sweet, and he talked kind of weird. Like maybe how royalty would talk. He said I reminded him of what he was fighting for."

Her lips slide to the side of her face. "You said he was here for a business trip?"

I nod. "No idea what kind of business. We never really got into details. I mean, what's the point? He's leaving."

Riley's arm wraps around my shoulder, which looks kind of funny because she's shorter than me. "Well, I'm glad he treated you right. He wasn't some scum asshole like the guys around here."

"Yep," I say, my chest heaving with a sigh. I can still feel the soft brush of his lips on mine, the beating of his heart beneath my fingertips.

The smell of his shirt.

I sigh. Just like every good thing in this world, Theo can't ever be mine.

SEVEN

Good Grace Shelter is one of the better group homes in the tri-county area. Most of the homes are reserved for what they call *behavior kids*, the kids who get into so much trouble that the state takes them away from their parents. I've been to a few of those homes, and as someone who tries to stay out of the disciplinary office, it was horrible.

But Good Grace isn't like that. There are some moody teenage assholes living there, but for the most part it's made up of orphans like Riley, or wards of the state like I was. People whose parents are in jail or are otherwise unfit to take care of their children. Most of the people who work there are nice and at least attempt to care about their job, but the place is still a total black hole that sucks away all the happiness the moment you enter.

The building is old, with wood paneling on the walls and water stained ceiling tiles. The furniture is all from the eighties, orange and yellow couches, dark green carpet. There's a rec room when you first walk in which has a couple old arcade games, several couches and two televisions. There's a pathetic shelf of books that are all too old and falling apart. Past the rec room you'll find the kitchen and eating area, and then a long hallway that stretches to the left and right. The right is the boys' dorms and the left is for the girls.

Even though I have since been checked out of living here, I still shudder when I come here with Riley. I still have nightmares where I'll suddenly be ten years old again, and Uncle Will doesn't exist and I'm back here, sleeping on a smelly mattress in bunk beds with roommates who are mean to me.

"Let's make this the last time we have a sleepover here," I tell Riley.

She brightens. "That's a good idea. Maybe we can get out of here in a week, when we get our next paychecks."

"Sounds like a plan."

Two guys argue over a football game on the television, but besides that, the rec room is nearly empty.

"Hmm," Riley says, seeing the same thing I notice in the corner of the room. You have to walk past the front office to get into the rec room, which Riley and I had avoided because we came in a side entrance in the kitchen that we're not exactly supposed to use after dark. There's an old bulletin board near the front door. People always post fliers for things they think will help out the group home kids. Religious papers, job openings, tutoring, lost dog fliers offering a cash reward. There's never anything good on there, and I know, because we've been checking it religiously for full time job offers ever since we graduated.

Right now, a lanky man with white blond hair stands in front of the bulletin board, surveying the papers there. He's wearing nice jeans and a crisp black shirt, the sleeves rolled up to his elbows. I'm not up to date with everyone who lives here at the home, but it's obvious by the expensive quality of his clothes that he's nowhere near being a home kid. He's also too old for it.

He pulls a couple of thumbtacks from the corner of the board and then flattens out a piece of paper right in the middle, pinning it on top of a few older fliers.

Riley walks right up to him. "Hi there," she says, wearing her signature customer service smile. "Is that a job offer you're posting?"

"Actually, yes," he says, turning toward her with his own charming smile. I wouldn't exactly call him handsome; more like friendly-looking. He's a little too thin and his beard is blonde and scraggly, like maybe he wishes he could grow it in thicker but he can't. He's probably from the local community college.

"How many openings do you have?" she asks. Her hands slide into the back pockets of her mini skirt and she gazes up at the flier. "My best friend and I need jobs, bad. Well, better jobs."

"We have a few openings, actually." He turns to look at me, his eyes roaming down to my skinned knees and back up again. "I'm Kyle," he says, extending a hand to Riley and then me. I do my best to shake it with authority, so I look like someone worthy of hiring. "I'm a scout for my company. We're looking for a few women like yourself who would be open to a wonderful opportunity."

"Awesome," Riley says. "We only have a high school diploma, but you must know that because you're posting here."

He chuckles. "We offer on the job training. Do you both live here?"

"Just me," Riley says. "But not for long. We're getting our own place soon."

Kyle's gaze turns to me. "You said your name was Cara?" I nod. He presses his lips together, as if he's summing me up, but I don't know what for. "Do you have strict parents who would object to you getting a new job?"

What a weird question to ask. "I don't have any parents at all," I say, holding my head up confidently. "I used to live here, too, but now I'm on my own."

This is normally where people give me that fake smile and wish me good luck on my endeavors. Employers don't want someone like me and Riley because they think we're weird and uneducated and probably addicted to drugs.

Kyle does the exact opposite. If anything, this news seems to delight him. "We're conducting interviews tomorrow," he says. "You should both come on by. We'd be happy to have two girls like you on our team."

"We will absolutely do that," Riley says, still beaming as if we've already been offered the job.

After he leaves, Riley rips his flier off the bulletin board. Since Riley's dorm has two other girls in it, we sneak into Margret's office to have some privacy.

"That guy was kind of secretive about what exactly the job is," I say, trying to quell some of Riley's excitement. "What if it's like, amateur porn or something?"

She rolls her eyes. "Those people are hired on the internet, Cara. See if the flier has any more details."

I spread out the paper on Margret's desk, flipping on her desk lamp so we can see it clearly.

NOW HIRING WOMEN AGES 18-25

Looking for an exciting opportunity?

We are currently hiring women aged 18-25 for full time employment beginning immediately. Room and board included. One year contract.

Salary: $100,000

Interviews: Monday, July 24th at Brook Falls Airport 1-4 p.m.

"HOLY SHIT," Riley whispers. "A hundred thousand dollars?"

"Did you say that loud enough?" I snap, looking around. If one of the night shift workers sees us in here, we'll get chewed out and Riley will be on lockdown for at least a week.

"I can't believe this," she says, a little quieter this time. "This is perfect. *Perfect!* Exactly what we needed!"

"I don't know," I say, exhaling. "This sounds a lot like porn."

"It is *not* porn, you party pooper! Plus, it comes with room and board, so it's probably some awesome camp counselor type of gig." Riley snatches the paper from beneath my hand and holds it to her chest like she's Charlie and it's the last golden ticket. "I knew the universe would take care of us."

Her excitement starts to tub off on me. Assuming the job isn't for something illegal or gross, could we really get hired for something that pays six figures? Do good things like this really happen to people like us?

A sharp pain radiates through my chest. Despite how much I've been telling myself to stop thinking about Theo, there he is, rising up in my thoughts again. I tighten my jaw and tell my brain to dump all thoughts of that boy. He is gone. He is just a memory now. I need to look forward to my future and stop dreaming about perfect guys with charming smiles.

"We'll go to the interview," I say, leveling a look at Riley. "But if it's anything remotely gross, we're out of there."

"Agreed," she says, her eyes crinkling at the corners. "There's no way I can sleep here when I'm this excited. Let's go back to your place in a few hours when the coast is clear."

"Thank God," I say, sinking into Margret's office chair. "I was really dreading sleeping over here tonight."

Riley giggles while she stares at the job flier. "Pretty soon we'll have a new place to stay. *Room and board*," she says excitedly. "With a shit load of money in our bank account."

Later, when my uncle and his girlfriend have fallen asleep and Riley is sleeping contently on the floor next to my couch bed, I lie awake and stare at the ceiling. That job offer does sound perfect, like the exact answer to all of our problems. But the chances of something like that happening are so slim, I have a hard time believing it. We'll probably interview and be skimmed over, pushed aside for better candidates to fill the positions. Or worse, what if one of us makes it but not the other? The whole idea of a perfect job just landing in our laps feels totally impossible.

Of course, meeting a guy on a Ferris wheel and then sharing the world's most toe curling kisses under the moonlight is also an impossible thing.

Maybe there is room for impossibility in my life after all.

EIGHT

The smell of bacon sizzling on the stove wakes me up the next morning. My pillow is over my face, something that usually happens after an uneasy night's sleep. Because of the darkness and the unusual smell of breakfast, for a split second, I wonder where the hell I am. Uncle Will and I aren't exactly the type of people who wake up bright and early and cook breakfast. We're more of the sleep in and eat cereal type.

But then I hear the high-pitched laugh of his girlfriend, Rachael, and it all makes sense. She's a pre-school teacher, and she spends all day telling little kids what to do. So, I guess it's become fused with her personality and now she spends all of her time off work telling my uncle what to do. They met on a dating app a few months ago, and although I'm glad that he's finally found someone that makes him happy, she's kind of...blah. I mean, I wouldn't choose her if I were him, but the heart wants what it wants.

"Brew some coffee, Will." Her voice is even louder now, and since she knows very well that my room is literally one folding accordion door away from the kitchen, I wonder if she's trying to wake us up.

I lean over and nudge Riley's shoulder. "Wake up."

"I'm awake," she says, rolling over to face me. "I couldn't sleep much since I'm too excited for our new jobs."

I groan and pull the pillow back over my face. This is *so* Riley. When she gets excited about something, no matter how impossible it is, she really lets herself get carried away with fantasies of the wonderful.

That's why I'm here to keep her grounded. Sitting up, I brush my hair back from my face. It smells faintly like saltwater, and suddenly it all comes back to me, like a punch to the gut.

Theo.

I breathe in deeply, forcing my shoulders to relax. *Forget about him.*

The folding door to the kitchen cracks open, sunlight spilling into my darkened room. "Oh good," Rachael says. "You're up." She motions at us with an oven mitt over her hand. "I made enough breakfast for the two of you so get out here before it's cold."

"Thank you," I say quickly, in case she changes her mind. "We'll be right there."

Riley turns me with wide eyes. "What is *that* about?" she whispers.

I shrug. "She probably feels bad for me since I'm all but homeless in a few weeks."

Riley begins gathering up the blankets she slept on last night. "Yeah, well the joke is on her. She doesn't make a hundred thousand a year and now we do."

I want to take her by the shoulders and tell her to stop getting her hopes up for something that most likely won't work out. But when Riley is in a great mood like this, it's a little contagious, even if her reasons are all misguided and make believe. So instead of bringing her back to reality—because reality will do its job eventually—I just sigh and get up, stretching my arms over my head. There will be time for disappointment later. Right now it's time for bacon.

There's a pile of bacon and pancakes on the small dining table, with four plates all set out for us. There's even orange juice, which Rachael must have brought with her because we never have stuff like that in our fridge. Riley and I barely make a sound, preferring to eat instead of small talk. Rachael and Uncle Will are going on about remodeling her apartment, so I'm not really paying attention until I hear my name.

"Yes?" I say, looking up from my plate.

Rachael smiles sweetly, but it's obvious she's faking her admiration. "You'll help with a garage sale, right? Maybe Riley could help too?"

"Uh, sure," I say, stabbing another bite of pancake. "Are you having a garage sale?"

Uncle Will clears his throat. "I am, actually." He gazes around at this small house filled with old, out of date furniture. "We need to get all of this stuff gone, and I'll split the money with you, like I promised."

"Oh. Right." Thoughts of Theo had taken up space in my mind while I ate, and although it's so stupid of me to let my mind run with fantasies, it's easier than remembering that I'm about to be homeless and Riley and I barely have enough money for rent.

"Thank you for that," I say, forcing a smile. "But I was actually thinking of something that might help us more than money."

Uncle Will lifts an eyebrow. "What's that?"

"Well, Riley and I have enough money for the deposit and first month's rent on an apartment, but we don't have money for furniture yet. Or anything that goes in an apartment, really. I was thinking maybe you could let me have some things, like my couch bed and the silverware and stuff like that?"

He nods. "That's a great idea. You pick out what you want and we'll sell the rest."

My heart leaps. Getting free stuff for our place will be a huge help. But as I look around, I see Rachael and Riley staring at me like I'm either an idiot or a nuisance, or something otherwise not worth dealing with.

"What?" I say to Riley. But Rachael speaks first.

"The garage sale is next week, Cara. Friday and Saturday and maybe Sunday if we don't get everything sold. You'll need to move into your apartment by then because we can't hold a bunch of stuff for you."

"Rachael," Uncle Will says, but she cuts him off with a sharp look.

"There's still time to do a short sale on the house," she snaps. "I'm trying to salvage your credit, honey. We can't let her stay in the house any longer just out of charity. She's an adult now, she'll figure it out."

"Of course," I say, feeling like someone's just let all the air out of me. "I'll call the apartments today, and we'll get moved in." It's a lie. We don't have enough money today. Maybe I can beg and plead and offer my first born child and maybe they'll take pity on us and let us start moving in tomorrow. It can work. I know it can.

"It won't be a problem," Riley says cheerfully. "What Cara hasn't told you is that we don't need any of that stuff because we're getting new jobs today."

"That sounds good," uncle Will says. "Where's it at? Is it full time?"

"Yes," Riley says. I give her a look but she ignores it. "The pay is really good and it includes room and board so, we're all set."

"Well that sounds a hell of a lot better than moving my crappy old stuff into an apartment," Uncle Will says with a laugh.

I sigh, rubbing my forehead. "Don't listen to Riley. We don't have the jobs yet and who knows if we'll actually get it." My uncle's shoulders fall and for some reason I feel like the bad guy here, when Riley is the one who falsely got his hopes up. "We're interviewing for the job on Monday."

"We're going to get it," Riley says with as much confidence as ever. "We talked to the talent scout already and he totally thinks we're a great fit. It's all but a done deal."

"But if it *doesn't* work out," I say through clenched teeth, "We'll need some of your stuff to take to our apartment."

Riley rolls her eyes. "Yeah, yeah. But it'll work out. I have a good feeling about this."

Rachael laces her fingers together under her chin. "Riley, please do all the talking when you get there, otherwise Cara's bad attitude will ruin both your chances of getting hired."

They all laugh, and I stab my fork into my food, choosing to ignore them. Unlike Riley, we can't all live in a fantasy world where jobs are given out just because you want it badly enough. Someone has to stay grounded to earth long enough to get us a place to live. Reality is painful enough without wasting time dreaming for something you'll never get.

NINE

Brook Falls Airport isn't like the massive airports you see on TV. It's privately owned and has only one runway. If not for the occasional small plane flying across the beach, I'd forget it even exists. I think super rich people use it to come and go, because no commercial airlines fly out here. They go to the massive airport in Houston.

It's Monday morning. The weekend seemed to take forever, what with working at the Surf n' Shop and trying not to think of my magical-but-not-magical birthday with Theo. Riley hasn't stopped talking about the stupid interview, and I haven't been able to stop worrying about coming up with the money to move out if we don't get the job.

"I guess we need to take a taxi to the airport," I say with a sigh. That means wasting some of our savings just for a small chance that we might get offered a job.

"Don't worry about that," Riley says, bobby pins hanging from her mouth while she twists her hair into a bun. "I called Chase and he said he'd drive us out there."

Relief falls over me. I feel bad that Riley is most likely leading the poor guy on, but a free ride is a free ride.

Riley and I get dressed in the best clothes we have for our interviews. For her, it's a knee length gray pencil skirt and matching blazer top that she found at the Goodwill. It fits her perfectly and was pretty cheap. I'm wearing a pair of black dress pants, also from Goodwill, and a blue satin blouse that I got for Christmas two years ago from Uncle Will. My black ballet flats aren't exactly business attire, but it's all I have.

I run the flat iron through my hair to take out all the frizz, and apply a little makeup so I look put together, like someone you'd want to hire and pay a ton of money. "Do I look nice, or slutty?" I ask after dusting some silver eyeshadow over my eyelids.

"Not at all." Riley cocks her head, studying me through the reflection in the mirror. "Maybe they want us to look slutty?"

I narrow my eyes at her. "If that's the case, then it's totally a porn job and we're not taking it!"

She laughs and turns her attention back to her own makeup, where she draws a thinner more sophisticated line of black around her eyes. "You worry way too much."

When Chase's Ford Escort arrives in front of Uncle Will's house, I start getting nervous. Although I'm pretty sure we won't be good enough for a job that pays this much, I still secretly hope we get it. We deserve a break, and maybe fate will be good to us for once. Maybe this will work out.

Only now that I'm looking forward to the interview, I'm now equally terrified I'll screw up.

Riley sits in the backseat with me and we practice interviewing each other while Chase heads to the other side of town to the airport.

"I think you're both worrying too much," Chase says, gazing at us from the rear view mirror. "Just be yourself and you'll win them over."

"Hey, I'm doing this for Cara's benefit," Riley says, giving him a flirty grin. "She's the nervous one, not me. I've got this in the bag. The job *will* be mine."

"That's the attitude," he says, nodding.

Chase pulls into the airport. It's even smaller than I thought it was from the few times I can recall driving past it as a kid. There's one entrance, a black asphalt road, and one tall tower in front of the runway.

"Good luck," Chase says, pulling over into the tiny three-space parking lot to let us out. "Let me know how it goes, and call me if you need a ride back home."

"I will," Riley says, smiling at him. "Thanks again for the ride."

We watch him drive away, and as his brake lights get smaller in the distance, I start to get a little more than nervous. "Um, where do we go?" I say, looking around at the deserted airport.

There's a hangar off to the left but it doesn't look like anyone is there. There are no cars anywhere, and no sort of welcome building or anything. Just the runway, the tower, and a private jet parked in the distance.

"There, I guess," Riley says, pointing to the jet.

I balk at her. "Are you kidding? That's on the runway."

She shrugs. "So?"

"We can't walk up to it. What if it, like, takes off or something? We'll get our heads chopped off."

Riley puts a hand on her hip, and gives me this exasperated look that's intensified because she's wearing her professional working-woman outfit. "Don't be silly. The flier said to come here, and that's the only place there is to possibly go. Look, there's someone now."

In the distance, a man walks toward us from the plane. Now I notice the plane's fold down stairs are out, and a red carpet runner extends from the bottom of the stairs and out from the runway.

As the man approaches, the butterflies in my stomach calm down a little. It's Kyle, the guy with the fliers at the group home. We're definitely at the right place.

"Glad you could make it," he says, extending his hand to both of us. "You're the first interviewees of the day."

"We're so punctual we should be hired first," Riley says, winking at him as we walk. If I had said something like that, it would have seemed stupid, but the way she did it was charming.

"I'll have to agree with you, Riley." Kyle motions for us to go in front of him when we reach the red carpet. "Ladies first."

Riley excitedly rushes up the jet's fold out stairs. I take my time, my heart beating with the hope and possibility of getting a new job.

Having never been on a jet before, I'm not sure what to expect. Reality is more amazing than my imagination. White leather seats fill the cabin, each one large like a recliner, with its own little wall mounted television and food tray. I can't pinpoint the sweet smell all around us, but I do know one thing: it smells like luxury.

"Welcome," a man says, startling me because I hadn't seen him. He's tall with square shoulders, dark skin and darker hair. He wears the kind of tailored suit that you'd expect to see on a man in a private jet. He rises from his seat toward the front of the plane. "We're so glad to have you." He smiles, revealing impeccably white teeth.

"This is Riley and Cara," Kyle says. "The girls I met at Good Grace."

The other guy nods. "Lovelier than you described, Kyle."

Riley dons this bashful smile and I'm not sure what expression I'm making. This whole thing seems weird. Two men on a private jet with no business logos or company information in sight. This kind of looks like the start to one of those Lifetime movies where the two girls end up chopped into pieces in some creep's freezer.

"I'm Henry," the guy says. "Where are my manners? Kyle, can you pour our guests something to drink?"

Kyle rushes off to fulfill his request. Henry turns a demure smile toward us. "My colleagues are on a lunch break, but since there's two of you and two of us, we can split up to conduct the interviews."

"Sounds great," Riley says, all beaming and peppy, like she doesn't think anything is weird about this.

But then again, maybe it's not. Maybe I'm overreacting. If a company can pay such high salaries, who's to say that conducting job interviews on a private jet is weird? Maybe that's how things are done with important businesses.

Kyle returns with two wine glasses filled high with a golden liquid that's darker and thicker than any wine I've ever seen.

"Thank you," Riley says graciously, taking the glass and immediately taking a sip. She's looking significantly more hire-able than I am, so I do the same thing.

"Yes, thank you." The golden liquid is sweet going down my throat, almost like it's warming my whole body. I immediately take another sip. I don't think it's alcoholic, but I've never tasted anything like it. If it weren't impolite, I would gulp the whole thing down in a heartbeat. With another sip, all of my nerves are washed away, leaving only a sense of peace and contentment.

Kyle leads me to the opposite end of the jet and Riley goes with Henry for our interviews. Kyle, with his white blonde hair and lanky limbs, isn't very intimidating as an interviewer. I'm relieved to have him instead of Henry, who seems more serious.

I take another sip of this glorious drink and sit in one of the leather seats that face my interviewer.

"Tell me about yourself," Kyle begins.

"Well… I just turned eighteen," I say, remembering to sit straight and poised like Riley and I practiced. "I got decent grades in school, and um, I liked art class a lot. I wouldn't say I'm very good at it, but I can appreciate the work it takes to make something with your own hands."

"Tell me about your home life," Kyle says.

"It's about to be nonexistent." His eyebrow quirks, so I tell him about my uncle and how he's losing his house and I have to get out immediately.

"That must be stressful," he says.

I nod, taking another sip of this golden, delicious drink. Maybe it's just my imagination, but with each sip, I feel less nervous and more confident. "Riley and I were saving to get our own apartment, but we're not going to survive long without a better job." I grin and point my glass toward him. "That's where you come in."

Kyle's boyish features smile back at me. "Cara, let me ask you a hypothetical question. If you were to move away without telling anyone, who all would notice?"

I snort. "No one."

He leans forward. "Give it some thought."

I bite my lip, embarrassed that my answer wasn't good enough for him. "Well, I guess my current boss would wonder where I went, but our job always has people flaking out, so maybe they'd think I just bailed." I blink. "I mean, not that *I'm* someone who would bail on a job—I'm not like that at all." Kyle nods for me to continue. He seems to be looking for a specific answer. "Normally I'd say my uncle would notice, but now that he's moving in with his girlfriend, he wouldn't care. He knows I'm moving out and I doubt he'd keep in touch with me after I do." My thoughts drift to my birthday and I take another sip of my drink. "It's not like I have a boyfriend or anything, and Riley is my only friend. So no one cares if I stay or leave."

"Your life seems lonely," he says, frowning.

I lift my shoulders as I gaze at the intricate marble pattern on the walls. "Not really. I have Riley."

"Do you enjoy expensive things?"

I pause, because I'm not sure how to answer a weird question like that. So I just tell him the truth. "I wouldn't know. I've never had expensive things."

"You'd have them with this job."

I brighten. "That sounds nice."

He nods. "It *is* nice. You'd have a very nice life if you took this job."

"Where can I sign up?" I say with a laugh. I'm trying to be funny but Kyle is studying me with an intensity that makes me wonder what he wants me to say to satisfy his piercing gaze.

He leans back in his chair, interlocking his fingers together. "What are your goals in life?"

"Honestly...I've never thought much about my future because it all seemed hopeless. But with a great job opportunity, I suppose I could do anything."

He seems to like my answer, judging by the subtle upturn of his lips. He leans forward, lifting his chin to see over the chairs. I look back, following his gaze to the other side of the plane where Henry is interviewing my best friend.

Kyle and Henry exchange a look that's full of meaning, only I'm in the dark as to what that meaning might be. Kyle stands up.

"You seem like a great match so far," he says, extending a hand to help me stand. "Henry will conduct the second part of the interview with you and Riley."

Relief floods through me. I'm moving on to step two, and so is Riley. Maybe this will work. Maybe she was right to be so optimistic after all.

"I'll refill your drink," Kyle says, taking the empty wine glass from my hand. That's odd. I don't even remember drinking it all.

TEN

Riley's eyes are filled with excitement, but she's hiding it well. I take a seat next to her and we exchange a knowing glance. We've made it to step two.

Henry's voice is deep and gravelly, like maybe he should have been born in a different era. "I'm delighted to say that the two of you have passed your interview with flying colors."

I sneak a glance at Riley and she beams at me, reaching over and squeezing my hand. Henry seems pleased as well. Kyle returns with my glass filled to the brim with the mysteriously amazing drink and I find myself taking a sip as if I can't possibly do anything else until I feel the warmth of it going down my throat.

Henry sits straight, even in the comfortable plane chairs. His cheekbones are prominent, which makes him look older than he is. I can't imagine him being more than thirty-five or so. "Allow me to explain the details of this job. Should you both accept, you can sign your contracts and begin working tomorrow."

A little nervousness comes back to me. This is the most important part of the whole day—seeing if the job is something we're actually capable of. What if it's manual labor we're not good at? Some skilled position requiring computers and software we don't know?

There's a nudge on my shoulder, and I look up to see Kyle point at my glass. I nod and take another sip.

The nervous feeling fades away.

Henry clears his throat. "This job is more like an opportunity instead of a job. You will not have to wake up early and report to a cubicle every day. You won't wear a uniform. You won't have to worry about sick days or sleeping through an alarm because none of those things matter with this job. With this job, you simply live on our premises and do as you please, occasionally accompanying us to meetings or on travels. You will never be in want of anything, and all of your needs will be taken care of. Medical care included."

I lift an eyebrow, but Henry continues. "The exact nature of my business with my colleagues is confidential, as it is highly important in regards to international affairs. Your job, should you accept it, will be as an assistant of sorts. My boss prefers to travel with beautiful women in tow. They—*you*—" he says, nodding to both of us, "Make us look professional, well-rounded. It pleases our clients to see how well we take care of our assistants."

I'm not exactly sure I understand, but Henry leans forward, his eyes glistening conspiratorially. "Plus, it's always lovely to have a beautiful woman in our midst. Wouldn't you agree, Kyle?"

My heart skips a beat. I look over at Riley, but she's holding onto her wine glass with a serene look on her face.

"Is this porn?" I blurt out.

Henry and Kyle both look amused, but Henry is the first to speak. "My dear child, no. This is an opportunity."

"We won't..." I swallow. "Be sex slaves or anything like that?"

Henry's eyes crinkle at the corners like I'm a toddler who just said something ignorant. Kyle snorts. "The only sex you'll be having will be of your own accord." He shrugs. "And probably not with any of us because we're busy men who prefer to find real girlfriends and not resort to sleeping with the staff."

"Well put," Henry says. Their answer makes me feel better, but still I'm confused.

"So what exactly is the job description?"

"It's simple," Riley says as if it's totally obvious. "They want us as trophy employees to parade around their high-value clients."

"Precisely," Henry says.

"That sounds..." I gnaw on my bottom lip. "Too good to be true."

"I assure you it is not." Henry brings his own glass to his lips, although his drink is pure whiskey, judging by the half empty bottle next to it. "You will be flown to our headquarters in Austin, Texas where you will be given a room and anything you need. You will live in luxury, in a life that is quite unlike the one you've grown accustomed to here in Sterling. There is only one catch," he says, gazing at Riley. "While everything you need will be provided by us, your salary will be paid in a lump sum at the end of your one year employment contract."

"As far as catches go, that one's not bad," Riley says.

"Does that mean you'll say yes?" Henry asks us.

"Can I talk to Riley in private?" I ask, my voice sounding meeker than I'd hoped for.

"Of course." If he's annoyed, he doesn't show it.

I stand and take Riley's arm and walk down to the far end of the plane, ducking into the little hallway that leads to a bathroom.

"So…" I say, whispering. "What's the verdict?"

"It's definitely not porn," she says, throwing me a wink. "I think it's perfect."

"I do, too." I gnaw on my lip, regretting how I stupidly left my wine glass in the cup holder back with Henry. Maybe it's just my imagination, but every time I drink from it I feel better. "I mean, we don't get paid for a year, but we get a free place to stay, so that's not bad, right?"

"It's amazing." Riley grabs my wrists and squeezes them. "He said we'll live in luxury. Can you imagine?"

"Honestly, I'm trying not to jump up and down like a dork," I say, unable to hide my massive smile. "There's nothing here for us. We have no future and we'll probably never even find a full time job here, much less one that pays all of our expenses and then gives us money at the end of a year."

"So we're doing it," she says, her eyes sparkling. "You sure you won't regret leaving Sterling for a year?"

I shake my head. There is nothing for me here but a meager stash of money and some old furniture from my Uncle Will. I have no friends besides the one standing in front of me, and any home these guys can offer will be better than a crappy apartment.

"You're all I need," I say. "Let's do it."

"I'll go tell them we accept!" Riley says. She turns and practically sprints down the narrow aisle toward the front of the plane, all of that grace and charisma she'd had from earlier now replaced with sheer joy.

Shadows fill the cabin near the stairs, and three men walk up and into the plane. I hang back near the bathroom and wait for them to pass, wondering if these are all of my new coworkers. They're all impeccably dressed, some more attractive than others. The hushed conversation of the two guys in front comes to a shop when they see me.

"Hello," I say softly. I give a little wave.

The first one, a tall man with the stature of a soldier and red hair shaved short, gives me a polite nod. "I almost forgot we were getting new girls today. Welcome to the team."

As they walk toward the front of the plane, the sound of heavy footsteps on the stairs make me pause. Another guy enters the plane, this one dressed in dark jeans and a black leather jacket.

My heart catches in my throat.

"What the hell are you doing here?" Theo says.

ELEVEN

I'M IN SUCH A GREAT MOOD, I DON'T NOTICE THE HINT OF ANGER IN HIS voice. "Theo?" I say, trying—but failing—to hide my grin. I've spent the last few days wallowing in self-pity because I thought I'd never see him again. And now here he is, somehow more handsome than I remember, standing right in front of me. "What are *you* doing here?"

"I asked first." He steps closer to me, his broad shoulders making an impassable wall in the narrow aisle of the private jet. His arms fold over his chest and my eyes go right to the veins on his forearms, the taut muscles beneath them. I want to slip inside his arms and feel them wrap around me again. "Cara, why are you here?"

"I'm getting a job," I say, blinking in an effort to slow my rapid heart. The last thing I need to do is melt into a puddle of lovesick goo right here in this expensive airplane, but seeing him after the last few days of missing him is doing crazy things to my insides. My mouth still tastes like that heavenly drink, but my throat is dry and I'm pretty sure my heart has lodged itself somewhere in my sternum instead of where it's supposed to be.

Theo hasn't shaved at all since I saw him on my birthday, and the shadowy scruff of a new beard makes him look dark and sexy. His hair hangs low over his brow, which pulls together while he studies me.

"Cara." His voice is hard. He grabs my shoulders but it's not at all like the passionate embrace we had on the pier. "Turn around and leave."

"What?" I blanch. "No way. I'm here for a job. It's a *good* job. I need this."

I need you. But I don't say that part out loud.

A muscle in his jaw flinches. "It is *not* a good job. You can't work here."

He says something else, too, but I don't hear it. I've become afflicted with tunnel vision, and all I see are his dark pink lips, twisted into a scowl.

And then I'm thinking something dirty.

I bet I could turn that frown upside down.

Desire takes over, forcing all rational thoughts out of my mind. It doesn't matter that I'm on a plane, wearing business attire, in the middle of a job interview. I launch myself toward him, my hands grabbing his shirt and pulling him forward. He freezes. I kiss him anyway. When my lips press to his, I feel his entire body loosen, tight muscles relaxing.

He sighs.

Somewhere in the back of my mind, I know this is weird. There's a tiny little voice telling me my new employers are at the other side of this plane and if they walk down here they'll see me with Theo, doing very inappropriate things for a new employee on her first day.

But it doesn't matter.

I. Can't. Stop.

"Kiss me," I whisper, my words hungry, my thoughts wrapped in desire for him and only him.

"Dammit," he whispers against my lips. Then he lifts me a little bit of the floor and pushes me backward, through a tiny door at the end of the hallway.

It's cooler back here than in the rest of the plane. I take a moment to look around, keeping my hands flattened on Theo's chest. I'm afraid if I let go, he might disappear on me again. I can't go another moment without being near him.

We're in a small bedroom. Well, the only small thing about it is the room size. The mattress in the middle of the space is huge, overflowing with cream colored silk sheets and fluffy overstuffed pillows with golden trim. The walls are curved, with a strand of lights built into them, giving the place a romantic glow. There's a mini fridge and a little television on the wall.

I turn back to Theo and slide my arms around his neck. That little voice that's been dancing around shouting warnings at me is back. She tells me that Theo's body language is that of someone who doesn't want to do this. He's standing rigid, his jaw tight, brows pulled together in a crease on his forehead.

But I tell that little voice to screw off because I don't have time for her right now. Plus, every time I kiss him, he melts right into it. He can't deny me just like I can't deny him.

"I missed you," I whisper, pulling up on his shoulders so that our bodies are pressed together. I need him. I need him so badly I can't stand it.

I run my tongue across his bottom lip. He pulls it into his mouth, then kisses me deeper. His hands, rough and calloused, slide up under my satin blouse and over my ribcage. I shudder, wrapping my arms around his neck to bring him closer.

Closer.

Closer.

I need this.

I need *him*.

Theo breathes in deeply, then sighs, pulling me back a few inches. "Cara," he says, his voice deep and penetrating. Those gorgeous amber eyes meet mine. "They gave you a drink, didn't they? The gris."

I don't know what that word is, but I know he's right. I nod, then go in for another kiss. "It's delicious. But it's not as good as kissing you."

A small groan escapes his lips. His head leans back as if he doesn't want to make out right now. But that can't possibly be the case. We're made for each other. He has to want me too, right? Pain slices through my chest. Theo is still resisting me. I frown.

"What's wrong?"

"Cara..." He breathes in and lets it out slowly. "We can't do this. You're not thinking right."

"I'm thinking perfectly right," I say, taking a step back.

But now that there's some space between us, my mind is whirling. My heart beats quicker and that little voice I'd been ignoring is suddenly screaming at me, jumping up and down and freaking out.

"Oh my god," I say, eyes wide. "I can't believe I did that. I'm on a freaking job interview!"

I cover my face with my hands. What's going on outside of this room? Are Henry and Kyle and everyone else watching, waiting for us to come out? Will I be fired on the spot? Riley will get to travel to Austin and be a trophy employee and I'll be stuck here.

And she can't even help me out with money because she won't get paid for a full year.

"Oh my god," I say. How could I have been so stupid? What sort of insane lovesick idiot am I that I can't even wait until after the interview to pounce on him?

Theo takes my hands, his thumbs tracing circles in my palms. "It's okay. Breathe. The gris is a special drink. It lowers your inhibitions." He chuckles. "That's probably why you threw yourself on me."

"Yeah," I say, forcing a smile. It all makes sense now. The drink, the warm soothing feeling I got with each sip. That's why I did this just now. That's why I threw myself at this guy and forced him to make out with me.

"Well..." I run a hand through my hair. "I wasn't making out with any other guys I saw," I say. "It was just you. Because well..."

"Because we have a connection," he says, his voice filled with sorrow.

"A connection," I say, feeling a warm tingle rise up in my stomach. "I like that."

He shakes his head. "Cara—"

I can tell whatever he's going to say is probably something I won't like. I don't have time for that now. "Why did they give me a drink that made me act like this?"

"It gets you to loosen up so you tell the truth in your interview."

"I guess that makes sense. Now how do I get out of here without looking guilty as hell? I need this job, Theo. I can't screw it up on my first day."

"Oh, yes you can. You're not accepting the job."

I back up, my heels touching the base of the bed. "Um, no. I am taking the job."

"No, you aren't. You'll go back out there and say thanks but no thanks and leave." Theo's expression has shifted from soft and romantic to stern. There's something in his gaze that frightens me, just like when he'd yelled at those drone kids on the pier. Something in him has changed. "How did you get here?"

"A friend drove us," I say, my voice much weaker than I want it to be.

"Us?"

I shrug. "Me and Riley. We're both hired."

His jaw flexes. "I'll drive you both home. Let's go."

He turns, reaching for the small handle on the bedroom door.

"No!" I grab his arm, digging my nails into his flesh. "I'm not going home. I'm staying here. I need this job. We can be together."

He rips my hand off his wrist in one quick motion. "You are not taking this job." He glares at me. "You and your friend are going home. And we *can't* be together."

"What the hell?" I say, rubbing my arm from where he'd grabbed me. "Obviously you work here, right? It's perfect."

He doesn't answer, he just keeps his gaze fixed on me. If I didn't already know him, if I hadn't seen into his soul that night we'd first kissed, then I'd be scared shitless looking at him now. But I stand my ground and try not to let him intimidate me. "We have a connection, you said it yourself. So why don't you want us working together?"

I laugh deliriously and throw my hands in the air. "Theo? I mean what the hell? This is perfect. We can be together. I can be your trophy assistant."

He scowls. "You will never be my assistant."

His words slice through me more painfully than a weapon ever could. Tears sting my eyes and I don't have the energy to hold them back.

"I don't understand."

"And you won't," he says, his expression softening. "Cara, I think you're amazing. And believe me, if there was another way, I would be with you. I swear to God." He touches my face, his thumb wiping off the tear from my cheek.

"So be with me," I whisper, glad to have the sweet side of him back.

And just as quickly as it arrived, it disappears again. Theo straightens. "That can't happen. You're going home."

My stomach drops. And then I get angry.

"I get it now. You already have a trophy girlfriend back in Austin. Is that it?"

His scowl doesn't change, but there's something behind his eyes that tells me he's in pain. I shake my head, disgusted. "You're a fucking asshole. You probably pick up some girl in every town you travel to, all while your real girlfriend is back at home waiting on you."

"Cara—" Theo sighs. "Please don't do this. You need to leave."

"No, you need to leave." Pain radiates throughout my heart. I can't believe I let myself get tricked into thinking Theo and I were perfect for each other. I can't believe I fell for a guy who only wanted one night with me.

I am an idiot. But I won't let that ruin my future.

"Get the hell out of my way," I say, reaching around him and yanking open the door. To my relief, no one is in this part of the plane. There's a loud conversation taking place up near the cockpit, with laughter and the sounds of wine glasses clinking together. Maybe they didn't even notice I was gone. I'll say I went to the bathroom.

I turn back to Theo. For a split second, that pain in his eyes spreads onto his whole face. He looks like a broken man.

I decide to break him even more, hoping he will hurt the way he's hurt me. "If you're lucky, I won't tell your girlfriend what you did," I hiss, and then I turn back around.

"What did I miss?" I say, doing some world class acting to make it seem like I'm fine and like nothing happened back there.

Riley hands me my wine glass. Her cheeks are pink, her eyes sparkling. The gris looks wonderful on her. "Kyle was telling me about this girl who wanted to work for them last year but she was terrified of airplanes and never got off the runway."

"Wow," I say, pretending like that's even remotely interesting. "That's a stupid excuse to turn down such a great job."

"Our pilot is amazing," one of the other guys says. "You don't need to worry at all."

"There he is," Henry says, his attention toward the back of the plane. "Theo, come say hello to our newest employees."

Theo walks slowly, that cool carefree expression back on his face. Just like me, he's acting. Acting like things are fine. Pretending he didn't cheat on some girlfriend back at home.

"I've had the pleasure of meeting Cara already," he says, taking me by surprise. When he looks at me, I look away. "I gave her a tour of the plane."

"Great." Henry nods. "This is Riley. She's best friends with Cara and we have the pleasure to have both of them on our team." To us, he says, "We work a lot, girls. So that bedroom back there is yours if you want it. We never sleep, do we?"

Some of the guys laugh and nod in agreement. I sneak a glance at every other guy here and none of them seem suspicious of me or what Theo and I just did back there. Good.

My reputation is still intact. I turn to Riley and hold up my glass. "Let's toast to the kindness of our new employers."

"Yes," Riley says. "To you all."

"Hear, hear!" one of the guys says. They all raise their glasses and we toast. Well, everyone except Theo, who is brooding in the corner.

Just to spite him, I turn to Henry. "So boss, when do we start?"

TWELVE

Up until now, Henry's personality had been a little dry, his demeanor nothing but professional and polite. But now he's joining in on the enthusiasm from the rest of us. "You'll start tomorrow. I'll fetch the contracts."

The three other guys on the plane introduce themselves to us, but I'm not really paying attention, other than noticing their names. Well, I catch one name. Russel is the guy with short red hair who looks like he walked right out of the army and into this company. He kind of looks like a first class asshole, but he seems nice enough.

I might be the only one who notices Theo slip off the plane. His fists are balled at his sides, shoulders tight. The plane shakes a little as he stomps down the stairs and disappears from my view. I try not to think about it. He may have played me for a fool on my own birthday, but that's over now. I've seen his true colors and I'm still deciding if I should tell his girlfriend when I inevitably meet her.

I probably won't say a word. This job is more important than revealing that one of my coworkers is a slime ball. Besides, maybe the girl already knows it. Maybe she'll break up with him on her own accord.

Riley and I are given a black leather folder and a heavy ball point pen. "You'll sign both pages and keep one for yourself," Henry explains. The folder is yours to keep as well."

"Sweet," Riley says, opening her folder. I open mine too and find that the contract is even shorter than the waiver to use the internet at the public library. I guess that's a good thing. This company is pretty straight forward with their amazingly awesome job opportunity.

Rosewater Industries: Employee Contract

I, Cara Blackwell, hereby agree to a contractual employment with Rosewater Industries, starting July 25th, 2017 and ending July 25th 2018, unless I choose to renew for another year.

I will keep all company business confidential.

I will keep all rules, regulations, etc to the best of my ability.

It's kind of vague, but Riley scribbles her signature on the page so quickly I don't think she's even read it all. I sign my name too, and hand the top page to Henry.

"Welcome aboard," he says. "You can go home tonight, pack up any belongings you want to take with you, and we'll send a car to pick you up in the morning."

"Awesome," Riley says. She turns to me. "A car," she says, wiggling her eyebrows. I know exactly what she means. We're already living a life of luxury and the ink on our contract hasn't dried yet.

"Girls," Henry says as we stand up. "Be sure to tell everyone you know that you've accepted a new job assignment." He smiles, but it looks more like a warning. "We don't want anyone reporting you missing."

THE CAR ISN'T JUST a car. It's a limo. Black and shiny, with a chauffeur who's even wearing a suit and hat. He opens the door for us and then drives us to Good Grace so Riley can pack up her stuff first.

The only luggage she owns is a duffel bag, so I help her stuff her remaining clothes into old grocery bags I find in the kitchen.

"Wow," Riley says when we're finished. One black duffel bag and three grocery bags rest on her bed. "When you put it all together like this, I don't really have much stuff. My entire life fits in just a few bags."

She exhales and then bends behind her bed, yanking her phone charger from the wall. "Oh well. New adventure awaits."

We stop at Margret's office to tell her goodbye. She's sitting at her desk, wearing red reading glasses and frowning at the documents in front of her. She brightens when she sees us.

"Hey girls, what's up with the bags?"

"I'm moving out," Riley says. "Cara and I got a job."

"Wonderful!" She stands and pulls us both into a hug, her floral perfume washing over us. "Where at?"

"It's in Austin," I say. "We're assistants for some huge company."

"Sounds great. Austin is beautiful." She pulls Riley into another hug. "I'll get you checked out from here. You call me if you ever need anything."

"That went well," I say as we leave the home and walk back to the limo. The pristine car looks all out of place parked here in the old, run down part of town. Our driver gets out and opens the trunk, loading up our bags for us.

"I'll miss her," Riley says. "But not anyone else from that place."

The two mile drive from the group home to my uncle's house is so much faster when you're in a car instead of walking. I kind of miss the walk. I've taken it so many times in my life, sometimes meeting Riley halfway so we could hang out, other times sneaking over there late at night to tell her something that couldn't wait until the next day at school.

"This is the end of an era," I say once we're in my old room.

"And the start of an amazing future," Riley adds. She pulls the black suitcase from the hall closet and drops it on my couch bed. Seeing the thing makes something twist up inside of me. Uncle Will bought it for me when he first took me from the home. I'd needed something to hold my clothes and the few toys I had, and he bought it for me. It was one of the first things anyone ever bought me that wasn't second hand from a thrift shop.

I let out the breath I'd been holding and move to my dresser. "Let's do this."

Once all my things are packed, I survey the rest of the room. The living room that's been turned into my room for the last six years. The stuffed elephant from the pier stares at me from my dresser, its little stitched on smile asking if I'm going to take him with me or throw him in the trash.

"We can't forget this little cutie," Riley says, grabbing him and placing him in the suitcase.

"Not yet," I say. I put him back on the dresser. "Let him stay out for tonight."

She has no idea what happened on that plane, I realize. No clue that the hot guy from the pier is also the asshole we'll be working with for the next year.

I'm about to tell her when someone taps on the wall next to the sheet that divides my room from the hallway.

"What's all that noise?" Uncle Will says.

"Come in," I say, pulling open the fabric makeshift door. "I have really great news."

Also, I'm happy to avoid thinking of Theo for the time being.

My uncle gazes around my room, his eyes landing on the suitcase. "You got the apartment?"

"Even better. We got the job."

His eyebrows shoot to the top of his forehead. I guess even he thought we had no chance of landing an awesome job. "That's good," he says, nodding to himself. "Really good. When do you leave?"

"Tomorrow morning. I'm just getting everything packed up here."

"Make sure to tell me goodbye before you leave," he says, pointing a finger at me. For a second I think he might get emotional, like maybe he realizes he'll miss having me around. It makes my stomach hurt, seeing him indecisive like that, because even though we're not the closest relatives ever, he saved me from that group home. He took me in when he didn't need to, and I'll forever be grateful.

"Thanks for everything, Uncle Will."

He waves my word away with his hand. "It was nothing," he says. It looks like he wants to say something else, but then he smiles. "I'll order pizza for dinner."

THIRTEEN

That stupid elephant stares at me from my dresser. Everyone in the house is asleep but me. The lights are out, only the soft glow from the porch light outside drifting in through the slats in my window. I can't see much of anything, just a little baseball sized shadow where I know the elephant is sitting, waiting patiently for me to make my decision.

Do I take him with me or does he go in the trash?

I throw an arm over my eyes. I don't have to look at the time on my phone because I checked it a few minutes ago. It's two in the morning, and I haven't fallen asleep yet. Riley has been passed out since eleven, having fallen asleep while we watched a movie on my laptop.

I lean over and look at her. She's balled up tightly on top of a pile of blankets. Her face is serene, her breathing steady. I would be as content as she is if not for Theo.

If not for my shattered heart.

For the millionth time tonight, I wonder why I'm so unbelievably pathetic. Once you find out a guy is a total ass, you should just shove him out of your mind forever. You should drop him. Forget him. Maybe stab a voodoo doll while thinking of his gorgeous amber eyes, the sharp lines of his face, the rough but gentle way he grabbed you in an embrace.

I sit up, shoving the blankets off me because I'm entirely too hot. I hate everything.

"Riley." I nudge her back with my toes. "Riley, wake up."

She stirs, and then because years of living in a group home has made her a light sleeper, she's awake, pushing up on her knees. "What's wrong?"

"I can't sleep."

She rolls her eyes. "So don't sleep."

"It's more than that." As much as I've tried to make myself stay mad about Theo, the hurt he's caused me is trickling in like the rising tide. I'm not just mad. I'm broken.

We'd felt so right together.

We *were* right together.

How could I have been wrong?

I look over at the elephant. "There's something I have to tell you."

As much as it hurts to relive my two days with Theo, I tell Riley everything. From the Ferris wheel ride to almost taking things too far on his hotel room bed. I tell her about the connection we had, the strange pull from my heart when I was near him, like even my soul wanted us to be together.

She listens like the best friend she is, not judging, not interrupting. When I get to the part where I saw him on the plane earlier today, she grabs my hand, her eyes wide.

My heart had been wounded before, but now, sharing all of these things out loud makes them feel even more real. My heart rips in half when I describe the anger in his eyes, the resentment he showed when I said I was taking the job no matter what he wanted me to do.

She squeezes my hands. "Oh, Cara. This is awful."

I don't remember when I started crying, but my cheeks are streaming with tears. "I know."

Riley moves closer to me, her knees pulled up to her chest while she rests her head on my shoulder. "How did you go so long without telling me?"

"I guess I thought I could get over it. I mean, the job is so important and we need it. I can't just bail because of Theo." Saying his name makes another piece of my heart break off.

I know exactly where the term heart break comes from now. It is more painful than any physical injury I've ever had.

"How could he have been so sweet one day and then so mean the next?" Riley shakes her head. "That just doesn't make sense. Maybe he was mad about something else and he just took it out on you."

"It doesn't matter. He doesn't want anything to do with me. As soon as I saw him on that plane, I almost burst into happy tears because I immediately pictured spending the next year with him." I swallow the lump in my throat. "I was so stupid I even told him I'd be his trophy assistant." My cheeks burn with embarrassment. "God, I'm so pathetic. He doesn't want me. He has another girlfriend back at home. She's probably way prettier than I am."

"Don't even go there," Riley says, looking at me. "You are insanely hot. You're a catch, you hear me, Cara Blackwell?"

I can't help but smile at the look she gives me. "I don't know about that."

"It's true. You can't be hard on yourself just because some douche bag screwed you over. You deserve better. You'll find better, okay? And then you can flaunt your hot new man in front of him."

I laugh. "That's not very mature."

"So what? Revenge is sweet."

I pick at my cuticles, wishing I could be as carefree and determined as Riley is. "I don't know how I'm going to survive this. I know it sounds stupid but...he was so perfect. He felt so...real. Now it's like I don't trust anything anymore. If my heart could lead me so far astray, how can I ever trust it again?"

She levels a serious look at me. "What do you want to do?"

"There's nothing I *can* do." I take a deep breath. "I just have to get over it."

Riley stands up and paces the room, her thumbnail between her teeth while she thinks. "We can back out."

"We signed a contract."

I'm not proud to admit it, but I spent the first two hours of the night trying to come up with ways to get out of going to Austin tomorrow. I'd even gone so far as to consider breaking into a jewelry store so I'd be arrested. In jail your rent is paid for and your meals are included.

Of course, that would be a horrible solution to having my heart broken. "We can't get out of this," I say, shaking my head. "We have to go. It's still the best option for our future. I just have to stop thinking about him."

"It'll get easier as time goes on," she assures me. "I mean, I wouldn't know from experience, but people always say that. *Time heals all*, and what not."

"Maybe I'm crazy," I say, looking into my lap. I almost shut my mouth so Riley doesn't hear me say the stupidest most insane thing I've ever thought. But Riley knows me, all of me, and not telling her would be lying. "Part of me still doesn't believe what happened. Like... I keep thinking maybe I imagined that Theo was so angry. He did kiss me back like he meant it. I could *see* it in his eyes, Riley. I felt it down to my soul. He liked me as much as I liked him, and then something changed, and he was mad at me, telling me to leave." My face crumples up in confusion. "Who does that? What is that?"

She's still chewing on her thumbnail. "I don't know. But if you want me to tell you there's hope for him coming back, I won't. Any guy who treats you like that doesn't deserve your attention."

"But I *felt* it," I say, unable to stop remembering what it was like when our eyes met, that tingle of energy that ran between us. It was like I'd known him my whole life.

And then, with no warning, Theo told me to go home.

Riley drops to her knees in front of me, taking my hands in hers. I can't see her eyes very well from the darkness in the room, but I know she's in her rare serious form. "Cara. If you don't want to take this job, we'll get out of it. I'll do whatever it takes. We'll get an apartment and we'll get another job here in Sterling. Just say the word."

"You're the best friend in the world," I whisper, tears still rolling down my cheeks. Regret flashes across her face, but she stays strong, refusing to back away from her word even though I know she wants to take this job more than she wants anything.

"You really are the best," I say, wiping away my tears. "But we're taking this job."

"Are you sure?"

I nod. "I'll get over Theo. Besides," I say, laying back down and pulling the blankets up to my chin. "We have nowhere else to go."

FOURTEEN

THE NEXT MORNING I WAKE UP WITH A PEACEFULNESS THAT ONLY COMES from sleep. It takes a few minutes before all the dread over Theo and the excitement over my new job comes back to me. It's a force of nature, the two opposing emotions fighting for space in my mind. One thing is for sure though, today is the start of an entirely new life.

Riley's voice filters in from the kitchen. I sit up and look around, finding that she's already folded up the blankets she slept on and put them at the foot of my couch where they normally are, waiting for her to sleep over again. Only I'm not sure what will happen to them now that we're leaving.

My uncle laughs at whatever she says. There's a smell of toast in the air, so I'm guessing Rachael isn't here today to make one of her amazing breakfasts. I get up and throw on the jeans and t-shirt I picked out the night before, which are now the only items I own that aren't tucked away in my suitcase.

As I'm buttoning my jeans, my eyes land on the elephant. Pain soars through my chest, making each beat of my heart feel like a little stab of agony. It's really not the elephant's fault, now is it? He's just a cute, super soft little animal. He doesn't deserve to be tossed in the trash, where he'd be covered in dirt and rotten food and God knows what else.

This is how I rationalize taking him with me.

Keeping the elephant is simply a kind act saving this inanimate thing from the dumpster. It's not because I'm so pathetic I can't let Theo go even though he's totally an asshole.

It's not like that at all.

Riley looks as though she's never seen a stressful day in her life. Her brown hair is swept back in a sleek ponytail, those wispy bangs she cut herself are parted in the middle and hanging down. She's wearing black leggings, her combat boots, and a silver sparkly tank top.

"Good morning, sunshine," she says when I walk in the kitchen. "You were sleeping so peacefully I didn't want to wake you up."

"Thanks," I say, running my fingers through my hair. Staying up most of the night stressing out really does help you sleep in the early morning hours.

"Riley makes the best coffee," Uncle Will says from his seat at the kitchen table. He takes a sip from his coffee mug and nods, as if to reaffirm the fact. "Why did she have to go and leave right after I discovered this fact? I should have had her making my coffee every morning."

"I'll show you how I did it," she says with a laugh. "I'm also an excellent toast maker but no one's complementing that."

"Dork," I say, rolling my eyes. Some toast pops up from the toaster and Riley puts it on a plate, then hands it to me. There's three kinds of jams and butter on the table. Toast and jam is one of our favorite breakfasts because it's easy and requires no cooking skills at all.

I sit next to Uncle Will, trying not to feel sad about how this is the last time we'll have breakfast here together. Even though we're both moving on to better things, it is a little sad, in a way.

Riley makes me a cup of coffee and then sits down while we eat. "You're not going to eat?" I ask, pointing a piece of toast at her.

"I've had a ton already," she says, cupping her mug close to her lips. "I've been up over an hour."

"I *would* say it'll be quiet around here with you girls gone," Uncle Will says. He looks thoughtfully around the small kitchen, his lips dipping into a frown. "But really, at Rachael's house, her kid is louder than both of you ever were." He chuckles.

"Oh shit," Riley says, looking at the time on her phone. She looks up at me, excitement dancing in her eyes. "Our car will be here soon!"

My stomach flutters. It's almost time.

When the limo pulls up to the front of the house, Uncle Will carries my suitcase to the door for me.

"Cara," he says, just before I step off the porch. I turn back to him and he pulls me into a hug. "You be careful, you hear?"

I nod, hugging him back. "I will."

"I'm just a call away if you need anything," he says with a thin smile. "Preferably don't need money because I don't have much of that."

I laugh. "No worries. We'll be fine. Good luck with selling the house."

"Thanks, Cara."

He stands on the porch and watches until our limo turns down the end of the road.

"I'm so excited," Riley says, laying her head back in the seat to look at the roof of the car. "I can barely function, I'm so excited."

I nod along, but I'm not sure how I feel. I think I might be so overwhelmed with every kind of emotion and it's somehow turned me into a zombie who feels everything and nothing at once.

But even I can't ignore that one feeling is louder than the rest of them.

What will I do when I see Theo?

The limo's tires crackle over the asphalt at the airport. More people are here today. Two cars are parked near the tower, and the massive metal door of the nearby hangar is opened, revealing a few small personal planes. None of them are as big as the private jet that still sits on the runway.

My stomach twists into knots as our driver loads up our bags onto the back of a golf cart. As much as I don't want to, I'm counting down the minutes until I see Theo again...

We ride up to the jet, we get out. My legs are jelly as I walk toward the stairs, much slower than Riley whose excitement is practically floating her up each one.

Henry greets us at the top of the stairs. He's wearing a crisp black suit and holding a glass of whiskey in one hand.

"Good morning, Riley," he says, stepping back so she can get on. "Good morning, Cara."

"Good morning," I say. If he notices how damn nervous I am, he doesn't say anything.

The jet is full of people, which makes me stop cold then I get to the top of the stairs. I recognize Kyle, and two of the other guys from yesterday sitting up near the front. A football game is on the television and they're watching it absentimdendly while talking about other stuff.

Three beautiful girls are also here. They all look older than me.

"Hi," Riley says, walking right up to them. "Are you new hires, too?"

The first one, the leggy girl with tanned skin and beautiful cascading hair, gives us both a look like we're something stuck to the bottom of her shoe. "Yes," she says finally.

It is clear she doesn't want anything to do with us. And I can see why. She and the other two are arguably more beautiful than Riley and I could ever be. A rock settles in my stomach.

Why did they hire us instead of more girls who look like them?

Riley doesn't seem to mind. "Come on," she says, slipping into one of the two chairs in the back row and pointing for me to sit in the seat next to her.

"Now that everyone is here, we'll be taking off shortly," Henry says. The stairs rise up and lock into place behind him. "Everyone, put on your seatbelt for the takeoff, then you'll be free to move around. And to my new recruits," he says, turning a pleased smile to the five of us, "Welcome to the Rosewater Clan."

"*Clan?*" Riley mouths, her brows pulled together. They were called Rosewater Industries on the contract we signed.

I shrug and get to work buckling my seatbelt. It seems weird having something so technical and boring in such a luxurious seat. Finally, once the buckle is in place, I can't hold back anymore. I have to look for him.

Most of the seats are filled, and all of the guys are up front.

None of them are Theo.

I hear the engine start up, feel the wheels roll forward while our pilot taxis us into place on the runway. I glance behind me, toward the hallway that leads to the bathroom and bedroom.

I didn't realize until now how badly I've been wanting to see him. I've replayed our time together over and over in my head. How he'd passionately kissed me back and then hardened and told me to leave. The smart logical part of my brain knows he's just a cheating asshole who was thinking with the wrong part of his body when he kissed me.

But the crazy, lovesick, ardent part of me can't let go of the fact that he seemed so genuine in those sweet moments we had. He didn't seem like a cheater. Like some ass who only wants to get laid. He felt real.

And I guess I've been anxiously waiting to see him again to see how he'd react this time. Maybe he'd be nicer. Maybe he'd apologize and say he's glad I'm here working for the same company. Maybe I was wrong about everything and he really does still like me.

Riley's hand is cold as she places it on my wrist. "Don't look for him," she says quietly. "It's not worth it."

I swallow. Leave it to my best friend to know exactly what I'm thinking. "I'm not," I say, but it's a lie and we both know it.

There's also another thing I know as the plane begins to take off, thrusting us back into our seats.

Theo isn't on this plane.

And I'm probably the reason why.

FIFTEEN

FLYING IS AMAZING. ONCE WE'RE IN THE AIR, IT IS UNLIKE ANYTHING I had imagined it would be. Riley and I gaze out the window, absorbed in our own little world while we slice through clouds and watch the earth get small below us. It is almost beautiful enough to take my mind off the missing member of our group.

Almost.

The guys all keep to themselves up at the front of the plane. They have laptops open and an endless stream of whiskey filling their glasses. Just like Henry had said, we're left alone for the entire two hour flight.

It's also pretty clear that the other three new girls don't want anything to do with us, but they all seem to know each other already. That's fine with me. Riley has always been my best friend and I don't care to make room for more.

Although we land at an Austin airport, our driver says we still have another hour to drive into the hill country before we reach our destination. The guys take off in their own car and the five of us new hires share a limo together.

Luckily, there's a television that drops down from the ceiling. Our driver says he only has the DVD of *Pirates of the Caribbean*, but we can send him requests for additional movies to keep stocked. I guess he's our personal driver from now on, by the way he talks. I should probably learn his name.

We all focus our attention on the movie instead of the awkward silence that stretches between us. There's a clear animosity radiating out from the other three girls, and I'm not sure why. We're all hired together, so what does it matter? It's not like we're still being interviewed, so we're not in competition with each other.

Riley leans over, resting her head on my shoulder. "Girls are weird," she whispers.

"Tell me about it," I whisper back.

Just when the movie starts getting interesting, our driver rolls down the wall that separates him from the back of the limo.

"We're here," he says, grinning at us in the rearview mirror. "I think the view looks the best from the road, so you might want to take it all in."

And damn is he right. Riley and I look out the window toward the left, where a sprawling estate tops the hilly terrain. It seems to go on forever, the ground giving way behind it to reveal a beautiful valley below. There's a long driveway with a gated entrance. Our driver opens the wrought iron gate with a remote on top of his visor.

Even the snooty other girls in the limo shut up and pay attention as we make the drive toward the estate. I can't exactly call it a house because that word is too trite for the mansion in front of us. It's made of white and sand colored stone bricks with a charcoal gray roof. There are three circular peaks lined with little square windows rising above the rest of the house, and a four car garage off to the left, an archway you can drive through separating it from the house. Between the arch, you can see out into a glistening blue lake in the valley below.

There's a circular fountain in front of the estate with a massive black ball in the middle, seemingly hovering on the surface while water pours around it. The cobblestone driveway circles around the fountain, lined on the other side with thick green landscaping.

Our driver pulls up to the front door and parks the car. As if she'd been waiting for us, a woman dressed in a black maid's uniform steps out one of the double front doors that are made of a heavy dark wood with wrought iron detailing on the front.

"Your bags will be brought in shortly," our driver says while he holds open the door for us. The girls are the first ones out, Riley and I trailing along behind.

The air smells fresh and like sunshine, a stark contrast from the rank smell of saltwater and dead seaweed from Sterling. I close my eyes for a moment, letting the sun soak into my skin. Whatever troubles I've had with Theo, they don't matter as much anymore.

I am home now. And I don't ever want to leave.

The housekeeper woman who greets us is probably about fifty years old, with dark hair that hangs in thick waves down to her shoulders. She wears bright red lipstick and a lot of mascara.

"Welcome," she says in a thick accent, stepping to the side while we all walk inside.

The foyer is tiled in marble. While everyone else gazes up at the spiral staircase that unfolds in front of us, the ornate artwork on the walls and dark wooden ceiling beams that contrast to the white stucco walls, I notice something on the floor.

Just inside the door, laid into the tile work is a brown tile banner, like a scroll that's been unfolded.

A castle for my love is engraved into the brown marble scroll. Beneath that it says: *Established 1999*

My heart warms. Whoever built this house made it for his love. Though it is modern, the round turrets on the outside definitely remind me of a castle. How romantic is that?

Riley takes my hand while we walk into the foyer, everyone gathering together near our new housekeeper. The guys are nowhere in sight, and honestly, it's a bit of a relief. If Theo's not here, I can just pretend he doesn't exist.

"Did you have a nice flight?" the housekeeper says, smiling up at us as she makes sure to make eye contact with everyone.

"Yes, very nice," Riley says, speaking before anyone else.

"It was fun," the tall girl with the killer hair says. She seems to be the leader of her group of girls, and now I guess Riley is the leader of ours.

"Wonderful," the housekeeper says.

"Hello, hello!" another voice says. A woman appears from around the corner. She looks a little older than I am, but not by much. She's wearing a beautiful but simple purple sundress and white ballet flats. She's curvy, with darker skin and beautiful golden hair. But the first thing I notice is the bracelet on her wrist.

It's a thick silver cuff bracelet, with ornate curls of metal that wrap around a gorgeous light blue stone in the center. It sparkles in the light from the skylights above.

"My name is Bethany," she says, clasping her hands together in front of her chest. "For the last two weeks, I've been the only girl here, so I'm so glad you've all arrived! It's been terribly boring."

"You have the same job as us?" Miss perfect hair says, leveling a judgmental glare at Bethany.

"I do," Bethany says, totally unaffected by the girl's rudeness. "Before we begin, let's go around and introduce ourselves. I was so overwhelmed when I arrived here a few weeks ago, so I don't want anyone to feel left out."

She turns her sweet smile to Riley and then places a hand on her chest. "I'm Bethany, as I've already said. It's so nice to meet you."

"Riley Winters," Riley says, holding out her hand. "It's super nice to meet you, too."

"Cara Blackwell," I say when it's my turn.

I pay close attention to the other three girls.

The bitchy one is named Jayla. In addition to being tall, thin, and gorgeous, she also appears to be wearing blue contacts to change her eye color.

The second girl is a little gothic, dressed in dark clothes and wearing a nose ring. She has a lot of tattoos on both arms and brown hair cropped in an angled bob. The most noticeable thing about her is her huge boobs that are spilling out over her lowcut tank top. Her name is Nia and I see her smile for the first time when she shakes Bethany's hand.

Jayla and Nia, I think, trying to memorize their names with their looks. The third girl shifts on her feet and looks nervous as hell when it's her time to talk.

"I'm Olivia," she says, waving to the group before she shakes Bethany's hand. "People call me Liv."

She's pale and thin, with hair so black it's probably dyed because it doesn't match her lighter eyebrows. She's wearing black skinny jeans and a red flannel shirt with Converse shoes. She seems like someone Riley and I could be friends with, so I'm not sure why she's hanging out with Jayla and Nia, who are both doing their hardest to look like stuck up bitches.

"Now that we're all acquainted," Bethany says, bouncing on the toes of her shoes, "Let's get to the fun part. The grand tour of your new home!"

SIXTEEN

The estate has a Spanish style interior, with white stucco on the walls and arched doorways. I could spend hours just admiring the artwork and the sculptures positioned at various places in the house. It is all so breathtakingly beautiful that I feel like I'm in a museum. I actually have to remind myself not to let my mouth hang open in awe as we walk around. Rosewater Industries hired us to be pretty, not to be gaping idiots.

There are several living room areas with huge leather couches and marble coffee tables between them. There's two fireplaces that are as tall as I am, also lined with marble. I don't see any televisions in these rooms, but with the view of the hill country outside, the large infinity pool in the back yard, and the game room, I don't think I could ever get bored. Maybe you don't need to watch television when you're living in such a great house.

Bethany shows us the gym, which is an actual basketball court upstairs from the four car garage. The wood floor is so clean it sparkles, and I'm not sure anyone actually plays basketball here because it doesn't smell like the sweaty gym from my old school.

Bethany leads us down a flight of stairs to another room off the back of the garage. "I've actually only been in here once," she says with an embarrassed smile. "And that was on my first day when I got the tour. But we're allowed to come here whenever we want, just so you know."

She pushes open a door and reveals a workout room. It has soft squishy mats covering the floor, mirrors on two walls, and every type of exercise equipment you can imagine. There's even a rock climbing wall on one side.

"Sweet," Riley says, gazing around the room like a child in a toy store. None of the other girls seem too impressed with it, and I could go either way. I've never been to a real gym before, so I don't know if I'd like working out. But the thought of getting strong, being able to fight my own battles, or run as far as I'd like sounds really good. Maybe I'll begin a workout routine. I've heard the endorphins from a good workout can cure depression. I wonder if it works on heartache, too.

We go back inside, using a side entrance that leads us to a kitchen I haven't seen before. The main kitchen is huge, with dark wooden cabinets, sandy colored granite countertops, and top of the line stainless steel appliances. This one looks more like the one back at Good Grace, only it's cleaner and newer.

"This is the service kitchen," Bethany says. "If you want food, just call down here and place an order and they'll make it for you." She pushes open a swinging door and motions for us to head out into a hallway. "But you can use the house kitchen if you want to do your own thing. I make cupcakes all the time. I also keep cereal in the pantry, but I don't mind sharing if you guys want some. I'm obsessed with cereal with marshmallows in it."

She leads us down the narrow hallway that comes out at the first living room near the front door. "Some girls put their names on food they don't want to share, and we all respect that."

"How do we buy the food if we're not getting paid yet?" Riley asks.

"You just place an order," Bethany says as if it's the simplest thing ever. "We don't have to pay for anything here, Riley. It's all provided."

"Clothes too?" Jayla says.

Bethany nods. "Anything you want. Rosa, this girl who recently quit after her year was up, asked for a custom aquarium to be built in her bedroom and they did it. They didn't even care. Our employers are awesome."

"They really are, aren't they?" I say, gazing around the house. "This is insane."

Bethany takes my hand and squeezes it. "It's amazing," she gushes. "I don't know why anyone would leave after a year. Living here is like being a princess."

"So, they really do treat us right?" Nia asks. Her eyebrows pull together in the middle. "It wasn't some sham to talk us into coming here?"

Bethany shakes her head. "No sham. Just a few rules that aren't a big deal at all, and you get anything you want."

"What kind of rules?" Jayla says, folding her arms across her chest. "I didn't hear of any rules."

Bethany waves a hand at her. "Totally not a big deal. Like, for example, they don't want you going very far away. So, like, you can go to the mall, or a concert around here but they don't want you flying off to Hawaii for the week or something."

Jayla rolls her eyes but doesn't say anything. I look at Riley and know we're both thinking the same thing.

This is awesome.

It's not like I've ever cared to go to Hawaii anyway.

"That doesn't mean you can't travel," Bethany says as she leads us upstairs and toward the left. "The guys travel a lot, and if you ask them they'll let you go. Rosa loved going to Mexico, and the guys knew that, so each time they went, they'd ask if she wanted to come. So, if there's some place you're dying to see, just let them know."

"Are the guys nice?" Olivia says. It's the first time she's spoken since she meekly introduced herself, so we all look at her. She shrivels back, clearly not a fan of all the attention.

"Yeah," Bethany says quickly. "I mean, none of them are rude or anything. Most just won't talk to you because they're busy doing their own thing. Alexo is super kind and he treats us all like royalty. You'll see."

"Who's Alexo?" Riley asks.

"He's the boss." Bethany says. "He's really nice. You'll meet him later at dinner."

On the first part of our tour, we explored the entire right side of the house, so this is all new territory now. I try to memorize everything as we pass it so I don't get lost once we're alone.

"This is my favorite room," Bethany says, pausing at the arched wooden door in front of us. We're in a hallway but it's much wider than most normal house hallways. It stretches on to the far end of the house, with doors on both sides that are all closed, keeping whatever is behind them a secret.

"Also, this is as far as we go here," she says, brushing some lint off the front of her dress. "Everything past this room is off limits. It's the guy's private quarters, nothing scary," she adds when she sees Olivia's panicked expression. "Okay, here we go."

The door opens into a dark area that's only about the size of a closet. The walls are black, and it's hard to see because the lighting is so dim. "Just turn right," Bethany calls out behind the crowd of us.

And then it all makes sense. This little square area just inside the door is meant to block the outside light from the hallway. When we turn, we're in a movie theater.

There are five rows of seats, each a comfortable recliner with its own armrests and cup holders. The floor is sloped downward to where a screen fills the entire wall. It's not quite the size of a real movie theater screen, but it's close.

"Any movie you want to see," Bethany says, her eyes alight with cheer. "Even movies in the theater right *now*, you can get them. You just type it in the computer over there and it'll start playing it. They have some kind of deal with the movie companies where we can get all of them. I'm a huge move buff, so sometimes I spend all day in here."

Olivia and Nia walk down to the first row and sit, testing out the chairs. Jayla looks bored. Riley pulls me into the back row where we sit too.

"The cook makes the best popcorn," Bethany says. "It tastes just like real movie popcorn. They also have any candy bar you want so just call in your order before your movie starts and they'll bring it to you."

Riley looks over at me, her face shadowy from the dim lighting. "How did we get so lucky?"

"I have no idea," I say. "Something tells me this year will go by entirely too fast."

I lean back in my seat and look up. The ceiling has been painted black as well, but there are tiny little dots of light scattered around like the night sky. It all hits me at once. The feeling of doom and dread that I've been holding back.

I've been on edge since we walked in the front door. I've been expecting Theo to be around every corner, beyond every door. But he's not. We've only see housekeepers since we've been here.

And now that some of the magic of this place has had time to settle, I'm once again thinking about him.

"Hey Bethany?" I ask, nodding for her to come over here.

"What's up?" she says, sliding into the seat next to me.

I feel so stupid asking, but it needs to be done. I'd thought Theo's girlfriend would be one of the other girls working here but Bethany is the only one, and she's already mentioned being single. "Do any of the guys here have, like, wives or girlfriends?"

She considers it for a minute. "I don't think so. I guess I've never really thought about it," she says. "Most of them are kind of too old for me to care, and you barely see them anyway." There must be some tell-tale sign on my face, because her eyes flash with recognition. "Why, do you like one of them?" she whispers.

"I was just curious," I say with a shrug.

Riley leans forward, putting herself in our conversation. "She was worried about becoming a sex slave," she whispers.

Bethany laughs. "Oh, no. Definitely not. These guys are great to us."

"Told you," Riley says, punching me in the arm. "There is absolutely *no* reason to think about those guys."

I give her a tight lipped smile. She knows exactly why I'm asking about the guys, and it's not because I'm worried about them being perverts. But she gives me this look and I know what it means. I'm supposed to forget all about Theo. I'm supposed to enjoy my new life and forget that he exists.

Easier said than done.

Because now that Theo isn't dating one of the girls here, and Bethany doesn't know anything about his personal life, I'm stuck even more clueless than before. What if he doesn't have a girlfriend?

Why would he have acted like that if he wasn't trying to stop his girlfriend from finding out about his affairs?

"What's next on the tour?" I ask in a futile attempt to shove thoughts of him out of my mind.

"The best part," Bethany says, standing back up. "I'm going to show everyone their bedrooms!"

The rest of the girls seem really happy about this, and they all head back out the theater room and follow Bethany to the staircase. She tells us our rooms are all in the same hallway upstairs.

I walk next to Riley in a daze, unable to pay much attention to what we're doing. I stare at the rug that stretches across the hallway, covering the hardwood floors. If Theo doesn't have a girlfriend, then maybe it was just me.

I wasn't good enough. He didn't want me forever. He just wanted me for a day.

SEVENTEEN

The upstairs hallway looks just like the one below it. Plush carpeting sags beneath my feet as we walk down the wide hall, the white stucco walls occasionally decorated with artwork. The whole second floor smells like cinnamon and vanilla, but I don't see any air fresheners anywhere.

"Let's see who's first," Bethany says. The cheer in her voice and the pep in her step haven't diminished one bit since she met us at the front door an hour ago. There's a stunning painting of a monarch butterfly to the left that catches my attention. The brushstrokes are so skilled, it almost looks like the thing could fly right out of the canvas.

"Looks like this room is Cara's," she says. The large wooden door has a nameplate next to it, my name carved into the metal. This isn't some cheap plastic thing like you'd see on a banker's desk. It's a real solid chunk of brass with my name carved in large, curving letters. It's beautiful.

"Go on in," Bethany says, motioning for me to enter into my new room.

"I want to wait for Riley," I say sheepishly, looking over at her. "So we don't lose each other."

"No worries, Riley is next door," Bethany says, giving me a wink. Down the hallway is another door to the left, but it seems entirely too far away for there to only be two bedrooms between them.

"Ooh!" Riley says, clasping her hands together. "We're neighbors!"

"Done on purpose, I'm sure," Bethany says. "They always put friends together. For the rest of you, your rooms are down the hall. You'll find your name on the door. My room is at the far end on the left, and you can come get me anytime you want."

Nia, Jayla, and Olivia immediately leave in search of their rooms. Bethany chuckles. "Well, I guess the tour is over." She gives me a knowing look and I kind of want to ask how old she is since she acts so much older than she should. "Go enjoy your room."

"I love you, but I'm dying to see inside," Riley says. She gives me a quick wave goodbye and then skips down the hallway to her door.

I put my hand on my door knob, which is the same brass as the nameplate. I have no doubt what lies beyond will be a gorgeous bedroom just like the rest of the house. It's so stupid that I let my brain wander off like this, but I'm suddenly thinking about how great it would be if Theo was on the other side, waiting for me.

One by one, the other girls disappear into their rooms. I watch Bethany's retreating form as she reaches the end of the long hallway and disappears into her own room. Then I turn the handle and step into mine.

The ceilings are incredibly high, trimmed with crown molding. Where the rest of the house has a Spanish flair, my bedroom is more elegant and classical, like an old Victorian house. My breath catches in my throat as I look around, closing the door behind me. My room is massive. Maybe even the size of Uncle Will's old house. There's a king sized bed against the wall, the mattress so tall I'll probably have to jump to get on it. White satin sheets cover the bed and dark wood night stands are on either side. Across from the bed is a wall of windows that overlook the backyard. I can see for miles in the hill country, nothing but beautiful sloping hills and trees, houses occasionally dotting the horizon. The whole wall isn't a window, but it's close. The glass panes stretch from the floor to the ceiling and go about halfway down the room. There's a tablet mounted into the wall and a curtain rolled up above the windows, so I'm guessing I can block out the outside world if I choose to, but for now the view is gorgeous.

To the left, past the windows, is a sitting area. Two plush armchairs that are wide enough for me and Riley to sit in are turned toward a television that's mounted on the wall. There's also a large bookshelf that's empty except for a few knickknacks. Between the shelves are a door.

I walk over and open it, my stomach fluttering around with nerves and excitement all at the same time.

It's a walk-in closet with rows and rows of shelves and hanger space. Some shelves are slanted for shoes and others are deeper and wider. There's a square seat cushion in the middle of the room, a crystal chandelier hanging from the center of the ceiling.

This closet is bigger than my entire room back at my old house. It's nicer than anything the kids at Good Grace group home have ever seen. My heart catches in my throat. A sudden feeling of guilt falls over me because I don't deserve this. I don't deserve any of it. Once the guys of Rosewater Industries realize I'm not that special of a person, they're sure to kick me out. Just like Theo did.

With a heavy sigh, I figure I better enjoy it while I can. I head back to the bed and rush toward it, preparing to dive on top of the sheets.

A square envelope with my name on it stops me from leaping into the air. It's placed on the pillows, and the handwriting is the only sloppy thing in this room.

I sit on the bed and open it. There's a single piece of cardstock inside, the same handwriting scrawled across it.

Cara,
It's not too late to leave.
-Theo

What an asshole. The note crumples beneath my fist and I throw it at the wall since there doesn't seem to be a trash can around here. So he is here. He does know I've arrived. And yet he's avoiding me, choosing instead to send passive aggressive notes trying to get me to leave. Well he can kiss my ass because I'm staying. I'm staying as long as they'll have me.

There's a quick knock at my door and Riley bursts in before I have time to wonder if it might be Theo.

"Oh. My. God." Her eyes are so wide I fear they're going to fall out of her head. "Can you believe this?"

I force a smile, even though Theo's letter has sucked all the joy from me. "What does your room look like?"

"Pretty much identical to this," she says. She spreads her arms wide and then spins around in a circle just like on that movie *The Sound of Music*. "I am so happy we did this," she sing-songs.

"It is pretty amazing."

"I might just live in the bathroom," she says playfully. "Who needs a pool in the back yard when you have a tub like that?"

My brows pull together. "Where's the bathroom?"

"You mean where's *your* bathroom." She skips backwards and makes a grand flourish toward a door on the right side of the room. I haven't even noticed it yet. "Here it is."

She pulls open the door, revealing a marvel in granite and marble. The bathroom, like everything else in this house, is entirely too big. A hot tub rests in the middle of the room, tiled stairs going up to it. There's a shower without any doors because a long tiled wall curves around until you get inside it. The showerhead is in the ceiling and Riley says it looks like rain is pouring on you when you shower. There's another tablet in the wall here that plays music, and you can change the temperature of the water and even have calming scented oils added to it. Riley has apparently already played with the one in her bathroom. The vanity stretches the length of the bathroom, with mirrors stretching from one end to the other, and bright lighting that is probably every makeup artist's dream. There's another closet in the bathroom filled with plush white bathrobes.

A whimsical chime fills the air. Riley and I look at each other. "Is that your phone?" I ask.

She shakes her head. "Sounds like it came from your room."

The tablet built into the wall next to my door is lighting up. It says there's an incoming call from Bethany. I rush over and press the answer button.

Her face appears on the screen. "Hey there! I thought I'd give you a call so you can see how this thing works. Pretty cool, huh?"

"Very cool," I say, although I'm hoping there's no way for anyone to see through the camera on my end when I'm not on a call. I make a mental note to put a piece of paper over it.

"You can call anyone in the house," Bethany explains. "Just pick their name from the menu. You can also call down to the kitchen to request food, or call the housekeeping number to order things like groceries or shampoo or whatever."

"Sounds good," I say.

"There's one more thing, and since Riley is there with you, I'll just tell you both instead of calling her later. We're having a welcome dinner for you all tonight. Alexo will be here specially so he can welcome you to the clan." Her face lights up. That's the second time we've heard this company being referred to as a clan, which is kind of weird. "So wear something nice and be ready at seven. I'll come by and get you all, okay?"

"What if we don't have anything nice?" Riley says.

"Yeah, this is the extent of my wardrobe," I say. I do still have the outfit I wore to my interview, but that would be pathetic wearing the same thing twice in a row around my employers.

"No worries, I'll have housekeeping bring you some things. Later, you can go shopping if you want, but they have a lot of stuff here you can choose from until then."

When the call is over, I'm so overwhelmed with information that I can barely think straight. They're going to *send up clothes* for us like we're some kind of princess or something.

"How amazing is this?" I say, looking over at Riley. We're both laying on my bed, staring up at the ceiling while we bask in how amazing our lives are now.

"And to think," Riley says, "We owe it all to your uncle getting laid."

"What?" I nearly choke on my own spit.

"We came home that night and had to leave because he was getting it on with his lady friend. Then we went to Good Grace and saw Kyle putting up the fliers. So in a way, your uncle's sex life was the best birthday gift ever."

I crack up laughing. If only he could hear that, I wonder what he'd say. But she's probably right. I'm not sure we would have seen the bulletin board in enough time to make it to the interviews if we hadn't walked in when we did.

"That's hilarious and horrifying and let's never talk about it again," I say, still laughing.

Riley sighs blissfully and tucks her hands beneath her head. "Can you believe how lucky we are?"

"Nope," I say, sighing just like she did. "This place is wonderful. Let's hope here's not a catch."

"Actually." A deep voice fills the room, startling us. I whip around, ready to grab the lamp off my nightstand and beat someone with it, but the man in my doorway is Theo.

His eyes are bloodshot as he says, "There *is* a catch."

EIGHTEEN

The whole world seems to stop. My body freezes, and all I see is Theo. His eyes plead with me; they're filled with a desperation that doesn't make any sense to me. Probably only a few seconds have passed, but it feels like ages before Riley breaks the silence.

"You must be Theo." The tone of her voice conveys a hidden snark that her eyes don't show.

"I am," he says, his eyes never leaving mine.

Riley touches my shoulder as she walks past me. "I'll let you two talk. Cara?" she says, making me look at her. "I'll be next door when you need me."

I nod, my throat too dry to talk. The room is silent except for the soft padding of Riley's shoes on my carpet as she leaves, then the click of the door closing behind her.

"Go away," I say. My arms fold across my chest, instinctively blocking my heart from the man who hurt it. "I don't want you in here."

"Cara..." Theo's head dips to the side and he runs a hand through his hair. I notice now that it's messy, unkempt and going in all directions. He's wearing jeans and his same Converse, with a black long-sleeved shirt that has three buttons down the center of the neck. It hugs tightly to his chest and the muscles over his broad shoulders. It's like he chose this outfit specifically to drive me crazy.

"Don't say my name." I'm proud with how strong my voice is. "Don't leave me letters, don't come to my room. Just go."

"Cara, we need to talk." He steps forward, and I back up until I touch my bed. I hate that butterflies flood into my stomach at the sight of him approaching me. I hate that he still makes my body react to him no matter how much I try to stop it.

"I don't want to talk," I say. Just like the butterflies who betray my stomach, my voice has also left me out to dry. It comes out weak, scared, and sad. "Just go away," I say, looking out my window. "Please."

"I'm not leaving until we talk."

Even when I'm not looking at him, I can tell he's getting closer because the delicious woodsy smell of his cologne is now all up in my personal space, doing wicked things to my insides.

I grind my jaw together. I can't let him see me like this, all weak and pathetic. "Fine," I say, still refusing to look at him. "If you want to talk, then fucking talk."

"I know you don't want to hear this, Cara," he begins, his voice low and honeyed just like the day I met him. "But you really need to leave. You shouldn't be here."

"Why?" I say, throwing up my hands. I turn to him, facing the guy who broke my heart head on. "Because I'm not good enough? I'm not as pretty as those other girls? I'm just some poor trash from Sterling and you don't want me sullying your precious mansion?"

"That isn't why," he says. He seems like he's trying very hard to be patient with me. "Also, this house is a rental. None of us own it."

I roll my eyes. "I don't care to talk about finances."

"Neither do I." Theo takes a deep breath and presses his fingers to his lips before he exhales. "We should sit."

"I'm not sitting. I'm not moving. Just tell me whatever you want to tell me and then leave." Disappointment flickers across his chiseled features, but it only encourages me to push on. "I haven't told your stupid girlfriend, if that's what you're worried about. I don't even know who she is."

"I don't have a girlfriend," Theo says, clearly frustrated. "Haven't had one in decades, for what it's worth."

I look at him disbelievingly. He's not more than twenty-something years old. Does that mean he's never had a girlfriend? I shake my head, not wanting to let my thoughts derail. There's no way a guy like him hasn't had a girlfriend in his life. He's a liar, just like all scumbags on this planet.

"Look, I'm not leaving, and nothing you can say will change my mind. I come from a total shit hole of a town and this place is the best thing that's ever happened to me. So even though you don't think I'm good enough, someone else does, and I've been hired, so drop it. Clearly, it's not up to you."

"Jesus, Cara," Theo says, through clenched teeth. "Just believe me. Please. You can't be here. I wish I could say more, but I can't."

I've drifted over to the wall of windows now, making sure to keep my back to Theo so I don't have to see him. There's something about looking at a perfect specimen of a man that really makes a broken heart hurt worse.

Theo appears next to me, his gaze on the beautiful landscape outside. "You are too sweet, and too kind to be here. You are the most beautiful girl I have ever known, and even if you weren't—" He pauses, exhaling. "Even if you weren't, there's something about you. You are charming and adorable. You've awakened things inside of me that I haven't felt in, well, a long time."

Tears sting my eyes, and I still refuse to look over at him. Instead, I fix my gaze on a little white house on top of a hill miles away and focus on my breathing.

Theo leans forward, pressing both hands to the glass above his head. "I am trying to protect you, Cara. I wish you'd believe me."

"You don't protect someone by sending them away." My throat feels like it's full of cotton balls.

Theo sighs, his head tipping forward, sinking between his shoulders. "Sometimes, that's exactly how you save someone."

I turn to him now. "Why don't you just tell me what's going on? If you don't have a girlfriend, then I don't understand. You acted like you liked me on the pier, and then you hated me on the plane, and now you're being nice again but still telling me to leave. If you're afraid I'll become some lovesick stalker or something, just tell me. I promise I won't. If you don't like me, then fine. I'll move on with my life."

He shakes his head. "That's not it, Cara. You have no idea how badly I want to throw you on that bed and make love to you."

My heart skips a beat. And then another beat. And then I might actually be dead because there's no way he said that. But when his gaze meets mine, it's filled with passion again. His jaw flexes with determination.

My eyes drift to his chest and I am unable to stop myself from imagining what it'd be like to be carried to my bed in Theo's arms. I clear my throat as heat rushes to my cheeks.

Theo chuckles and steps away from the window. "But that's just a temporary fantasy," he says, his voice so low it makes my toes tingle. "If I truly had my way right now, I'd never leave your side again. I would make you mine forever. Until this entire planet implodes—you would be mine."

My breathing is shallow. He's now just a few inches away from me, his sultry gaze peering at me just like he's done in my dreams lately. I don't know when it happened, but now his fingers are interlocked with mine, our hands clasped together between us.

When my heart starts beating again, the ache in my chest brings me back to reality. *Don't touch me.* The words run through my mind but I can't say them aloud. I want his touch as much as I don't want to admit it. I want the sensation of his calloused palm sliding across my cheek.

But deep down I know this man will hurt me again, just like he already has. This is some kind of trick and here I am falling right into it again, without even the help of a glass of gris. I let my hands fall from his and I step away.

"I don't believe you."

"Let me take you home," he says. His tongue flicks across his bottom lip. It takes everything I have not to reach up and kiss him. Instead, I shake my head.

"This is my home now."

"Let me take you back to Sterling. Please."

I laugh sarcastically. "I don't have a home. My uncle's house is being sold. I literally have nowhere to go back to."

"I'll buy you a house." His hands slide down my arms, leaving a trail of goosebumps behind. "It doesn't have to be in Sterling. Anywhere you want. I'll buy it for you. I'll come visit every chance I can."

"Fuck that." I shove him, hard, and he steps backward. "I am not some whore you can buy off," I say, gritting my teeth to stop tears from flowing. "I'm also not a charity case."

"Cara, that's not it. Please," he comes toward me but I back away. "Let me help you. Anywhere but here, Cara. Please."

I have never seen a man as desperate as Theo looks now. What's worse is that it's getting harder to hate him.

"Why are you doing this?" I say, not even bothering to hold back my tears now. "Why are you playing with my heart? Don't you see how much this hurts me?"

"I'm trying to help you," Theo says softly. His hand cups my cheek as he gets closer. "Hurting you is the last thing I want."

"Then why can't I stay?"

His thumb slides across my cheek while he watches me with a deep sadness in his amber eyes. "I can't tell you why, love."

I close my eyes and lean forward. Theo wraps his arms around me as my face presses against his chest. I feel his chin rest on top of my head, feel the warmth of his hands locking together behind my back. His heart is pounding, just like mine.

"Do you really care about me?" I whisper, my lips against his chest.

"More than you know," he whispers back. "More than I ever thought possible."

I don't know why I believe him, but I do. Maybe I'm the stupidest girl in the world. "Do you feel it?" I say, looking up at him. "The…connection…between us?"

"From the moment I met you." His bottom lip pulls under his teeth, revealing a raw side to him that he's tried to keep hidden. My breath catches in my throat. We stand here, looking into each other's eyes, and right now I realize that I don't care if I'm being an idiot. I want Theo, and I trust Theo and that's all there is to it.

"If you really care about me, you'll let me stay."

He frowns, then pulls me closer and kisses my forehead. "Me caring about you is exactly why you can't stay."

NINETEEN

I have an electric type of attraction to Theo. I feel it between our bodies, holding us together like magnets. I sink my hands into his back pockets and gaze up at him. "What if I refuse to leave?" I say playfully. "Would you still want to be with me?"

"Of course I would," he says, his voice pained. "But you would regret it."

"I'd never regret being wrapped up in your arms."

He groans, a blissful sound that makes his knees bend a little. "You're killing me. Absolutely killing me."

"But I get to stay," I say, grinning like a dork.

He shakes his head, tightens his hold on my waist. "You can't."

"Yes, I can."

Some of the playfulness fades from his eyes. "We'll talk about this later. There's still time to change your mind."

I smirk. "Giving up that easily, huh?"

He shakes his head, an evil but sexy look spreading across his face. "I haven't given up. I just can't resist you anymore."

I'm still processing his words when his lips find mine. That electric feeling between us intensifies when he kisses me. I feel it from my mouth down to my feet, and it is absolute euphoria.

My hands tangle into his hair, and then I'm lifting off the floor and he walks us to my bed. It's like the hotel room all over again when he gently lays me down, his gaze filled with hunger as he crawls up the bed, his body hovering over mine.

Except this time I won't push him away.

I haven't won the war yet, but I won this battle. Theo is now making out with me instead of begging me to leave for some stupid reason he won't tell me.

I let all worries of that slip away while I fall further into bliss. His kisses trail down my neck, to my collarbone. I close my eyes and let the sensation of his lips flood my whole body with pleasure.

His tongue flicks across my neck and then he kisses the same place and my whole body shivers. My hands dig into his shoulders. I let my nails drag down his back lightly.

He leans into my touch, his muscles tightening as he hovers over me on the bed. I want him closer, need him closer.

I bring my hands up to his face, then pull him toward me for another kiss. His tongue tangles with mine, his breath warm and delicious.

There's this surreal feeling between us as our bodies move together, our clothes annoyingly in the way. I can't explain it, but Theo is unlike any other guy. It's like he was meant just for me. Like his entire existence on this planet was formed by fate, waiting for us to find each other.

The feeling is so powerful I can barely breathe.

"You are so beautiful," Theo whispers, his face casting a shadow over mine. I don't know what to reply, but luckily, I don't have to.

His lips find mine again, and I revel in the way this boy kisses. Like a fucking god. I melt into him, letting him take the lead, letting his hands roam up my shirt and over my breast.

When his lips find my collarbone, I gasp, and a little whimper I can't hold back escapes me. Theo chuckles to himself. "You will be the death of me," he whispers. "The actual death of me."

"So long as it takes a while," I say between kisses. "I'm not ready for you to go."

He laughs, somewhat ironically. "Don't worry. I won't."

I slide out from underneath him and press his shoulder, motioning for him to roll onto his back. Waves of electricity are flowing through me, and I'm nervous as hell to take charge like this, but I want more of him.

I bite my lip and move forward, putting my hands on either side of his shoulders.

Then something vibrates in his jeans pocket. I jump off of him, the unexpected noise startling me.

"Shit," he mutters, stretching out his leg to grab his phone. His face hardens as he looks at the screen. "I have to take this."

Sitting up, he grabs my face and pulls me in for a kiss. "I'm so sorry."

"It's fine," I say weakly as I watch him stand up and straighten out his clothes. He puts the phone to his year. "Yeah," he says sternly, his eyes far away. "I'll be there."

Sliding the phone back in his pocket, he turns to me. "Dinner is at seven."

"I know," I say, still breathless from our make out session. "Will you be there?"

He nods. Some trace of that phone call is still obviously on his mind right now. "Meet me at the pool at six. Just you, no one else, okay?"

I bat my eyelashes at him and pat the bed. "You don't want to meet somewhere else instead?"

He grins, then shakes his head. "No, love. This is important."

I sigh. "You want to talk about stupid things again."

"Yes. But it's important."

He walks up to me and takes my hand, pulling it to his chest. "Promise you'll meet me at six."

"I promise," I say, rolling my eyes. "But you won't talk me into leaving."

"Just be there," he says with a resigned sigh. "Six o'clock. Alone."

"Fine," I say, dragging out the word so he knows how stupid I think it is.

"Good," he says, kissing my forehead. "I'll tell you everything you need to know. And then you'll be begging to leave this place."

I frown and let out my breath in a huff. "You've admitted you have feelings for me, Theo. So stop trying to get rid of me."

"I would never do such a thing," he says, his voice slow and sexy. "You'll understand it all soon." He gnaws on the inside of his lip and it gives me great satisfaction knowing he doesn't want to leave me. "I just have some things to take care of," he says with a sigh. "But then I'm all yours. And I'll convince you that you need to leave, but you'll understand why."

I roll my eyes. "Unless you're going with me, I'm not leaving."

He hides his annoyance with a smile. I guess it's kind of sweet that he doesn't want me to know his true feelings when it comes to being annoyed with me. Still, I'm not sure anything he tells me will convince me to leave this ridiculously awesome living situation. I mean what would be better than living in luxury with the guy of your dreams?

I can't think of anything.

TWENTY

Shortly after Theo leaves, a garment cart is rolled into my room by the housekeeper who first greeted us at the door when we arrived. "Formal wear," she says, giving me a small nod before turning to leave.

"Wait," I say. She turns back to me.

"You need anything else, dear?" Her thick accent is beautiful but I'm not sure where it's from.

I shake my head. "I just wanted to know your name. I'm Cara."

"My name is Malina," she says, dipping into a quick bow. "I'm the head housekeeper. Let me know if you need anything, dear."

"Okay, thank you," I say. "It's nice to meet you," I call out as she leaves. There's a very uncomfortable feeling in my stomach when I'm around her and I'm not sure I'll be able to get used to it. I've never had a housekeeper or anything in my life. I don't like the idea of telling someone else what to do. Maybe I'll talk to Henry about it. I'll ask him to let me do my own stuff so the housekeepers don't have to.

I turn toward the garment rack. It looks like one of those things bellhops use to cart around suitcases in hotels, only this one has a rail across the top where a few dozen outfits are hanging. Each one is in a clear plastic bag, and I flip through them, admiring the beautiful colors and fancy fabrics.

Theo will see me in one of these dresses tonight. I have to make sure I pick out the exact perfect one, one that will make him so attracted to me that he won't be able to stand asking me to leave.

I grin as I look through each dress. They are all low cut, sparkly, and probably very expensive. I want to try on every single one and parade around like a princess.

But before I do, I call Riley on the wall screen.

"Heyyy," she says, dragging out the word. Her face is entirely too close to the screen, and it makes me laugh.

"You don't have to stand so close, you know."

"Yes, I do," she singsongs, flitting her eyes upward. "You can't see my dress until I come over there. It's too pretty to be seen on a stupid webcam."

"You already picked one out?" I say, glancing back toward my dresses that aren't even out of their bags yet.

"The moment I saw it, I knew it was perfect," she says, her face still hovering hugely on my screen. "If you want, I can help you pick out yours and then you can tell me all about lover boy, who by the way, is totally hotter now than he seemed at the pier."

I roll my eyes. "Yes, come over."

"Hey, Cara," she says, her voice taking on a different tone. "Remember when we were kids and they put us in two different dorm rooms at the home because we talked too much and they wanted to separate us?"

"Of course I remember. They separated us in school, too," I say with a laugh. Riley and I weren't ever *bad* kids, but we talked and giggled too much when we were together. It annoyed every teacher and caretaker we ever had.

Riley says, "Remember how we stole a butter knife from the kitchen and cut through the drywall so we'd have a little window to be able to talk to each other face to face?"

Now that's a memory I had forgotten. We got in so much trouble for cutting that small square into the wall. They made us fix it and then we had bathroom cleaning duty for two months.

"I remember," I say. "What's your point?"

She grins. "This is just like that. Only better because we're talking through technology instead of a hole."

The call ends.

When Riley taps on my door a few seconds later, I open it to reveal a girl who barely resembles the one I've known most of my life. She's chosen a black form-fitting dress that's so long it trails behind her a little bit. It has a plunging neckline that makes her boobs look bigger than they actually are, and she even looks taller than normal.

"Whoa," I say, as she does a little spin for me. "You're totally hot."

"I know, right?" Riley's hair is pulled up in a messy bun with strands of her bangs expertly hanging around her face. She's styled the bun with some rhinestone hairpins and her makeup looks more classy sophisticated than her usual grunge style.

"You did all of that in the ten minutes since they delivered your dresses?" I say. "Did you also find some magic powers in your bedroom?"

"Nah," she says, waving her hand at me as she walks over to my wall of windows. "I was bored waiting on you and lover boy, so I got started on my hair and makeup before the dresses arrived."

"His name is Theo," I say.

She shrugs. "Oh, but calling him lover boy is so much more fun because you get that embarrassed look on your face."

"I hate you," I say, turning my attention to the dresses.

Riley walks to the other side of the garment rack and peeks at me through two of the dresses. "You *love* me!"

I stick out my tongue at her. "Okay so, here's the deal. I'm going to tell you what happened with Theo, but I want to just say it all fast and then not dwell on it, okay?"

Riley lifts an eyebrow. "Oh-kay." She pulls a dress off the hanger and shoves it toward me. "This is the one."

"I want to try all of them on," I say, putting the dress back on the rack. "I'll start from one end and work my way down."

She takes the dress again, shoving it toward me. "Trust me, this is the one. Now tell me about lover boy. Do we hate him or love him?"

"We don't *hate* him," I say, taking the dress she hands me and walking over to my bed. "But we're not sure if we love him yet."

"Love is a strong word for someone you just met," she says with a nod. "So, what happened? Did you make out?"

"Riley!"

She puts a hand on her hip, a gesture that is so like her, but looks so unlike her since she's currently dressed like an actress going to the Oscars. "It's obvious you did. You're looking guilty as hell right now."

I roll my eyes and pretend I'm not blushing. I can't even focus on the dress in front of me right now because thoughts of what Theo and I did on this very bed a little while ago are running through my mind.

"He wants me to leave," I say, turning to Riley. She still has a hand on her hip, and now her pink glossed lips pucker into a frown.

"Still?"

I shrug. "He begged me to leave and quit this job. He even said he'll buy me a freaking house if I want, just as long as I leave."

"Damn," she says. "What the hell is he hiding here?"

"He said he doesn't have a girlfriend." I bite my lip. "And then we totally made out."

Riley chuckles. "So, that's good news and bad news. Why on earth would he want you to leave? He works here, right?"

"Yeah, so it doesn't make sense, unless he doesn't really like me. But I swear he does, Riley. I can feel it."

She frowns. "Maybe he has an issue with the boss, that Alexo guy. Maybe he's about to quit and he thinks they won't let you date him or something if he does?"

"I like that idea better than my idea of Theo having a secret girlfriend," I say. "He wants me to meet him at the pool an hour before dinner so he can explain things to me." I make air quotes around the word explain. "So I guess I'll know more then, but I have no intention on leaving."

"Cara, if the boy is going to buy you a freaking house, maybe you should leave, if it means being with the guy you want."

I shoot her a look. "I can't leave you! I can't leave a hundred thousand dollars. And I don't even know Theo that well. I mean, I think he's the greatest guy ever, but I need time to get to know him better."

"I guess we'll have to see what he says." Riley looks at the clock on my wall. "We have an hour until you need to meet him, so get this dress on and I'll do your hair and makeup."

"I didn't bring any makeup," I say. "Can I borrow yours?"

"Oh honey," Riley says, rolling her eyes. "You spent so much time kissing that boy of yours that you didn't bother checking your vanity. The whole bathroom is stocked with stuff. Brand *new* stuff. We're talking Sephora level makeup in there, and all of mine matched my skin tone perfectly, so I bet yours does, too." She snaps her fingers at me. "Now get the damn dress on!"

I pull the dress from the bag. It's a deep purple gown that's made of a satin type fabric that seems to flow like liquid under the lights. I run my fingers down the skirt, imagining what it'd look like on me, hugging every single curve I have. Like Riley's dress, this one is form fitting and sleek.

"Get dressed," Riley says. "We're going to make lover boy's jaw drop so far he'll have to use duct tape to hold it back up."

She disappears into my bathroom and I shrug off my clothes, then carefully slip into the dress. There's no size on the tag, but somehow it fits me like a second skin.

It's sleeveless, with metal in the bust area to hold the chest part up over my boobs. The skirt flows down to my feet, looking like rippling water with every step I take. I can't help it—I twirl around.

I choose a pair of black heels from the bottom of the garment rack and slip them on. I'll need to practice walking for the next two hours if I have any chance at all of not looking like a total idiot at dinner.

"What do you think?" I ask, walking carefully into the tiled floor of the bathroom.

"You're a babe," Riley says with a grin. She gazes at our reflection in the large mirror that stretches across the wall. "This is why they hired us. They saw two scrappy teenagers with potential. Now, go take that off so I can do your makeup."

I groan and turn around, my heels clacking on the floor.

Once Riley has finished my makeup, I start getting really excited and nervous for the night ahead of me. Thanks to her killer makeup skills, I look just as hot as she does. Elegant, but not overdone.

Riley keeps my hair down, saying I look more mature that way, but she straightens it and sweeps a part of it to the side, pinning it back with a barrette that has purple gemstones that match my dress.

We spend at least ten minutes admiring ourselves in front of the mirror, and then there's a knock on my door. All the blood rushes from my face as I go to answer it, expecting Theo since it's only a few minutes until six.

Unfortunately, it's another housekeeper. She's holding a tablet in her hand as if it were a clipboard. "I'm getting some shopping done," she says by way of greeting. "Can I get your orders?"

"Um, I don't really need anything," I say, turning to Riley.

"What did the other girls order?" Riley asks.

The housekeeper looks down at her tablet. "Shampoo from a store called Barneys, nail polish, a bigger television, new laptops..." She looks up at us. "Anything you want that's local. The Barney's shampoo isn't local so I have to order it."

I consider it for a moment, but there's not really anything I need right now. The bathrooms are filled with amenities and I'm not one for special shampoo so I can use the stuff they have in here with no problems.

"Maybe some magazines," Riley says. "Like fashion and women stuff. I need fashion tips since my wardrobe just got a whole lot bigger."

The housekeeper makes a note of it in her tablet. "Anything else?"

I'm coming up blank. Never in my life have I been asked a question like this. I run my whole life based on the cheapest possible outcome, the bare necessities. Now I have a blank canvas before me, a woman offering to buy anything I want, and yet I can't think of a thing. "No, I guess I'm good for now."

This seems to surprise her, but she nods anyway. "Most items you can order through here," she says, tapping the screen near my door. "But things you need immediately, let me know and I will run to the store."

"Okay, thanks."

"So," Riley says. "Do you travel with the guys of Rosewater Industries?"

"No, ma'am, I just work for the house. I am contracted out to whoever rents it."

"Do you like these guys?" Riley asks.

She nods. "They are nice. But I am paid to work, not to have an opinion. Have a good day."

After she's gone, Riley says, "Do you think it's weird having these people we can boss around?"

"Very weird." I start to rub my forehead, but then I remember the face full of makeup that Riley has so carefully applied, and I stop myself. I have to stay perfect for Theo and for the dinner later where we'll meet Alexo, the real boss of this place.

"It's almost time for your clandestine meeting," Riley says, nudging me with her shoulder. "Let me know how it goes. And remember, if you make out down there it's going to ruin your makeup."

The thought of another kiss with Theo lights up my insides, but I give Riley a sarcastic look and shoo her out of my bedroom. I really don't think we'll be making out by the pool, because being told to pack up and leave isn't exactly romantic. Hopefully Theo doesn't try too hard, because no matter what, I'm not changing my mind.

TWENTY-ONE

The house is quiet as I make my way downstairs and out to the pool. The only person I see is a maid dusting some of the statues in a sitting room. She doesn't look up at me as I walk by.

The back of the house has a large back porch that stretches from one end to the other. A white concrete handrail lines the porch, and recessed lighting makes the pathway glow as I make my way toward the pool. I'd heard this type of pool called an infinity pool, and I understand why now that I'm seeing it up close.

The back half of it just drops off, the water flowing over the edge. From the back porch, you'd think the pool went on forever because the water looks like it's spilling out into the lake that's actually pretty far away from where we are on the hilltop. Really, it just dips over the side and cycles back into the pool. The water is a gorgeous blue that reflects the sun as it begins to descend beyond the horizon.

There are patio chairs and lounge chairs near the pool, and closer to the house there's an outdoor kitchen and two televisions hanging from the ceiling.

I don't see Theo yet, so I walk up to the porch handrail and lean on it to take some of the balance work off my high heels. I realize I'll probably have to wear fancy clothes a lot around here, so I better spend my free time practicing walking in these things.

The rest of the backyard slopes downward and the grassy areas fade out into thick groves of trees. I spot a small golf course to the right of the property, the grass expertly landscaped and unnaturally green.

To the left, there's a tennis court and the gardens, which Bethany had told us were very beautiful. She said it made her feel like she was Elizabeth Bennet in *Pride and Prejudice* when she walked through the gardens, and somedays she dreamed she'd run right into a modern-day Mr. Darcy when she went walking alone.

I didn't bring my phone and I don't have a watch because that wouldn't match my dress, so I don't know what time it is. But as the minutes stretch on, I know it's after six and there's still no sign of Theo.

I walk down to the pool and stand at the water's edge, watching my reflection wobbling back at up at me. In the distance, the blue sky turns shades of red and orange, casting a stunning sunset glow on the landscape before me. I glance back at the house, but I don't see anyone through the windows. However, I do find a wall tablet in the outdoor kitchen. I check the time.

6:18

It's hard not to let disappointment sink into my bones when another ten minutes pass and Theo still hasn't arrived. I try to look like I'm not bored, worried, and embarrassed as even more minutes go by. I wonder if Theo is upstairs somewhere looking at me through a dark window, laughing to himself for setting me up like this.

But that's just my imagination. He wouldn't do that.

I take another walk around the pool. I gaze out at the breathtaking view of Texas, and I casually look around for Theo. My toes are killing me in these shoes, but I don't want to sit down and risk wrinkling my dress.

My thoughts go in a million different directions as I stand around like a loser waiting for a guy who isn't showing up.

I count to one hundred in my head and promise myself I'll leave if he's not here by then.

And then I count to one hundred three more times.

Birds sing and squirrels chase each other through the tree branches in the yard. The sound of the pool filter churns beneath the water, and somewhere in the distance I can hear an airplane soaring through the sky, but I can't see it in the clouds. I gaze out at the wonders of nature before me and stay focused on the sound around me, hoping that soon enough one of them will be Theo's footsteps.

But by 6:55, he's still not here.

I take a deep breath and walk back inside. It takes every ounce of energy I have to keep my expression serene, like I don't have a care in the world. I'm not going to be the girl who is full of drama on her first night here.

On my way to the dining room, I see the maid again.

"Excuse me," I say, going over to her. "Is there a second swimming pool here?"

"No, ma'am," she says. She points in the direction from where I came. "Just that pool back there."

"Thanks," I say. "That's what I thought."

Swallowing the lump in my throat, I look for Theo on the entire walk to the dining room. I see Nia and Jayla in gorgeous shimmery dresses, but they ignore me as if I were part of the help instead of one of the girls who live here.

I need Riley right now, but there's not enough time to find her before dinner begins. Hopefully she'll be waiting in the dining room when I arrive.

And hopefully Theo will be there, too, with an explanation for why he made me stand around feeling lonely and stupid for an hour.

TWENTY-TWO

The smell of roasted garlic fills the air as I enter the dining room. The other girls are here, standing next to each other, all in dazzling gowns. Riley rushes over to me, a magical smile on her face.

"It smells so good in here," she says, gazing around. "And the food's not even out yet."

"I can't even begin to think about food right now," I say quietly. My eyes divert around the room, to the faces of Kyle and Henry who are standing in the nearby sitting room having a glass of wine. To Nia and Olivia and Jayla, all huddled together like wallflowers at a high school dance. There are two men dressed in black tuxedos with long tails, standing straight-backed and ready for service near the dining table. The other guys from the plane are here, mingling with Henry and Kyle. Everyone but Theo is here.

"What happened with the talk?" Riley whispers while pretending to fix my hair.

"Nothing. He never showed," I whisper back. Riley's face flashes with concern, so I smile all happily so no one thinks anything weird is going on with us. We need a no drama night so we look good in front of our new boss.

"I don't see him here, either," she says, gazing around casually, a pleasant smile fixed on her face.

"He got a phone call earlier and said he had to take care of something." I shrug, ignoring the tightness in my chest. "I guess he's not back yet."

She squeezes my elbow reassuringly. "He'll be back. Don't worry."

"Welcome!" The booming voice comes from the hallway. We all turn toward the man whose black suit is tailored perfectly. His presence is like a force of nature the moment he enters the room.

The guys immediately stop talking and the other new girls seize up like they've been frozen in place with fear. I look over at Bethany, who only got here a few seconds before Alexo, and she's smiling happily, so I relax as well.

Alexo is not as tall as some of the guys here, but he definitely looks like he's in charge. He has olive skin with shoulder length dark brown hair, the ends sharp and slicked back. His beard is trimmed neatly, his square jaw making him look a little more stern than handsome. Although he is definitely handsome in a traditional sense. I'd guess he's probably in his late thirties.

"My name is Alexo," he says, spreading out his arms in greeting. "I'm so honored to welcome our newcomers to the clan." He takes a moment to gaze at each of us, a sweet smile on his lips. "Unfortunately, a matter came up that can't be put off, so I will have to miss dinner tonight. I'm so very sorry, as I know it would have been delightful getting to know you all."

He checks the time on his watch, which is one of those gold and massive designer things that swallows his wrist. "I usually save the clan initiation ceremony for after dinner, but tonight we'll do it before."

Riley and I exchange a glance. *Clan initiation?* Why do they keep calling us that? It reminds me of a group of vampires or something.

Alexo flicks his wrist in a *come here* gesture, and five maids walk out, each holding a black velvet pillow like the ring bearers in a wedding. Only instead of a ring, each pillow carries a beautiful silver bracelet.

"Bethany, sweetheart," Alexo says. "Would you like to help me initiate your new roommates?"

"I would love to," she gushes as she hurries over to him. She doesn't stumble at all in her high heels and I really hope that kind of skill is in my future.

As the maids follow Alexo toward us, I realize the bracelet looks just like the one Bethany wears. That's kind of cool, actually. It's like a gift for everyone, maybe to make us feel like a family.

Or a clan. Whatever that means.

Alexo stands in front of us and I'm reminded of the Olympic medal ceremony. Everything feels so formal. The guys line up behind Alexo, their hands clasped behind their backs. There's still no sign of Theo, but I try not to worry about him. One thought that does cross my mind is how on earth will we be together happily if he's always dashing off to take care of business?

I shrug the thought away.

"Ladies, I am so honored to have you here with us," Alexo begins. "Your job may not be backbreaking or hard, but I assure you, you are doing a great service to the Rosewater clan. Just like my darling Bethany," he says, turning to her with a smile, "You are all about to become the lifeblood of this clan. Your beauty and charm all help make us better men. With your presence, you are helping us achieve our goals and obtain success in our greatest missions."

He reaches for the first bracelet which is in front of Jayla, who of course has positioned herself to be first in line. He holds it up and I notice a deep blue marbled stone glisten in the light. "With time, you will realize what a valuable asset you have been to the cause, and your legacy here at the Rosewater clan will endure forever. Now, I'm sure you have been told there are only a few rules here as part of your employment," he says, his voice taking on a more serious tone.

"The first and only rule that you must follow at all times is this:" He twists the bracelet in his hand, then reaches out his other hand to Jayla. She puts it in his palm. "You must never remove this bracelet. Not for showering or swimming. Not for anything. Jayla, dear, do you vow to wear this bracelet every moment of your time here?"

"I do," she says formally. He slips the band around her wrist. She beams, then brings it closer to admire it.

Wearing a bracelet all the time is kind of weird, but then again, a job like this *is* weird. Maybe it has a tracking device in it to make sure we don't run off or go into the private areas or something. Oh well, I think. That's not really a big deal. I'm here for the money and the luxurious living.

And maybe for one of the guys.

Alexo moves to Nia and says the same thing, for which she also agrees.

When it's my turn, I hold out my hand and Alexo's fingers are cold on my wrist. "Cara, sweetheart, do you vow to wear this bracelet every moment of your time here?" he says.

"I do," I say, smiling sweetly at him. He may have an intimidating presence, but this man's kindness also shows through. I have no doubt he won't let anything bad happen to us while we're here.

The bracelet slides onto my wrist. It's a silver bangle, rigid like every other bangle I've ever known, and maybe it's just my imagination, but the moment it touches my skin there's this split second sensation like it has formed exactly to my body. I look down at it, at the beautifully ornate curls of silver that wrap around the band and hold the blue stone in place. It's not loose or tight. It fits perfectly.

It's so beautiful it takes my breath away. I'm staring at it so long I miss Riley's oath, but soon the bracelet is on her wrist too and she turns to me, smiling wide, her eyes sparkling.

This is kind of crazy, and I know it sounds weird, but in this moment, I do feel like I'm adding something to the Rosewater clan. Like I'm doing something great by being here, even though I'm not really doing anything at all. As I gaze around at the guys, I feel a sense of belonging with them that I hadn't felt earlier.

The thought hits me as if it were put there on purpose. These guys would do anything for us. I don't know why, but I just know it. They would.

This really is a family.

A clan.

"It was such a pleasure to meet you all," Alexo says. The maids walk out of the room taking the pillows with them. "I promise we will have time to talk later, but I must take my leave now. Please enjoy dinner." He gives a slight bow in our direction and then turns to leave, waving sharply toward the guys.

I am so happy I could burst. I keep sneaking glances at my bracelet as we walk toward the table in the dining room. The servers pull out our chairs for us and everything.

This night is so wonderful and the food smells amazing. The only thing that's missing is Theo.

TWENTY-THREE

Although the stress over Theo had taken away my appetite, the moment a plate of fresh pasta is set in front of me, my mouth starts to water. I guess I'm no good at starving out my feelings. A lifetime of eating crap food from school cafeterias and group homes has left me without the ability to turn down delicious food, no matter how depressed I am.

And it is so delicious. I have to take great measures to eat like a lady and not just tip the bowl to my mouth and shovel it all in.

The conversation is lively around the dining table. The table itself is bigger than it needs to be, expanding from one end of the room to the other. There's high backed chairs and a fancy gray tablecloth with a floral arrangement in the center of the table that's long enough to reach across the whole thing. Everything is so elegant it looks like it came straight out of a magazine.

There are two empty seats at the table; the one at the head of the table for Alexo, and then one almost directly across from me. Theo's chair.

I twirl some pasta around my fork and try to imagine how dinner would be tonight if Theo were there, watching me. I'd most certainly not be able to finish all the food in front me. The imaginary butterflies in my stomach would see to that. But now he is gone and the butterflies are asleep, so I eat without any problems.

It's hard to ignore that huge empty space in the table and participate in the conversation. Luckily, Riley holds her own and talks enough for the two of us.

I find out more about the girls, who all seem excited to talk about themselves. Jayla goes on and on about how her dating life wasn't going so well after having split up with three older men who were all married and didn't want to leave their wives for her. She chose to take a sabbatical and get a job instead.

But by the way she's been eyeing Russel all night, I'd say she hasn't stopped dating at all. I wouldn't be surprised if she makes a move on him soon.

Russel is probably in his late twenties, so he's not too old, and he's not wearing a wedding ring so I can only assume he might be single. That's already a step up for Jayla, in my opinion. But Russel is tall and pale, with reddish brown hair the distinct personality of a drill sergeant. Like the asshole kind of sergeant you'd see in a movie about the military. On first glance, Jayla with her long brown hair and permanently prissy face, doesn't really seem like a good match for Russel. But then I think about how she's kind of totally stuck up and gives off this *don't talk to me* vibe, and maybe they would work well together.

It's too bad Russel doesn't seem to notice she exists.

Nia and Jayla were friends before they started working here, just like Riley and me. Only they both came from Silver Valley, which is an undeniably rich part of Texas. Maybe that's why they don't want anything to do with Riley and me. They can smell the poor on us. They know we weren't brought up in fancy houses like they were.

Nia's only good qualities are that she wants to be a singer, and when she sings a little for Kyle when he asks, she's actually pretty good. Also, her boobs are huge, which I guess is a good thing for the guys. I don't really care too much about that, and her personality is enough to make me want to roll my eyes.

After half an hour of Jayla and Nia talking about themselves, Henry asks Olivia where she's from. She's also from Sterling but she was homeschooled so we never saw her while we were growing up. She tells us that she was sick of living there and wanted to move away from her overbearing parents who swore they would disown her if she did leave. Olivia wants to travel the world, and you can tell she's really passionate about it in the way her eyes sparkle when she talks.

Henry tells her he can have that arranged if she'd like, and she beams so brightly I fear the centerpiece will catch on fire.

In all, dinner goes well. I don't have to talk much which is good because my thoughts are on Theo. When dessert is finished, Henry rises from his seat to address everyone.

"I think it's time for drinks in the courtyard," he says. "Ladies, dinners together are a rare occurrence, and most nights you'll be left to your own devices. So because we're all gathered here tonight, I say we spend a little more time together."

The courtyard is on the side of the house between the gardens and the pool. It's a cobblestone area with a fountain in the middle and beautiful flowers around all of the sitting areas. Unlike most fountains I've seen, where it's either a shooting spray of water or it has a bird bath in the middle, this one has a wild Mustang lifting up on his rear legs. He's a handsome horse, even if he is only concrete. The water fountain is centered around his legs, as if he's running through a river and splashing it up all over the place. It's very Texan.

Riley and I take a flute of champagne from the tray of a nearby waiter and we're both disappointed that it's not gris. It's just plain old champagne by the taste of it. Smooth jazz plays through hidden speakers and everyone mingles in this sophisticated way that's all new and thrilling to me.

We talk to Kyle for a little bit. He seems to be the youngest guy in the group and he's definitely the happy go lucky jokester around here. He talks forever about some stupid comedy show on late night television that he loves. I'm about to fall asleep to the sound of his voice, when someone appears on my left and touches me on the elbow.

I spin around and find Theo.

Gorgeous Theo, in dark jeans and a black shirt. He's slightly out of breath like maybe he ran out here, and his brows are pulled together.

"Can I talk to you for a minute?" he says, glancing apologetically at Kyle and Riley.

"Sure thing, man." Kyle waves us goodbye and Riley gives me a quick *good luck* wiggle of her eyebrows.

"Let's walk," Theo says. He leads me away from the courtyard and away from the gardens. We're headed toward the driveway of all places. He glances over his shoulder, his lips twisted in a smirk. "I missed you like crazy, by the way."

"I waited for you," I say, not hiding the annoyance in my voice. "I felt like an idiot."

"I'm sorry, Cara. This shit took longer than I thought it would." His voice is low, like he's afraid we'll be overheard. "I didn't have your number or I would have called you."

"No need for my number," I say. I have to hurry along to keep up with his long strides. "I can't pay the bill much longer so it'll get shut off soon."

"The clan will buy you all new phones. They're probably already ordered by now." He says this like it's a bad thing, but I guess it is since he wants me to leave.

"I'd hold your hand but that's probably not a good idea so soon," he says, giving me a half smile. He keeps walking further down the driveway and my feet are killing me in these heels.

"How far are we going?" I ask, exasperated and still annoyed. A simple apology doesn't really help smooth over the embarrassment I felt hanging out by the pool for an hour.

"Far enough so we're not overheard." He cuts a sharp look at me. "When we return, make sure you look all flushed and flirty like I've just been seducing you, okay?"

I roll my eyes. "Isn't that what you do every time we're together?"

His serious expression turns into a sly grin which makes my stomach tingle. "Oh, I *like* you," he says slowly.

Finally, he stops walking. "This is far enough."

I can see the main road from here and I'm pretty sure I could scream and no one would hear it. "So," I say, turning toward him.

"So." He studies me, his eyes going from my eyes to my lips and back. Then he steps forward and takes my face in his hands, tilting it up for a kiss. I'm trying to be mad at him, but damn, this kiss is amazing. "I missed dinner, but Alexo isn't here yet, so we haven't missed the ceremony. There's still time."

"What ceremony?"

His lips press together like he thinks it's the stupidest thing ever. "The bracelet ceremony."

I lift up my right arm. "You mean this bracelet?"

Words can't describe the look on Theo's face. Something like rage, anger, fear, and disbelief all cross at once, distorting his handsome features into something that terrifies me. He steps back like the bracelet just punched him in the face.

"Cara, no," he says, taking my arm in his hand. He shakes his head. "Goddammit, no."

His shoulders slump, and all of the air seems to deflate right out of him.

"What is it?" I say, yanking my arm back.

He's silent for a long time, his face tipped toward the ground.

"Theo?" I say, pushing him in the shoulder. "You can't just say that and then go silent on me."

He looks up at me. All of the light has faded from his features. "Why would you do this?" he growls, his jaw tightening. "Why the *hell* would you put that on?"

"Excuse you?" I say, stepping backward. "It's just a stupid bracelet. You can't yell at me for this! I should be yelling at you for standing me up at the pool!"

"Jesus, Cara. It's not just a bracelet." He runs a hand across the top of his head, making a fist in his hair. He turns around and stares up at the sky. "God, this is all my fault. I should have been here."

"Why are you freaking out?" I ask softly. "You told me to wait by the pool and then you didn't show up. What was I supposed to do?"

He turns back to me, his eyes now bloodshot and his hair all messed up from where he grabbed it. He looks like a broken man, like someone cut him open and took out all of the important pieces then left him here to die. "Why didn't you just listen to me?" he says, his voice a desperate cry of pain. "Why didn't you just *go home?*"

"I need this job, Theo."

He shakes his head. "It's not a job. I—dammit," he breathes. "I can't believe this. I should have—I didn't—" He exhales and then gets angry again. "Of course this would fucking happen. I meet a perfect girl and this shit fucking happens."

Now he's practically on a tirade, pacing a line in the driveway. He chuckles deliriously. "This is my life. This what I get. I was called to that job and I fucked up and I didn't save you. I don't deserve the happiness, so I don't know why I thought I could get it. And now you—sweet Cara—"

I rush up to him and put my hands on his shoulders, forcing him to stop pacing. "Theo," I say, looking into his eyes that are now the color of the sunset. "You sound like a crazy person. Why can't we be together?"

He bites on his lower lip, watching me like he's been called off to war and will never see me again. "I am not allowed to tell you," he says, closing his eyes. "I almost did. I was going to earlier. But now it's too late."

"Why is it too late?"

"You should have just gone home," he says, turning away from me.

"You know what?" I snap as anger rises up in me. "I am better than this. Why the hell am I standing here wishing you'd be nice to me when you're being weird as hell?" I shake my head. "Forget it. You want me to go home? I'm going home." I fling a finger toward the house. "That's my home. And don't fucking come see me anymore. You are no longer welcome in *my* part of *my* new house."

It rips my heart in half to say the words, but I don't understand why he's being so weird about this. He likes me, and then he doesn't. He wants to be with me, and then he's ranting that he can't. It just doesn't make sense.

And I am better than this.

So I kick off my heels and hold them in my hands, and then I walk as fast as I can toward the house. The sooner I cut myself off from Theo, the better I'll be.

TWENTY-FOUR

In all of the romance movies Riley and I have seen, there's always this part where the girl gets mad and runs off.

And in the best ones, the guy chases after her.

I may be pissed off and sick of being toyed with, but I'm secretly hoping Theo does just that when I stomp away from him. If he follows me, it'll mean he cares.

I'm only a few feet away when Theo jogs up to me and gets in the way so I can't keep walking toward the house. "Wait," he says, taking my hands in his.

My breath hitches. He smells amazing, like cologne and wine. The stubble on his jaw is thicker since I last saw him and I want to feel it scratch against my cheek again. I *hate* that these feelings exist at all because it'd be so much easier to turn him down if they didn't.

"I shouldn't have yelled," he says, squeezing my hands. His eyes never leave mine. "I'm sorry."

"It's fine," I say quickly. "Now let me go."

"Not yet." He dips his forehead until it touches mine, and I have to close my eyes to keep myself under control. "I still want to be with you, Cara." He places a kiss on top of my head. "It's just...everything is wrong now."

"Would you just tell me why?" I say, pleading with him. "I don't understand and you're acting like I should know already, but I don't. You're leaving me in the dark and it's bullshit."

I can see the pain in his eyes. He looks down at my arm, at the bracelet. "Everything changed when you put this on. I'm not mad at you—I'm just— I'm just mad. I wish I'd been here. I *should* have been here." He exhales, then moves forward, wrapping his arms around me and holding me close to his chest. I breathe in the scent of him, and revel in the way his chest feels against my cheek. "I still want to be with you. You still bring out something inside of me that I like. It's just—" Another sigh. "It's just not the same anymore. And I know I don't deserve you forever, so I guess I'll take you while I can have you. I'll be happy as long as I have you, but I will never forgive myself."

I pull back and look up at him skeptically. "What's the big deal?" I say, holding up my wrist. "If you don't like the bracelet, I'll just take it off."

"No!" Theo's eyes widen in fear as he launches toward me, but it's too late. I pull the bracelet off with my left hand. It all seemed so simple at first. I would toss it in the grass, say I lost it, and Theo would be happy.

But that doesn't happen.

The moment the metal leaves my wrist, my vision blurs and blackens around the edges. My heart beats like a jackhammer and my muscles stop working. I gasp for air. I fall forward. My eyes focus on my wrist, where the bracelet had been. There's a dark blue mark there, an oval with weird symbols in it, right on my skin like a tattoo.

My chest burns in agony, desperate for air and my mouth is open but nothing is happening. Everything darkens. I'm falling.

I'm drowning from the inside out.

I'm dying.

Something cold snaps back onto my wrist and a sudden jolt of energy slams into me chest first, like I've just been thrown onto a transformer. Precious air flows into my lungs and I keep gasping, the need to breathe overwhelming my every other sense. My vision comes back and Theo is there, watching me with worried eyes. I blink and choke and breathe in deeply.

He's holding me up by my arms, his grip tight.

My heart pounds so hard I can hear it in my ears. Blood rushes through me as if a floodgate had sucked it all dry and now it's filling every vein in my body back up. My senses come back to me one by one: clear vision, the piney smell of the outdoors, the sound of crickets chirping and a plane flying overhead. Theo's breath, ragged like mine. I become acutely aware of his hands on my arms and I yelp in pain because he's squeezing too tightly.

He lessens his hold and I look down, surprised that I'm actually standing on my own two feet. The black heels are lying scattered on the driveway.

I look down at my wrist. The skin seems normal, but I'm not about to move the bracelet to see if that blue image is still there. I must have imagined it. I don't have any tattoos.

"What the hell was that?" I say, wincing because even my throat hurts now.

"That is what happens when you remove the bracelet," he says softly. "It is bound to you until you die. And if you take it off, it'll drain all the life from you. You wouldn't have lasted more than a few seconds if I hadn't put it back on."

Fear slams into me, extending out to my every nerve. "What the hell is it?"

He looks down, his lips pressing together.

"Theo?" I say. My voice sounds just as panicked as I feel. I keep reliving that moment over and over again, the horror of what it felt like consuming me to the core.

"I almost died just now?"

"Yes."

I am breathless again, but this time it's from fear. "For a moment there...I thought..." I turn my wrist over and examine it again. The bracelet, so shiny and beautiful, doesn't look like it'd ever be capable of doing that to me. It doesn't look like it can do anything. It's an *effing bracelet*. An inanimate piece of metal and gemstone.

"I thought I saw a blue circle on my skin," I say over the sound of my pounding heart. "Just before my vision went black, I saw it. It had little symbols on it."

"This is an immortality bracelet," Theo says. He cradles my hand in his palm, leveling his gaze on me. "And what you saw was the immortal mark."

TWENTY-FIVE

Everything—my breathing, my heartbeat, even the crickets—are silent for a long moment. I watch Theo, knowing the meaning of the words I just heard but not believing them. Not *wanting* to believe them.

Immortality? That kind of thing is a myth, a made up concept that entices made up characters like Lord Voldemort. People live and die and humanity has been like that forever. We age, we get old, we kick the bucket. There's just no way anything else is possible.

Is he messing with me? As much as I want to laugh and call him on the joke, I can't stop thinking about that horrifying moment when I took off the bracelet. My body has never felt like that before, and I fear I'll never be able to forget how horrific it felt to be without the bracelet on my arm. That wasn't natural, it wasn't normal.

It was...

"I'm gonna need you to explain a little more," I say finally.

Theo glances back toward the house. "You should probably be sitting down when I tell you."

With a shrug, I drop to my knees and then sit on the grass, probably ruining this elegant purple gown. When I'd put it on earlier today, I'd pictured this night going in a completely different direction. You know, in a normal direction. Maybe I'd even get to make out with Theo by the end of the night.

But now I'm sitting in the grass next to Theo, who kneels down beside me, his elbow resting in his knee, this thumb and index finger sliding slowly across his brow.

Making out is the last thing on my mind.

In fact, I'm freaking out so much I'm not sure anything is on my mind.

"You *cannot* repeat a word of this to anyone," he says, his voice low as he peers up at me through his eyelashes. He keeps glancing back toward the house, as if someone will suddenly spot us way out here. As if that would be a very bad thing. Theo, the calm and sexy guy I met on the pier, looks very unnatural like this. He's worried. He's in pain. He's a guy with a lot of secrets that are probably hard as hell to contain.

I hold my chin up high because Cara Blackwell isn't a liar. "I won't say a word."

"Not to anyone," he stresses, looking me dead in the eyes. His voice is still low, so low it's hard to hear. "Not Riley, not anyone. You cannot say a word, ever, for the rest of your life."

"Okay..." I say as trepidation builds beneath my ribcage. "I won't."

His lips form a flat line. "You will be the first to die if you tell anyone. And then whoever you told would quickly follow you to the grave."

"You're being really morose," I whisper back, trying to lighten the mood. I don't get the feeling that Theo is threatening me here, it's more like he's the one who was threatened and now he's risking it all by telling me.

"What the hell happened with my bracelet?" I ask.

He takes my arm in his hands, this thumb sliding across my skin just above the silver. "This blue gem is a lapis stone. It was created by an alchemist in the year 1532 after he spent a lifetime studying ancient Greek and middle ages texts on the elixir of life. I don't know how the bastard did it, but he made a stone capable of giving immortality. He made several of them in fact. About two hundred." Theo gazes up at me, pain flickering in his eyes. "Alchemy is real. When he couldn't figure out how to turn metal into gold, he discovered another thing. Immortality."

Chills prickle over my skin. People have searched for immortality for centuries, but just like getting Spiderman-like superheroes is just fiction, I've always thought living forever is just as unlikely to ever happen.

"Does this mean I'm immortal?" I ask.

Theo's face falls. He looks at the ground, his hand still holding onto my wrist. "No, love. It means your life is being given to an immortal."

I try to swallow and my throat tastes like acid. Tears sting my eyes. I don't fully understand what's going on but the solemn expression on Theo's face has me more frightened than I've ever been. My body shakes uncontrollably. This is worse than the time I had to walk home after midnight and was run off the road by a car full of drunk assholes. It's worse than going hungry, or being beaten with a belt from a foster care mom.

This is worse than everything.

He continues, "These stones work as a battery of sorts. They press to skin and they slowly drain the life from the person. That person's life force is then transferred to the person who wears the stone's mate. They will remain immortal so long as they have a donor wearing the bracelet."

"So...I'm keeping someone immortal by wearing this bracelet?"

He nods and I frown, then look down at my hands, which are alive and normal. "But I'm still alive so..."

"Most girls last a year or two." His voice is so soft I barely hear it. When he looks at me, there are tears in his eyes. "That thing is slowly killing you, Cara."

Maybe I should cry, or scream. Or laugh and tell him this is all so impossible there's no way it's real. Instead, I don't do anything. I stare straight ahead, my gaze focused on a sloping hill in the distance, the dark sky beyond it. There are a few stars out tonight, and the moon hangs toward the left. I have the sudden realization that people have been staring at this very moon for centuries. For thousands of years. How many of them have been immortal?

I have just been given a death sentence, and I don't even know how to react.

"That mark you saw," Theo says softly. "It was dark blue. That's because you're still filled with life and your essence is strong. As time goes on, it'll get lighter, and then it'll fade away completely."

"And then they'll replace me." It's not a question, it's a fact.

His voice cracks. "Yes."

We sit in silence for another long moment. Theo is still kneeling beside me, and I can feel how uncomfortable this is for him. Good. Let him feel bad. Let him feel like absolute shit.

"Why didn't you get here early enough?" I say, looking up at the stars. This far in the country, they sparkle and shine without any light pollution from the big city. I let out a breath until my shoulders sag. "Why didn't you meet me at the pool and tell me all of this earlier?"

"I'm so sorry." Theo runs his palm down his face. "It is forbidden to speak of the clan's true purpose. I couldn't tell you in you room. The tablet near your door is triggered to listen for certain words, immortality being one of them. Should any girl start to question why she's there, they know about it the moment they figure it out."

My eyes widen, and seeing the horror on my face, he says, "No one's listening to you all the time. This isn't the government or anything," he says with a roll of his eyes. "It's a piece of software on the tablets. If it hears a certain word, it'll start recording and it'll send it to Alexo."

"What happens then?" I ask.

He looks at me. "A person would be immediately killed to protect the secret. That's why I couldn't tell you on the plane. I couldn't tell you in your room. I had to wait until we were truly alone. I was going to meet you at the pool and walk down here and tell you." He swallows and I watch his Adam's apple bob up and down. Just a few minutes ago, I thought he was the most handsome man in the world. I thought I'd never be able to focus on anything else when I was near him. I thought we could live happily ever after.

But now boyfriends and kissing and all of those things seem so stupid and trivial.

Theo presses his forehead to mine and sighs. "I'm so sorry, Cara."

"Me too," I say.

And that's when it hits me.
I have just been given a death sentence.
This is not a drill.
This is real life.
And real death.

TWENTY-SIX

Overwhelming panic consumes me. My heart pounds like it's fighting to get out of my body and drops of sweat bead along my forehead. I start hyperventilating until stars fill my vision, and even then, I can't stop. Theo is talking to me, his voice low and urgent, but I can't understand any of it. It's just noise against the backdrop of my panic.

I am dying.

This thing is killing me.

I'll be dead before I'm twenty years old.

"It all seemed too good to be true." When I talk, it sounds like someone else's voice. Some other stupid girl who just ruined her life, not me. I am so far consumed in panic that I don't even feel like myself anymore. But I know it is me, deep down.

Theo doesn't say anything. There's really nothing to say. All he can do is watch me fall apart as the realization that I am going to die cascades over me like a lead blanket, suffocating me.

"I feel like I should be mad at you," I say, shaking my head. "But it's not your fault. You tried to warn me. I can only be mad at myself."

He starts to say something, but now that I'm aware of my own impending demise, I have a lot of questions. "How long do I have?"

"Two years at the most. If you stay calm and don't injure yourself or get sick, your life force will be stronger and last longer."

"That's why they let us live in luxury," I say. I'm smiling, but I am not happy. I've probably gone completely insane.

He nods and I see the hint of a scowl cross his face. "If you take care of your life donors, they last longer. This clan is one of three clans, and they are arguably the most humane of them all."

"There's more clans?" I say with a snort. "This whole time I thought that word—*clan*—was so weird. It's like this ancient, weird, word you never hear on a normal basis and they kept saying it."

"They are ancient," he says. "Alexo is two hundred and fifty-nine years old."

My heart catches in my throat. When I had met Alexo, however briefly, there *was* a calm demeanor to him. That of someone who has lived life long enough to be able to stop and smell the roses. He wasn't a fast talker. He took time to look at all of us when he performed the ceremony.

A sardonic thought comes to mind. Ceremony is probably the worst word to describe condemning five young women to an unnaturally short life.

"What about the hundred thousand dollars?" I ask. Maybe I can send it to Uncle Will and he can use it to make his life better.

Theo frowns. "A lie. You will live in luxury while you're here, no doubt, but you'll leave here in a body bag. They use the high salary as an incentive to lure in women."

I flinch as soon as he says *body bag*, and I can tell he feels bad about it. He reaches out and cups his hand to my cheek. "Cara..." he breathes. There are a million emotions behind that one word, and I find myself wanting to hate him and love him all at the same time. Why did this happen?

Why is my luck so impossibly shitty?

Theo sighs. "I will never forgive myself for letting this happen to you."

"But you let it happen to other girls," I say, my stomach clenching into knots. "You're letting it happen every day."

"I'm trying to make it better, Cara. I swear to you. I—" He stops, his forehead creasing as he looks at me. "That day I saw you on the plane, I've never been more horrified. I wanted you out. I wanted to save you. Some of these girls they hire are just vapid idiots and I've been able to look the other way, but with you—" He sighs, then lowers his lips and presses them to my forehead. "With you, I felt my entire heart get ripped out at the idea of you becoming one of their pawns."

A tear rolls down my cheek and I don't wipe it away. This is all too much. I can't handle it, I can't function or even begin to fathom what the hell is going on.

Part of me still hopes that maybe it's all a prank, some mean hazing joke to convince me that immortality exists and that I am on the wrong side of it. I imagine myself in a parallel universe, where this really is a joke, and we can all laugh about it later.

There's a rustle in the grass near a wooded area of the yard. Theo straightens and curses under his breath.

In one swift movement, he pushes me on my back and then dives on top of me, his hand sliding down to my hip.

"Stop crying," he breathes against my ear. "Pretend we're making out."

"Is someone out here?" A man's voice calls out.

Theo's lips press to mine. My eyes close on instinct and a flood of warmth rushes through me from the kiss. But it only lasts a second because my heart doesn't have room in it for kissing guys at the moment.

Still, Theo keeps up the charade as the footsteps grow closer and then a guy says, "*Damn*, son!"

Theo jumps up, doing a fantastic job of pretending to be startled. "Can a guy get some privacy?" he says, giving Russel this ridiculously douche-bag level grin. I've seen the same look on college frat guys. I can't believe for a second that Russel actually believes Theo's act, because anyone who knows him should know he'd never act like that.

"Of course, of course," Russel says. He holds up his hands innocently and takes a step back. "I lost the spare keys to my four wheeler out here so I was just looking for them. I'm glad to see you're finally enjoying yourself here, Theo." He winks at Theo and then gives me a smile. "Carry on."

Theo rocks back on his heels and watches until Russel has disappeared back into the wooded area. I sit up on the palms of my hands and try to catch my breath.

Even while knowing I'm about to die, a kiss from Theo can still take my breath away.

"I'm sorry about that," he says. His teeth bite down on this bottom lip. "It is not the time for shit like that, but I couldn't let him think we were talking. I'm not exactly on excellent terms with these guys."

"Why?" I say sarcastically. "Because you disagree with their heinous lifestyle?"

"Er, sort of." He scratches his neck. "There are so many more aspects to this than you know. More than I could possibly tell you in a night. Immortality—it goes deeper than that. The clans don't always get along and there are some very bad people after this one."

His tone is so ominous it makes me shrivel in fear. I hitch up the bottom of my gown so I can bend my knees so I can get more comfortable. I don't plan on leaving until I know every detail of this horrific thing I've gotten myself into.

"Wait," I say as I think over what he just said. "Why are *you* here? You're not..." I don't want to say the word. "You're not...immortal, right? You're not one of them?"

"I am not one of them," Theo says evenly. "I would never lie to innocent people and then steal their life force from them." He runs a hand through the grass, then looks up at me. I smile a little, because I know I can trust Theo. He's broken this huge secret because he also trusts me.

"I'm glad," I say, reaching for his hand.

"It's more complicated than that, love." He reaches for the collar of his shirt. Pulls it down.

There's a thick silver chain around his neck. A blue gemstone pendant presses against his chest.

"I am not a member of the Rosewater Clan," he says softly. "But I am immortal."

TWENTY-SEVEN

Theo braces himself. He must expect some kind of backlash from me, but I'm all out of energy. At this point, God Himself could come down from the heavens and hand me some cotton candy made from clouds and I wouldn't be surprised. This is all too surreal. I can't function. I can't understand.

"How old are you?" I ask.

"Ninety seven."

"How old were you when you became...like this?"

"Twenty two."

I nod and then look at my hands because I'm unable to meet his eyes right now. My mind is a swirl of thoughts, emotions, and fear.

"We need to get back," Theo says. He rises and offers a hand to help me up. "I'll answer any question you have, but we need to get off the premises first."

I let him pull me up but I drop his hand as soon as I'm on my own feet. I brush the dirt and grass from my backside and then try to see the back part of it in the moonlight. Luckily, it's already pretty dark and the dress isn't showing any dirt.

"Here's the deal," Theo says as he picks up my shoes and carries them in one hand while we make the trek back to my house. "You should act enamored, like we just met and we are crushing on each other. It needs to be believable, okay? They can't suspect anything."

I roll my eyes. "It would have been more than believable if you'd never told me about this epically huge and terrifying secret world of people," I say. "It would have been *actually* true."

"Listen—" He reaches over and squeezes my hand. "I know you're dealing with a lot of shit right now. I remember when I found out about immortality—but we can't let them know anything is out of the ordinary."

I nod. Even though we're both doomed to die soon, I don't want to let anything happen that would put Riley's life in danger. "I'll be the best damn actress on earth," I say.

He smiles down at me. "So, what's our story? We met and you fell head over heels for me at first sight?"

I roll my eyes. "We met and *you* fell for me at first sight. I wasn't really feeling it, but you begged and begged and asked me to go on a walk with you, so I obliged."

His grin is so cute it almost makes me forget about the horrors of what my life has become. "I suppose we can go with that story…"

"Good," I say, bumping into him with my shoulder. He smiles, and I smile back, and it hurts my insides because everything is not okay. Nothing will ever be okay again.

This is literally hell.

We make it back to the party and although my mind is reeling with the severity of the situation, I try to stay calm. I make swoony eyes at Theo and hold onto his elbow and act like I'm totally in love with him. It comes easily, all this swooning. In another world, he might have been my soul mate, after all.

Riley walks over to us, a glass of wine in her hand. "Where have *you* been, lady?" she says all flirty like, like she knows exactly where I've been. She doesn't even look like the same person to me now that I know the terrible secret of the bracelet on her wrist.

"It's my fault," Theo says. "I, um…requested that she take a walk with me."

"I see," Riley coos, giving me flirty eyes. If this were any other time and any other moment, I'd give them right back to her. I'd be eager to rehash the entire night with her once it was over. Now, I can't think of a single thing to say.

"Hey man," Theo says, nodding toward Kyle who's been hanging out with Riley this whole time.

"I see you met Cara," Kyle says, seeming genuinely kind about my obvious attraction to Theo and not crass like Russel had been. "Did you take a tour of the gardens?"

"Something like that," Theo says. His smile is a little crooked. We are losing this battle of pretending like nothing is wrong.

Every few seconds my brain screams *you are going to die* in my head. I no longer have the energy to tell it to shut up.

"We're thinking of going to get some ice cream," Theo says. "Will you let the guys know we'll be back in an hour?"

"Sure thing." Kyle doesn't suspect a thing. Riley winks at me as we walk by and I do my best to smile back at her like this is all fine. This stupid smile is the biggest lie I've ever told.

In the garage, Theo heads toward a dark gray Jeep Wrangler. It's the only vehicle in here that's not some expensive sports car. He holds open my door for me and I climb inside.

"I know it's not the time to say this, but you look unbelievably sexy tonight."

I stare at the dash. "Yeah it's not the right time for that."

Once we're a few miles from the house, Theo's thumb taps the steering wheel. "Listen, Cara." He sighs and then takes a deep breath.

I look over at him. Normally when someone says something like that, they say more than just that. He pulls to a stop at a red light and looks over at me.

"Okay so, don't get your hopes up but...most of today's immortals don't really know much about how the lapis stone came to be. We join a clan, we learn how to stay alive, and that's all we do."

"What does this have to do with me?" I say, leaning back in my seat.

"It means I'm going to the ancient archives and I'm going to find a way to save you."

Chills prickle over my whole body. It's as if I fell off a skyscraper and suddenly someone caught me before I hit the ground. "I can be saved?" I say, my voice cracking.

"I said don't get your hopes up," he says, focusing on the road. "It might be possible. I remember a long time ago, I'd met this man from Greece who was five hundred years old. He'd had a wife who died during childbirth. It was such a long time ago, but I seem to remember him telling me the story of how they first met, and if I'm remembering correctly, she was his life blood for a time. Like..." he squints like he's trying to remember. "I'm pretty sure that's how the story went. So that would mean he had a way to cut off the stone's powers and save her from dying as a life blood."

Hope surges through my veins. "Do you still talk to him?"

Theo shakes his head. "He killed himself."

"I thought you were immortal?"

"Immortal is not the same as invincible, I'm afraid. We die almost as easily as you do." Theo exits onto a darkened back road with a rickety wooden fence lining each side. "But if there's a way, what I'm telling you Cara, is that I'm going to find it."

Tears spring to my eyes and I reach over and grab his hand. "Thank you."

He flashes me a smile. "We have about two years. That's enough time to scour the planet for the information I need."

I breathe a sigh of relief that takes the last hour of pain right out of me. "I sure hope so."

"Do you want ice cream?" he asks. "We might as well do something while we're out here."

I shake my head. "Let's just drive. I'm not done asking questions."

He steers with one hand and holds onto my hand with the other. "Anything."

A million questions come to me at once. "Where do you get your power from?"

He hesitates a second. "Terminally ill people. Drug addicts. People on death row."

"So you're like a mercy-killing-killer?"

He frowns. "I suppose."

"Do the people know you're killing them when you do it?"

He nods slowly, his eyes still on the road. "I make a deal with them. I offer them something they want more than life and in exchange they wear the band." He lifts his shoulders. "Most of my donors are men, so I had the lapis stone set into a leather men's bracelet instead of the silver ones you have."

"What do you offer them?" I ask. It's hard not to blurt out all my questions at once.

"The man wearing my stone right now has stage four colon cancer. I offered to fund his two daughter's college savings accounts. He didn't even hesitate to take the deal."

"Does it make him die faster?" I say.

"Yes."

I look out the window, watching the fields roll by. There's mostly nothing out here, but occasionally the scenery will be dotted with a cow or a house. "That seems like you'd have to get new donors more frequently."

"I do," he says, frowning. "Usually once a month. But unlike the others in the Rosewater clan, I can't justify the death of a healthy innocent person, even if it means going two years without finding a new donor."

"You're a good man," I say.

He smiles sadly, his eyes meeting mine. "Not good enough."

I tilt my head and watch his thumb as it slides across my palm. "You mentioned other clans... what's the deal with that?"

"It would take longer than a car ride to tell you the history of the three clans. I was made immortal in 1920, during the great depression. I was a member of the Embrook clan for all of that time, up until a month ago when I joined Rosewater."

"So...what do these clans do?"

"Mostly they stick together. You can't develop long lasting relationships when you never age. There's no getting married and having kids and living in suburbia until you retire. Clans stick together and travel around the world, never staying one place for very long. As with any group of people, there are disagreements between the clans. Some are more reasonable people than others."

"And what is Rosewater?" I ask. "Are we good or bad?"

He looks at me, his face covered in shadows. "I'm not sure yet."

After driving for an hour, I decide to stop the inquisition. There's clearly a lot to learn about this new type of person, and I won't learn it all overnight.

Theo and I switch to other topics, like music and food and traveling, and for a little while, it almost feels like we're on a real date. A normal date.

Ever since Theo revealed that there's a way to change me from a human battery to a normal persona again, my anxiety has lowered tremendously. I no longer feel like I'm choking, and I can enjoy this alone time with the guy who's occupied so much of my thoughts lately. Now the only weird thing is that I'm sitting here with someone who should be a wrinkly old man. It's a little unusual.

When we arrive home, a few of the sports cars are gone from the garage and the party outside is over. Theo parks back in his spot and leaves the engine running. He cranks the radio until it's so loud it's annoying, and then he leans over to me.

"I might be in love with you," he whispers against my ear, the warmth of his breath sending a shiver of delight down my neck.

I can't help the goofy smile I get. "You should be thinking about other things than that."

He takes my hands and then presses his forehead to the side of my face. He exhales slowly, then whispers into my ear again. "I will find a way to save you."

"Save me first," I whisper back. "And then you can fall in love with me."

TWENTY-EIGHT

When I wake up the next morning, I know something is off before I even open my eyes. My bed sheets are as soft as a rose petal. This is not the ratty comforter I slept on in Uncle Will's house. The room doesn't smell like old furniture and dirty carpet either. It smells like a five star hotel. Like clean linens and soft vanilla.

I stretch and breathe in deeply, finally remembering where I am. And then I remember the bracelet, light as a feather on my arm, and sparkling as if the sun is shining on it at all times.

How can something so beautiful be so evil?

Laying on my side, I shove my arm under my pillow so I don't have to look at it. And then I hear it; the distinct sound of someone softly breathing next to me.

Someone is in my bed.

I freeze. Memories of last night come back to me. After Theo had revealed his horrifying secret and we drove around and talked, we came back home. He walked me to my room and we said our goodbyes. His kiss was soft and affectionate, and part of me had wanted to bring him inside and spend hours sitting on my bed with him, asking more questions and just enjoying being around him.

But the other part of me was sick to my stomach over my impending demise. The whole idea that immortal people exist is really hard to wrap my head around. So, I'd said goodbye to Theo and went alone into my room, even though the very act of leaving him made my chest ache. But thanks to that ache, I remember, very clearly, that he didn't come inside with me.

So why is someone sleeping next to me?

Carefully, I turn over, hoping that I won't wake up…Riley?

I sigh and sit up in bed. My best friend is sleeping next to me, the covers pulled up to her chin. Her makeup from last night is washed off, her hair hanging wildly around her pillow.

My eyes drift to her bracelet that's halfway peeking out of the comforter. My stomach hurts. Riley's life is slowly being siphoned away too. We are both in the same sinking ship and I can't tell her about it.

I'd promised Theo I'd keep the secret no matter what, but as I sit here and stare at my best friend, the girl who's always been there for me and has never lied to me, I don't know if I can do this. Keeping it a secret would be the biggest betrayal ever.

Maybe I can wait until Theo finds a cure for us and then I'll tell her. It's not like I'm lying to hurt her, I'll be lying to protect her so she never has to feel the sheer terror I felt last night when Theo told me about the clan and what they're doing to us. I shiver just thinking about it. Then my mind wanders into worse territory.

What if I hadn't met Theo and totally fallen for him? What if Riley and I had accepted this job and then been doomed to a death we didn't see coming? My heart aches as I watch my best friend sleeping.

If Theo can't fix us, we would have been better on the streets.

It's still early morning, so I lie awake for another hour, watching the rising sun through my wall of windows. In the distance, the lake shimmers a deep blue color and speedboats zoom around on the water. Those people are living their normal lives, enjoying a warm summer day on the lake. Their biggest worry right now is probably what they'll have for lunch, or if they have enough gas in the boat to go for one more loop around the water.

Riley's soft breathing hitches, and then she yawns and stretches. I roll over, propping my head on my palm.

"Good morning," I say sarcastically. "Did you sleep well?"

She grins at me, then yawns again and stretches her arms over her head. "I certainly did."

"You do know we're in a mansion, right?" I say, lifting an eyebrow.

"Yep."

"And you do know you have your own bedroom?"

"Yes, I do know that."

I give her a look. "And you have your own bed in that bedroom?"

She rolls her eyes. "I couldn't sleep all by myself. The bed was too big and too comfortable and everything was too quiet. There's no sounds of people snoring or girls bitching at each other here. The group home was so noisy all the time." She sits up on her elbows and pouts at me.

I throw a pillow at her. "Just let me know if you're going to sneak into my room next time, okay? You almost gave me a heart attack when I realized someone was in my bed."

Riley's lips curl into a smirk. "If I let you know beforehand, then it's not really sneaking, Cara."

I throw my other pillow at her.

AFTER A VIDEO CALL to Bethany to inquire about breakfast, she tells us that we can eat in the main kitchen or just have food brought up. Riley wants to order food to our room because it's fancy and chic, and I agree with her but only because I don't feel like seeing anyone right now. I may not be friends with the other girls in the house, but I can't look them in the eyes now that I know what I know.

I'm starving, but I have to eat slowly because of all the crap I'm dealing with right now. Riley and I eat breakfast and then spend some time playing on the laptop in my room, looking for clothes and accessories to order since the other girls have already ordered a ton of stuff to be paid for out of the clan's massive pockets.

Riley has a blast. She's excited and smiling and doing little happy dances when she finds some cute new clothes and combat boots to order online. She has a long list of things to buy and her enthusiasm grows stronger with each new website she visits.

I'm doing my best to pretend like I'm also excited. I'd promised Theo and myself that I'd keep this secret from everyone, including Riley. I toy with this secret for hours, going on into the day. After we eat lunch—also delivered to our room—I still can't shake these thoughts.

Should I tell Riley?

Should I keep my promise to Theo?

Girl Code says I should tell Riley anything I know that she doesn't, regardless of what I've promised to a guy. But Girl Code was invented for juicy gossip and embarrassing secrets. I am pretty sure that when humanity decided that girls should treat their best friend with total and complete honesty, they had no idea that immortality existed.

Plus, even if I were to tell her, I couldn't do it here where the walls are listening.

"Oh my God," Riley says, her eyes lighting up with the glow of the computer screen. "You would look so hot in this outfit. Look how cute it is!"

She spins the laptop around, showing me a fashion model dressed in some designer cut off jean shorts and a black button up shirt with a golden elephant printed across the front.

I nod absentmindedly because I'm having a really hard time focusing.

"Should I order it for you?" Riley asks.

"Sure."

"Cool." She taps on the keyboard, copy and pasting the link into a document she's going to send to Malina later.

I'm sitting next to her on a purple ottoman by the desk and computer that came in my room, and I'm gazing out at the beautiful view, watching sailboats and jet skis out on the lake. I get so caught up in my own thoughts that I don't realize Riley's been talking to me until she shoves me in the arm.

"Sorry," I say, giving her a half smile. "That lake is just so beautiful, I can't stop looking."

Riley's smile softens. "Cara, you're my best friend. I'm not stupid, okay? I know when you're keeping a secret from me."

My blood turns cold. "You what?—I'm... I'm not."

She laughs. "You *so* are!"

Fear grabs onto me, and I'm wondering how she knows. Did I talk in my sleep? Can she read it on my face?

And then Riley just rolls her eyes like I'm a dork. "You're totally obsessed with Theo now," she says, patting me on the shoulder while she makes this little pout to embarrass me. "You're head over heels for this guy and now it's taking over your every thought."

Relief washes over me. Riley has no idea about the real secret. I try to smile. "Yeah, he's pretty great." But even memories of that good night kiss, of the way he said he was falling for me—none of that helps quell the fear in my stomach right now.

There is a very real possibility that Riley and I will die soon, and it is a secret I have to keep to myself until the very end.

My eyes tear up and my stomach lodges itself in my throat. And then a tidal wave of fear slams into me, knocking me to my feet. I pace across the room as the horrifying reality of my situation falls over me again. Just like last night on the grass, I am consumed with panic. I can't control it and I sure as hell can't stop it.

We are going to die.

Riley calls my name, grabs my arm, but I don't really notice it. My vision has gone blurry, my hearing is dull over the roar of a high-pitched ring in my ears. I can't breathe. I can't focus. I can't think.

The only words in my mind are playing on repeat.

We are going to die.

We are going to die.

We are going to die.

TWENTY-NINE

Theo calls it a panic attack. And I guess he's right, even though I don't want to admit it. There wasn't anything wrong with me, not medically at least. I just freaked out so bad that I panicked until I couldn't control it. My body couldn't handle it, and neither could my subconscious.

After I blacked out from hyperventilating, Riley called Theo on the tablet. It was smart thinking on her part, even though she couldn't have possibly known it. He's the best person to deal with me now because any other guy in the house wouldn't have known why I was freaking out. It could have caused a lot of unnecessary attention if she'd called someone else.

I woke up in Theo's arms with a wet towel on my forehead. Now it's been about an hour, and Theo hasn't left my side.

We're on my bed. He sits with his back against the headboard and I'm laying diagonally across the mattress, my head in his lap while he brushes his fingers through my hair. It feels heavenly and I keep closing my eyes and focusing on breathing steady to keep my heartbeat normal. Theo's presence keeps me grounded. The thought of him leaving right now sends another shock of panic through me.

Riley has dragged a chair over to my bed, and she sits there watching me with her head in her hands, elbows on her knees.

"You sure she'll be okay?" Riley asks for the hundredth time.

Only this time Theo doesn't say the same thing he said each time before. He says, "She needs fresh air." He peers down at me. "Do you feel up to walking? Let's go to the gardens and talk privately."

Riley stands and folds her arms over her chest. "Where Cara goes, I go."

Theo doesn't hesitate. "I'm afraid I need to speak to her alone."

Riley holds her ground. "Absolutely not."

I give her a sad look and I hope she realizes how truly sorry I am about this. "I really should go alone."

"Are you freaking serious?" Her voice is angry, but her eyes soften and I can tell she's really just hurt.

"No," I say. Theo looks at me and I turn to him. "I can't keep this from her. She's my best friend."

His eyes widen, his jaw tightening. "Not here," he mouths.

Realizing that what I just said could sound damning to someone listening in, I think quickly and change the wording. "I mean...well, yes Theo and I are kind of an item, I guess you could say." I look at Riley, wishing I could tell her the exact truth right now. "And I wanted to keep it a secret from you but I can't. So...maybe we should all go out to the gardens and talk about it."

"That's pretty much all there is to know," Riley says, lifting an eyebrow. "You two have the hots for each other. I mean, duh."

Theo holds up a finger, looking at me. "I don't think you should tell her," he whispers so quietly I barely hear it.

"I trust her," I whisper back.

He nods once. "Then let's go talk."

"You're both being really weird," Riley says after we've reached the gardens. Theo holds my hand, probably just for show, but I can't help but hate how our first real hand holding is ruined by thoughts of this immortality crap. I should be swooning hard right now, but instead all I can think about is death.

And immortality.

And how crazy it all is.

It's just after noon and the sun is beating down on us. Even while walking under a shady path near the trees, it's still so hot I want to rip off my clothes and dive in the pool.

We're way past the gardens now, on the edge of the property near a wooden fence. On the other side, the land stretches on for miles. "You can still change your mind," Theo says softly so that only I can hear it.

I look down at our clasped hands. I wish I didn't also see my bracelet, the beautiful piece of death that is strapped to me, immovable, and unrelenting.

"I have to tell her," I say, gazing up at him. I hope he realizes how important this is to me. "I've done the math; I've tried spending half an hour without telling her the secret. It sent me into a panic attack. Theo, I can't keep this from her."

I'm so emotional, I forget to whisper.

"Um...guys?" Riley says, walking up to us. "What the hell is going on?"

Theo looks at me. "We're telling her?"

I nod once. "We're telling her."

And so we tell her. Right here in a field, surrounded by the Texas heat and the scent of pine trees. We tell her everything.

She takes it well, all things considered.

Riley looks down at her bracelet. "Okay so...let's just find a way out of it."

"We don't know if there's a way out of this," I say with a sigh. "Theo thinks there might be a way but he'd have to find it."

She shrugs. "So find it."

My mouth falls open because she's being so weirdly calm about this. "It might not be that easy." Doesn't she see how fucking bad this is?

Riley nods a little and then looks at her bracelet again. "Think about it... there's some fancy alchemy shit in this stone that does something amazing. Someone found a way to transfer my life into someone with just a *stone*." She looks up like the answer is obvious, but even Theo looks a little confused.

She rolls her eyes and continues, "There's a way out of this. I am confident. We'll find it, and we'll be okay. Hell, I think Cara and I should become immortals too," she says, wiggling her eyebrows. "That sounds awesome."

Oddly, this thought has never occurred me. Becoming immortal? Living *forever*? Would I really want to do that? It means I could stay with Theo forever...

I gaze over at him and find him looking right at me. He doesn't say anything for a long while. Riley finally speaks up and puts a hand on my shoulder. "This is crazy freaky, don't get me wrong. But...there's a way out of this." She throws her hands in the air. "There *has* to be. Newton's third law, or whatever. If something makes you live forever with the stone, then something else can make us not die from the stone. We'll figure it out."

"So when *I* find out, I panic so bad I black out, but when you find out, you're all '*oh well dudes, this is totally fine*'?" I take in a deep breath and let it out in a huff. "Why can't I be like you?"

"Because you're sensitive," she says, gazing at me with admiration. She brushes her bangs behind her ears. "I like that about you. But I'm not, and I see things like they are and that's what makes us a badass best friend duo."

It's totally the wrong moment for it, but I laugh. "I can't believe I thought I could keep this from you," I say. "Telling you is probably the best thing I could have done."

"Now that you both know, you absolutely can't tell anyone else," Theo warns. "I am serious."

"I understand," Riley says. She runs her fingers across her lips, pretending to zip them closed.

Theo rests a hand on the fence post and gazes out at the pasture. "We've been around for centuries. There is a lot of information I don't know about the lapis stone or the origin of immortality. I agree with Riley, there has to be something. I just need to find it."

"We'll help," Riley says encouragingly.

Theo shakes his head. "Absolutely not. You two must go on as if everything is normal. You play the part of someone who's enamored to be here in this mansion with all of these free things being thrown at you." Theo runs a finger down my arm. "If either one of you seems even remotely off, even for a minute, they'll catch on. You'll both be killed."

"You don't need to tell me that twice," Riley says with a laugh. "One death threat is all I need to keep my mouth shut."

"Me too," I say because Theo looks really worried about it. "Riley and I will act normal. Everyone already knows you and I have a thing so I'll just pretend to be super excited about my new crush." I poke him in the ribs and it gets a little grin out of him.

"Okay," he says, exhaling. "Let's get back to the house."

This time when Theo grabs my hand, it feels real and not like a charade. He keeps glancing over at me as we walk and it makes me shy and googly-eyed and all kinds of crazy because he's truly the most handsome guy I've ever known.

And although he wasn't there to stop us from getting into this situation, he's here now. He's going to get us out of this.

For the first time in the last twenty four hours, I feel like everything might actually be okay.

"So about immortality," Riley says. "What's a girl gotta do to become one of you?"

Theo's eyes darken, his expression going cold. "We're getting too close to the house. Can't talk about it anymore."

The house is still pretty far away, so it feels like an excuse to avoid the subject altogether. Now that Riley's brought it up, I'm curious as well about what it takes to become an immortal. But I'm not sure I'd like the idea of living forever. It's all just too much to handle right now.

As soon as we walk inside, we find Malina in the foyer, talking to a woman dressed in white scrubs.

"There you are," she says, looking me and Riley. "I tried your rooms but couldn't find you."

"What's up?" Riley says.

"This is Cynthia. She's our weekly masseuse. I was wondering if you two would like a massage today while she's here?"

Cynthia nods. "I have a partner with me too, so you could get massaged together if you'd like."

Riley looks at me, her lips turned up in a smirk.

"I have work to do," Theo says, even though I know the work he's talking about involves totally going against the clan's rules to try and save us. "But you two could probably use the stress relief."

"Hell yeah," Riley says. "Sign me up!"

"Me too," I say as I let go of Theo's hand. I'm a little nervous to let him leave after he's spent the morning with me helping me calm down. But I have

Riley now, and my secret is safe with her. I'm feeling better, more optimistic. "I'd definitely like a massage," I say.

"The Rosewater clan loves to take care of its employees," Malina says as she walks us upstairs and to the room that's set up with massage tables, soothing music and scented candles.

"They certainly do," I say, giving her a grin that probably looks like I'm crazy. "Speaking of, can I get a ninety inch television for my room? And an iPad?" I glance at Riley who is giving me the ultimate look of approval. "Also, I'd like a motorcycle. Hot pink."

"Of course," Malina says, lifting an eyebrow. "I'll get it ordered right away."

I've never even been on a motorcycle, but can't help but smirk.

The Rosewater clan gives out expensive things in exchange for taking a life. If they want my life, the least I can do is make them pay for it.

THE IMMORTAL TRUTH

BOOK TWO

Copyright © 2019 by Amy Sparling

All rights reserved.

First Edition March 14, 2017

Cover image from bookcoverscre8tive.com

Typography from FontSquirrel.com

No part of this book may be reproduced in any form or by any electronic or mechanical means, including information storage and retrieval systems, without written permission from the author, except for the use of brief quotations in a book review.

❦ Created with Vellum

ONE

Riley stomps her feet as she follows me through the kitchen and out toward the garage. Her mouse like face is all pinched up and pretend-angry. "I was two seconds away from a delicious peanut butter and jelly sandwich," she gruffs, twisting her lips down so she can pout like a child.

"Get over it," I say. But I don't let go of her arm. She has to see this and it can't possibly wait until after she's had her sandwich.

"What's up with you and PB&Js anyhow?" I say as I pull open the service door to the hallway and let her go first. This is a shortcut to get to the garage instead of walking through the entire house and out the front door and then over to it. The service hallways get to everywhere much faster.

"What do you mean?" she says, her face back to normal and no longer being sarcastic. She'd just opened the jar of peanut butter and had two slices of bread laid on a plate when I burst into the kitchen and demanded that she follow me.

"We have a professional chef who will cook anything you desire," I say. We've been living in this mansion for two weeks and it's still hard getting used to that fact. "Why stick with the same sandwiches you've had your whole life?"

"It's *because* I've had them my whole life that I want them," she says. "I know what I like."

"I guess I can't argue with that." I do see where she's coming from, but my meals have been pretty extravagant lately. I've taken Bethany up on her offer to tell me all of her favorite chef-cooked meals, and so far, she's been right about all of them. Last night I ordered smoked salmon with fettuccine alfredo and it was freaking amazing. Our chef also does something magical with the garlic bread. Forget the pool and the free stuff and the movie theater room—the food alone is almost worth giving up my soul.

A knot forms in my stomach. *Ugh, Cara.* That was a bad joke. Totally not even funny.

Nothing is worth giving up my soul, and yet I've unknowingly traded it anyway. It was just two weeks ago, when my best friend Riley and I happily signed up for an all-expenses-paid "job" here in Austin, Texas. All we have to do is live in luxury and wear this beautiful bracelet that has a glowing blue stone in the middle of it.

Seems perfect, right?

Wrong.

The stone is an immortality stone, and whoever wears it gives their lifeblood to the immortal person who has the other half. They get stronger and continue living forever, you get weaker and eventually die.

None of that was mentioned in the job description.

It's been a weird two weeks. Part of me is continually impressed and awed every day that I'm here because we're truly living in luxurious splendor that girls from Sterling can't even imagine. We're in a mansion with housekeepers and servants and we get anything we want for free. There's a ninety inch television now mounted on the wall in my bedroom simply because I asked for it. Riley now has a collection of over two dozen combat boots and enough clothes to fill her closet that's the size of a freaking classroom. We are in want of nothing here, but in exchange, our lives will be cut short. None of the other girls know this, and we aren't supposed to know it either. Sometimes I can absorb myself in our beautiful surroundings and allow the fear of dying to slip from my mind for an hour or two. But it always comes back. The dread, the fear, the uncertainty of a quick impending death.

It always comes back.

It doesn't help that Theo has been gone this whole time. He's the one immortal who knows that Riley and I know the secret of immortality, and he's vowed to find a way to save us.

"You're doing it again," Riley says. We're just in front of the door that leads to the garage, but she stops and turns around, giving me this look that's mostly concern and a little bit annoyed.

"I'm not doing anything," I say. I hold my head high and put on the fakest smile ever.

Riley sighs, her arched eyebrows coming to a point in the middle of her forehead. "You are acting like you've been dumped or something." She smacks my shoulders. "Suck it up! Your loverboy will return in no time."

She's my best friend, so she knows these things about me. There's no reason to deny it, even though the words are on the tip of my tongue. I'm so used to denying it to myself lately.

We're in a narrow service hallway, and I lean my shoulder against the wall. "It just hurts."

"Why?" Her voice is bubbly as she stares at me with those big brown eyes of hers. "You're in love! He's totally all about you, Cara. So stop being all mopey when he's gone."

"Maybe that's why it hurts so bad," I say, picking at my cuticles. There's not much to pick at because Riley and I recently got manicures and now my cuticles are perfection. I heave a sigh. "It's like...I went my whole life being alone—"

"Ahem," Riley says, looking offended.

I roll my eyes. "*Romantically* alone. I've been romantically alone all my life and then I meet him—it's like...like I've met my soul mate. And I'm pretty sure he feels the same way." There's a little flutter in my chest as I think about Theo's smile, that cocky little smirk he does. The way his eyes lower when he looks at me, the woodsy scent of his cologne.

I make my hands explode outward. "And poof—he's gone. And I'm back to being alone."

"*Ahem*," Riley says again. "You have me. Now what did you want to show me?"

Sunlight spills onto our faces as we press through the thick metal door that leads to the garage. It's not your typical family garage with two car spaces and years of junk piled up on the sides.

This place has a tiled floor, a dozen sports cars, some SUVs, and a fully stocked bar. It's like a car person's wet dream in here. I don't even have to show Riley what we came here to see because it's so obvious you can't possibly miss it.

"Oh...my...God..." she says, eyes wide as she rushes up to the hot pink motorcycle sitting at the far right of the garage. "You got one!"

"Yeah," I say with a chuckle that sounds kind of hysterical. "I mean, I remembered saying I wanted one, but I can't believe Malina actually ordered it for me."

I'd gotten the call this morning around nine a.m. There was a delivery for me, which is kind of weird because most of the time Malina just drops off the packages at my bedroom door. This one was in the garage. I kind of forgot I'd even requested it a few weeks ago. I was kind of freaking out when I'd realized that Riley and I are now trapped by these immortality bracelets. Since the guys in the Rosewater clan were taking my life in exchange for letting me live in luxury, I'd demanded a few things. I got an iPad, which isn't really as cool as you think they are when you're too poor to afford one, and I also got the insanely huge television in my room. Honestly, it's too big for anyone, especially for a bedroom. But it's all mine and it cost twenty grand and the guys paid for it.

The hot pink motorcycle? I kind of forgot about that.

Now it's here, freshly removed from its crate. The delivery guy took it out for me and put it on the kickstand, but he didn't seem like the friendly sort who would tell me how the thing works. He just handed me a set of keys that were also pink, told me the gas tank was filled, and promptly left.

I reach into my shorts pocket and pull out the keys. "Do you know how to drive this thing?"

"Drive it?" Riley says. "I didn't even know motorcycles had keys!"

We laugh and I pocket the keys again. "Maybe I'll just look at it all the time instead of drive it." I run my hand across the smooth pink gas tank. Not only is the bike pink, it's been painted with this iridescent pearly type of paint that looks beautiful under the bright garage lights and probably even better in the sunlight. The tires are sharp black and the wheels are a shiny aluminum pink as well. The word Ninja is on the side, so I think that's the brand or something.

"I would say we should ask for a car," Riley says while she walks around the bike. "But getting chauffeured around is so much cooler than driving. But with this thing..." She taps the handlebar. "It's kind of badass. We need helmets."

"Already taken care of," I say, nodding toward the wall. There's a rack of helmets over where two other motorcycles are. One of the bikes, the black one on the left, is Theo's. He took a car when he left. I avoid looking at it because it only reminds me of him. "The two hot pink ones on the end were delivered with the bike," I say. "I guess Malina knew you'd want one too."

"That woman sure knows how to anticipate our needs," Riley says while she reaches up and takes one of them down. She pulls it over her head, and with her tiny body it makes her look like an alien bobble head toy. She puts her hands on her hips. "How do I look? Like a sexy biker chick?"

"You look like a girl in Hello Kitty pajamas," I say.

Her big bulbous head wobbles around on her shoulders. "Eh, I can be sexy in Hello Kitty." I can't see her eyes under the dark plastic visor, but I'm sure she's smiling.

I'm smiling too, and it feels good to be happy about something. All the fun of manicures and back massages and lounging by the pool have been muted by my constant missing of Theo. I'm glad he's trying to find a way for us to take off these stupid bracelets and survive, but I'm having a hard time dealing with him being gone.

Finding your soul mate and then having him leave really kill the happiness of finding your soul mate.

"So, should I get one too?" Riley says, still admiring my new bike. "Or maybe I'll just let you drive me around all the time?"

I laugh. "I don't even know how to drive a *car*, Riley. This thing might just be a shiny decoration. I wonder if I could bring it to my room."

"Aw, come on!" she says, removing her helmet and holding it in front of her chest. "You totally have to ride it! It'll be awesome!"

I'm still debating if I'm brave enough to hop on a motorcycle when I hear the soft click of the door shut behind us. I turn around, hoping it's just one of the guys because I'm not exactly friends with most of the girls here besides Bethany.

Reality is better than I'd hoped. Standing there, just a few feet away, is the man I've been missing like crazy for two weeks. Theo's brown hair is wild on top of his head. He's wearing a black t-shirt that hugs tightly to his biceps, and jeans that hang low on his hips. He's all I've wanted to see for these last two weeks and yet now I'm frozen in place, suddenly intimidated by how damn sexy he is.

He grins and glances at my new bike. "What do we have here?"

TWO

"Oh my God."

Something takes over my body—love, or maybe craziness, or just delusion. I run across the garage and throw my arms around Theo. I need the reassurance that he's really here right now and that I'm not just seeing a mirage because I miss him so much.

Comfort folds over me as Theo holds on tightly, lifting me off the floor. I clamp my arms around his neck, burying my face into his shoulder, inhaling the scent of him that I've missed so so so much.

"I'm glad you're home," I say against his shirt.

He chuckles and softly puts me back on my feet. "I can tell," he says. He holds onto my waist, and as much as I don't want to let him go, I loosen my grip a little so I can look up at him. His eyes are such a gorgeous shade of amber, it's a little freaky.

I gaze up at him, letting my fingers slide through his hair.

"I missed you more," he says, his voice low. And then he's kissing me. And it feels just as wonderful as all the other times he kissed me, only my heart reacts like some kind of drug addict who hasn't had a fix in a while. It's almost painful, being this close to him.

Riley clears her throat. "Uh, lovebirds? There's another person in the room."

"Sorry," I say sheepishly as I let go of Theo and force myself to take a step backward.

"What's up, Riley?" Theo says, giving her a friendly nod. It's annoying how he can speak all calmly and normally where I'm still trying to catch my breath over here. Theo's presence is like a magnet, drawing me in so tightly it's hard to let go. My heart thumps in my chest, excitement and giddiness making me unable to look away from him.

"Just admiring Cara's new wheels," Riley says, nodding toward the bike.

"A Kawasaki," Theo says, sliding his hands in his back pockets. He nods once. "Nice."

"It's a Ninja," I say, pointing to the black writing on the front fender.

Theo's fingers slide down the back of my arm, leaving a trail of goosebumps in their wake. "It's a Kawasaki Ninja," he whispers into my ear. "It's a great bike. I used to have one."

"Was it Pepto Bismal pink?" Riley asks with a cheeky grin.

"It is not Pepto Bismal pink!" I say, moving to stand in front of my bike as if to protect its feelings. "It's badass Kawasaki Ninja pink."

"Nah," Theo says, tapping the handlebar with his finger. "They don't make them in pink. This was a custom job. Malina probably called our motorcycle guy and had him custom paint it." He tilts his head while he gazes at the pink. "Although it *does* kind of look like Pepto Bismal..."

I punch him in the stomach and three of my knuckles pop. "Don't hurt yourself," Theo says, giving me this cocky freaking grin.

"You are so annoying!" I say, smacking him since my punches do nothing.

He laughs and then grabs me by the arms, pulling me into him. "It's just so easy with you."

"Oh my Godddd," Riley groans, throwing her head back. "You two are so gross it's going to make me puke myself to death."

"That'd be a terrible way to go," I say, curling my nose. I turn back toward Riley, and now Theo is directly behind me. I feel his finger tracing circles on my lower back and it makes it very hard to concentrate. But Riley has turned serious now. She bites on her bottom lip and stares at Theo.

"So, where did you go again? Some business thing?"

"Yeah, just boring business stuff," Theo says with a sigh. I can tell by the look in his eyes that he's slipped into actor mode. The walls are listening in this mansion and since immortality is strictly forbidden from talking about, we have to be sneaky. Theo shrugs. "Someone has to keep you girls living in luxury."

"Well, we appreciate that," Riley says. "So...did you do any new business? Or just the same old stuff?"

Theo glances at me. We're talking in code here, but we never really invented a code to begin with. What she means to say is, *did you find a way to save our lives from being taken by this stupid immortality bracelet?* But she can't exactly say that.

"No new business," he says, shaking his head. He takes my hand and runs his fingers over the bracelet on my wrist. "I didn't meet any new clients, or do anything new. Just the same old stuff."

Disappointment rolls over me. That has to be code for no. No, he didn't discover anything. No, he can't save us yet.

Riley looks down at the floor for a long moment. "Maybe next time your trip won't be as boring."

"Hopefully," he says, giving her a small smile. I look up at him, feeling a mixture of emotions that are hard to separate. How can I be so totally in love with someone and at the same time be scared shitless because I've been sentenced to die within a year from this bracelet?

Of course, the first part makes me blush when I think it. I'm not *in love* with Theo. There's just no way. You don't love someone after a few days of knowing them. I certainly know better than to tell him something like that so soon into this weird immortal relationship. Every time we're together and the words feel like tumbling out of my mouth, I remind myself that Theo is ninety seven years old and I am eighteen and when I die he'll still be here, alive.

So my loving him isn't something to worry about right now.

Riley's phone goes off and she pulls it out of the little front pocket of her Hello Kitty pajama pants. "It's Kyle," she says, glancing at the screen. "He wants me to go to the mall with him to help him pick out some new shoes."

She makes this face as she types out a quick reply. "That boy is totally useless without someone telling him what to do," she says. "I assume you two are going to go jump each other's bones, right?"

I glance up at Theo and he winks at me. "Probably," I say.

Riley rolls her eyes. "Then I guess I'm going to the mall. Call me when you two dorks are done looking longingly into each other's eyes!"

We watch her until she disappears on the other side of the door. Theo grabs my belt loops and pulls me toward him. He's so much taller than I am that I have to throw my head all way back and stand up on my toes to kiss him.

"You have a very understanding best friend," he says between kisses.

I shrug. "She also enjoys dressing other people. Picking out stuff for Kyle is like her favorite hobby."

Theo sways a little, then dips his lips down to my neck. I love these kinds of embraces. I close my eyes when his lips press against my flesh. I've missed this so much.

"Do you think he and Riley have a thing for each other?" Theo asks.

"Eh, I doubt it."

"Would she tell you?"

"Totally," I say, but it comes out all high pitched because he's assaulting my neck in kisses now and it tickles. I push him away and he just holds on to my hips tighter, but at least he stops tickling me with the scruff of his chin.

"I don't really see them being a couple," Theo says. I love how he can hold a conversation with me right in the middle of a make out session. I try to keep up, but it's hard to focus.

"I don't either," I say, my words distorted by his lips. "But they do seem to be good friends."

"Kyle's an okay guy. He joined the clan a few months before I did."

"He seems nice enough," I agree. I wish I could say more, like ask how old he is and how long he's been immortal, but those kinds of questions are off limits here.

"Have you taken her for a ride yet?" Theo says, throwing me off.

"Huh?"

"The bike."

"Oh," I say. I've totally forgotten it was even here. I didn't really remember we were standing the garage, to be honest. Everything around me disappears when I'm in his arms. I shake my head. "No, I don't know how to ride one."

"Got the keys?"

I fish in my pocket and hand it to him. He takes the key in one hand and then touches the bottom of my chin with the other. He brings my lips up to his. "Will you get the door, beautiful?"

I nod, unable to say anything because *damn*, that was sexy. On the wall, I hit the button that makes one of the garage doors roll up. Theo straddles my new bike, puts the key in and starts it. A low, and if I'm being honest, sexy growl of the engine fills the air.

This bike is so freaking cool.

"Hop on," Theo says, motioning for me to join him.

"Do I need a helmet?" I ask.

He shakes his head. "I won't hurt you."

I slide onto the back of my new bike, and hold onto his stomach. Theo puts the bike in gear and slowly rides out of the garage. Sunlight washes over us as we ride down the long winding driveway. We're going slow enough that I can look around and enjoy the view of the sloping Texas hill country. At the end of the driveway, there's a wrought iron gate and Theo pulls up to the keypad, putting one foot on the ground while he punches in the code to open the gate.

Then we're free. Theo starts off slowly, probably for my benefit, and then soon we're soaring over the empty county roads around our home. The wind whips my hair and the sun bites my skin, but I've never felt so free in my life.

I am terrified and thrilled. We lean in the corners and the bike glides over the streets, her shiny pink paint looking totally badass.

When we get back home, Theo stops while the gate slowly opens for us.

"What'd you think?" he asks.

"You have to teach me how to ride this thing," I say. I'm panting and I don't even know why. "It was amazing. I've never felt so..."

"Free?" Theo says.

I nod. "That's exactly it. Will you teach me?"

"Of course," he says, flashing me a sexy smile that makes my toes tingle. "But first, we have some lost time to make up for."

THREE

Theo's fingers lace into mine. He leads the way through the service hallway and back into the house. When we reach the stairs, he starts to turn right. I stop.

"My room is this way," I say, lifting an eyebrow. With our hands still linked, I tug him in the correct direction. He's been gone two weeks, but did he really forget where I live?

The corners of Theo's lips twist up in a grin. "My room has a better view."

He starts walking again, in the wrong direction. It feels so weird going this way since all the girls in the house live on the left side of the massive hallway at the top of the stairs. This part of the mansion is technically off limits, but I guess it will be fine if I'm being escorted by the guy who lives here.

Of course, rules and propriety aren't what's got my stomach in a tightly wound knot.

I've never seen Theo's bedroom before. It only occurs to me right now, as my flip flops patter across the thick hallway carpeting, that I've never been to Theo's room. We've always gone to mine. I've never even thought of his room, which is kind of stupid of me because of course he has one. It's weird feeling so unbelievably close to someone only to realize that we don't really know much about each other.

My nerves tingle with anxiety as we pass each door and I wonder if it's his room or not. What will it look like? Will there be forgotten hair ties on the nightstand from other women he's had before me?

I recoil at the thought. Surely Theo is smart enough to remove anything like that before inviting me to his room.

We walk all the way to the end of the hallway before Theo stops at a door.

He reaches into his pocket and takes out a key, shoving it in the deadbolt. We don't have deadbolts in our rooms, but we can lock them from the inside.

"Am I allowed to be here?" I ask meekly.

"Of course." He twists the key and the lock clicks open. Then he pushes open the door and grins. "Ladies first."

My first thought is that Theo's room is small. But that generalization only makes sense when comparing it to my room, because by all normal standards, his room is still pretty big.

The walls are wallpapered in an eggshell white, and the carpet is the same color, plush and unmarred with dirt or signs of wear. He has a king-sized bed that's so tall I'd have to jump to get onto it, and it's covered in crisp white sheets that are tucked in perfectly. I venture in further, not wanting to look at the nightstands on either side of the bed because I am a jealous weirdo. There's a large wooden wardrobe to the left, a curved wall to the right made of the same kind of stones that make up the outside of the house. The curved wall is parted only by a large wooden door that looks very heavy and old. The whole place reminds me of a modern castle, like how the outside of the mansion looks. Where Riley and my rooms have been made up into contemporary, and kind of girly, masterpieces, Theo's room is very much a manly space.

At the back of the room, the corner walls open to large windows and a little seating area with three plush white lounge chairs. There's a gorgeous and antique brass chandelier hanging from the ceiling. I notice it matches the large one hanging over his bed. There are other wall mounted sconces with lights that look like candle flames on the walls. It gives the whole place a romantic glow, but the mid-morning sunshine pouring in from the windows keeps everything light.

I stop in front of the windows and gaze out at the sloping fields below. This is a completely different view from the one on my side of the house. You can't even see the lake over here.

I feel Theo walk up behind me, his body so close to mine it makes the hairs on my arms stand up, as if they too are hoping to touch him. Just thinking about him gives me that tingly sensation in my stomach, but when he's near me, it's like a whole tsunami of emotions flood into me. It's a miracle I can even stand up straight. "I thought you said your view was better," I say, folding my arms over my chest. "You can't even see the lake from here."

His fingers brush my hair to the side. I feel his legs step closer, touching my butt, as he leans forward, his lips hovering just over my ear. "Wait for it," he says. "Your room has a better view on most days. But not today."

I look back and nearly bump into his face with my cheek. "Are you messing with me?" I ask accusingly.

"No ma'am. I'd never do such a thing."

I give him a look and he just smirks like he's got it all figured out. "Give it a minute," he says, nodding back toward the window.

I roll my eyes, but I turn back around anyway, and gaze out the window.

The mansion is on a hill so we can see everything down below. The grass is green and trees fill up the spaces between houses. There are also some cow pastures dotting the area, but we're so far away the cows look like ants.

And then, I see it. To the left, mostly hidden behind a bunch of pine trees, are big bright colors. Like spheres or massive bounce houses or something.

"What is that?" I ask.

Theo's hands slide up my hips, his chin resting on top of my head. "You'll see."

Another minute passes and the colors seem to get bigger. Or, more accurately, they get higher. Soon I realize exactly what they are. Hot air balloons, at least two dozen of them, all lifting up into the sky at once.

I am frozen in place, too captivated by the balloons and by Theo's hands on my waist to move or say anything for a long while. Together, we watch the balloons rise and begin to glide across the sky, spreading out from each other at very slow speeds. My favorite ones are the rainbow balloons with each color vibrantly filling the sky. There are a couple of branded ones with company names I've never heard of printed on the fabric.

I sigh and lean back into Theo's chest. "I guess you win. Your view is better today."

He chuckles and turns me around until I'm facing him. "It doesn't have to be a competition. We can share the best of what we have with each other. That way we both get to experience it."

I slide my hands up his chest. "You really are amazing, you know that?"

He actually looks bashful for a split second before that cocky grin comes back. "I don't know about that."

I shake my head. "Totally amazing. I don't really deserve you at all, but I plan on keeping you as long as I can."

It takes him a second to smile. In that second, I see a thousand emotions flicker across his eyes, and the reality of my words hits me like a jackhammer. I'm an idiot for saying them of course. Theo is immortal and I am dying and we can't be together forever. A sickening feeling comes to me as I realize maybe that's all he wants from me. A quick fun fling that he doesn't have to commit to because I'll be gone in a few months anyway. I wonder if he was even looking for a cure at all? Maybe it's all just a lie to placate me.

A darkness settles over me in the very next second and I know Theo notices it.

"Talk to me, love." He nudges my chin with his knuckles. "What's wrong?"

"Besides the obvious?" My words are all choked up.

A fine line appears between his eyebrows. "Cara, love. Don't think like that."

I look down. "It's impossible not to."

"You're doubting me." The seriousness in his voice gives me chills. "Cara Blackwell, I swear to you I will—" He stutters when he realizes we can't exactly say the right words here, where anyone could be listening. His eyes meet mine.

"I will make this right," he says in a low voice. "I won't let anything happen to you."

My chest feels like I've been covered with ten of those radiation vests they make you wear at the dentist when you get an x-ray. It's all too much to think about right now. This is the kind of deep shit that will drive you crazy if you don't keep a tight rein on it.

"Let's just make out," I say, trying to be lighthearted.

Theo quirks an eyebrow and I hit him playfully on the chest. "Come on, you know you want to."

"Of course I want to." He runs a hand through his hair, making it more wild than normal. "I always want to."

I push him backward until his legs hit the nearby lounge chair and he sinks into it. My heart starts pounding because I'm being flirtier than I have ever been with anyone, but I need this distraction from real life. I move forward and put my hands on the chair's arms while I climb onto his lap, straddling him on the chair.

Theo leans back, sinking into the cushions. "Take your shirt off," I say, surprised at the confidence in my voice.

In one quick movement, his black shirt is tossed to the floor and every gorgeous tanned muscle of his chest is on display. He leans back again, putting his hands behind his head, which makes his arm muscles tighten. "I like where this is going," he says, wiggling his eyebrows at me.

I swallow. "Don't make fun of me, or I'll stop."

He pushes my hair behind my ears. "I'd never do such a thing."

His voice is deep and sexy and it stirs something inside me. I lean forward and kiss his neck, lightly at first because I have no idea what I'm doing. Then I move to his collarbone and kiss him the way he kisses me, hoping he'll like it as much as I do. His hands loosen from behind his head and they go straight to my thighs which are pressed up against him. I'm wearing shorts so I feel every inch of his calloused hands sliding up my legs and back down them. His touch lights a fire inside me, but still, I keep on, running my tongue up Theo's neck to his ear, grinning when that makes him groan in pleasure. I pull back and he turns toward me, and then I kiss him.

The stubble on his chin is prickly, but I don't care. I love the feel of his lips on mine, his tongue flicking across my bottom lip.

He wraps one arm around my back, pulling me to him until my boobs are pressed so tightly to his chest that they kind of hurt. But it all hurts in a good way because I can't seem to get enough of him. He holds me tightly while his other hand grips my thigh and we make out like we've been doing it our whole lives. A warm tingle starts in my lower belly and I rock my hips against him. A low growl rumbles in his chest and the next thing I know, my shirt is lifted over my head.

I grab onto his shoulders and kiss him, feeling the warmth of his hands traveling up my bare back and sending chills all throughout my body.

When his fingers slide under my bra strap, something brings me back to reality. I freeze. Theo breaks our kiss and slides his hand down to my waist.

"Sorry," I stammer. The moment is ruined and I lean back a little, biting my lip as I look at him. "I'm not—I just—"

God, I'm a loser. Tears sting the back of my eyes. Theo gives me this small smile. "You're not ready," he says, his eyes focused on mine instead of my cleavage which feels so very exposed right now.

"I'm sorry," I say again. Heat flushes my cheeks and I feel so freaking stupid. "I *am* ready. I just—I don't know, let's start over."

I lean down to kiss him again but he stops me, pressing a finger to my lips instead. His eyes meet mine. "There's no rush, Cara."

I sigh. "But I feel bad."

"Don't," he says. "I'm not going to rush you, love. We have plenty of time."

When I don't say anything, he grabs my shirt off the armrest and gently pulls it back over my head. "I am more than happy just being here next to you. Everything else will come with time."

He's being really romantic, so I just nod and sink down against his chest, letting him hold me and stroke his fingers through my hair. But what I wish I could say is that we don't have time. We have money and luxuries and anything we could ever want.

Except time.

FOUR

The Last Stop Café is a remnant of the past, a little preserved restaurant tucked into the countryside that's otherwise been taken over by modern society. It's narrow like a train car, and the outside is a shiny silver metal. There's even the original sign out front, a big red circle with neon lights around it. The inside has been lovingly restored to look like it did when it was brand new. I know because there's a black and white picture of the original restaurant on the wall when you walk in. Everything still looks essentially the same, only now the waitresses wear jeans and t-shirts instead of baby blue waitress dresses.

Theo and I slide into a shiny red booth at the far end of the café. He's taken me here a few times for breakfast and also for milkshakes. He swears the milkshakes are almost as good as they were in the thirties when they used real ingredients without fake sugar and preservatives. It's been a few days since he's been home, and we've spent nearly every second together. Luckily, we haven't had another awkward shirtless moment again, but Theo hasn't pushed our make out sessions very far. I'm still pretty embarrassed about it, but he's acting like everything is normal between us.

"Waffles are just sugar and carbs," Theo says while looking through the laminated menu.

"But they're *so* good," I say.

He nods. "I think I'll get them this time, even though there's no protein or nutrition whatsoever in them. They might as well be putting a slice of birthday cake in front of us."

"Are you tired of your scrambled eggs and bacon?" I ask. That's what he always gets.

He peers at me through his eyelashes. "I would be perfectly happy with my normal breakfast if *someone* didn't get waffles piled high with whipped cream every time we come here." He pokes me with his menu, but his smile is playful.

"Am I throwing you off your rigorous diet?" I say, rolling my eyes. "Trust me, you and your god-like body can handle some carbs for one day."

He grins and sips from his coffee. "Waffles weren't really a thing for the first few decades of my life."

I stop drinking my orange juice mid-sip. Theo doesn't talk about his past, like, ever. "Yeah?" I say. Now I'm incredibly curious.

He nods. "Pancakes were a thing. We had little diners and soda shops like this everywhere in the forties and fifties."

I gaze around the café. Where I see a retro and quirky diner holding onto the past, Theo must see what life was like for him all those years ago. "Is it weird getting used to modern society?" I ask, keeping my voice low. Just because we're out of earshot from the clan doesn't mean we're safe from nosy strangers.

He shakes his head. "I've been here the whole time, so I saw the world grow and change. I guess I grew and changed with it."

"What was your favorite decade?" I ask.

He doesn't even take the time to think about it. "This one."

I feel my cheeks get hot. "Why's that?"

"Because I met you." His finger reaches out and taps my hand from across the table. "Plus, cell phones are amazing. And the special effects in movies?" His puts his finger and thumb together. "Perfection."

I laugh and bury down the questions I'm dying to ask him. It would take way too long to discuss all the things I think about when I'm lying awake in bed, plus Theo has never talked like this with me before. I don't want to rush him into it. I'll just let him take his time.

When the waitress comes, we order the same thing and I ask her for a cup of coffee to go with my orange juice. Theo watches her walk away and then he turns to me. "You're a very polite person," he says, his head tilting. "I like how you speak to everyone with respect."

I rip the top off two sugar packets and pour it into my coffee. "What do you mean?"

"Our waitress. You're kind to her. You're kind to everyone. You'd be surprised how many people treat servants like shit."

I shrug while I think it over. He seems so genuinely interested in this subject. "I try to be nice to everyone. And just because someone's serving me doesn't mean they're below me. Hell, she's got a job. She's contributing to society. All I'm doing is..."

I fade off because it's better than talking about the truth.

Theo seems unaffected. "You're beautiful inside and out," he says. "I really like that."

I'm probably making a really goofy grin right now, so I try to cover it up with small talk. "So, what's up this week? Any good movies we could go see?"

His lips press together. "Actually..."

My bottom lip curls out. "Please tell me you're not leaving!" I whine. "I just got you back!"

"Sorry, love."

Our waitress brings our food so we're forced to sit here quietly as if we're not discussing an immortal clan of assholes who steal life from innocent people. When she's gone, Theo leans forward.

"I have a friend in Greece. He's a member of my old clan and I reached out to him a few weeks ago. He finally got back to me and he might have some knowledge that will help me save you."

"He's from your old clan?" I ask while I cut my waffle into pieces. "Is that allowed?"

He shrugs. "Technically maybe not. The clans keep together and avoid other clans, but he and I are close. We've always been close." When he sees the look of concern on my face he covers his hand over mine. "I promise I'll be fine. I trust him."

I nod but I can't seem to take the frown off my face. "So, he might be able to help us..." I say carefully. I'm not like Riley, so I can't get all excited easily like she does. "How old is he?"

"He was twenty one when the constitution was signed."

"The *American* constitution?" I ask. He nods. I frown. "That's not very old."

In any other circumstance, I'd think being two hundred and fifty years old is old as hell. But after Theo came back from his first trip a week ago, he'd taken me on a motorcycle ride out to the boonies and told me about the trip. It was a total bust because his sources were too young. Immortality has been around since the middle ages. It seems like all of the pertinent information about the stones died out over the years.

Theo puts on a positive attitude and I can see in his eyes that he's trying to make me feel better. "He's spent the last century in Greece. Greece is ancient, love. There are libraries dating back hundreds of years and a few immortal historians who are even older than that. My friend thinks he can get me a meeting with them."

A flicker of hope dances in my chest. "That would be good," I say, still trying to keep my excitement to a minimum.

"But if anyone asks, you don't know where I went," Theo says. "I'm sorry it has to be this way, but I can't let the guys think I've gotten too close to you because they know I'd risk telling you the secret."

"I get it," I say, taking a bite of sugary delicious breakfast food. "I'm just a dumb bimbo you make out with."

He frowns. "I don't like that at all."

I roll my eyes and reach over and steal a bite of his whipped cream. "It's all an act. It keeps us safe."

"You have a point," he says with a sigh. "Every day I wish I could go back to that night on the pier and save you from taking that bracelet." His eyes seem far away as he gazes out the window and into the parking lot.

"You can't think like that," I say. The waitress drops by and refills our coffees, so we fall into silence again. When she's gone, I lean over and whisper, "Even if you'd stopped me, you'd still be immortal and I'd still be mortal."

He peers at me through his thick eyelashes. "Maybe this trip to Greece will fix both of our problems."

That's so damn cryptic I don't even want to ask what he means. Could Theo really give up immortality to be with me? Could I ask him to?

I stab my fork into the waffle and shrug the thoughts to the back of my mind. This new life I've fallen into keeps getting deeper and deeper. It's easier not to think about it.

"So where does Alexo think you're going?" I ask.

"He thinks I'm securing some old bank accounts." Theo grins. "Actually, I *am* doing that, so it's kind of a happy coincidence."

"Securing bank accounts?"

He nods. "The clan members befriend wealthy people all over the globe. They use their powers of persuasion—usually with heavy glasses of gris—to bequeath these people's fortune to the clan." Theo turns his hand up. "It's shady I guess, but we've all done it. I personally stick to men who've made themselves wealthy in an unethical way. They make me their beneficiary and when they die, it all goes to me."

"That's kind of evil and kind of genius," I say.

He shrugs. "It takes a lot of money to live forever."

FIVE

The month of May is always hot, humid, and gross in Sterling. The Texas heat sure knows how to ruin a perfectly good day by coating your skin and clothes in sweat and making it hard to do anything that's not relaxing under a shade tree with an iced tea. Even on the beach in Sterling, it's still always just too damn hot.

But here at the mansion, we're hours away from the beach and there's practically no humidity here. It's hot—Texas hot—but it's easier to handle when you're living in a mansion. Theo left three days ago, and this time I followed him outside and kissed him and watched him get into the back seat of the car just before the chauffeur took him to the airport. Just like in every sappy movie ever, I stood there in the heat, my bare feet on the grass because the cobblestone driveway was searing hot, and I watched the black car fade away and around the corner, taking my love far away from here. It was pretty pathetic, but I stood there. I felt the pain of seeing him get further and further away. Theo called me when he landed in Greece and told me he was settled in at a hotel. Even with today's cell phone technology, he still sounded like he was on the other side of the world. I can actually feel a pain in my chest, deep down and aching, when I think about how far away he is from where I am now.

I am totally in love and I can't tell him about it. At least not until we find out what the future holds for me and Riley. Either way, I don't see how I could ever truly be happy here. If Theo saves me from the immortality bracelet, I'll grow old and die and he won't. If he can't save me, I'll die within a year. And he won't.

Whatever happens, I don't end up with Theo in the end.

It is because of this very real and very terrifying situation that I've spent the last three days trying to distract myself from thinking about it. Riley has been here with me the whole time, and I can tell she's trying to stay cheerful for my sake. Together we've had a massage every day for the last three days. We got our toes done and then had our nails redone even though they were still pretty from last week's manicure. I chose a deep purple shellac polish that has just a hint of sparkle. Riley's nails are black.

We watched YouTube videos on how to ride a motorcycle but we were to chicken to test it out in real life without Theo here to teach us. Actually, I'm too chicken. Riley keeps saying she thinks I'll do great, but I always back out just before we go down to the garage and try it out. The last thing I'd want to do is fall over in the driveway and scratch up my shiny beautiful bike.

Every afternoon, we order dinner from the kitchen and then settle into the movie theater room and watch movies. It's only been three days but we've seen every film that's currently in theaters, except for two horror films because I hate horror films, and this one drama film about a med student that has a lot of graphic depictions of surgeries.

In the mornings, we hit the gym and play on the rock climbing wall. Even with a harness and fancy climbing shoes and gloves, I still can't get to the top of the stupid wall. Climbing is hard and the stupid wall has shown me just how weak my upper body strength is. Riley actually gets a little higher than I do, but we still suck at it.

We've also taken advantage of the bright summer days and swam in the pool. That's really the only place we socialize because Jayla, Nia, and Olivia are in there pretty much every day. Even Olivia, who used to be a pasty pale, is now a golden sunshine princess in her purple bikini. I don't know what Bethany does in the daytime, but she's never at the pool. I've considered asking Riley if we should invite her to hang out with us, but then I always chicken out. Not only am I kind of anti-social in general, preferring to stick with Riley who's been my best friend forever, but being around the other girls makes me really nervous right now. We know a secret they don't, and it's simply too hard to hope that I won't accidentally say anything. We're not exactly friends with them, but their lives are being stolen as well. It's hard to keep a secret like that.

On the fourth morning of Theo's trip, I wake up to the sunshine sparkling through my wall of windows. I throw back the sheer curtains so I can see the hillside in all its beauty, with the sparkling blue lake below.

I get dressed in a pair of blue and black plaid shorts and a white T-shirt and slide my feet into my flipflops. After I've brushed my teeth and pulled my hair back, I'm about to go get Riley, but she beats me to it.

"Hey," she says as she lets herself into my room. "I love those shorts."

"Thanks," I say, doing a little curtsey. She's the one who bought them for me from some online store. Riley cares a lot more about shopping than I do, so I just let her get whatever she wants for me. Riley has always been the wild spirit out of the two of us, yet when it comes to this immortality thing, she's actually the calm one. She's gone all wise and enlightened on me, and she doesn't even seem worried about our predicament. Riley thinks we'll be just fine. For once, I really wish I could be more like her.

"So, what should we do today?" she asks as she plops on my bed. I'm not as good at making my bed as the housekeepers are, but I've tried making it look nice so they won't have so much work to do when they come by later.

"We've seen every movie," I say as I check the time on my phone. "And the girls are having a pool party with some of the guys today." I make a face.

Riley laughs. "Yeah I got the e-invite from Nia on my tablet. I mean seriously? Who sends out invitations for a pool party at the house you live in when the only guests will be the people you *live with*?"

I shrug and try fitting my phone in my pocket only to realize the pockets are stitched closed and are merely for decoration. With a frown, I put my phone on the nightstand. It's not like I'll be hearing from Theo anyway because he'd told me this morning that he'd call me tonight.

"I think Nia is just trying to be like some Hollywood starlet or something. I don't know." I'm surprised it's not Jayla throwing the party. She's little miss attention whore around here. Maybe Nia is trying to one-up her or something.

"Kyle said I should go, but I told him I'd rather hang with you." Riley sits up on my bed. "So what kind of things are we doing today to take your mind off loverboy?"

I roll my eyes. "Shut up."

"I'm just *playing*," she says, emphasizing the last word. "But I'm kind of bored of all our usual things."

"Where haven't we been yet?" I ask. There's beautiful flower and butterfly gardens outside on the property, but that involves walking in the heat and Riley and I are pretty much over anything involving sweating. Also, the irony of suddenly having too many things to do is not lost on me. Even glamorous lives can get boring.

"There's a library, right?" Riley says, her brows squishing together skeptically.

"I think so." I walk over to the tablet on my wall and touch the screen to wake it up. There's a map of the house on here, because of course there is. This whole place is like a modern castle of luxury. I scroll around on the screen until I find the library. "It's off the hallway near the large den with all those concrete statues," I tell her.

She stands up and flattens my sheets to fix where she'd messed them up. "Sounds good. Maybe they'll have some steamy vampire romances."

I pull open my bedroom door, casting one last glance at my phone and wishing I could talk to Theo. "I'm pretty sure a house this nice isn't going to have books like that."

"You never know," Riley says, pointing a finger at me. "You have to think positive."

I laugh at her ridiculousness. After a long walk downstairs, we find a massive wooden door that's at least fifteen feet tall. It's always been closed when I've been down here, but according to the map, it's a library. I push it open and the smell of books envelopes my lungs.

"Whoa," Riley says as we enter the library which is filled with books but devoid of any other people.

The room is round and stretches up to the second floor. It's definitely the part of the house that makes that round castle turret feature on the outside of the house. The whole perimeter of the room has bookshelves that go nearly to the ceiling, where the roof breaks away into skylights. There's even one of those ladders on a rail that allow you to roll around the room, getting books off the high shelves. Riley goes straight to it.

The dark wooden floor is covered with a maroon plush rug and there are a few sitting chairs in the middle of the room. A fireplace near the wall isn't lit, but I imagine sitting near it with a book in the winter time, cuddled next to the fire with a hot cup of cocoa.

Riley climbs to the top of the ladder and pushes herself around the room. "I feel like Belle from Beauty and the Beast!" she says, throwing her arm in the air. "Too bad I can't sing, or I'd totally be singing right now."

"Dork," I say as I venture around the room, looking at the books on the lower shelves. There's a mixture of leather-bound books that look very old and new hardbacks in many different genres. I even find a young adult section near the fireplace and I realize that years of having girls my age come and go as lifebloods is probably the reason these books are here. No doubt, they've probably had a few bookworms succumb to the immortality bracelet before Riley and I got here. My stomach tightens as I run my fingers down the book spines, stopping on a vampire book. I recognize it because it was turned into a movie a few years ago.

"I found your sexy vampires," I say, pulling out the book and holding it up.

"Oooh!" Riley says. She climbs down the ladder and walks over. "I think I will actually read this thing. I've heard it's got some good sex scenes in it."

"Some things you don't need to share with your best friend," I say as I hand her the book.

"Just wait until I find the scenes," she says, rushing over to one of the armchairs and opening the book. "I'll read it out loud to you!"

Now that the ladder is free, I can't help but walk over to it. I may be a legal adult now, but who hasn't wanted to play on a rolling library ladder before? I push it all the way over to the far right of the room, where the railing stops for the doorway. I climb up to the very top to where the books are old and look like they've been here forever.

The air smells musty up here, and I make the mistake of turning around to look at Riley. I'm at least twenty feet in the air, so it makes me dizzy. Luckily, Riley is now absorbed in her book and doesn't see me freak out up here. I turn back around and grip the ladder with both hands.

I lower my foot one rung, and then bring the other foot next to it. When I look up, I'm facing a black leather book with a shiny spine that's twice as thick as the other books. I don't know why, but I can't take my eyes off it. Something makes me want to touch it. So I do. I reach out and press my finger to the spine.

Nothing happens.

I exhale, feeling really stupid right about now. Why am I suddenly focusing on some stupid book? It's not like touching a book will do anything. I'm about to make my way down the ladder, but I still can't shake the feeling I got when I saw that book. I reach up and pull it out a little bit. Something shiny on the front cover catches my attention, so I pull the whole thing off the shelf.

My breath catches in my throat. There are no words on the cover of this book, just a shiny leather binding and a small blue stone set into the middle of the cover.

I would know it from anywhere, because I see one just like it every single day.

It's an immortality stone.

SIX

I run my fingers across the stone. It could be my imagination but the way the lights roll over the surface of the beautiful blue makes it look like the thing glows, if only for a second. Like it's got power inside of it that's dying to get out.

"Whatcha doing?" Riley calls out, making me jump. I clutch the book to my chest as I descend the ladder.

"I found something."

"Is it *sexy*?" she coos, making flirty eyes at me.

"This isn't a joke, Riley." I look toward the door, making sure it's closed. I'm pretty sure everyone is out at the pool right now, but it doesn't make me feel better about the idea of being caught. I lower my voice. "The library isn't off limits, right?" I ask. I can't remember what Bethany told us on the first day except that the guy's quarters are a huge no-no.

"No..." Riley's eyes widen. She folds down the corner of the page in her vampire book and sets it on a nearby end table. "What do you have?"

I turn the book over and show her the front cover. Curious, she holds her wrist up to the book, matching her bracelet to the stone on the cover. They look identical. The only thing the book is missing is the intricate silver bracelet wrapping around the stone's edges.

"Well open it up!" she whisper-yells.

I kneel to the floor and put the book on the rug in front of me, keeping my back to the door behind us. Riley sits next to me too, and the air between us fills with anticipation. Could this be the answer we need?

Slowly, I lift the front cover. It's much heavier than a normal hardback book. The inside pages are thick and smell musty like the old books at Sterling's antique bookshop. I flip the blank first page. The next page is some kind of title, printed in dark black ink in a language I don't know. I turn a few more pages and my excitement wanes. They're all useless to us because none of it is written in English.

"What language is this?" I whisper.

Riley frowns as she watches the pages. It appears to be like an encyclopedia, the pages lined with two columns of writing and occasionally there's a diagram or a drawing. They're simple drawings, like pie charts and sketches, but it's nothing we can understand without reading the subtitles.

"You know what this looks like?" she says, pointing to the heading at the top of a page.

"Those sorority house letters," I say. There were quite a few of them near Sterling College.

"Yep," Riley says, running her fingers over the print. "Alpha, Beta, Kappa. Stuff like that."

Chills run down my spine. "It's Greek."

"Isn't that where loverboy went?"

I shoot her a look because I hate how she won't call him his real name. "Yes."

"Is that where..." she stops, trying to work out how to talk about the subject without talking about it.

I shrug. Theo said ancient alchemists created the immortality stone. I wasn't exactly an A-student in school, so I have no idea if Greece was considered a home of alchemy back in the middle ages. I sigh, my shoulders falling. I am just a stupid teenager. I don't know anything about life or history or science. How the hell can I even hope to solve this problem? A few weeks ago I didn't even know immortality exists. I am stupid. I am worthless.

And I definitely don't know Greek.

"We're so screwed," I whisper.

"We are not," Riley says, grabbing my arm. "Theo will help us." Her voice is the faintest whisper, but it fills me with a new hope.

I nod slightly and turn the page on the book.

A full-page drawing fills the left side. It's an outline of two human bodies standing side by side. One has a circle drawn on the chest, the other has the same circle on the chest, but little jagged lines are drawn around it. Greek writing explains what's going on, but I don't need to read it to understand. These are the immortality stones. This is the information we need.

"Do you see this?" I whisper.

Riley's phone beeps and she leans over to check it. "Shit," she says, scrambling to her feet. "Put that back."

I lean over and look at her phone, seeing a text from Kyle.

The boss is looking for you two. Be warned, he'll probably want you to come swimming. ;-)

"Shit!" I jump up and close the book. The library might not be off limits, but this book would raise some questions, especially if Alexo saw us attempting to read it.

I rush over to the ladder and scale it quickly, my former fear of heights diminishing in place of the real fear of Alexo. The book slides back into its place easily. I push myself several feet away and let the ladder roll to a section of cookbooks and encyclopedias. Two seconds later, the tall library door opens.

"There they are," says Alexo. He sounds pleased, not angry so I hope he doesn't know what we were up to.

"You have such a great selection of teen books," Riley says. I climb down the ladder and walk over to join her, trying really hard to make it seem like I'm not hiding anything. You'd think I'd be good at it by now, but I'm still scared shitless anytime I'm around another immortal guy in this house.

"She's really into vampires," I say over the lump in my throat.

Alexo is impeccably dressed, as usual. Today he's in a charcoal gray suit with a deep blue tie. "Vampires," he says, lifting an eyebrow. "Good luck finding one of those in real life."

Riley chuckles. "Yeah...too bad that magic stuff isn't real. Of course, I'd be all over Harry Potter if *he* was real. He's better than a vampire, I think."

She does it so effortlessly, all of this shallow small talk that makes us seem innocent and in the dark about reality. All I can do is stand there next to her, my heart pounding like crazy, while she covers for both of us.

Alexo's thin lips twist into a smile. "There's a pool party outside. The music is a little...loud for my taste, but the whole gang is there. I wanted to extend an invitation to the both of you."

"Oh...that sounds fun," Riley says. "We actually planned on going down there soon."

"Excellent," Alexo says. He turns his gaze to me. "I spoke with Theo this morning. He's doing well."

"That's good," I say, exhaling slowly.

Alexo's knowing grin softens. "He's very fond of you."

"Oh?" I say. I mean, I know he is, but it's kind of cool to hear Alexo say it, although I do worry that he has some kind of ulterior motive.

He nods once. "I'll see you outside. Feel free to bring some better music. Something without so much screaming and techno garbage added in. I miss the days of real music played on real instruments."

Riley fakes a charming laugh. "I can do that. Jayla's music is usually of the trashy nightclub variety. I don't like it at all."

"I couldn't have said it better myself," Alexo says, his smile as charming as his voice. "See you soon."

SEVEN

It's Sunday and all the guys are home. All of them except the one I care about, who is still traveling and attempting to find a way to save us. It's been another week, another seven days of loafing around this mansion and missing Theo like crazy. I simply can't take it anymore. Every morning I wake up and check my phone and every morning he's texted me something vague and sweet, but it never says he's on his way home. My life has somehow become more boring since finding out I'm about to die.

A relationship through text messages and long distance trips might work out for some couples. It'd even work out for me if the guy I was dating was just some normal loser from Sterling. If I didn't really care about him, this would be fine. But I care about Theo more than I've ever even dreamed of caring about another guy. It's never been like this before. I've never had crush this strong. I've never felt so completely empty when I was separated from someone. It's like I've been turned into some lovesick idiot straight out of a romantic comedy. Like I'm Rapunzel locked in a tower and desperately going crazy waiting for my prince to come save me, but all he ever does is send me text messages saying he'll save me one day. Ugh.

Normally I get by fine each day. I hang out with Riley and we do stuff to take the boredom away. It always seems like we're the only ones here since the guys are usually gone and the other girls keep to themselves. But today, the guys are actually home and, they're all hanging out outside on the massive covered stone patio that overlooks the infinity pool.

When we woke up this morning and Jayla and the other girls weren't already out here, Rile and I decided to claim the pool as our own and have a pool day. Then Kyle and Russell appeared with beers and meat for the grill. Now Henry and Alexo are here too, all sitting under the patio while we swim in the pool. It would have been rude to get up and leave when they arrived, so we stayed. Now I'm thinking it's even weirder that we're here, living this lie of being perfectly happy.

It's like we're one big happy family, except we're not. Riley and I can't exactly get up and leave without a good explanation, plus it's scorching hot today and the pool is beautiful and refreshing so I like being out here. The guys are all very nice, and I used to like and respect them. You know, until I realized they were immortals, and now it's hard to look at them the same way. Even Kyle, sweet and innocent Kyle who is the youngest immortal of the group, he's still aware of what's going on here and that makes him an enemy as well.

The other bad thing about being around the guys is that Riley and I have to be actresses the whole time. We keep our conversations light and stupid, chatting about what we imagine teenage girls would talk about if they weren't aware of their own impending death. Riley even goes off talking about how Ryan Reynolds is the hottest actor ever, and I can't even contribute to the conversation because I'm too busy thinking that Theo is the hottest guy ever, hands down, of all time forever and ever. Of course, thinking about him only makes me sad, so I end up sitting in the shallow end of the pool, my arms resting on the stairs while I gaze out at the landscape below us.

"Cara," Alexo calls out in his honeyed voice. I realize now that I recognize what his voice reminds me of. Those old black and white movies where the men were always in suits and the women were always in housewife dresses with perfectly curled hair. He sounds like one of those guys.

I turn around, fake smile plastered on my face. "Yes?"

Even outside in the middle of the summer, Alexo wears a black fitted suit, his shoulder length black hair slicked back like he's the villain in an action movie.

He nods toward the house. "I think I just heard the car drop someone off."

He gives me a playful wink and it feels like all the happiness that left with Theo is suddenly back again.

"I'll be back," I tell Riley as I launch myself out of the pool. She rolls her eyes and waves me away. One of the servers leans down and hands her a fruity frozen drink with an umbrella in it.

"Would you like one too, miss?" the woman asks me.

"No thanks," I say, as I look around for my towel. Where the hell is it? Then I remember I never even grabbed one when I came down here. I was too distracted thinking about Theo to remember a towel. *Stupid*, stupid.

In the distance, I see Theo step out onto the patio. He's wearing jeans and his signature black shirt, with dark sunglasses.

"Theo!" I call out, unable to hide my excitement. I run along the side of the pool, up the three stairs to the patio, and then I run straight into his arms.

"Whoa," Theo says as I leap up, wrapping my arms around his neck, my legs around his torso. "Hey there," he says, holding on to me. Water drips down to the stone pavers beneath our feet, and it occurs to me a second too late that I am sopping wet in a hot pink bikini and Theo is fully dressed. At least my hair is pulled up in a messy bun, so it's dry.

I lean back and kiss him, still latched on him like a spider monkey. "Sorry I'm wet," I say.

He grins and glances behind me. "Maybe you should get down," he whispers.

"Why?" I say, but I climb off of him and land on my feet. Then I see what he was looking at. Everyone is watching us. Even Kyle, who's manning the grill is turned toward us, spatula in hand, jaw open.

Oh my God, I'm so embarrassed.

I clear my throat and run my hands down Theo's mussed up shirt. "Sorry about that," I say.

I've got him all wet, but the wettest part is right on his chest where the padding in my bikini top pressed against him and squished out water. "I'm... really really sorry," I say. "I was just excited to see you."

His head dips toward mine, that sly smirk on his face. "It's not a problem, love."

"Burgers are almost ready," Kyle calls out. "You want one?"

Theo looks at me, lifting a brow. "You want to eat here?"

"Not if we can eat somewhere alone," I whisper, giving him a look that means I want to talk about his trip, not exactly run off to make out, but that we should pretend that's what we're doing. It's a lot of emotions to convey in one look, so he probably doesn't get it.

Theo winks at me, then looks up to Kyle. "No thanks. I think we'll hit up Cara's favorite diner in town."

"Cool beans, man," Kyle says, going back to the grill.

I turn to Riley, who waves me away without a second thought. Normally I'd feel bad ditching her to hang out with my boyfriend, but she knows as well as I do that Theo has information for us. We can't both leave to talk to him because that would be suspicious.

"Where's your towel?" Theo asks.

"I forgot it," I say with a shrug.

"Why doesn't that surprise me?" he says as he opens the door to the house and steps back for me to go first.

"Shut up."

In my room, I close the door and then grab the small dry erase board Riley got for us the other day. We use it to write messages to each other that we can't say aloud. Theo eyes me curiously as I quickly write out: *I wish we could talk right now, dammit!*

His smile softens and he takes the board and marker from me.

"We should get dressed," he says while he writes. "You look hot as hell in that bikini, but if we're going to lunch you should probably put on normal clothes."

He turns the board to me, where he's written: *No way to fix you yet. I did learn some interesting stuff though.*

Right after I read it, he wipes it clean with his hand. My heart sinks. No fix yet.

"We should definitely go to lunch," I say, hating how weak my voice sounds. "I feel like I could eat my feelings right about now."

Theo's fingers slide down my cheek as he gazes at me. "Don't stress."

My eyes drop to the floor. "Easier said than done."

The air conditioner kicks on and blasts me with cold air, sending chills all over my body. I shiver and Theo takes off his shirt, then uses it to wipe the water off my face and arms. I watch his chest flex and move, the immortality necklace staying perfectly in place over his sternum. "A towel would probably do a better job of this," he says, frowning.

I laugh. "Yeah, but I like seeing you take care of me."

"Oh, I'll take care of you," he says, his voice deeper than usual. He gives me a sexy look and my insides melt. My face must be red by now, too.

"Shut up," I say, rolling my eyes to lighten the mood. I head into my closet and quickly find some shorts, a new pair of panties, a bra, and a shirt. I bundle them all up into a ball and then step back into my room. "You should go get a new shirt so I can get ready," I tell him as I walk toward my bathroom.

"How long is that going to take?" He tosses his wet shirt over his shoulder and I focus on the immortality necklace around his neck so that his muscular chest doesn't derail my thoughts.

"Just a few minutes. I need to get makeup and stuff."

He frowns. "That's going to take forever. Just throw on some clothes and let's go."

I shake my head. "I look like shit and I still smell like sunscreen."

"You look fucking amazing Cara, and sunscreen is good for you because we'll be out in the sun. Especially if we take your new bike, which I figured we would so I can give you lessons."

I get excited at the idea of riding my bike again, but still, I feel all gross and ugly right now. I heave a sigh. "Ten minutes."

Something dark falls from the clothing in my arms. Theo grabs it, lifting the pair of my black lacy panties in the air. "You dropped this," he says with a smirk.

Okay, I am definitely red now. I snatch it from his hands and ball them in my fist. "Thank you," I say sarcastically as I turn toward my bathroom. "I'll be out in ten minutes."

"Make it fifteen and I can join you," he says. I'm not sure if he's playing or not, but suddenly I am too nervous to function properly. The idea of showering with Theo is…well…awesome. But I'm not sure I'm up to that right now.

Theo puts his hands on either side of the bathroom door and drops his head down to mine. His eyes shine with mischief as he kisses me. "It is so easy to get you flustered," he whispers, then kisses me again.

"I hate you," I whisper playfully.

"You love me," he says just before he plans a kiss on my lips. "I'll be back in ten."

I nod slightly and watch him leave. Every fiber of my body is alight with desire. If it weren't for the immortally bracelet beating him to it, this boy would be the death of me.

EIGHT

Theo and I take the new motorcycle out to a high school parking lot. Since it's summer and school is out, there's no one here and the vast open space will be good to learn how to ride this thing. This time Theo insisted that I wear a helmet since I'd be driving by myself. I tell myself I'm excited to learn how to ride this thing all the way up until Theo and I climb off the bike and he motions for me to get on it.

"I'm scared," I say, clutching my helmet in my hands.

"You're not going to ride it now, I just want to show you the controls," he says. He lifts the bike off the kickstand and holds it upright by the handlebar. "Climb on."

I set my helmet on the concrete and walk over to the bike. "Don't let it fall..." I say as I climb on.

"I won't let you *or* the bike fall." Theo grins. "You're both too valuable. So, here's the throttle," he says, tapping my right hand that's holding onto the grip.

"I knew that," I say with a smile. "That's about all I know, though."

"Okay, this handlebar lever is the brake," he says, tapping the shiny silver levers. "It's the best one to use on the street." He walks over to the left side, shifting his grip on the bike's handlebars so I won't fall over. My toes barely tap the ground when I sit on this thing, so I'm more than nervous about my ability to drive it.

"Over here is your shifter. You click it down once for first gear, and then up five times for the higher gears. It's just like in a car...you start out in first or second, then go up a gear every ten miles an hour or so. You have to pull in the clutch when you do this or you'll strip the gears."

He taps the left handlebar lever. "That's your clutch."

"That's a lot of information." I shift forward on the bike, letting my feet rest on the pegs instead of the ground. Theo holds the bike upright and I grab the handlebars, which feels a little uncomfortable because it's not like sitting on a bicycle. I have to lean forward to reach and my balance feels off.

"Your body steers the bike more than the handlebars do," he explains as he moves to the front of the bike, putting his legs on either side of the front tire to hold it up. "You'll lean left to turn left, right to turn right. It's just like how we lean when I'm driving."

I nod. "That's scary."

"It is at first, but you'll get the hang of it."

"Tell me about your trip," I say, sitting up on the bike. I wanted to wait until after the motorcycle lesson to grill him on the trip that kept him away from me for a week, but I can't help it. I'm dying to know, even if he's already told me he didn't learn anything.

Theo leans the bike back until it's resting on the kickstand. "Well...what do you want to know?"

"What'd your friend say?" I ask. I get off the bike.

Theo runs a hand through his hair. He shaved recently, so his jaw is smooth, and I see the muscles flex as he swallows. "I met with Damien, and told him about my situation."

"That's your friend from the other clan?" I ask.

He nods. "We've been friends a long time. He shares the belief that we should only use dying humans as lifebloods, so we get along well."

He seems sad, and I'm not sure why. I step closer and reach for his hand. "What did he say?"

Theo sighs. "He thinks I'm an idiot for getting involved with a human. Especially as a member of the Rosewater clan, he doesn't think it's very smart."

"What does our clan have to do with it?" I ask.

He drops my hand casually and takes a few steps back, looking at the bike as if he suddenly needs to check the engine or something. "Immortals don't *fall for* humans, Cara. We tend to use humans for our personal gain, not turn them into love interests."

"But what does Rosewater have to do with it?"

"It's complicated, Cara." Theo adjusts something on the bike, a little black knob that twists ninety degrees. "Damien is just looking out for me, and I can't say I blame him. Alexo chewed me out after I left you to shower."

My blood turns cold. "What?"

Theo looks at me, his expression blank. "Yeah, after I grabbed a new shirt, Alexo pulled me into the study and told me I was being entirely too careless by making you like me as much as you do. That the..." He flashes me a grin, "charming display of affection you gave me at the pool—well, it made him nervous. I'm still new to the clan so I don't think he trusts me fully. He warned me against falling too hard for a lifeblood because he's afraid I'll crack my composure and tell you about the stone."

"Kind of like how you already have?" I say with a sardonic laugh.

He nods. "I told him you were just a fun girl but that my intentions were... carnal only. He believed it."

I swallow.

Theo runs a finger down my arm. "Cara, my feelings for you are very real."

"I know," I say, nodding. "I understand. But I don't care about Alexo. I care about you finding a freaking way to fix this."

He smiles sadly, his lips turning down in the corners. His eyes are on me but he feels so far away.

"Why did you leave your old clan?" I ask.

"It's complicated." Some strands of my hair have escaped their ponytail and he brushes them behind my ear. "But that doesn't matter right now, because all that matters is getting the bracelets off you and Riley."

"It kind of does matter," I say, frowning. "I still don't understand how these clans work. It just sounds like a weird underground group of immortals who all hate each other."

He chuckles. "That's pretty accurate. The stones were invented ages ago and they were given to the elite of the time. Mostly men, mostly wealthy guys who all knew each other. Only, over time they disagreed on how immortality should be governed and they branched off into their own groups."

I listen intently, hoping something in this story will hint at how we can break the stone's power. Theo thinks for a moment, like it's hard for him to say what he's saying, or maybe—and it kills me to think this—maybe he's hiding parts of the truth from me.

"I'm relatively young compared to other immortals. I'm like a child to some of them who are centuries old. I'm not privy to some information, like Damien is. Anyhow, over time, immortals were slain for their stones and the people who took them became immortal themselves. Most of the originals aren't alive anymore, and like I said before, a lot of the knowledge has been lost over time. But there's one thing every clan agrees on, and that's that we must keep immortality a secret. Once someone knows about it, they'll do whatever it takes to become immortal themselves. Since the stones are limited, that means they have to kill to get one."

"How did you get one?" I ask.

"Damien was my boss," Theo explains. His face softens from the nostalgia as he talks. "It was during the Great Depression. I worked as a delivery boy for his milk company. My parents kicked me out because they couldn't afford me, so I was on my own. He took a liking to me, I guess. He became like a father to me. One day when I was twenty one and had started my own woodworking business, Damien approached me and gave me the stone. A member of his clan, the Embrook clan, had chosen to end his life, so Damien revealed his immortality and me to join the clan."

He presses his lips together. "Honestly, I thought maybe he'd drank too much moonshine that night because he sounded full of shit, but I took the stone to be nice." He taps the necklace beneath his chest. "The original stone's owner still had a lifeblood in the city, so she became my lifeblood the moment I put the necklace on."

He looks down at his chest. "I've never taken it off. Damien made me a murderer that day. He thought he was helping, but I've often felt like the burden of immortality makes life not worth living." There's regret in his eyes as he says, "Yet here I am, taking terminal life bloods and telling myself it's ethical because I'm helping their families." He chuckles sarcastically. "Really I'm just a coward who won't admit that I should just die."

"Theo." I put my hand on his chest. "Don't say that."

"I'd had enough of this shit before I met you," he says, his jaw tightening. "I needed to do something. So I joined the Rosewater clan. I needed a purpose if I was going to keep myself alive any longer."

"What does that mean?" I ask, and my voice seems to take him by surprise because he flinches, then his golden eyes fix on mine and he smiles.

"Nothing to worry about, love." He leans forward and places his lips over mine in a soft, slow kiss. "Damien took Riley's approach on this. He said there has to be a way to remove the immortality bracelet and spare your life. He's going to help me find it."

"Well...that's good," I say, staring at Theo's shirt, knowing his necklace is underneath the fabric. "It's not exactly what I wanted to come out of your trip, but it's something."

"It's only been two months, love." Theo grips my arms tightly and kisses the top of my head. "I'll fix this."

"What did you mean by finding a purpose?" I ask. I've never seen Theo look so resolute as he did a minute ago, and then he changed the subject like it was nothing.

"Eh, I was just talking. Immortality makes you very lonely, but then I met you and now my goals are different."

I frown. "It seems like you're hiding something from me."

"You need not worry, Cara."

He sounds so confident I want to believe him, so I nod and ignore my intuition that's telling me he's being weird about this.

I take a step back and look at him. "This last week..." I exhale and then take a deep breath. "This last week felt like my heart had been ripped out, Theo. I can't keep sitting here suffering in that mansion without you while you jet off and do whatever you're doing. I know you're helping and all, but I just can't stand it."

"I feel the same way." He bites on his bottom lip. "That's why I'll take you with me on the next trip. I can't be away from you anymore."

A fire lights up inside of me. When I made this confession, I thought he'd comfort me and tell me stupid things to make me feel better. But this is much better than what I'd imagined. "Good," I say.

He grins. "You're mine, Cara Blackwell. I'm sick of being away from you."

I lean against his chest, wrapping my arms around him tightly. His chin settles on top of my head, the familiar gesture he always does when we embrace like this. I'm still curious about why he left his old clan, but I don't want to kill the moment by bringing it up again.

I breathe in his cologne and think about asking if I can keep one of his shirts like the dork that I am. He'd probably let me. I look up at him and he smiles. Then his eyes glaze over and lose focus.

"Theo?" I say as his body seems to soften, all of his muscles going limp.

And then he crumples. His eyes close, his head falls back, and I'm not strong enough to hold him upright. We both crash to the hot asphalt. "Theo!" I press on his chest, squeeze his hand. He's out. His skin pales, his lips turning blue. I pound on his chest and call his name, but he doesn't react. He doesn't move. He doesn't seem alive at all.

NINE

Theo winces. The tiny gesture sends hope soaring through me. "Theo?" I plead.

His eyes flutter a little and then go still. He's on his back in the abandoned high school parking lot. I'm kneeling next to him, my hand pressed to his chest. I feel a heartbeat, but it's slow, weak. I lean forward press my fingers to his lips. He releases a shaky breath. "Theo? Wake up!"

I'm not sure when I started crying, but tears splash onto his shirt. His eyes flutter open again, his face contorting in pain.

"Call Kyle," he says, his eyes meeting mine before they close again.

I call Kyle as fast as my fingers can work the phone screen. He takes forever to answer, and when I finally hear his voice after four rings, I'm yelling. "Kyle! It's Theo!"

"It sounds like Cara," he says with a laugh. The freaking idiot, this is not a time for jokes. "Theo is—I don't know," I say as I keep my hand pressed to his chest, desperate to feel the beating of his heart. "He passed out. He said to call you. He looks...he looks like death."

"Where are you?" All the lighthearted joking has left his voice.

"The high school parking lot."

"I'll be there in a minute," he says before hanging up.

I drop the phone and grab Theo's clammy face in my hands. "Theo? Please wake up," I say, tears falling down my face. He'd told me that immortality didn't mean invincibility, but now I'm seeing firsthand what he meant. He's not okay. Maybe he's sick. Can immortals get sick?

Time seems to crawl on forever even though we're only about ten minutes away from the mansion. I sit here, the hard parking lot digging into my bare knees as I lean over Theo, shading the sun from his face with my body. He's still breathing and his eyes flutter every few seconds, but he's not talking. When his eyes open, they're unfocused, unaware.

I lean forward, resting my forehead on his. A blue glow emanates from underneath his shirt. I blink, thinking it's just a trick of the sunlight, but it's still there. I reach down and push the collar of Theo's T-shirt down, revealing his necklace. The blue immortality stone is glowing, a bright blue like a flame is beneath the stone. The surface moves like a fuzzy television screen, and as I watch, the brightness slowly gets dimmer.

Kyle arrives in a Camaro, barely slamming to a stop before he flings open the door and rushes toward us. He yanks down Theo's shirt just like I had done, but he doesn't seem surprised when he sees the glowing stone.

"I have to take him to the, uh, hospital," Kyle says. Normally he's so tall and lanky and carefree that he seems like a dork. Now he's dead serious. "Sorry Cara, but you can't come with us. I have the driver coming to pick you up. He'll be here any second," he says as he scoops up Theo and carries him to the passenger side of the car. He slams the door closed and jogs back around to the driver's side. All the while I'm still kneeling on the ground, tears streaking my face. Kyle offers me a small smile. "He'll be okay. I promise."

I nod and watch as he peels out of the parking lot and drives away, leaving me along with the motorcycle I still don't know how to drive. What the hell just happened?

If Theo really will be okay, I'm not going to get answers until he's back.

I grab my helmet and pull it over my head as I try to remember everything Theo told me about the bike. One down, five up. The clutch is on the left, brake on the right. We're only a few miles away from the house. I slide onto my bike; its shiny pink paint the opposite of how I feel right now. The motor cranks to life as I turn the key, and when I pull back slightly on the throttle, it roars just like when Theo does it. My heart pounds and nerves mix with worry in my chest. Balancing the bike with my toes on the ground, I pull in the clutch and press down on the gear shifter, putting it into first gear. Slowly, I let off the clutch and give it some gas. The bike launches forward, shaky and unsteady, but I hold on. I switch to second gear and give it a little more gas. There aren't any sharp turns on the way home. I have the gate code memorized now.

Theo thought I could handle driving this thing. I'm going to prove him right.

RILEY SITS NEXT to me on the loveseat in Theo's room. I've pulled it up close to the window so I can see the moment Kyle's Camaro gets back home. From this side of the house, you can see the driveway and about half a mile of the road that leads to it. The cars are tiny, but I'd recognize the red Camaro anywhere.

"You sure you don't want any water?" Riley asks. She's been trying to give me that bottle of water for an hour and half now, but I shake my head just like I did every other time she asked. My stomach hurts from worry. I can't eat or drink anything.

It's been an hour and a half with no word. When I got home, I parked my bike and burst through the house, only to find that all the guys were gone. Alexo is on a business trip, according to Malina. There's no one here to update me on Theo's status, and even if the guys *were* here, they'd probably lie to me. This is clearly something happening with the immortality stone, a thing I'm not supposed to know about.

I didn't ask permission to go into Theo's room, but I did it anyway. I grabbed Riley, the dry erase board, and my phone charger and then I marched us straight into this side of the mansion.

I explained the entire event to Riley on the dry erase board. We've barely talked out loud in this room since we got here but she's been writing back to me, telling me it'll be okay.

I was so close to getting answers, I write.

She furrows her brow. *what do you mean?*

I sigh. "He was telling me about some old friends," I say aloud, figuring that's not very incriminating to voice. "And then he just collapsed."

Friends who know how to fix us? she writes

"Yes," I say, turning my gaze back to the road outside. Still nothing. I pick up my phone and call Kyle again, but it goes straight to his voicemail.

I leave another text for Theo, wondering if he'll ever see it.

I miss you. Please come back to me.

"This is bullshit," Riley says, breaking the silence a few minutes later. "Why can't Kyle update us on the freaking situation? Your loverboy passed out! What if he has a brain tumor or something?"

She's talking so loud, I almost wonder if she's doing it on purpose, just in case someone is listening to us. I don't even care if I'm not being told the truth right now, I just want to know if he's okay. And no one is here to tell us anything.

Theo's wall screen starts ringing. Riley and I look at each other, and then I jump off the loveseat and rush over to his door, where the screen is mounted into the wall.

It's a video call from Alexo. I hesitate to answer, but then Riley pushes the button for me, and Alexo's face appears on the screen. He's in a hospital, by the looks of it.

"Hi Cara," Alexo says. "And Riley, I figured you'd be with your best friend." Small smile.

"I'm um," I stutter. "I only came to Theo's room because I can see the driveway better and I wanted to know when he got home."

"You're fine, sweetheart." Alexo doesn't seem concerned with my being in the wrong side of the mansion. "Theo made you his beneficiary my dear, so you're welcome in his room any time you'd like."

"Beneficiary?" Tears spring to my eyes and all of the air seems to suck out of the room. Alexo's eyes widen and then he laughs.

"Oh, sweetheart, no. Theo is fine." His eyes crinkle at the corners and I take a deep breath as I try to come back down from the horror of thinking he had died. "I just wanted to let you know he's at Methodist Hospital recovering nicely."

"What happened to him?" I ask, knowing I probably won't get the real answer.

"Rare blood disorder," Alexo lies with a skill I've never seen before. "Poor thing needed a transfusion. But he got it, and he'll be fine so don't you worry. It might be a day or two until he gets home, though."

"Oh," I say, my heart sinking. I'm so sick of Theo being gone. "Can I come see him?"

"I'm afraid not, dear. He's isolated." Alexo shrugs like *what can you do*. "Some hospital procedure. They won't let anyone back there, but they said he'll be back to normal soon. He might need to leave for more transfusions in the future, so you can be warned of that. If you ever see him get pale again like that, you just give us a call and we'll get him to the hospital, okay?"

I nod, the lump in my throat making it hard to talk. "Okay."

Alexo's narrow eyes and pointed nose reminds me of a fox. "Rest easy, dear. We'll see you soon."

When the call ends, Riley touches my shoulder. "Well...that's good."

"It's also freaky that he called right after you were talking about it," I say, giving her a look that I hope she understands. We are not alone here. We're given anything we want, but we're probably being watched the whole time. My stomach churns.

The wall screen lights up with another call, this time from a number that's not saved into the contacts list. That's because it's Theo's number, calling his own bedroom.

I answer the call, anxious to see him, but his face isn't in the screen. His hands are, and they're holding a piece of paper.

don't say anything

I keep quiet, and a second later, Theo lowers the paper. He's holding his phone up with one hand, and the paper in the other. He looks like shit, all pale with sunken eyes and dark circles under them. He motions for me to wait a second and then he turns the paper over and holds it up to me.

My lifeblood died. Kyle is helping me find a new one.

I motion for Riley to get me the dry erase board and I write out a message to him.

Alexo said you're in the hospital

He smiles and instead of it lighting up his face, he looks like the living dead.

I am, he mouths, turning the camera to show the empty waiting room of a hospital. He scribbles something on a paper and holds it back up to me.

looking for a new lifeblood

hurry up I write on the board.

He nods and then he holds his fingers to his lips and blows me a kiss.

When the silent call is over Riley says, "Holy shit."

he looked like shit, she writes on the board.

"I can't sit around here worrying anymore," I say aloud. "I'm going to go crazy. Alexo said he's fine, so I believe him." I add that last part just to suck up to the guy who might be listening to me.

"Well, let's do something to take our mind off of it," Riley suggests.

"I have an idea," I say. "Want to go for a ride on the Ninja?"

TEN

I'm pretty sure I didn't sleep all night. Theo texted me that he'd tell me when they're heading home, so I left his room for my own. It felt like I was kind of a weirdo stalker being in his room even though he didn't seem to mind. Honestly, the urge to snoop was a little overwhelming and I didn't want to be that girl who goes through her boyfriend's things.

So I spent most of the night in my own bed, staring at my bracelet. It's weird how it works. The silver bangle fits snuggly but not too tight. Just like any other bracelet, it shifts up and down if I jiggle my arm, and I can twist it all the way around on my wrist. I just can't remove it. To any bystander, it looks like a normal bracelet. Beautiful and intricate, with a stunningly blue stone in the middle. Its beauty only makes me hate it more.

When there's a knock at my door, I know it's Riley. It's around nine in the morning, and I yell for her to come in.

"You want some breakfast?" she says, poking her head inside my door. "There's pastries and donuts in the kitchen. I'll bring us some."

"Apple popover," I say, sitting up in bed. "And coffee."

"Coming up!" she says cheerfully before leaving me alone again. I go to get out of bed, and the door opens again. "By the way," Riley says, "What did Theo say about that book we found?"

"Shit." I press my palm to my forehead. "I totally forgot to ask him."

She tisks. "Lovebirds. You are completely worthless around him."

She leaves again, and this time she doesn't come back immediately after closing the door. I stand up and stretch, feeling like a zombie from lack of sleep. I really hope the kitchen has some strong coffee this morning. I can't believe I forgot to ask Theo about the freaking book. We were even talking about his trip to Greece, and it totally slipped my mind. Maybe Riley is right—I'm worthless around him.

Even *I* think it's a little sad how quickly and completely I fell for Theo. I barely knew anything about him and I was already mentally wrapping up my heart to present to him on a silver platter. I know it sounds crazy, but I don't care.

Theo is mine now and he's all I've ever wanted. Especially in this messed up world where immortality exists and my life is at stake, Theo is all I want.

That's why I need to make things right with that book. Still in my pajamas, I put on some socks because the library floor is wooden and no doubt cold. Plus, it'll mask my footsteps. The pajamas are a decoy; no one ever does anything sneaky when they're not properly dressed. No one will notice me steal that book.

I stroll through the hallway, happy that no one but a maid sees me. It's still early enough for the girls to be asleep and the guys to be doing whatever business stuff they do on weekdays.

I slip into the library and look around casually, like maybe I'm just here to browse in case anyone is in here. But the room is empty and majestic just like the first time I came here. The ladder is still where I'd left it. I slide it over to the far right and then climb up quickly, not letting my fear of heights bother me this time.

The book is in my hands in no time. I grab a couple of inconspicuous books about the ocean and sandwich the book between them. Then I hold them close to my chest and book it back to my room.

Riley arrives a few minutes later with a tray of coffee and entirely too many donuts and pastries.

"What's that?" She says as she sets the tray on the table in my sitting area.

I put a finger to my lips and then hold up the book. Her eyes widen. "I like where this is going," she says, grabbing a pink iced donut and taking a bite. "Let's enjoy some classic literature together."

I sip from the piping hot cup of coffee and take a bite of my apple popover while Riley flips through the mysterious book. Our chef makes the popovers fresh in the mornings and they're so good I always eat too many. Today Riley has brought me four of them, so she's clearly not trying to help me stay healthy.

"We need a translator," Riley says with a frown. We've officially flipped through every thick parchment page of this ancient book. Everything is in Greek and the drawings are impossible to decipher.

"Google has a translation page," I say, getting up to get my computer.

"Wait—" Riley holds up her hand to stop me. "This song is my jam." She leans over and cranks the volume on her phone's music player, blasting the room with the new Lady Gaga track.

"Our computers might be hacked," she whispers against my ear. With the music going, there's no way we'll be overheard. "Like...maybe they'll see what we look up."

"You're right," I say. My heart sinks. I had been determined to decipher some of this book before Theo got back. Maybe I could have found something helpful for our situation. I pick up my phone and turn it over in my hand. The clan pays for our phone bill, so it's probably being tracked as well. If not, I could take pictures of the pages and send them off to some language specialist to get it translated. But if it talks about immortality and other secretive things, that wouldn't work either because I'd be sharing the secret.

"I feel like shopping," Riley says. She flashes me a sneaky smile and then stands up, pulling out her ponytail and then redoing it. "I heard about those virtual reality things at the stores and I really want one, but if I order it, it'll take two days to get here."

I know she's lying for the sake of keeping our secrets, but I'm not sure where she's going with it. "We should see if we can get the driver to take us to an electronic store."

Then I get it. Computers. We should get a new computer, one that isn't potentially being watched by the clan. "Oooh, I want a new cell phone case," I say excitedly to join in on the charade. "Best Buy has a lot of them. We should go."

"Let's eat breakfast first," she says, reaching for a donut hole. "Then we'll spend the rest of the day deeply involved in a virtual reality."

She winks and I hold back a laugh. Now I finally feel one step closer to finding an answer to our problem. We'll get this thing translated and we'll find out the way to remove these bracelets.

Then I'll only have about a dozen other problems to work out, like how I'm supposed to date an immortal when I'm finally mortal again.

One step at a time.

ELEVEN

MALINA GIVES US SOME PETTY CASH IN THE AMOUNT OF TWO THOUSAND dollars. All it took was a sweet look from Riley and the request of money for shopping. Some aspects of this life are so incredibly easy it contrasts with the hard parts, like not being able to speak freely in our own bedrooms. Our driver drops us off at Best Buy and says he'll wait for us in the parking lot.

Theo texts me as we're walking into the store. It's a picture of himself, and although he looks adorable, it's even cuter when I imagine him snapping a selfie like a modern day twenty-something. Selfies certainly weren't a thing when he was my age.

His text reads: *Do I look better?*
I write back: *You look much more alive*
New blood, he replies. *of the live variety*.

It makes my stomach ache to think of the dying soul who agreed to be Theo's lifeblood. Although, I guess it's a much better deal to agree to die quicker in exchange for Theo giving his family money. The people he uses for his immortality were already dying anyway, which is much more ethical than what the Rosewater clan has done to me and the other girls. We were healthy before we were shackled with the bracelet. Sure, they give us free stuff and let us live a nice life, but the cost is far greater than a few months of fun. Plus, we didn't agree to give our life to the clan. Theo's lifebloods agree. My heart swells with pride for Theo, and his moral way of handling his situation. I'm glad he never let himself die in the past, because then I wouldn't know him.

I miss you, I text him. I feel like I say that phrase too much, but I always mean it.

be back later tonight. midnight or so, he texts. *Oh, and I miss you far more than you miss me!*

I type: *come see me as soon as you're back! Don't even knock on my door, just come in!*

He sends me a smiling emoji and I grin. When I look up, Riley is gone. I'm standing alone in the middle of the store. An employee in a blue polo shirt nods at me. "You need some help?"

"No, thank you," I say. I put my phone away and search the store for my best friend. It feels awkward being around all of these normal people who are here doing normal things, like shopping and socializing and checking out new cell phones. A few months ago, that was me, just a regular person like everyone else. Now I feel like an outsider, someone from another planet where my alien life is not even remotely close to being like theirs.

Riley is in the computer section, leaning over a table of laptops and smiling flirtatiously with the guy who works here. He's short and chubby, and his nametag says his name is Juan. Not to be mean, but he just looks like the kind of guy who would know a lot about computers. He has thick black framed glasses and he's breaking a sweat just having to talk to Riley, probably because she's adorable and it intimidates him.

"Did you get lost?" Riley asks me when I join them.

I don't bother answering because getting lost in my own thoughts is not something I want to admit to right now.

"So, you need a laptop that can't be tracked," Juan says after giving me a polite smile. "But you have to use someone else's internet connection? That'll be a little impossible because you can control your computer but not the connection you're using."

Riley sighs. "I don't know if this will work," she tells me. She turns back to Juan. "What about if we just want to use Google translate. Is there a way to block anyone from seeing that we're on that website? Or, like what we're typing on it?"

Juan's brows furrow. "What exactly are you trying to accomplish here?" He holds up his hands, "But don't tell me if it's something illegal because then I can't help you or I'll get fired."

I explain to him that we just need to translate a foreign book, and Riley tacks on a lie that it's a surprise for our dad who monitors our internet activity. I don't know if Juan believes that or not, especially since Riley and I look nothing alike to be sisters, but he nods along as we tell the mostly fake story of needing to translate a book.

"If all you need is a translator, why not buy a translation software?" Juan steps back and runs his hand down his face. "That'll work perfectly, actually. I can sell you a gutted laptop that has no internet connection at all, and you install a software that translates all known languages, and you can just use that instead of the internet."

"They have software like that?" I ask, feeling a surge of hope again.

He nods and taps his fingers on the shiny tabletop in front of us. "We sure do. It's like forty bucks. And a basic laptop with no internet connection runs around three hundred."

"Money's not an issue," Riley says, beaming up at him. "How soon can we get this?"

AT HOME, Riley works to install the translation software, which takes forever because our cheap basic laptop isn't very fast, but Juan assured us it'd get the job done. I get on my own laptop and fill out the survey at the bottom of our sales receipt, giving Juan all five stars and praising him in the comment box. It makes me feel good to know that his manager might see it and give him a raise or something.

Now that Theo is on his way home and we have a solution to figure out the book, I'm feeling a thousand times better. Unfortunately, not sleeping last night has caught up with me, and I find myself drifting in and out while Riley and I work on the new computer.

"You should take a nap," Riley says after my fifth yawn in a row.

I shake my head. "We have stuff to do."

"I can do it," she says, reaching over and turning up the music again. "We have to type in each letter of each sentence on each page," she says, sounding oddly optimistic at the mammoth-sized workload ahead of us. "You take a nap and I'll work."

"Fine," I say, scrunching up my face like a child. I hate to admit it, but I'm the one who discovered what the bracelet does, and I kind of want to be the one to translate the book and save the day. But Riley is right—this is going to take a while. We've decided to translate the entire thing and keep the English version on a document on our new computer, even though chances are the first part of the book is just explaining immortality and doesn't get to the part we need until the very end. As much as I don't want to admit it, I can probably sleep for an hour or two and I won't miss anything.

Then I'll be refreshed for when Theo gets here and we can tell him what we're up to and maybe he can help us. I kick off my shoes and take down my hair and climb into my bed, leaving Riley on the floor near my window, working diligently.

As soon as my head hits the pillow, I'm asleep. When I wake up again, it's to the sound of Theo's voice.

TWELVE

The bed sinks a little as Theo's body forms a shadow next to me. It's not bright enough in here to see him, but I smell his cologne so I know it's him. Otherwise, I'd probably be screaming for help. "You awake?" he whispers.

I'm exhausted, and waking up now feels painful because I'd like to keep sleeping. But it's Theo, and I want to see him more than I want to be refreshed. I sit up on my elbow, blinking away the last bits of sleep. Through the window in my room, moonlight sprinkles in, the sun having disappeared hours ago.

"Mmhmm," I say, reaching out to him. I grab his shoulder and pull him toward me. He falls into my arms, then shifts to lay beside me. He's on top of the sheets and I'm underneath them, but I hold him close to me while we share my pillow.

"What time is it?" I ask.

"Just after midnight," he whispers. He smells a little different up close, like the leather interior of Kyle's car that he keeps religiously clean. "Why's Riley sleeping on the floor?"

I turn around and look toward the sitting area of my room. In the glow of the moonlight, I can see that Riley is passed out, her arms and legs tucked up in the fetal position. The open laptop is dark next to her. No telling how long she's been asleep.

"Long story," I say, exhaling as I snuggle against his chest. "I'll tell you in the morning."

When I open my eyes the next time, Theo is watching me, his head propped up on his elbow. My eyes widen. He looks like a new person. Still the same guy, of course, but new. Like he went to a spa or something. I hadn't realized he'd had dark circles under his eyes, or that his skin was paler than usual until now that all of those things are gone. Theo's dark hair is shinier, swooping over his head like a GQ model. His skin is tight and golden again, his golden eyes sparkling in the morning sunlight.

"Hey beautiful," he says, flashing me a wide smile. He dips down to kiss me and I jerk away, putting my hand over my mouth. His brows flatten. I've offended him.

"Sorry," I say under my hand. "Morning breath. You are *not* getting anywhere near these lips until I brush my teeth."

He chuckles. "How about I go get us breakfast?"

I nod, still keeping my lips protected with my hand. "I'll be kissable by the time you get back."

Once he leaves, I jump out of bed and brush my teeth with a fury, using my mouthwash twice to make sure I will taste good. Then I run the brush through my hair and dab on some lip gloss. Theo's already way out of my league and the last thing I want is to have him see me looking like a disgusting morning-breath zombie.

Riley is still asleep and I'm about to nudge her awake when Theo returns and renders me speechless. He seems taller, his muscles more pronounced. His jawline, fuzzy from stubble, is sharp. And those eyes. Theo looks like a fucking Roman God and now I can't concentrate.

"Why do you look so good?" I ask, the words falling out of my mouth before I can think of better ones that make me sound more educated.

He sets the breakfast tray down on the table. "Um, thanks?"

"I'm serious," I say, abandoning my sleeping best friend while I walk over to Theo. I grab his cheeks and press the skin backwards and forwards. "You look amazing. I mean, you're always crazy hot, but *damn*. Something's changed since I last saw you."

"It's um," he says, tapping the necklace under his shirt. "The new *donation*. I should have seen the signs coming days before I passed out," he says with a sigh. "I was too caught up in—other things—" he says, giving me a flirty wink, "—and I didn't pay attention to my own body. Normally, I can feel when I need a new...*blood transfusion*."

Ugh. It's so weird to talk about using live humans as immortality lifebloods, and it's even weirder to call it a blood transfusion for the sake of keeping up the lie. I wonder who is wearing Theo's bracelet now. I wonder how long they have, what they accepted as payment in return for giving their life to Theo, a man they don't even know.

"Well, let's not let that happen again," I say, playfully poking his stomach, and even that seems harder than usual. "You scared me."

He kisses my forehead, his lips lingering on my skin. "It won't happen again."

Riley stirs on the floor, then sits up and yawns. "You're back," she says, raising her hands above her head in a stretch. "We have something to show you. Wait—" She blinks. "Damn, you look good, loverboy."

If anyone else had said that to him, I'd be seething with jealousy, but Riley can get away with it. She's the kind of best friend who can speak her mind, appreciate a hot guy, and not try to steal him away from you. I don't know what I would do if I didn't have her by my side.

"He got some *rest*," I say, emphasizing the last word. "Now he feels a lot better."

We eat breakfast and spend time sneakily catching Theo up to date on the ancient Greek book and our new translator computer. It takes a while, since we have to whisper some things and write out the more complicated things on the dry erase board. Theo hasn't seen the book before, but he doesn't think it'll amount to much simply because, in his words, "Alexo is too careful to leave something like that laying around."

Still, we're going to translate it anyway because it's the only lead we have. It takes about an hour to eat breakfast and explain everything with Riley and Theo. There's something special in the way Theo is acting, even when we're talking about serious topics. He keeps looking over at me, that smirk I love on his lips. It's like he can't stop looking at me, and I start to wonder if there's something in my teeth. A trip to the bathroom tells me there's not, and that I look pretty much normal. So why is he being like this? He can't possibly have missed me as much as I missed him over the last two days. He was busy getting a lifeblood and trying to feel better and all I did was wait around and miss him like a pathetic dork.

When we're done catching him up on what's been going on, he tells us to hide the book so we don't get caught with it, but we have a better idea. Riley has her digital camera, which has no access to Wi-Fi because it's really old. We snap a picture of every page of the book and then load it onto our new laptop.

Keep the laptop hidden Theo writes on the board. *No one will be snooping in your rooms, so it should be fine here. Just don't let anyone see it.*

I take the board from his hands and erase his message so I can write: *don't worry we've got this.*

He leans over my shoulder as I write, and when I look up at him, he kisses me. Just like that. Riley makes this exaggerated gagging sound and shoves the last bite of toast into her mouth.

"Okay guys, I'm out of here. There's so much sexual tension in this room I think I'm gonna vomit."

Theo laughs and I want to bury myself in a deep hole and never resurface because she's totally right. Normally Theo and I can't keep our hands off each other, but it's extremely bad today. He's acting head over heels for me, and I'm loving every second of the attention, even if I don't know what caused it. As soon as Riley leaves, Theo walks over to my door and locks it. Then he takes out a small roll of electrical tape from his pocket. I watch him curiously as he puts several layers of tape over the small speaker on my wall tablet.

"Not foolproof, but if we whisper we should be fine," he says in a whisper to prove his point.

"Genius," I say at a normal volume. Now I'm getting all kinds of ideas, like buying some of that foam from soundproof music booths and taping it over the tablet. Of course, it'd look suspicious if Alexo or Malina ever saw it. Maybe we can make something removable to take off when we leave the room.

"You are so beautiful when you sleep," Theo says, his head tilting as he watches me from across the room.

"You're being extra flirtatious today," I tell him. I put my hands on hips and glare at him. "What's your angle?"

"My angle is that I'm totally crazy about you."

I break into a smile. "That's good to know."

"Yeah?" He saunters toward me, that grin of his turning sultry and his eyes softening. I can practically feel the dirty thoughts floating through his mind.

"Mmhmm," I say, still trying to keep my cool, but now he's so close and so handsome that it's hard to stop my knees from wobbling.

In a swift motion, Theo scoops me up, his hands under my legs and neck. I squeal as he carries me to the bed and then lets me fall on top of the plush mattress. My whole body warms as he slowly crawls onto the bed, lowering himself on top of me. His hands are on either side of my pillow, his lips just inches away.

"Come here," I whisper, and he does.

His kisses are ravenous, his body grinding against mine with an urgency I've never felt before. I grab his sides and feel the muscles ripple under my fingers as he bends down and trails kisses down my neck. The scruff on his jaw tickles, but his lips feel amazing.

"I still think you seem different," I whisper against his shoulder.

"You could say I'm energized," he whispers back. His hand slides under my back, pulling me off the mattress and closer to his body. My skin tingles from the heat of our skin, until everything feels electrified. He presses a kiss to my collarbone and then moves lower, kissing down to the top of my bra, and then to the front clasp in the middle.

I am fully on board for whatever comes next, but he stops. His lips are pressed to my cleavage, one hand under my back and the other bracing himself on top of me. I exhale slowly, trying to get my thoughts to stop being so fuzzy with desire. Theo slides up and kisses me on the mouth. "Just testing my self-control," he breathes, a grin playing on his lips. There's some glitter from my lip gloss on his lips and I reach up and kiss it off of him.

"What if I don't want you to have self-control?" I ask, trying to be sultry and flirtatious.

"You do," he whispers back just before he kisses my neck. "We haven't been together very long, love."

"So?" My voice is breathy. I can't concentrate with him so close to me, with our bodies pressed together and all of these annoying clothes in the way.

He rolls to the side, leaning on his elbow while his other hand gently slides down my ribcage, to my thigh and then back up. "I come from a time where men could wait longer than a few weeks," he says, his eyes turning serious. "What we have is real, Cara. There's no need to rush anything."

I swallow. Now reality is back, slapping me with the coldness of real life. "I guess you're right."

"You're a virgin, right?" he says, although I'm not sure if it's a question or a statement.

I nod and look away. There's really no point in lying to him. He'd see right through me. "All the more reason to take our time," he says with a gentle smile as he runs his fingers through my hair.

"Won't that drive you crazy though?" I ask, staring at his shirt because I can't meet his eyes. "You're a guy...and guys like... well..."

"There's more to us than sex, Cara." He frowns. "*You* drive me crazy, but in a very good way. Besides, there's still so many things I want to learn about you. I don't even know your favorite color, but I'm guessing it's pink because of that bike out in the garage."

"I guess it is pink," I say. "I've never really thought about it. What's yours?"

"Hmm... blue," he says after a moment's thought. "The kind of blue in a deep ocean."

"I like this game," I say as I snuggle against him. "I don't even know your last name."

"Theodore Price."

"Theodore? That's cute."

He rolls his eyes. "Makes me sound old. I've been Theo most of my life. I don't have a middle name because my parents didn't seem to care about those things."

"Did you have any siblings?" I ask.

"An older sister. She died of pneumonia when she was six."

"I'm sorry," I say.

He shrugs. "I don't really remember it. My old life was so long ago. And it was a harsh, unforgiving life at that." His lips brush against my forehead. "I'm happier now, with this life." He swallows. "Tell me about your family."

"I don't know who my dad is," I say simply because this is the sort of sad thing that everyone considers to be a tragedy but it doesn't really bother me. "Mom was a drug addict. She left me at a McDonald's one day, and the state took me and put me in a foster home. My uncle Will adopted me when I was twelve and then I lived with him until recently. My life has kind of been pointless so far. I hope I can change that soon, but with the way things are going..." I look at my bracelet. "I might die having never accomplished anything."

"You won't be tethered to that forever," he says quietly.

I run my fingers down his shirt and then up his arm, to his jaw and down his neck until my fingers touch the silver chain of his necklace. "What else would you like to know?" he asks.

Maybe it's the closeness I feel with him in this moment, or it's knowing my room is sound-proofed with the tape, but I say exactly what I'm thinking. "Who's your new lifeblood?"

"Well, it's a guy with cancer," he says quietly. "I don't really want to talk about that though."

It feels like a massive rejection and I can't keep the pain off my face. "Cara," Theo says, nuzzling against my cheek. "It's—" He sighs. "Talking about that right now just pisses me off because of things that don't have anything to do with you."

"So why can't you tell me?" I ask.

His lips press into a flat line. "Kyle talked my ears off while we were gone. He wouldn't shut up about the benefits of getting a girl lifeblood, like how they do with you and the others." His expression hardens. "I told them when I joined the clan that I'd use my own lifebloods and that I wouldn't conform to their ways. They agreed, and now I'm being pressured to change. Normally Kyle is a cool guy, but he just wouldn't stop trying to talk me into it. I get the feeling Alexo was pressuring him to convert me."

"Why would they care?" I ask.

He presses his lips to my forehead before talking. "They see it as a sign of not being fully committed to the clan. I hoped things were going to work out, but now it seems like I need to conform to their ways to be seen as one of them."

"Are you going to?"

He gives me a look like I should know better than to ask such a thing. "Of course not. But that's the problem. If they start questioning my loyalties to the clan, we're going to have a problem."

"You are loyal to the clan though," I say, peering at him while he stares at me, a serious look on his face. "Right?"

He smirks for a flash of a second and then he's back to looking serious. He glances back at my taped over tablet and then says quietly, "Not exactly."

THIRTEEN

Silences stretches out like a rubber band between us, and although a million questions are going through my mind, I don't want to speak and snap the rubber band. Theo watches me curiously, and it's like he's both dying to know what I'll say and also somehow relieved that he just confessed this to me.

I lean forward. "You're not loyal to the clan?" I whisper. A thousand feelings flit through me at once, but the biggest one is fear. Of him.

I can't even imagine what this clan will do to a member who isn't loyal. They kill us humans if we figure out what's going on, so the punishment for an immortal is probably worse. Theo doesn't say anything, but now I can't shut up.

"This isn't good!" I whisper. "What if they find out?"

I put a hand on his chest, feeling the steady thumping of his heartbeat pushing against my fingers. "But we're in the clan together," I say, my voice still a whisper. "Why wouldn't you be loyal to it?"

To me, I think.

Theo reaches for my hand and pulls it off his chest, then brings my knuckles up to his lips. They are soft as they graze the back of my hand.

"You deserve answers," he says.

And then that's all. He doesn't say anything else, like, oh I don't know, the *answers* he's referring to. He's insane if he thinks I'll be okay with this.

I sit up and pull out my ponytail then fix my hair again. I need to keep my hands busy or I'll start strangling him, or screaming, or I don't know what. "Well, are you going to tell these answers to me?"

"Of course." He smirks, then dips his head into a slow nod. "But not here."

Sliding off my bed, Theo stands and stretches his arms above his head. "Let's go for a hike today."

THE IMMORTAL TRUTH

"A...hike?"

He nods, then brings his elbow across his chest to stretch it out. "I need some sunlight and wide open spaces. And you."

He leans over the bed, to where I'm now sitting, and stretches over to kiss me on the lips. "Get dressed and I'll come get you in half an hour."

"Will I get answers on this hike?" I ask, giving him the stink eye, both because I don't like waiting for important information and a hike sounds kind of, well, athletic.

He taps my nose with his finger. "Of course."

CHEF PACKS us a lunch in this really cute woven basket with wooden flap top. It's exactly the kind of picnic basket you see in children's books, and I never even knew they were real. This one is fancy though, the red plaid lining is actually covering a gel pack so it keeps the food cool. Theo loads it up in the trunk of the Camaro and then we ride out into the wide open spaces on the outskirts of Austin.

Since it's ungodly hot outside, I chose to wear a pair of white shorts and a light pink tank top. I opened a new pair of Nike running shoes from the box and put them on for the first time since I ordered them online. When I think of hiking, I think of cargo pants and walking sticks, ugly hats and a compass. I didn't want to look that dorky, so hope my outfit is decent for hiking. Of course, what I really hope is that Theo isn't actually making us go hiking.

Theo's hand rests on my bare thigh as he drives. I look over at him and take in his outfit—tan cargo shorts and a blue T-shirt. He looks like a regular college guy, maybe one who plays sports. It's so weird to think that the rest of the world sees a normal, super attractive guy when they look at Theo. And I see someone who's a hundred years old, with even more secrets than that.

"How much further?" I ask after fifteen minutes of riding in a comfortable silence. As long as Theo's hand squeezes my thigh every few minutes and he looks over and smiles at me, the silence is never awkward.

"Not much," he says. He lifts one finger off the steering wheel and points toward the horizon. "There's a state park up there with great hiking trails."

We pull into the park and it's mostly empty. Two decked out SUVs are parked at the end of the lot, and they're the kind of car that screams: *My owner does a lot of hiking.*

We're in a sports car, and I feel like that accurately portrays my hiking ability.

Theo slips a backpack over his shoulder and then grabs the picnic basket.

"Need some help?" I ask, feeling guilty that I didn't bring anything.

"Just your company," he says, tossing me a smile.

The park covers five hundred acres, according to a sign on the side of the first trail. There's trees dotted around with shade to break up the hot summer heat, and the trails are mostly gravel and dirt. The terrain slopes gently up and down, but it won't be like mountain climbing or anything, so that's good.

We take off on the Parrot Trail, which is marked by handmade wooden signs. "I don't think Alexo is in charge of the clan," Theo says as soon as we start on the trail.

I look over at him. "Why do you think that?" I ask. "He seems pretty in charge to me."

"I think someone else is pulling his strings," Theo says, glancing at me before stepping up on a huge rock that blocks our path. I step up too, and follow along beside him, trying not to sound out of breath because this hike is already kicking my ass.

"So, who is really in charge?" I ask.

Theo shrugs. "I don't think we've met him. It's not someone at the house."

"Does Rosewater have other houses?"

"Oh yeah," Theo says with a chuckle. "Most of them are like this one, a rental. And that alone tells me something is weird here. The other two clans are ancient and rich, and we have our own properties. We wouldn't rent something, we'd own it. That way we know every inch of the place and no landlord can suddenly decide to take it back. That way it's *ours*."

"Theo?" I ask.

"Yeah?" he says, slowing his pace as we reach a rocky part of the trail.

"You keep saying 'we', as if you're not a part of this clan."

"I'm not, Cara." He exhales and faces forward. "I'm from Embrook."

"Well, I know, but...you switched over to Rosewater."

"Under false pretenses."

I stop walking. Luckily my abrupt halt happens to be under a large shade tree, so I don't have to squint at Theo. "Babe, you're scaring me. I don't understand any of this shit, but I do know that I am a member of Rosewater and you should be too if we want to be together."

Theo puts a hand on my cheek, and then thankfully lowers it a few seconds later. It's so hot outside I'm not all about physical contact right now.

"I'm in Rosewater for a mission, love. As soon as it's over, I plan to take you back to Embrook with me."

I lift an eyebrow. "But you said Rosewater was the nicest clan to the humans."

He tilts his head and bites on his bottom lip. "They definitely are. But you'd be under my protection, so you'll be fine."

I look down at my toes. The formerly white soles of my shoes are now singed with dirt. "You keep talking about a mission, but in my mind the only mission that matters is you helping me and Riley get rid of these bracelets."

"Love, that is first and foremost my most important mission." He smiles softly. "But before I met you, I temporarily left Embrook and joined Rosewater so that I could fulfill another mission. I need to find out who is really in charge of this clan and get to the bottom of their motives." He sets the picnic basket down and leans his back against the tree. "When that's over, we will either have disbanded Rosewater permanently, or we'll be at war with them." He shrugs. "Regardless, I will go back to Embrook. It's where I was sired, and it's where I'll die. The Embrook clan is my home."

Something cracks apart inside of me. This other clan I don't know anything about might be Theo's home, but Theo is *my* home. "So I guess meeting me was epically bad timing in your life," I say with a snort of laughter that chills me to the core. I don't want to be a part of another clan. I didn't want to be a part of a clan at all.

"You could say that," Theo says, his lips stretching into a smile. "The only reason I'm alive today is because I took on the mission to discover the secrets behind the Rosewater clan. I never meant to fall in love, and I certainly didn't think it'd be with a human."

I frown and look away, but Theo steps in front of me, his hands resting on my hips. "Cara, you are the best part of my life. I have learned that falling in love when you don't expect it is the greatest thing that could ever happen to anyone."

"Really? Because it seems like I'm fucking up your weird secret mission."

"Impossible," he says, pulling me closer to him. "This mission was fucked up from the start."

I roll my eyes and I can't help but smile. It's so hard being serious around Theo, especially when he stands so close to me, his hands roaming up and down my back. All I want to do is lean in close to his chest, close my eyes and let the whole world fall away.

Instead, I force myself to start walking down the trail again. "So, in addition to fixing me and Riley, you're trying to find the real boss of the Rosewater clan."

"That's correct," Theo says, falling into step beside me.

"So why do you think it'd lead to war?"

"Rosewater is a baby clan," he explains. "Immortality is centuries old, and the original clans are tightly woven allies. Rosewater appeared out of nowhere almost two hundred years ago, and that's the thing—no one knows how they came to be. None of the elder immortals in the other clans have ever heard of Alexo, or anyone else in the clan for that matter. He appears to be a few centuries old, but we don't know him."

He sighs and runs a hand through his hair. "Honestly, I don't know all the details. The elders in my clan have been studying Alexo for decades, always trying to infiltrate his clan and figure out what the hell they're up to. If anyone's at risk of exposing immortality to the world, it would be the Rosewater clan. We needed someone to find out who's really in charge. I volunteered, and maybe it's because I'm the youngest member, they agreed. We had a very public—" He looks at me, "And *fake*, of course—excommunication of my membership with Embrook. We spread the rumors that I'm hard working and I just didn't believe in their ways of doing things, and that I wanted a clan I could believe in. I was supposed to charm my way into Rosewater."

Theo steps on top of a fallen tree trunk and then drops to the other side. "Ironically, Alexo sought me out. I joined a few months ago, and got to work. Then I met you." He bumps into me with his shoulder while we walk. "I wish I could say you distracted me from my mission, but really, I was getting nowhere with it. I believe my elders and if they think someone else is secretly running the clan, then they're right."

He sighs. I step on a flat piece of rock and it wobbles, throwing me off my balance and sending me flailing. Theo steadies me with his quick reflexes and then smacks a quick kiss on the top of my head. "I have no idea how to find the real head of the Rosewater clan. That's why I'm focusing on fixing you and Riley first." He flashes me a smile, but I can tell he's upset about his first mission.

"Okay...so if someone else really is in charge..." I say, pondering the new information he's just revealed. "Why is that a bad thing? Rosewater seems nice. I mean, all of you immortals have to take a human life to prolong yours, and you've said the other clans aren't so nice to their lifebloods like Rosewater is. We live in luxury. I mean—they lied to us which is literally ruining my life, but at least they aren't mean. So why are they considered bad by the other clans if they're the nice ones?"

"That's exactly why," Theo says. "They're kind and humane, and so far, all of the clan's business transactions have been fairly by the book. Rosewater doesn't cheat, or steal." He meets my eyes. "And that's why they can't be trusted. No immortals act like that. They are ruthless. Not kind."

I follow Theo as he branches off the trail and into a grassy meadow between tall pine trees. "So...because they're good people, they're bad people?"

"No one uses their immortality like that, Cara." Theo sets the picnic basket on the grass and turns to me. "My mission is to find out who's in control and what we should do to stop it. The elder clans are not a fan of this new clan who appeared out of nowhere and started conducting international business that makes them billionaires. That's just not how things work. No one uses their immortality that way. They're hiding something."

"Okay," I say resolutely. "I am loyal to you, not the clan, so I'll help you any way I can."

"That's sweet of you, love, but this is dangerous. I'd prefer knowing you're safe at the mansion until I finish my mission and take you home with me."

I roll my eyes. On top of the picnic basket is a folded blanket, so I take it out and spread it down for us. "Let's have lunch first, and then we can talk more about secret immortal missions and the risks they pose by letting me help you."

Theo chuckles. "We can talk all you want, but I'm keeping you safe and there's no way around that, love."

FOURTEEN

Theo and I spend the rest of the day together. After our picnic lunch, we head back to the car and drive an hour away, only stopping when we find an outdoor outlet mall. The whole place is set up to be enjoyed outside. It's built on a manmade Riverwalk, and there's water taxis (which are just boats) that take you down from store to store. Theo and I spend the day as tourists, hands interlocked while we browse the shops, eat snow cones, and pretend to be normal people doing normal things. I need these bits of normalcy to cling to each day, because every new bit of information I learn from Theo makes me long for my old life, where things were black and white and magic stones didn't exist.

It's six in the evening by the time I realize I haven't heard from Riley all day. I send her a text, but she doesn't reply. Theo tells me I worry too much because Riley is pretty strong and can handle herself, but I ask if we can go home anyway.

"Of course," Theo says, squeezing my hand. We've reached the end of the strip of stores at this enchanting outdoor mall, and it only makes sense that we head home now.

Ever since we left the park, we haven't talked about the clans or the mission or the fact that this bracelet is still on my wrist, sucking the life from me. As much as I care for Theo, it feels like my relationship with him consists of talking about terrible things I never knew, and then pretending things are fine.

Something has to change soon, because I can't keep living like this.

As soon as we drive up to the gates at the beginning of the property, it's obvious something is going on. It's dusk, and the sun is orange-red in the horizon, but the house is lit up. Every spotlight in the yard is turned on, loud music thumps through the night, and the driveway is filled with limos and town cars.

"What the hell is this?" I ask as Theo navigates around the limousines toward the garage.

"Just another party, I'd say."

"Does this happen a lot?" I gaze out the window while a chauffeur opens the door for a leggy woman in a golden mini-dress.

"More often than I prefer," Theo says with a sarcastic snort. "Alexo loves parties."

The music is louder this close to the house. I send Riley another text, this time asking where she is. If it were me left alone today, I'd probably be hiding out in my room while this party rages on, but knowing Riley, she's probably in the thick of it, having the time of her life.

"Can we just sneak up to my room?" I ask while we're still safely hidden in the garage from the crowd outside. Theo frowns and clicks the lock button on the Camaro's key fob.

"I'm afraid not, love. We should at least make an appearance first."

I heave a sigh, even though I knew he'd probably say that. "I'm totally not dressed for a party," I say, gazing down at my shorts and sneakers.

"No one cares," Theo says, coming over to my side of the car. He slides his hand in my back pocket, but it's too small so it feels like only two of his fingers actually go inside it. "You want to go upstairs and change really quick?"

I shake my head. "What's the point? I'm not here to impress anyone but you, and you're already impressed." I poke him in the chest. His phone rings, and he exhales. Peering at the phone from his pocket, he frowns. "Go on to the party and I'll catch up with you."

I want to whine and ask if I can stay, but I also want to keep my boyfriend and not lose him because I'm acting like a child. I know that look on his face—someone from his old clan is calling him. He always seems frustrated when they call him, so I'm not going to add to it. I smile sweetly. "See you out there!"

Most of the party is on the back porch and swimming pool area, but people spill into the gardens as well. There's a stage set up to the left of the pool, where a real life DJ spins records or does whatever it is DJ's do. He's kind of cute, all tattooed and grunge-rock.

Beautiful women in gorgeous dresses are everywhere, so much so that it's kind of easy to ignore them. I don't recognize anyone immediately, except for Alexo who is talking to three very uptight looking men in suits across the yard. I make my way toward the pool, and my intuition is right.

Riley is here, sitting on the edge wearing her purple striped bikini with her feet dangling in the water. She's smiling at someone—Kyle—who emerges from the deep end of the pool, a tiny silver trinket in his fingers. "Found it!" he calls out, swimming over to her.

"You're my hero!" Riley says in this high-pitched playful voice. Kyle hands her the trinket, which I see now is an earring, and she loops it back into her ear.

I walk up to her. "You're not supposed to wear jewelry in a pool, you know."

She startles when she hears my voice, and then she turns to me, eyes sparkling and smile wide. "Cara!" she sings, throwing her wet hands around my legs in a poolside hug. "You're here!"

"I'm here." It doesn't take a genius to realize that Riley is just a little bit drunk. "So, what's going on?" I ask, bending down and sitting on the edge of the pool. I get to work taking off my shoes so I can let my feet hang in the water next to Riley.

"We're having a party," she says.

"I can see that," I say sarcastically. "But why?"

She shrugs. "Who knows?"

"Random party," Kyle says while he treads water in front of us. "I didn't know about it, either, so don't feel bad."

"Who are all these people?" I ask him as I shove my socks into my shoes.

He gazes around and then wipes some water off his face. "Hell if I know. That chick over there in the white dress is a famous country singer."

Riley and I look in her direction, and find the girl in question standing with three handsome guys who are all vying for her attention. She looks bored and keeps gazing off into the distance as if she'll find something more interesting out there.

The pool water is cool and refreshing as I let my tired feet sink into it. We did a lot of walking today, so sitting down feels wonderful. I notice all the other girls from the mansion are also here in the pool. Well, all of them except Jayla, which is kind of weird. Olivia and Nia sit next to each other on the pool steps, sipping fruity frozen drinks. They seem bored without their leader Jayla here. Bethany is flirting with a guy who looks like that professional basketball player from Houston who just got drafted out of college. I don't know much about sports, but I remember him because he was all over the news and he has this really cute dimple in his left cheek.

Kyle and Riley get into an argument over who is the better swimmer, and I gaze back toward the house, to where I can barely see the side of the garage. Theo is there, talking on the phone and pacing back and forth. His expression is stern, but not mad. Russell branches off from a group of people and walks over to Theo. He gets off the phone and shakes Russell's hand and they talk for a bit. Russell is the tall army guy of the group, the one Jayla really likes. Although now that she's gone, her squid-like attachment to him has been replaced by two other women who are now inserting themselves into Theo and Russell's conversation.

Except—ugh—both of the women have their eyes on Theo. I watch like a hawk as one floozy puts her hand on his arm and laughs as if he's the most hilarious guy ever. My blood starts to boil, but I turn away and look back at the pool, telling myself to calm down. Floozies will be floozies after all. It's not Theo's fault women see him and hope to flirt their way into his pants.

Still, I can't help but feel a little weirded out by the whole thing. I keep my attention on the pool in front of me, occasionally nodding along with Riley as she talks about how great her swimming skills are. But deep down I'm judging my knees, how they're knobby and boring. My legs aren't long and sleek like some of the women here. My hair is blonde and stringy, not golden, silky, and long like a model's hair. Compared to the women here, I am just plain. I'm basically a kid compared to them. What does Theo even see in me? Before I was here, did he flirt with the women at these parties? Did he take them back to his room at the end of the night like I know the other guys will do?

"I need a drink," I say, pushing myself up from the edge of the pool. Riley barely notices me leave because she's too busy in a splash war with Kyle.

Feeling nervous and inadequate, I make my way up to the back patio where the kitchen staff is ready to serve drinks, only when I get here, I don't want alcohol. I just need some fresh air.

I walk over to the far side of the porch, out of the way from the rest of the guests. The sun is nearly gone now, leaving only traces of color in its wake. I lean against the railing and close my eyes and try not to question everything about everything. I've given my mortality to the clan, and my heart to a guy who is entirely too handsome for me. Maybe it'll be fine if Theo never finds a way to save me from the bracelet. Then I could die tragically and he could go on with his unending life.

I sigh, knowing I'm being dramatic. But emotions are painful for me now, now that life is all messed up and crazy. As much as I care for Theo—as much as I'm pretty sure I love him—I know I'm just a nobody. I'm not good enough for Theo, not by a long shot.

The breeze carries the scent of a familiar cologne my way. I blink, breathing in the smell that makes my knees weak. Footsteps approach, a warm hand softly touches my lower back. Theo's breath tickles my ear and my whole body lights up to the touch of his chest pressing against my back.

"There she is," Theo whispers as his hands slide around my waist, the sensation sending tingles right down to my toes. "The most beautiful girl at the party."

FIFTEEN

I slide my hands on top of his. "Aren't we just a charmer?" I say.
"I speak the truth."
I look back at him, my lips pressed into a disbelieving line. "You are being a charmer, Theo. Look around. There's famous women and supermodels here."
"And I still stand by what I said."
I roll my eyes, but heat fills my cheeks anyhow. Theo twists me around to face him. My butt leans against the concrete railing of the porch and I love the way his strong arms feel as they're wrapped around me. I hold onto his shoulders and gaze into his eyes. They're golden like the sunset from a few minutes ago.
"I don't know why you like me so much," I say, sliding my fingers through his hair. "But I'm glad you do."
His smile is warm, and one little dimple appears in his left cheek. "What's bothering you, love?"
I shrug. "Nothing."
He narrows his eyes at me.
I sigh. "It's really nothing...but if you *have* to know—"
"I have to know," he interjects.
I roll my eyes. "I saw those beautiful women talking to you and Russell and it just—ugh, I don't know. I know you're not going to cheat on me right here or anything, and it's not even about that—I just..."
Lines appear in his forehead and his hands grip me tighter. "You just what, Cara?"
I glance down at the front of his shirt. "I just feel inadequate."
"Let's get out of here," Theo says, his eyes sparkling with a renewed energy.

"Let's go to my room. I'll make you feel adequate, I promise." He winks and all of my insides melt.

I know I'm blushing, but damn. I don't even know what to think about an offer like that. I swallow. "Did you date those kinds of girls before you met me?"

"Nah," he says, shaking his head. "Those girls aren't my type."

Something like a jealous monster takes over and I immediately want to tell him he's lying, that every guy dates girls like that if given the opportunity. But Theo's standing here, wrapped up in me, his gaze on mine like I'm the only person in the world who matters, and for some reason, I believe him. He wouldn't lie to me about something like that. That's just not like him.

"Okay," I say, nodding. "Sorry I asked."

"You're welcome to ask anything you want, love. But *I'm* going to ask once again that you come back to my room with me."

He pulls my hips against his and kisses me so hard I can't breathe for a second. "Please?" he whispers against my lips.

"How could a girl say no to that?" I say breathily. My heart is rushing a mile a minute now, all worries and jealousies are fading fast now that Theo's giving me that hungry look of desire.

He kisses me quickly. "Let's go."

I hold his hand as we weave back through the party guests, toward the house. I wave at Riley when we slip past the pool but I'm not even sure she saw me because she's having fun in the water. I'm immensely relieved that Riley has found a way to enjoy her time here without me. I feel terrible ditching her all the time for Theo, even though she claims she doesn't mind. Maybe she really doesn't. She's always been the more independent one of this friendship.

Inside, the music from the party is dulled. Not many people hang out in here, so Theo and I are alone as we make our way to the grand staircase. Now that the party noise is dulled, and I can smell Theo's cologne, hear our footsteps as we go up the stairs, I start wondering what exactly he has in mind when we get to his room. A thrill of excitement rushes through me as I realize I'm ready for anything. As long as I'm with Theo.

We turn the corner and make our way into the long hallway of rooms where the guys live. There's an excitement, a charged energy that flickers between the two of us. I can't wait to get into his room and wrap myself up in his arms.

I'm grinning at Theo as we walk, so I don't see when a figure steps out from nowhere. Theo's gaze hardens. I look forward and find Alexo, dressed in a sleek black suit. His black leather shoes are so shiny you could see your reflection in them. His dark hair is slicked back, resting on his shoulders.

"Theo, there you are." Alexo's voice is cold and calculating. Theo freezes. "I'm afraid I need you to come with me," Alexo says, but his expression anything but regretful.

"Sure," Theo says, dropping my hand. If he's upset, he's hiding it well.

Alexo's piercing gaze turns to me. "Don't you worry, Cara." His eyes flash as he smiles. "I will bring him back in one piece."

SIXTEEN

I can't believe I once thought that dating was hard in high school. I remember lamenting to Riley about how much guys sucked back then. I'd finally like some guy who liked me back, and then I'd spend hours and hours waiting for him to text me hello or even acknowledge that I existed. High school guys were always promising they'd call you and then forgetting. I spent so many nights lying awake in bed, cell phone clutched to my hand, as I waited for something from a guy.

Now that I'm dating an immortal and living in a mansion, those old high school dating days seem so easy. I would love it if Theo had just forgotten to call me. As it is, an entire night and morning goes by and I haven't heard a word from him just because he's lazy like one of those high school guys. Instead, I didn't hear from him all night and I know it's not because he's forgetful, it's because he's with Alexo.

The suspense is killing me. Alexo's expressions are so hard to read. He always looks like he's up to something, and at the same time he looks like he knows what you're up to as well. I tell Riley exactly what I know about the situation—that Alexo showed up and requested Theo's presence last night. I can tell her that part in our bedrooms because there's nothing secret about it. I can also tell her how much it bothers me and how much I miss Theo and how I hate that he hasn't called or texted me yet.

But as long as we're in this house, I can't tell her the truly important stuff, like Theo's epic clan secret and his real reason for joining this one. It's too much to write down, and since it's such a huge betrayal of the Rosewater clan, I don't even want to write it in this house. No, this is the kind of thing we have to talk about far, far away from the mansion.

I ask Riley to stay in my room tonight because I'm driving myself crazy with worry. Once again, she showcases how great of a best friend she is by ordering ice cream and freshly baked brownies from the kitchen. We eat and watch movies and Riley tries to comfort me, but it's not working.

"They're probably off doing some business stuff or whatever," Riley says as she digs her spoon into a pint of rocky road ice cream. "The guys have to work a lot to be as rich as they are."

"Something tells me this isn't work related," I mutter as I stab at my ice cream until it's mushy and more like a milkshake.

"Do we need to talk about this?" Riley whispers, her brows pulling together.

I nod.

"Do you know something?" she says, her voice so impossibly quiet that I have to read her lips to fully comprehend. I nod again.

"Let's go get breakfast in the morning," I say. "There's this cute diner in town that serves chocolate chip pancakes."

"Cool," Riley says casually just in case anyone is listening in. "There's nothing I love more than ending a night with sugar and then starting the next morning with sugar."

RILEY IS ENTIRELY TOO on board with my idea of taking the Ninja to the café the next morning. I mean, I was mostly kidding myself when I said it. We should have our personal driver take us, because that would be the safest, most reasonable option.

But the hot pink motorcycle in the garage is calling my name.

"Do you know how to get there?" Riley asks.

"Yeah, it's literally just down that road about twenty minutes." It's the same café Theo took me to, and it's pretty much the only place I know how to get to. I check the time on my phone, trying not to count the hours up in my head. Let's just say it's been a long time since Theo left with Alexo. Riley grabs both helmets off the shelf and hands one to me. "I trust you, bestie. Let's take this bad boy for a spin."

"She's a girl," I say, patting the motorcycle on the gas tank.

"My bad." Riley pulls the helmet over her head. "Let's take this bad girl for a spin."

"Okay, that just sounds dirty," I say with a laugh.

I push the bike out into the driveway and then crank the engine. It roars to life, sounding like it's just as excited as I am to go for a ride today. Nervous energy stabs at my insides, but it's quickly overpowered with adrenaline. Riley climbs on the bike behind me and we take off, slow and steady at first.

Once we're on the main road, we fly around the curves and the bike practically drives itself. There's no cars on the road, another luxury of living in the middle of nowhere, so the ride is painless and exhilarating. I get a little nervous when we pull into the gravel parking lot at the café because Theo had warned me that gravel and motorcycles don't go well together. But I drive slowly, creeping along until I'm in a parking spot up front.

"That was so much fun," Riley says, pulling off her helmet. "I want a bike now."

"You should get one," I say, tucking my helmet under my arm. "Then we could be badass biker chicks together."

The café door jingles as we walk inside. Three older men in a booth are watching us. "Damn girl," one of them says. "You're pretty good lookin' for a biker babe."

"Y'all two lesbians?" the other one says, lifting an eyebrow curiously.

"That is none of your business," Riley snaps at him as we walk by.

I suppress a shudder. Those creepy old men have nothing better to do than check out two freaking teenage girls. Ugh.

Our waitress is the same one from when I was here with Theo, but she doesn't seem like she recognizes me. She is considerate though, and seats us at a booth on the opposite side of the restaurant from those creeper men.

"Okay, it's time to spill," Riley says, flattening her hands on the red table in front of us. "What's going on to make you so freaked out?"

"For starters, Theo is betraying the clan," I say quietly. We're far away from Alexo's prying ears, but I still don't like talking very loudly about these matters.

Riley's eyes go wide. "What the hell does that mean?"

We order lunch and I explain everything I know to her, about how Theo came from Embrook and he's here specifically to spy on Alexo and find out who's really in charge.

"That makes sense," Riley says, nodding while she picks at her BLT. "If you're in charge of an immortal clan, you'd be smart to make sure no one knows who you are."

"It's weird though, because apparently, the other clans are all very much in the open about who they are. The leaders know and respect each other."

"Theo said Rosewater was a baby clan?" she asks as she dips a fry into ketchup.

"Just a couple centuries old, which is apparently a baby clan," I say with a snort. "They're screwing up the order of things. Plus, there's only a finite number of bracelets and so you can't just go creating new immortals all willy-nilly."

"So someone started a new clan and had enough bracelets for..." Riley counts on her fingers. "Like six people to become immortal." She leans forward. "So where did they get the bracelets?"

I shrug. "That's the issue. Where did this clan come from and what's their end game? Theo has to find out who controls Alexo and he's doing it all secretly while pretending he had a fall out with his old clan and he joined Rosewater for real."

"So that's why you're worried about Theo," Riley says, a somber expression on her face. "If Alexo found out that Theo's lying to him, he'll be pissed."

"He'll be more than pissed," I say. The knot in my stomach tightens. "I don't even want to think about what would happen."

Riley gently kicks my foot under the table. "Hey, it'll be okay. Theo's smart and he knows what he's doing." She shakes her head. "Hopefully he also knows how to fix us," she says sarcastically as she stares at the immortality bracelet on her wrist. "Now he has two missions and, not to sound like a bitch, but only one of those missions saves our lives, so...I hope he gets on that soon."

"Oh my God." I sit a little straighter in the booth. "Oh my God."

Riley holds a fry in the air, lifting one eyebrow at me. "What is it?"

"I have an idea." I chew on my bottom lip as I think. "Theo has two missions. One of them is his real mission and the other one he took on to save us—"

"You're just saying things I already know," Riley says, rolling her eyes.

"Shut up, I'm getting to something here." I take a deep breath as the ideas roll around in my head, making me excited and scared and giddy all at the same time. "Why don't we take away one of Theo's missions? That way he can focus on the important one."

"The *important* one is saving us, right?"

I nod. "Theo has to find out who's in charge of Alexo and the clan, but he can't do it if he's pretending that he's loyal to the clan." I lace my fingers together and stare at Riley. "So we'll do it for him."

Riley's eyebrow stays lifted. "We'll spy on Alexo?"

"Yes." When she puts it that way, it's kind of a terrifying thought.

"But we're already translating a book to try and save ourselves."

"Trust me, I haven't forgotten," I say, exhaling. "We're getting nowhere with the book translation. We should help Theo find out more about Alexo."

Riley sighs and gives me this sad look. "Cara, I don't know. We're already risking a lot by translating the book, and now we're supposed to risk even more by spying on Alexo?"

"Don't call it spying," I say. "Maybe it's as easy as you flirting with Kyle, and maybe ask him if there's other members of the group, maybe get him to spill something."

Riley shakes her head. "Kyle's a vault. He never talks about the clan, like ever. I figured it's because he doesn't want any details to slip that will let me know about the immortality thing, since he thinks we don't know."

I start to object but Riley stops me. "Cara. Our number one mission is to get these fucking bracelets off of us, and survive while doing it." I look at my bracelet while she talks, and I know she's right. She puts a hand on mine. "Theo can do his own thing with Alexo, but right now we should focus on the bracelets and translating the book. Honestly, now that I know Theo has another mission to worry about, I think it's even more important that we find a way to take off these bracelets ourselves."

I look up and find Riley's eyes pleading with mine. "The prince doesn't always swoop in and save the princess, you know. I mean, I trust Theo and I like him, but if he's preoccupied with his other mission then we can't trust he'll also fix this one. Sometimes the princess has to save herself."

My throat feels like it's full of cotton balls. I nod. "And sometimes the princess has to save everyone. You keep working on the book. I'll spy on Alexo."

SEVENTEEN

At some point, you'd think I'd get used to going hours and hours without hearing from Theo. You'd think I'd learn to go on with my life and stop clutching my cell phone, taking it with me everywhere—even the bathroom—on the off chance that I might hear from him.

You would think that. But you'd be wrong.

This isn't some jealousy issue, or a case of me being a clingy girlfriend. The fact is, Alexo "borrowed" Theo two days ago, and he's still not back. I know I can't get texts or calls from Theo while he's with Alexo, so every minute that passes with radio silence from him is a moment I worry about his well-being. What if Alexo found out Theo's a double agent?

What if Theo's being tortured at this very moment?

What if I'm just making this all up in my head and Theo's totally fine? A girl can dream.

Now that it's Riley's personal mission to translate the book, I didn't see her for the rest of the day yesterday. She's being stubborn, locking herself in her room to translate ancient Greek, and trying to make me feel bad for wanting to work on something else. I get where she's coming from, but I also feel that what I'm doing is right as well.

Well, what I plan on doing. I stayed up all night trying to figure out how to spy on Alexo, which is not only hard on a normal day, it's impossible since he's not at the mansion right now.

In the morning, I slip my phone into my back pocket just in case Theo calls, and I head down to the kitchen for some cereal. The smell of coffee lets me know I'm not the only one awake at seven in the morning, but I don't expect to see so many people here.

Kyle, Russell, and Henry are all sitting at the bar stools at the kitchen counter, drinking coffee and chatting with the chef who is cooking bacon and eggs. They all turn to me, weird looks on their faces like maybe they were expecting me.

But when they see it's just me, they turn back around.

"Good morning," I say, trying to act like that wasn't weird.

"Morning," Kyle says, flashing me a bright smile. "The coffee is great today. Chef added cinnamon to it."

"Cinnamon, really?" I crinkle my nose.

Henry nods. "You should give it a try. It tastes better than you might think."

"Okay, I guess I will," I say, taking the coffee mug the chef hands me. It smells like coffee and Big Red gum. I take a tentative sip and the nod. "Not bad at all."

Kyle holds up his coffee mug. "Told you!"

"What can I get you?" the chef asks me while he moves the scrambled eggs around a large pan with a wooden spatula.

"Nothing. I just want cereal," I say. A full homecooked breakfast always makes me sleepy and sluggish, and today I need to be alert for my brainstorming session on how to spy on Alexo. I glance back around the room.

"I take it Alexo isn't back?" I ask.

Henry shakes his head. "I haven't heard from him."

"Missing Theo, huh?" Kyle says, frowning. "Damn, I wish I had a girl who missed me."

"We all miss you when you're not here," I tell him while I pour a bowl of Lucky Charms.

He snorts. "Yeah, but not in the same way."

Russell says my name, his deep voice booming over the sound of sizzling bacon. I turn to him. "What's up?"

"Malina came to us this morning," he says slowly, and it triggers all kinds of panic in me. Is he going to mention the secret laptop and the book? Has Malina been snooping through our stuff? Then he exhales and says, "She's worried about Jayla. Says she hasn't left her room in two weeks."

I frown, trying to remember the last time I saw her. She definitely wasn't at the party the other night, and she hasn't been at the pool lately, either. "That's weird," I say.

Russell nods. "Do you know what it could be about? Is she upset? Sick?"

I shrug and grab a spoon from a nearby drawer. "I have no idea. We're not exactly...friends," I say, suddenly feeling guilty for keeping my distance from the other girls.

He nods. "Have you heard anything from the other girls? Any idea why one of them might stay in her room for days on end?"

I genuinely try to think of something, but Riley and I pretty much keep to ourselves. "No, I don't. I'm sorry. I could go check on her if you'd like?"

"You can certainly try," he says, sipping from his coffee. "But don't get your hopes up."

"We've all been by her room," Kyle says, frowning. "She's ignored all of us, and she's even ignoring Nia who was her friend before she started working here."

Okay, now that seems kind of weird. "Maybe she's overwhelmed with how great this place is," I offer, trying to come up with a solution that makes sense, because now even I'm getting a little worried about her. "All this luxury and free stuff... it's kind of crazy and maybe she just needs some time to cool off and unwind and like, feel normal again."

"Are you overwhelmed being here?" Russell asks.

The answer is yes, a thousand times yes. But I say, "No. I love being here."

This makes all three of them smile, even Henry who has been looking sternly upset since I walked in here a few minutes ago.

"Let me know if you hear anything new," Russell says.

"I will," I promise.

WHEN I GET BACK to my room, Riley is there. She's dressed for the day in jeans and a blue flannel shirt, which says she means business, because normally she'll lounge around in her pajamas for as long as possible.

"You're still alive?" I ask as I close the door behind me, carefully balancing the bowl of cereal in my hand. "I figured you died, or was abducted by aliens since you ignored me all night."

Riley rolls her eyes. "Sorry. I just needed to focus on this book. I have the first two chapters translated."

"Wow." I leave the cereal on my nightstand and go over to her. She's sitting on the floor, which is her usual style ever since the days of never having enough desks at the group home to do homework. The laptop is in front of her, and the Greek book is open in her lap.

"Here you go," she says, handing me the laptop. "It's really just an introduction—nothing we don't already know."

I read the document silently. It starts out talking about how immortality has been invented and harnessed, and that it is a real thing. I kind of skim a little bit because just like with ancient history books, they go on and on and on instead of getting right to the point.

All of chapter one is just an introduction, filled with poetic ramblings about the kinds of greatness and power one could have if they were immortal.

Chapter two gets a little better.

The finite amount of immortality stones ensures that only the slightest fraction of humanity will achieve the greatest fate available: immortality. The Creator has transposed two hundred lapis stones, or immortality stones as they are hereby referred as, and two hundred stone mates. The wearer of the lapis stone must have a human mate wear the pair, or the immortality connection will be broken, and the immortality lost.

I read through the rest of it, but Riley is right. None of it says anything we don't already know, and there's certainly not any information about how to stop being a human life blood once you've become one.

"This is only chapter two," I say, handing her back the laptop. "The good stuff probably comes later."

"You're right," she says, and there's optimism an excitement in her eyes. "I just totally love astronomy, don't you? Although black matter is kind of hard to comprehend, but I'm hoping they explain it better later in the book."

She winks at me, back to talking code in case anyone is listening. I sigh and stare at the book in her lap. I'm thrilled that she's translated so much of it so soon, but it's also a little discouraging because I haven't even started on my mission yet.

"We should probably put it back soon," I whisper. "What if someone notices it's missing?"

She nods. "I was thinking the same thing," she whispers back. "I downloaded the pictures of the pages to the computer so it's time to ditch this thing."

By the time we finish reviewing what she's translated, my cereal is soggy and ruined. But I'm not hungry anymore. I'm eager to get this book back so we're not implicated if any of the guys should go looking for it. Then I'll start on my own mission while Riley gets back to hers. I already have a plan, too. I'm going to sneak into Alexo's bedroom. He's not here and he probably won't be back any time soon, so the best way to spy on someone when you can't spy on the person is to spy on their stuff.

Piece of cake, right? A giddy thrill rushes through me.

"I'll go put this back," I say, tucking the book under my arm.

"Take these too," Riley says, handing me a stack of romance novels that will look innocent enough should anyone see me in the hallways.

"You can stay in here if you want," I tell her. "But I might take a while coming back...I have...something to do."

She eyes me curiously. "Something a princess should do?"

I grin. "Precisely."

I don't run into anyone on the walk to the library, which is a relief but it doesn't stop my heart from beating erratically in fear. I slip in through the massive and heavy library door, closing it softly behind me. The romance novels go on a lower level, but I'm still scared I'll get noticed in here, so I keep them with me as I make my way toward the ladder on the right side of the room. Once this spooky immortality book is back on the shelf, I'll be able to breathe easier.

I climb up a few steps on the ladder. A sudden voice makes me jump out of my skin.

"Read anything good?" The voice is feminine, soft. My brain immediately knows it's not Alexo or one of the guys, but I can't help the little squeak of fear that escapes me. I whip around, nearly falling off the ladder.

It's Jayla. She's wearing black leggings and a black long sleeved shirt while she sits in the corner of the room, her knees tucked up to her chest.

"Not really," I say, answering her question. My voice is raw and scratchy, probably from hyperventilating. Now that someone has seen me get up on this ladder, I can't exactly leave. I turn back and scale up to the top as quickly as possible, sliding the book back into place while my body shields exactly which book it is from her view.

Then I climb down and replace the rest of Riley's trashy romance novels. I can feel Jayla's eyes on me as I work.

"Romance novels," I say, shrugging one shoulder. "They're always better than real life."

She just stares at me. Her dark skin is paler than usual. Deep purple circles rim her eyes, and her normally gorgeous black hair is messy, pulled into a ponytail that looks like she's forgotten all about it for the last few days.

"Are you feeling okay?" I ask, scared to get any closer to her. She looks violently ill.

She shakes her head, her eyes drifting to the floor.

"I can call an ambulance for you," I say. "You need a doctor."

"I don't need a doctor," she says, her voice stronger than she looks. "I need something, but a doctor is not it."

A shiver slides up my spine. Her voice is eerie, fearful. "Can I get you some water or something?" I ask.

Her eyes flit to mine and her jaw goes rigid. "Leave me alone."

"Okay," I say, holding up my hands. This girl needs help. But she clearly doesn't want any help from me.

EIGHTEEN

The next day, I wake up eager to get back to my personal mission. I spent the entire day before doing recon on the mansion and Alexo's room. I pretended that I left something in Theo's room, so I needed to walk down the forbidden hallway to retrieve it. To my disappointment, none of the nameplates on the doors in that hall were Alexo's. I was just about to give up when I noticed an unmarked door at the very end of the hallway. Opening it, I saw nothing but a long staircase going straight up to the third floor. But the sweet masculine aroma in the staircase told me all I needed to know. It was Alexo's room.

Now, I am armed with weapons of deception: a half-empty bottle of whiskey, a pair of men's sunglasses and a DVD of Mr. Robot season one. Two things that belong to Theo. One that belongs to the bar in the sitting room downstairs.

I pour some whiskey in my mouth and slosh it around, wincing because this crap is gross. It feels like fiery vomit, and it's actually worse when you don't swallow it. I spit it into my sink and allow a couple of drops to fall on my shirt for maximum drunken stench. My plan is to act, look, and smell drunk. That way if I get caught going through Alexo's room, I can pretend I got lost along the way to Theo's room to return his stuff. It might be a stupid idea, but it's all I've got.

I still haven't heard from Theo, and I allow that to fill me up with courage. It means they're not back at the mansion yet. I have plenty of time to snoop through Alexo's things without the fear of being caught.

I wake up at five in the morning and make my way through the house, shuffling on my feet like I'm drunk, just in case anyone sees me. I stay quiet though, my socked feet soft on the floor. Soon, I am at the end of the hallway, facing the door that leads to the stairs.

I take a deep breath and open the door. The soft glow of the sunlight from the third floor just barely illuminates the stairs before me. I close the door behind me and carefully walk up, taking each step achingly slow so as to keep quiet. My heart thunders in my chest, but I clutch Theo's things tightly, holding on to the lie that I'm drunk and trying to find his room.

At the top of the stairs, I face a room that's larger than mine or Theo's. The walls are dark wood, with candelabras hanging every few feet. Alexo's bed is the biggest bed I've ever seen, made up with white silk sheets and a ton of pillows. There's a sitting area, a bar, and doors that probably lead to the bathroom or closets. At the top of the stairs is an office area with a high ceiling that has skylight windows.

I go for the desk. Every drawer is locked. He has no computer, and not even any televisions in his room. As I look around, I realize there are no modern devices at all in Alexo's room. Everything is big, immaculate, and clean. I make my way to the end tables next to his bed, but there's nothing in the drawers. It's as if he's never in here at all.

I take a deep breath and continue my search. The bar is filled with alcohol and nothing else. I check behind the few paintings on the walls but there's no hidden safe or books on immortality. The entire room is spotless.

I scrub my hands over my face, smelling the stench of whiskey on my fingers. I groan in frustration. There's nothing here. Not even a wall tablet, or an alarm clock. The closet is filled with suits and shiny leather shoes, and nothing at all of any interest to me. I pull open all the doors, but as I suspected, they lead to a bathroom and two closets. There's no secret hide out, no bookshelf that might be a false wall to a hidden room. Frustrated, I look around the room once more, making sure I've left everything exactly how I found it, and then I make my way back to the stairs behind his desk.

And then I notice it. The door on the other side of Alexo's desk. It's made of the same dark wood paneling as the wall, but I still can't believe I missed it on my first look around the room. I shove the DVD in my back pocket and put Theo's sunglasses on top of my head so I don't drop them.

A new spark of excitement fills my bones as I make my way to the door, twisting the silver handle slowly. The door swings open, revealing another set of stairs. They also go down, just like the door I used to get here, but they lead somewhere else. It's dark at the bottom, no sunlight filters in from wherever these stairs end. I reach for the handrail and then slowly lower myself down each step, feeling in the dark to make sure I don't fall. The light from Alexo's room gets dimmer and dimmer, and the stairs seem to go on forever. I can't be sure but it certainly feels like I've been walking down many more steps than I walked up to get to Alexo's room.

Finally, I step forward and there's no more steps beneath my feet. Just solid, hard flooring. My vision is nearly pitch black. I turn around and look up at where I'd left the door open just a crack. There's a sliver of light up there, but it doesn't illuminate the area down here.

I turn back and hold out my arms, feeling for whatever lies ahead. I touch a wall in front of me, and feel down until my hand closes over a cool metal doorknob.

Curiosity claws at me and I'm dying to know what's on the other side. This could be the answer to all of my questions. It could lead me to who is in control of Alexo.

I twist the handle slowly, and then the door at the top of the stairs slams shut.

NINETEEN

My breath catches in my throat. Footsteps walk away from the door at the top of the stairs.

"Damn drafts," someone says. It almost sounds like the deep gruff of Russell's voice, but I can't be sure. But it does calm my pounding heart a little bit. If he thinks the door was open because of a draft, then he doesn't suspect that someone is down here. I clutch the half empty bottle of whiskey to my chest, frantically reminding myself that I'm supposed to act drunk if I'm caught. I turn back around, my hand finding the doorknob again. I have no idea what's beyond this door, but I can't go back up the stairs if someone is up there.

I take a deep breath and prepare to make an exit through this mysterious door. If I'm lucky, maybe it goes outside.

A shrill female scream freezes me to the floor.

I turn back around, staring at the sliver of light emanating from the bottom of the door at the top of the stairs.

"What are you doing to me?" a girl screams. I know her voice, and a shudder ripples through me. I can sense her fear, feel the terror in her voice.

It's Jayla.

"Let—me—go," she says with a huff.

"Ain't happenin', sweetheart."

Now I know for sure that's Russell's southern twang of a voice. I know I should leave, turn around and run out that door and forget I ever heard any of this, but I can't. Curiosity takes over.

And if I'm being honest, even though I'm not friends with Jayla, I don't like the sound of what's going on up there. Whatever is happening, she doesn't deserve it.

Carefully, I lean forward, putting my hands on the stairs in front of me since I can't see them very well. I crawl up them slowly, only stopping when my eyes are level with the slit under the door. I see Jayla's bare feet standing next to Russell's heavy boots. There's another pair of shoes—Nike's with blue laces. Those belong to Kyle.

The sounds of Jayla struggling to free herself makes a knot form in my stomach, but she should know that she'll never escape Russell's grip. He's too strong and she's too small.

"You really fucked up kid," Russell says with a tisk that sounds like he might actually feel bad for her. "You should have kept to yourself. Followed the rules."

"You should have told the truth!" she says. "Tell me what I am! What did you do to me?"

The door across from Alexo's office opens. It's the first door I came in from, the one directly across from the hidden door I'm peeking out of. Fear solidifies in my bones as I watch the shiny leather shoes walk into the room and make their way over to Jayla and Russell. I study Kyle's shoes, but he's not moving. He's also not speaking.

I wish I could see better, but as I press my face to the final stair, all I can see is the bottom of everything on this floor.

"Get away from me!" Jayla yells as Alexo's shoes slowly click across the floor toward her.

"Jayla," he says, his voice smooth as honey. "You knew the rules when you accepted this job, did you not?"

"What did you do to me?" she hisses.

"I gave you a place to live," he says. "I gave you everything you could have wanted."

"You cursed me!" she screeches. Her feet shift as she struggles to free herself, but Russell holds her tightly by the arms. "This bracelet is a poison!"

"You shouldn't have tried to take it off," Alexo says plainly, like she's the one in the wrong here.

"I know your secret," Jayla says, sounding like she's talking through gritted teeth. "I found out what you did." She takes a ragged breath and I lean in close. "You're a *succubus*!"

"Am I?" Alexo says, clearly amused. "Do explain how you figured that out."

"I knew you were hiding something. I followed you, and I saw that you have secret meetings with a woman who wears a necklace that looks just like my bracelet."

The room goes silent, and Alexo's shoes shift on the floor. I think Jayla is onto something. More importantly, she might have found who Alexo works for.

I wish I had brought my phone so I could record all of this and take it back to Riley. But since I don't have it, I strain and focus to remember every word I hear.

"You're a demon!" Jayla says. "I looked it up online. You make us wear bracelets so you can stay here on earth and if we try to remove the bracelets, we die!"

Alexo chuckles now, but Jayla talks over him. "The internet told me all about you. You're evil!"

"I think that's enough talking for now," Alexo says. He turns and walks away from her, directly toward me. I freeze, right here like a sitting duck on my hands and knees on the staircase. His shoes get closer and closer, and then they turn toward the wooden desk. I breathe a sigh of relief as Alexo leans down, inserts a key into one of the desk drawers, and opens it. He retrieves a syringe. My stomach flips over.

He walks back to Jayla. It sounds like she's started crying, but I can't see her face.

"You are wrong," Alexo says, his voice like venom. "Hasn't anyone ever told you that you can't believe anything on the internet? Demons don't exist, child. But immortals do."

Jayla cries out in pain. Within seconds, her body goes limp, sinking to the floor. Russell steps backward to avoid the fall, and Jayla's long black hair splays out all over the shiny hardwood floors.

Alexo just killed her.

"Now," Alexo says, clapping his hands together in front of his chest. "Russell, you'll need to head into town and hire a new recruit. We can't be down a lifeblood for very long."

"Yes, sir," Russell says. "There's a women's shelter about seventy miles from here. No one would miss someone from a shelter."

"Just make sure she's not a drug addict," Alexo says. "Kyle—" Tears spring to my eyes as I watch Alexo's shiny shoes turn toward my friend who has been silent this whole time. "Take the body to the east balcony. Throw her off. We'll say she slipped."

Kyle sighs. "I wish there was another way."

"Fine with me," Alexo says. "You can create an elaborate death scene if you want. Just get it done and make it believable."

"That's not what I meant," Kyle says, his voice low. "I don't think she needed to die. She just—we could have bribed her or something. Made her keep quiet and let her live out her remaining days here."

"Humans don't keep *quiet*," Alexo says. "Teenage girls have no integrity in them at all. You are young, but you'll learn. If they break the rules, they die." Alexo turns on his heel. "Dispose of this damned body. I need a drink."

He saunters off toward the bar in his room. Kyle bends down to pick up Jayla, gingerly cradling her lifeless body in his arms.

"Use the back exit," Russell says, gesturing toward the hidden door. Toward me.

Kyle's shoes turn in my direction. I spring into action, climbing back down the stairs backwards on my hands and knees. When my heels press against the door behind me, I turn and yank it open, then push it closed as quietly as possible. Kyle and Russell will be at the top of the stairs any moment. I have to get the hell out of here.

I look around. I'm in a hallway that looks nearly identical to the first hallway that leads to all the guy's rooms, only this is the only door, and the hall is narrow like a service hallway. There are no windows, no place to hide, just a metal door at the far end of the hallway.

I take off running toward the door. I run like my life depends on it, because it probably does. If I'm caught, I can't lie my way out of this. I fly down the hall, my socks sliding on the thin carpeting. Once I reach the door, I push it open and burst outside into the humid, hot summer air. The bottle of whiskey flies out of my hand, but I leave it. There's no time to waste. There's a wooded area next to the fence that runs along this side of the house all the way up to the garage. I run toward the garage, my socks getting covered in dirt and leaves along the way. When I reach the front of the house, I tuck around the corner, then lean against the closed garage door, panting for breath. They can't see me now.

My legs are shaky and worn out as I walk across the front of the mansion, the cobblestone driveway hot on my feet. I pass up the front door because a servant would welcome me inside if I went that way. Instead, I keep walking until I get to the gardens. I need time alone. I need to cool off and compose myself before I even think of stepping foot inside that house again.

Jayla is dead.

Jayla has been murdered.

Jayla knows that Alexo meets with a woman.

What if the man in charge of the Rosewater clan is actually a woman?

My thoughts spin in a vortex of fear and curiosity as I walk aimlessly through the garden. I try to take deep breaths but they all come out ragged. My chest aches in a way it's never felt before. I just watched a girl get killed for doing exactly what I did that day with Theo. She tried removing her bracelet and discovered that something was very wrong.

Now she's dead.

I turn the corner of the garden, past a line of rose bushes. In my dazed state, I walk straight into someone.

Nia yelps, then turns around. Her short brown hair is sleek and cute today. I stare at the butterfly tattoos on her shoulders because I can't meet her eyes.

"Sorry, I thought I was alone," Nia says.

"I should apologize to you," I manage to say. "I just walked right into you."

"The gardens are so pretty, it's easy to get distracted."

I nod, fearing that the lump in my throat might cut off my airway any second now.

"Listen," Nia says. "Um, have you seen Jayla today?"

I stare at her so long she asks the question again. "Yeah," I breathe. All the sounds of nature outside have been replaced with the pounding of my heartbeat inside of my ears. "I uh, saw her in the library this morning."

Nia's eyebrows lift. "You did? What was she doing?"

The poor girl's face has so much hope on it now, that I wish I hadn't said anything. I shrug. "She looked kind of upset, I guess. I tried talking to her but she didn't want to talk to me. She just...wanted to be left alone."

I realize in the moment that I'm describing a girl who's depressed. That if Kyle goes along with the body dumping, it'll look like Jayla committed suicide. No one should be blamed for their own death when they were actually murdered.

But what can I do? If I say anything, I'll be next. Nia will be killed, too. They'll take all of us out and find five new unsuspecting girls to give their mortality way.

I have to keep quiet.

Nia smiles. "Well, she's been weird lately but at least she finally left her room, you know? I think maybe she's homesick."

"Yeah," I say, exhaling as I turn around, ready to get the hell out of this conversation. "Maybe she is."

TWENTY

My entire world is upside down. I've never seen anyone die in front of my own eyes before. And this wasn't just a death. It was murder.

My vision is blurry, my pulse is racing, and my mouth is dry. I don't know how I manage to make it all the way back inside the mansion and up to my room. My legs work on autopilot, making me move even though my brain is freaking the hell out.

This is bad. This is so bad.

Poor Jayla, dead because of the clan. They caught her snooping around. They found out that she knew something was up.

That doesn't look good for Riley and me. We've been so careful but suddenly it doesn't seem careful enough. The whispers and dry erase board—it's not good enough. They're going to find us.

They will kill us too.

I burst into my room so quickly that Riley jumps. She's sitting on my floor, laptop in front of her and the book in her lap, just like how I'd left her earlier this morning.

"Jesus, Cara," Riley says, putting a hand to her chest. "You scared the hell out of me."

"I just—" I stop talking. I clamp a hand over my mouth. I want so badly to tell her every gory and horrific detail of what just happened, but I can't say a damn word of it in this house. I have to get out of here. The walls feel like they're closing in on me. I pull off Theo's sunglasses and toss them on my bed, then put the DVD on my nightstand. Several deep breaths don't slow my racing heart.

Riley lifts an eyebrow and then nods toward my nightstand. "Theo called you."

"I don't care."

My voice sounds like someone else's. Riley's eyebrows pull together and she stands up, eyeing me like I've gone insane. "What's going on?" she asks. "Did you two get in a fight?"

My heart is screaming at me to play it cool. Act normal. If the clan spies on us through the tablets in the wall, they might be on high alert right now because of Jayla. Maybe they're worried she told one of us something. I have to be calm. Act normal.

"No, not really," I say, trying to keep my voice calm. "He's just always gone so I'm kind of over it."

Lies. It's all a lie.

And Riley knows it.

Her eyes widen and she puts a finger over her lips to silence me. She looks around, finding the dry erase board and then she scribbles something on it.

What's going on? I know you're lying

we need to get the hell out of here, I write back. *We need to talk—privately!!!*

"Wanna go for a ride on the motorcycle?" Riley says.

I shake my head, but then I think twice. If we have the driver drop us off somewhere, I know I won't be able to maintain a normal act in front of him. The only other way to leave is of our own accord so no one can tell I am positively freaking out.

"Yeah," I say. "Let's go for a bike ride. Maybe get some ice cream?" My stomach churns at the thought of food. I don't think I can ever eat again.

The wind whips my clothing and hair as we zoom through the country roads that lead away from the mansion. Riley holds onto my stomach tightly, but if she's scared she hasn't said anything. My eyes sting with the threat of tears and I have to keep blinking them away. Every time I think about Jayla, about this impossible situation, I want to cry.

Crying won't solve anything though, so I push on, driving my motorcycle farther than I've ever been. We go past the diner, past the high school. We cross through an intersection and I just keep on driving until half an hour has passed.

"We stopping any time soon?" Riley calls out when we slow down for a stop sign.

I don't know where to stop. Fields fill my vision as far as I can see. Pastures and farmland and slanted hilly terrain stretch on forever by this old two lane county road.

I put the bike in first gear and push on, driving a little further until I see a large oak tree on the side of the road. I pull over and park my bike under the tree, rolling it so that the tree blocks most of it. I don't know who I'm kidding though—if the clan has my bike GPS tracked, they'll know exactly where I am.

Riley pulls off her helmet and shakes out her hair. "What the hell is going on?"

I shake my head. "Not here," I whisper.

I start walking, the motorcycle key gripped in my palm. I cross under the barbed wire fence of whatever farmland is in front of us and I walk.

The bike could be tracked, or bugged, or fitted with hidden cameras for all I know. I can't risk it, so I walk, my shoes trudging through the high grass that's as tall as my waist. Riley follows behind me, no doubt annoyed, but she doesn't say anything.

When we're so far into the field that my bike is just a tiny dot near the old oak tree, I stop walking and turn to her.

"Jayla is dead."

Riley stares at me for a long moment, her dark hair whishing softly in the breeze. In all my years of knowing her, I don't think she's ever been this quiet.

A tear falls down my cheek. I am mourning the loss of an innocent girl, the loss of our mortality. The fear of losing everything on top of all we've already lost. Riley just watches me for a long moment, neither of us saying anything.

Then I tell her everything.

"Holy shit," Riley breathes, closing her eyes for a moment. We stare at each other, both of us dumbfounded and terrified, and I just nod.

"Holy shit is right," I say. "I don't know what to do. I keep wondering if I could have prevented this, if I'd only stayed with her in the library or tried to help her or something."

Riley shakes her head and pulls a long blade of grass out of the ground. She twists it around her finger. "Clearly she'd already known something was up by the time you found her in the library. If you'd stayed, they might have thought you were in on it, too."

"She's dead, Riley." I blink away tears. "I can't believe this happened."

Riley exhales. "What do we do now? We need a plan."

"We have to act normal. We have to pretend to be happy and carefree and not give off even the slightest hint that we know anything."

She nods. "We can do it."

"And...the book," I say, biting my lip. "Maybe we should delete the photos and clear out the computer and just forget about that for now. It's too risky if we get caught."

Riley's face contorts, and I know it's not what she wants to hear right now. Finally, she nods. "Yeah, it's too risky. I haven't translated enough information to learn anything anyway."

"As for Alexo," I say, remembering what Jayla had said. "We should find out who this woman is that he meets with."

"Absolutely not," Riley says, dropping the blade of grass she'd been playing with. "No more spying, no more playing detective. We'll let Theo handle it all."

"He doesn't have time to do it all," I say, groaning in frustration. "We have to help."

"If we get caught, we'll end up like Jayla."

"And if we don't do something, we will end up like her anyway. Dead in a year with no future whatsoever."

Riley can't argue with that. "We'll be careful. I'll talk to Kyle...maybe I'll say something like why aren't there any women in the clan and I'll give him this girl power guilt trip. Maybe he'll tell me about the woman in an effort to let me know that there *are* women in power here."

"That could work," I say, but thinking of Kyle makes me remember what he had to do today. Theo is right; Kyle is a good guy underneath it all. He's just stuck in the clan like the rest of us.

"I wonder what Jayla found online," I say, thinking back to what she'd said just before she died. "She thought Alexo was some kind of evil creature, but she mentioned that they talked about the bracelet on some message board. What if there's information out there about how to remove it?"

Riley seems skeptical. "You'd think the immortal clan leaders would make sure that wasn't online."

"I don't know," I say as optimism awakens inside of me. "If the clans use lifebloods but never tell them what they're actually being used for, maybe they don't look online for people talking about it. They're all old as hell, after all. I don't even think Alexo knows how to use the internet. We could get a secret computer, like a library somewhere or something, and search for bracelets you can't remove."

"We would need to do it far, far away from here," Riley says. "Who knows how far their tracking goes."

"I have an idea," I say, shivering from the wave of nausea the idea gives me. "It's...well...it's kind of a bad idea."

Riley folds her arms across her chest. "What is it?"

"Jayla did all this research on her own before she got caught. We should figure out what she knew. Maybe it'll make our search easier."

"How can we get information from a dead girl?" Riley asks.

"Easy," I say, reaching for my motorcycle keys from my pocket. "We search her room."

TWENTY-ONE

When we're back at the mansion, Riley's phone beeps. I park the motorcycle in its spot in the garage and put my helmet on the shelf. Riley makes a weird *hmm* sound while she looks at her phone.

"Theo just texted me," she says quietly as if she's afraid he's hiding in the garage and will hear us. "He wants to know if you're okay because he can't get ahold of you."

I sigh and try to think of what to say to him. I'm crazy about him, as much as you can be crazy about someone, but this is something I need to be alone for right now. Well, not *alone*. I need Riley, and we need answers. If Theo knew what we were up to, he'd put a stop to it. As much as I'm dying to see him and curl up in his arms, we have to take care of this first.

"Tell him I'm sleeping," I say. "Say we were up late last night and I'm still asleep and you'll have me call him when I'm up."

She nods as her thumbs fly across the screen, sending him the text. "He's here, you know," she says as she slides her phone back in her pocket. "He could see us walk inside."

"That's why you'll go first," I say, feeling so guilty I could die. "Look around and then wave for me to follow you if the coast is clear."

"Maybe you should just tell him," she says as we enter into the garage through the service hallway.

I shake my head. Jayla is dead, killed at the hands of the man in control of the clan. Theo has spent the last few days on a secret trip with that same man, doing God knows what. I need to figure out as much information as I can before I see him, or I might crack from the weight of it all and fall apart the moment we see each other again. Plus, I can't shake the thought that Theo has bad news from Alexo. Like maybe Alexo talked him into leaving me because I'm just a pathetic human. Maybe it's something worse. I have no idea what happened with Theo and Alexo, and I just can't bear to face him right now.

I need to find out what Jayla knew.

Riley walks ahead of me, stopping before every turn to look through the house and make sure Theo isn't there. Luckily, it's still pretty early in the morning, and we don't run into anyone. When we make it to our hallway of bedrooms, I breathe a sigh of relief. I'd half expected to see Theo hanging out by my door, waiting for me to wake up. The hallway is empty, and so is the feeling in my stomach as we walk toward Jayla's bedroom. Her name is still on the brass plate outside the door. Her death is still fresh. I wouldn't doubt if they're still waiting for someone to discover her body, lying splattered on the concrete where Kyle and Russell dumped her. At least then they could act innocent about the whole matter, like they had no idea she was dead beforehand.

My stomach flips at the thought. That is not the way anyone should be laid to rest.

Jayla's door swings open when Riley tries the knob. I'd almost expected it to be locked, almost looked forward to being turned away before we started. But I press on, slipping into her bedroom and closing the door behind us.

The place is in shambles. The bed is unmade, the comforter kicked to the floor. Clothes and shoes are scattered around, and her television is on the news channel, the volume muted.

"Whoa," Riley says under her breath. The sound sets off alarms in my mind. I grab her arm.

Don't talk, I mouth to her. Then I bring my lips to her ear and whisper, "They could be monitoring the room. They don't need to know we're in here."

She mimes zipping her lips closed and we walk further into the room, taking in the chaotic state of the place. Jayla was always so put together and beautiful. This doesn't feel like what I'd imagine her room looking like, not at all. This is the room of someone internally tortured, someone suffering. I wonder how long it's been since she tried to remove her bracelet and discovered the suffocating feeling of death that comes with trying to separate from the immortality stone.

Riley goes through Jayla's dresser and nightstands, but they don't turn up anything interesting. I check out the closet, looking inside her purses and the pockets of the dirty clothes she left on the floor.

Her computer is password protected, so we don't bother trying to get into it. I consider stealing it and trying to guess the password back in the safety of my room, but I think better of it. The clan would surely find out if I took Jayla's computer, and they'd want to know why.

Riley holds up her arms in defeat after a few more minutes of searching. Her eyes meet mine and I can tell she's wondering if we should just leave because there's nothing here to find.

I'm about to agree with her, but then I get the idea to look where I used to hide things when I lived in the group home.

I slide my hands under Jayla's mattress. Toward the foot of the bed, I touch a notebook. I shove my other hand under the heavy memory foam and retrieve the spiral notebook, eyes wide as I show it to Riley. I set it on the bed and flip it open, but all the pages are blank. My heart sinks. Riley takes the notebook and holds it up to the light, maybe checking for invisible ink or something. Something small falls from the pages and lands on the carpet. It's a little black SD card, like the kind they put in cell phones. I take it and shove it in my pocket. *Jackpot*, I mouth. Riley grins.

We turn to leave and then there's a knock on Jayla's door. Shit. Riley turns toward me, eyes wide. Then she points toward the closet door and rushes over to it to hide.

"Jayla?" the soft voice on the other side of the door is Nia's. Riley comes out of her hiding place and we both stare at the closed door while Nia says, "Are you in there?"

We don't make a sound.

"Jayla, I wish you'd talk to me," Nia says, her voice pleading. "Whatever is bothering you, I can help. Just talk to me."

My heart shatters for this girl and her friend who is never going to open that door again. Nia doesn't know the grim reality yet. She still has hope, still thinks that there's a way to save Jayla from her all-consuming depression. My heart breaks all over again.

"I'll come back later," Nia says through the door. "If you need anything at all, just call me, okay?"

I press my forehead into my palm as the next few moments pass. Riley just stands there, her expression solemn. After a few minutes have passed, I make my way to the door and slowly open it, peaking outside.

Nia is gone, and the hallway is empty.

I motion for Riley to follow me and we rush back to my bedroom, the memory card weighing a million pounds in my pocket.

TWENTY-TWO

I check my phone the second I'm back in my room. I have three missed texts from Theo after he tried calling me this morning. Seeing his name on the screen sends a twinge of guilt through me. I want to see him, I really do. But some things are more important right now.

Leaving my phone on my bed, I take out the non-Wi-Fi laptop Riley stashed under my bed and power it on.

Riley paces behind me, chewing on her thumbnail. "I really hope this isn't a dead end," she says, walking a few steps and then turning back to walk the opposite way. "If this is some stupid stash of selfies or something, I'll be pissed."

"She wouldn't have hidden if it wasn't important."

"She'd hide it if it's all naked selfies," Riley says with a sigh.

Now doubt creeps into my mind, but I shove the memory card into the computer anyway. It seems to take forever to pull up the folder on the screen, even though it's only a few seconds. The memory card has only one folder saved to it. It's called Untitled.

I click on it, revealing just one file. A video saved with a file name that sends a shiver down my spine.

If_I_die.mov

"Now we're talking," Riley says, kneeling down beside me. We're sitting on the floor, as always, and it occurs to me now that we do almost everything on the floor out of habit from living at the group home where desks and tables weren't abundant. I guess you can take the girl out of poverty, but you can't take the poverty out of the girl.

Riley plugs a pair of earbuds into the computer and hands me one. We each put one in our ear to keep the noise of the video quiet. I look over at my best friend, then I double click on the video.

Jayla's face appears on the screen. Her tanned skin is radiant like it used to be, her eyes are missing the dark circles she had this morning. Her hair, dark with soft highlights, hangs wavy around her shoulders. She looks like she's taking the video on her cell phone, and she's in her room, sitting on her bed.

"Okay," she says. That one word is loaded with emotion, but it takes her a minute to say anything else. "This thing—" She holds up her wrist, twisting it around so the camera can get a good view of her immortality bracelet. "It's evil. It's magical. I don't really know what it is, but it's bad. I tried taking it off the other day because I wanted to do some painting and I didn't want to mess it up."

She gazes at her wrist and the camera shakes since she's holding it up with her other hand. "I can't even begin to describe what happened when I tried to remove it but…I felt like I was dying. No, I know I *was* dying. I would have died if I didn't put it right back where it goes, here on my wrist. This clan I joined, these guys with lots of money—they gave me the bracelet and I was told never to remove it. I thought it was just a joke, like some stupid fraternity promise or something, but I was wrong."

She looks right into the camera and all I see is fear behind her blue eyes. "I don't know how, but this bracelet is magic. And I can't take it off. I did some research online and I found these forums of people talking about bracelets that kill you if you remove them. I won't say what the website is on here because I don't want to implicate these people. They are good and honest people and they tried to help me. They told me that evil people use bracelets with powers like this. It's sucking the life out of me."

Chills prickle over my arms. She got that part right. I glance at Riley but she's watching the computer screen intently, her jaw rigid.

On screen Jayla sighs. "It's like they're using me and the other girls here for some kind of magic. I don't understand. I don't know what they're doing to me. I feel normal on most days, but now I can't stop thinking about it. Every day I look at this bracelet and I want it off. The people online said there's no way to remove it."

I don't hear what she says next. My hopes crash straight through to the floor and tears spring to my eyes. Riley curses under her breath.

"She's wrong," Riley says.

I nod in agreement but I'm not feeling very confident about that. On the computer, Jayla starts crying. "Something terrible is going on here. I've been following the leader of this clan and trying to figure out what he's doing. Every few days he goes to the balcony in the library and he talks to someone on the phone. I've never gotten close enough to hear what they say, but when they talk on video chat, I can tell it's a woman. She always looks pissed and Alexo doesn't seem like the same guy he is when he's talking to her. He seems like a scared little kid. I think she's making him do this to us. I think she might be a witch or something."

Riley reaches out and pauses the video. She turns to me, her expression blank. I stare at her for a moment, and then play the video again. There's only a few seconds left and I'm too anxious to hear what Jayla has to say.

"I'm going to get to the bottom of this and try to save all of the girls here. I don't know what they're doing to us, but it's not good. Nia, I told you to check under my bed if I ever go missing, so if you're watching this well..." She looks down. "That's not a good thing. It means I failed in taking off this bracelet and it killed me. It means I didn't succeed, but you still can. I want you to do everything in your power to find a way to remove yours, okay?" In the video, I hear the ringing of her wall tablet. She looks back, the phone camera shaking. The video turns into a picture of the floor, and then her feet as she walks over to her tablet. She brings the camera back to her face. "I'll record more later."

The video ends. I pull out my earbud and close the folder on the computer. "That didn't help us much."

"We know about the woman now," Riley says, her voice low. "Where's the library balcony?"

I shrug. I didn't know the library had a balcony. There's skylight windows at the top of the turret, but that's all. "Maybe there's another library?" I ask.

Riley nods. "We'll find it. I wonder if we should show this to Nia?"

I shake my head and slam my hand over the laptop. "No way. It'll only—" I press my lips to her ears and whisper so as not to be overheard. "It'll only get Nia killed as well. No one can know about this and keep it a secret, it's too much."

"You mean no one except for us?" Riley says, giving me an evil grin.

It's so scary I start laughing. "I am scared out of my mind," I whisper, even as I'm still smiling. It's not a happiness that's soaring through my veins right now—it's terror. Sheer, unhindered, terror.

"You need your boy," Riley says. She leans up and takes my phone from the bed, then hands it to me. "Call him. Talk to him."

"I don't know about that..." I say, looking at the phone in my hands.

"Cara," Riley says, putting a hand on my shoulder. "If you can't trust Theo, there's literally no fucking thing left in this life to count on."

"Yeah." I unlock the phone screen and press down on his number. "You're absolutely right."

TWENTY-THREE

With a heavy sigh, I look down at the phone screen. Theo didn't answer.

"I'm sure he'll call right back," Riley says, giving me an encouraging smile.

I know she's right because Theo always calls back, but this feels important. It feels cosmically important, like something he needs to know *now*. I shouldn't have kept Jayla's death from him this long. I shouldn't have ignored his call this morning. I need Theo's advice on everything that's going on.

"We should destroy this," I say, holding up the tiny memory card. There's nothing on it that's so important Theo would need to see it. We'll just tell him what happened. Right now, I'm terrified of Alexo paying us a visit and seeing what we're up to.

"Fine, fine," Riley says loudly. She holds up her hands in surrender. "I am a terrible artist. Destroy it if you have to, and I'll just try to create something better next time."

I snort because she's still trying to make it sound like we're not up to anything special in here, should anyone be listening.

"I think I'll set it on fire," I say, heading over to my desk where there's a lighter I use on my scented candles.

"Do it in the metal trashcan so you don't burn the place down," Riley says.

I take out my scissors and cut the tiny thing into pieces, and then, holding up each piece with a pair of tweezers, I put the lighter to it. They burn and curl up and warp in shape and when I'm pretty sure it'll never be able to have information extracted from it, I scatter them in three different trash cans, throwing away other stuff on top of it for good measure. All the while, I'm waiting for Theo to call me back. I kind of want to go down to his bedroom and see if he's there. But if he was, he would have called me. So I wait.

Riley goes back to her room, but not after giving me strict orders to call her as soon as I hear from Theo. I get tired of waiting around by the phone, so I take a hot shower. I hadn't realized how badly I needed to wash away the horrors of this morning until the water splashes on my skin and rolls down my face. I let the shower steam up and I toss my head back and let my hair get soaked. The hot water is searing, turning my skin pink, but I don't make it colder. I like the pain. I like knowing I still feel it. I am alive and Jayla is not. Her fate could have easily been mine or Riley's, had we been caught.

We have to be safer.

We have to be careful.

We have to take down Alexo and this whole fucking clan.

All the mirrors are foggy when I finally step out of the shower. My fingers are wrinkly, but I feel a little better. Jayla's death was a horrible injustice, but it has made me stronger in my resolve. I will fight with Theo to find a way to save not only me and Riley, but the other girls. I will find this woman, find whoever is in charge of Alexo, and I will take them out. I don't know what that means for the future of Theo and me, but I do know that living as a lifeblood is no life at all.

When I step back into my room, the scent of Theo's cologne fills my lungs. I look around for him, but no one's here. There's a note on my nightstand and I rush over to it.

DIDN'T WANT *to disturb your shower. Call me when you get this.*
-Theo

I GRAB the hair tie off my wrist and wrangle my wet hair into a messy bun on top of my head, and then I call Theo.

"Hey love," he says, his voice gruffer than usual.

"Come over," I say.

"I uh, I can't right now." There's a shuffling sound on the phone.

"What's wrong? Are you okay?" I'm whispering into the phone because I can't help myself.

"I'm fine, love. I'm just—" a sigh, "Busy. Give me a little bit, okay? I'll come see you soon."

I exhale and fight back the urge to tell him to get his ass over here right freaking now. Whatever he's up to, it's clearly important and related to the clan. We still have to keep up appearances.

"Fine," I say with a sigh. "I just miss you." I let my voice get all sweet and loving, just in case anyone is listening.

"See you soon," he says quietly.

I head over to Riley's room next door, hoping she can calm me down. I am so sick of waiting and so sick of needing answers and not having them. I'm also getting really tired of my mind replaying Jayla's death over and over again. Though I didn't see the moment the life left her eyes, I did see her body collapse to the floor. I may never stop seeing that image in my mind.

Riley has her TV turned on to a movie about three housecats who have adventures while their owners are away. It's clearly for kids, but there's something about the innocent fun of the movie that makes me feel a little better right now. I can't handle real life at the moment. I've been given entirely too much reality to last a lifetime.

I sit next to Riley on her couch, my head leaning on her shoulder while we watch the movie. Half an hour passes in what feels like five hours and I still haven't heard from Theo. Whatever Alexo had him doing when he took him a few days ago, it's probably been interrupted by Alexo's need to murder Jayla. Maybe they're back to doing whatever they were doing.

I'm sure Alexo doesn't shed tears for the girls he disposes of. We're all just batteries to him. Disposable, replaceable.

My phone sits in my lap, screen up so I can see if he calls. By the time the credits roll on the movie, I'm starting to go completely insane with worry and impatience. "What the hell is taking him so long?" I say, staring at my phone in my hand.

Riley turns up the volume on the TV, making the song playing over the movie credits impossibly loud.

"I love this song!" she shouts, cupping her hand to her mouth. "Let's dance!"

Only she doesn't get up to dance. She stays right here on the couch with me, turning so that our knees are touching.

"I've been thinking," she says quietly.

I snort sarcastically. "Me too."

She shakes her head. "No...not about what happened, but about the *after*."

I narrow my eyebrows and Riley continues, staring at her bracelet. "We keep them alive," she whispers. "It's one bracelet per person...someone has a stone themselves and we have the matching bracelet."

"Right," I say.

Her eyes flit up to meet mine, her voice the barest whisper under the loud music. "So, who was Jayla keeping alive?"

My heart skips a beat. I hadn't even thought of this, but Riley's right. When Theo's lifeblood died, he passed out and nearly died himself until he got a replacement. When Jayla was killed, Kyle and Russell were there, and they seemed fine. Alexo warned that they needed a replacement soon, but no one seemed like they were about to die without her bracelet.

"Henry?" I guess.

Riley shakes her head. "He was downstairs playing pool. I played a game with him while you were gone. He seemed fine."

"That's weird," I say with a shrug. I look at my own bracelet. "I wonder who we're keeping alive?"

Riley shudders. All around us, the music plays on. Some long ballad sung by a woman with pipes like Celine Dion. "I don't even want to know," she says.

TWENTY-FOUR

We're halfway through another movie, this one a comedy about college sororities, when Riley's wall tablet makes an awkward sound. It's like a wailing alarm, and it's unlike the normal phone call sound. We both walk over to it and see a message flashing on the screen.

EMERGENCY MEETING
ALL RESIDENTS MEET IN THE DEN IMMEDIATELY

The image flashes over and over until Riley presses the button at the bottom of the screen that says Accept. "I wonder what this is about?" she says, looking at me with an expression that tells me she knows exactly what it's about.

Bethany gives us a tentative smile when we meet her in the hallway on our walk downstairs to the den. Nia and Olivia are about thirty feet ahead of us, talking to each other in quiet voices. Jayla's door remains closed.

At the bottom of the stairs, two housekeepers stand there, their expressions blank. We turn into a hallway that leads to the den and Theo is there, standing alone, his hands in his pockets.

He wears jeans and a black long-sleeved Henley shirt even though it's hot outside. His dark hair has been combed back so it's not as messy as usual. He's standing there, straight backed and rigid, but he melts when he sees me.

"Theo," I say, falling into his arms for a hug. I've been dying to talk to him all morning, but now that we're around everyone else, I have to keep my mouth shut.

Theo's arms squeeze around me in a quick hug and then he takes a step backward. "Let's get in the den," he says, his voice heavy. He doesn't even look at me when he says it, but his hand rests on the lower part of my back as we walk into the sitting area where everyone else has gathered. Alexo, Henry, Russell and Kyle are all here, standing together on one end of the room. Bethany and the other girls look slightly confused, but no one seems worried.

Theo's arm stays wrapped around my back as we stand next to an armchair. Riley leaves Bethany's side to join mine.

Alexo steps forward. He's wearing the same suit from earlier this morning. He looks impeccably put together. You'd never even know he murdered someone just a few hours ago.

"I have gathered everyone here today to reveal some tragic news."

My eyes flit to Nia, who's expression morphs into fear the moment Alexo speaks. His voice is cold, unwavering, and straight to the point.

"I regret to inform everyone that Jayla has passed away. She was found this morning and taken to the hospital, where it was discovered that she had a rare heart condition."

I guess Kyle made this one up. It definitely sounds better than suicide or accidentally falling off a balcony.

"What?" Nia says, her voice breaking.

"I'm so sorry, my dear," Alexo says. The fake compassion in his voice makes bile rise up my throat. "I know you were close to her."

Nia bursts into sobs, her knees giving out and sending her to the floor. Olivia kneels down beside her, throwing her arms around her shoulders to comfort her.

Bethany looks stricken, her face pale. Tears fill her eyes. I look over and find Alexo staring straight at me.

"This is horrible!" Riley says, her voice cracking as if she's truly hearing the news for the first time.

"I'm sorry, love," Theo says in my ear, his hand warm on my back.

Then it hits me.

I better act sad real fast.

I bite my lower lip and will the tears to come like they had earlier this morning. But now that I'm standing in the same room as Jayla's killers, I can't cry. I can only feel anger, hatred, resentment.

I turn around and throw myself into Theo's chest, burying my face against the soft fabric of his shirt. It's a great cover because Theo wraps me in his arms, his head resting on top of mine, and he comforts me as if I'm really crying. I throw in a few shoulder sobs for good measure, but the tears just won't come.

From the other side of the room, Alexo continues on a pretend diatribe to the girl we lost. "Jayla wasn't with us very long, but she was a kind soul and was always very fun to be around. She will be missed terribly. Nia, I know you two were close, so I've arranged to have some grief counselors visit should you or anyone else need someone to talk to. I think we should all come together during this time and help each other mourn the loss of our clan member."

He continues like that, rambling on and on. Bethany joins in, and suggests that we all get together tomorrow to share stories of Jayla and have a little memorial for her. I keep my head pressed against Theo's chest, because I have nothing to add to this conversation. We are in a room filled with lies, and grieving girls who don't know the truth.

Theo runs his fingers down my back. "You okay, Cara?" he says softly, peering back to look at me.

I look up at him and he flinches. His eyes narrow and he studies my tearless face. "Cara?"

"Yes?" I say softly, not even trying to fake tears anymore since I know they won't come.

"What's going on?" he whispers. From the other side of the room, Nia's sobbing continues. Alexo is talking to her now, trying to comfort her and it makes me sick. He has no right.

"Cara," Theo says again, his hand reaching up to my cheek. His eyes dart upward, scanning the room before he looks at me. "I know you two weren't friends but I thought you'd be sad."

"I was," I whisper. "Earlier today."

His expression darkens. I fake a sniffle and say just loud enough for people to hear, "I think I need some fresh air."

"Of course," Theo says. He guides me out of the room, all the while I'm holding onto his arm, pretending to cry.

When we're outside, he turns to face me. "You know something," he says. "Alexo told us no one knew about her death yet."

A sardonic laugh escapes me. So that's where Theo was when I called him —having a secret meeting of immortals while they discussed Jayla's death, and the real reason she was killed, no doubt.

"Alexo doesn't know everything," I say. "I knew about Jayla and I also know something else."

Theo's eyes flash but he doesn't say anything. A sly grin slides across my lips. "I know who Alexo reports to."

TWENTY-FIVE

In the evening, Theo and I go for a drive so I can finally tell him everything that's happened since he was gone. He takes one of the trucks from the garage, and it's a huge Texan-sized monstrosity of a vehicle. There's four doors and the front passenger seat is so huge I feel like I'm in a motorhome instead of a truck. We try going out for dinner, but when we get to the Italian restaurant's parking lot, neither one of us are hungry. My stomach hasn't felt right since I saw Jayla killed earlier this morning. It was only a few hours ago, but it feels like it's been much longer that I've had the weight of this situation on my shoulders.

Theo leaves the restaurant and pulls into an empty parking lot of what looks like it used to be a grocery store before it closed down. The doors are boarded up and a real estate sign says it's for sale, but it looks like it should be condemned.

Theo runs his hands down his face and then puts them back on the steering wheel. "Tell me everything," he says.

I unbuckle my seatbelt so I can turn to look at him. "First, I want to know why Alexo took you away for a few days."

"He took me to Vegas." Theo's eyes focus on the empty store in front of us. "He said he wanted to get to know me better since I'm new to the clan, so we went from bar to bar, casino to casino, doing what Alexo calls bonding." He makes air quotes when he says the last word. "Basically, he was feeling me out. He doesn't like that we're dating, doesn't like that I refuse to take a lifeblood in the same manner that the rest of them do. I reiterated my loyalty to the Rosewater clan and did a lot of lying my ass off to keep him happy."

I feel a twinge of jealousy at the idea of Theo being in Vegas, most likely surrounded by attractive girls that Alexo would prefer he use as a lifeblood. "I guess that's better than what I thought," I say, shoving aside the jealousy.

"What did you think it was?" Theo asks.

I shrug. "I thought he would be torturing you for information or something. I don't know. It felt ominous."

"Well, it *felt* like torture," Theo says with a chuckle. "Being away from you—keeping myself in check so I don't say the wrong thing. It was hell."

"I'm glad you're back," I say, reaching for his hand.

"Me too." He gazes at me a long moment. "Time to spill what you know."

I sigh. "I don't even know how to explain everything that happened."

Theo squeezes my hand. "Start with the beginning."

I tell him about how I ran into Jayla at the library when I was putting back the book. Then, although it gets me a disapproving look from Theo, I tell him how I went snooping around Alexo's room to get information. His face falls when I describe Jayla's murder and he holds my hand so tightly, his jaw clenching in empathy.

"I can't believe you had to see that," he says.

"It was my own fault," I say. "But I'm glad I did. Now I know the truth, and I know that Alexo's lie about Jayla dying accidentally isn't really what happened. And because of that, I was able to find out who Alexo's taking orders from."

Theo sits up straighter. "If I hadn't seen Jayla's death then Riley and I wouldn't have gone snooping in her room. We wouldn't have this information, and we'd be no closer to solving this problem, so in a way, I don't regret what I did." Tears sting the back of my eyes as once again, Jayla's lifeless form appears in my mind. "I'm sorry she's dead, but I'm trying to make some good come from this."

I tell him about the video Jayla left after her death. I've never seen Theo look so serious. I thought he'd break out into a smile or something after I told him about the woman Alexo meets on the balcony.

"What's wrong?" I say. "This is our lead. This is a good thing."

In the back of my mind, I know it's not *the* good thing. It's *a* good thing. Finding a way to remove these bracelets should still be my top priority, but if I can help Theo solve his mission from the Embrook clan, then we're one step closer to dedicating all our time to saving me and Riley.

"This is good news," Theo says. There's a crease in his forehead as he thinks. "I'm just trying to figure out where to go from here. We need to destroy that video immediately—if Alexo finds out you watched it—"

"Don't worry. It's taken care of," I say. Theo flashes me a smile.

"So what do we do now?" I ask.

"I have to find a way to see this woman he talks to on the balcony. Maybe set up some cameras or, well no that won't work." He frowns and reaches up to turn the car's air conditioning vent toward his face. "Alexo no doubt has his room blocked from bugs or video devices. I can't slip anything in there without him discovering it. And his cell phone is untappable. I'll have to get the information in person..." His tongue flicks across his bottom lip while he thinks. "There are plenty of places to hide on the balcony. I'll stake it out, wait for him to go out there and make a phone call."

"Where is the balcony?" I ask. "I've never seen it."

"There's a hidden door just like the one in Alexo's room. It's near the fireplace and it'll take you up a flight of stairs to the balcony. It's long and wraps around most of the back of the house. There are trees and hedges up there, plenty of spaces to hide."

Theo looks at me, smiles and then says, "They leave it off the house tour for the lifebloods. I figured it just wasn't important, but now I realize Alexo uses it as his private meeting space, so I guess he doesn't want anyone to know it's there. Guess I'll start spending my evenings hanging out up there until I can catch him in the act."

"Cool," I say. "I'll wear all black so I'll be hidden."

"No you won't."

I feign innocence. "Should I wear green or something, to blend in with the plants?"

"You're not coming, Cara. It's not safe."

I cross my hands over my chest. "You promised me you'd take me on your next mission."

"Cara—"

I reach over and press my finger to his lips. "You don't get to object. You promised me, and I'm going."

"It's not safe," he says with my finger still over his lips.

"I don't care. You know what's not safe, Theo?" I hold up my wrist. "This damned bracelet. I'm already dying, and I'm coming with you."

He sighs, his breath warm on my finger that's still covering his lips. "Fine."

I smile. "Good."

I go to take my finger away but he grabs it, then pulls my hand forward so he can kiss my knuckles. "I missed you terribly," he says with his lips on the top of my hand. "So, so much."

"I missed you more," I say, leaning over to rest my head on his shoulder.

"Come here." Theo shoves the center console up until it forms a middle seat in the front of the truck. I slide over closer to him and he takes my knees in one hand, and wraps his other arm around my shoulders. In a quick movement, I'm pulled into his lap.

"That was fun," I say, unable to hide my smile, even in the middle of all these things that are wrong in the world.

"This will be more fun," he says, kissing me.

I close my eyes and lose myself in the embrace. Theo's lips taste like heaven. They're soft and warm and they know exactly how to kiss me in the way that makes my toes tingle.

I wrap my arms around his neck and hold him close, shivering when Theo's hand slides down my thigh, then back up again. We make out for several minutes, and the world fades away. We're no longer in a dirty old parking lot. We are just us, together, in love, and steaming up the windows.

Theo moves his seat back and I twist until I'm on top of him, my legs straddling his. He kisses my neck down to my collar bone, and my hands get all tangled up in his hair. I love the feeling of him. I love how he holds me, how he makes me feel like I'm the only girl in the world.

Theo's hands slide up my shirt, sending a trail of heat up my skin. I'm reminded of that first night we had together, back when he was a handsome stranger and I had no idea what horrors existed in the world. I lean in and kiss him, taking myself back to that day when we were just strangers, but I knew he was the one for me.

"Theo," I whisper against his lips. "I want you."

"Then let's go home," he breathes.

I sit up, frowning. "I said I want you, and you want to go home?"

A soft smile plays on his lips. "I'm not making love to you for the first time in the front seat of this truck that doesn't even belong to me."

I bite my lip. "But I want you *now*."

He runs a hand down my cheek, then kisses me softly. "Baby, I want you every second of every day. Let's make it special."

I grab his shoulders. "It can be special here," I say. "Not at that house where lies are told and people are murdered and the very bed I sleep on was given to me as a bribe for my mortality. I want you, and I want you now. Here, in the middle of this stupid town, where it's just me and you."

His hands grip my hips, and he leans his head back against the headrest. "You make a compelling argument."

I grin. "The backseat is huge," I say, winking at him in what I hope is a sexy way. I crawl off him and into the backseat, which really is massive, and then I curl my finger at him, motioning for him to join me.

Theo gets out of the truck and walks to the back door. When he opens it, the way the overhead parking lot lights shine on him makes him look like a statue in a museum. The card under him would read: *Perfect Specimen of a Man*

He climbs in, closes the door and presses the lock. "Are you sure about this?"

I nod and pull off my shirt to prove my point. I reach behind my back and unhook my bra, then let it fall to the floorboard.

Theo stares at me with kind eyes, and the hint of a smile on his lips. He takes off his shirt, too. I lie back on the seat, my heart pounding as he lowers himself on top of me. He tugs at my leggings and they come off easily. I am nervous, but I want this, and I pull him to me, kissing him with everything I have. I want him to know how I feel, deep down, under all of the drama and complications of life, I love him.

Theo's skin is warm against mine. He's careful not to hurt me, and he moves slow, his eyes watching mine to make sure I'm okay. I run my fingers down his back, feel the ripples of his muscles. Theo presses against me and he sighs with pleasure, his breath tickling my neck.

"You are," he breathes as he rocks back and forth.

"I'm what?" I whisper.

"Stunning." He kisses my neck.

"Beautiful." He kisses my breast. "Absolutely beautiful."

I can't help but smile as he makes love to me. He is gentle, and sweet, and he takes his time. I feel safe with Theo. I feel loved.

I know without a shadow of a doubt, that this is where I belong. And that's why I will fight to stay with him until the day I die.

TWENTY-SIX

"It's time," Theo says. Riley and I are in the middle of painting our nails, and I look up at Theo, wondering if he really means it this time. We've spent the better part of three days hanging out on that balcony, waiting for Alexo to show up. Everyone thinks we're locked up in our room, having crazy sex or whatever, and that's the lie we've chosen to stick with. Even Riley is in on it. Alexo and the other guys don't suspect a thing.

I cap my nail polish, frowning because I've only got two nails done and they're not dry yet. I reach for a cotton ball and rub off the wet polish. "How do you know?" I ask.

We can't talk details, but we can talk vaguely, and that's what Theo does now.

"Trust me."

"That's my cue to leave," Riley says, but she stays right where she is because everything we say in my room is a freaking lie. "Have fun, lovebirds."

I sneak out with Theo, hand in hand. We head to the kitchen, where we run into a couple of the guys and Theo tells them we're going on a nature walk. He grabs two bottles of water for show and then we slip into the library.

The hidden door is nearly imperceptible, and if Theo didn't know exactly where to push, I'd never be able to find it. I wonder what other secrets this mansion has as we walk up the narrow staircase to the balcony. Theo and I have had some wonderful chats in our time up here. The balcony door makes a lot of noise when you open it, so there's no chance Alexo would overhear us. We've chosen a place to hide out that's behind a thick wall of ivy. Behind it is a wall and then the sloping of the roof, so we're pretty sure Alexo would never bother to come this way.

We go there now, and I sit on the concrete bench that's been long forgotten behind the overgrown ivy and flowers. Theo sits next to me.

"So what makes you think this won't be another wasted day?" I ask as I brush his hair out of his eyes.

"Alexo got a call while we were having a business meeting just now. He stepped out of the room to answer it, and I excused myself saying I had to take a piss. I really just spied on him. He told the caller he'd call back in forty five minutes." Theo looks at his watch. "That's ten minutes from now."

"Sweet." This is the first lead we've got, and it'll be the first time we're not just blindly waiting around up here for something to happen.

He leans in for a kiss and then stops when the balcony door creaks open. My heart leaps with the thrill of finally being able to spy on Alexo's phone call.

Soft footsteps cross the balcony, going straight to the ledge. I lean forward and peek through a small opening in the vines. It's not Alexo.

It's a woman.

Dressed in a sheer flowy sundress, she's tall and beautiful, with black hair cropped short around her heart-shaped face. It spikes out in all directions, but somehow it looks amazing. Her lips are pink, her skin pale. She wears several rings and has black polish on her nails as she taps them across the top of the balcony railing. I can only see her profile from here, but I can tell from the side of her face that she's one of the most beautiful women I've ever seen.

She stands there, silent and contemplative. I tear my eyes away from her and look at Theo. His eyes are wide. I want to ask him if he knows who she is, but I don't dare to speak right now. I don't even want to breathe for fear of making a sound and alerting her to our presence.

Minutes pass and the door creaks open again. I peer through the vines, my heart thumping hard as I watch Alexo step onto the balcony, his eyes on his phone.

"Alexo." The woman's voice is soft, but fierce.

He shrivels when he sees her, and nearly drops his phone. "Lady Em!" He clears his throat. "To what do I owe the pleasure of a personal visit?"

I look at Theo, mouthing the words *Lady Em?*

He shrugs and turns back to the scene in front of us.

"Your own idiocy is the reason I am here, Alexo." Lady Em turns sharply around to face him. That's when I see the necklace splayed across her chest and my heart catches in my throat. The ornate collar-style piece of jewelry is exquisite, a silver design that spreads across her entire chest. And it has about a dozen immortality stones in it.

Theo draws in a sharp breath. He sees it too.

Alexo clears his throat and takes a step backward. "Lady Em, as I said on the phone, things are perfectly in order."

"In order?" she says, her voice higher this time. "You lost a lifeblood today because she didn't follow your rules. It is not hard to enforce one single rule onto children you've bribed with cash and luxury!"

"Lady Em, all I can do is tell them not to remove the bracelet. I can't follow them everywhere to make sure they comply."

"You *scare* them into complying!" She puts a finger on his chest. "You tell them you will end their lives if they even *try* to go against the rules, do you understand me?"

"I don't feel that would be the best course of action, Lady Em. I create a comradery with our lifebloods. I take lonely girls and make them feel like they're part of a family. They don't take off the bracelet because they want to preserve their place in the family."

"And that works out so well, does it? We lost a lifeblood today, Alexo." Lady Em sighs and then steps closer to him. "You better hope she didn't talk to the other girls. You better pray she didn't post something on the internet!"

"We are investigating that right now," he says calmly. "Her computer history was wiped, but we've got the best IT guys trying to recover anything they can."

"Of course it was wiped," she says with another sigh. "If she posted about the bracelet, or told any outsiders about it, this could be the end of us, Alexo! We would be found out. You know Dover clan has people scouting for us. They've no doubt got a trace on the internet as well. You talked me into this—this *humane*—treatment of lifebloods, but I'm about two seconds away from throwing them all in a fucking dungeon!"

Alexo sighs, grabbing the bridge of his nose. "Lady Em, we know that doesn't work. We've tried it. They just rip off the bracelets and let themselves die. The lifebloods need a reason to wear it. They need to be bribed and they need to stay healthy and happy or else their use to us wanes within a couple of months. This is the only option."

"We could take away access to the outside world," she says. "No cell phones, no internet."

"How long will that work?" Alexo counters. "Young people can't live without internet these days. They'll leave."

Lady Em inhales sharply, then turns back to look over the edge of the balcony. "I did not risk everything in Dover to create a clan that would not hold up even a few decades," she says, sounding almost somber now. "I will not fail, Alexo."

"You won't fail, my lady. You have my word."

"What have you done to fix this?" she says without looking at him.

"We're being careful. We're vetting the other girls, making sure Jayla didn't tell any of them about her suspicions."

"And?"

"Her best friend is clean. I think she knew better than to put her at risk like that, especially since she thought we were demons. But we have one girl who needs further investigations. Riley, the spunky one I told you about."

My skin turns cold. Why the hell would Riley be under suspicion? I'm the one sneaking around with Theo. I'm the one hooking up with a member of the freaking clan.

"What does she know?" Lady Em says, turning back to face Alexo. Her sheer gown flows in the gentle breeze. With her smoky eyeshadow and bright blue eyes, she looks like she should be on the cover of a fashion magazine.

"She is the only girl who didn't show any emotion when we announced that Jayla had died accidentally," Alexo says. "I found it unsettling, but as Kyle has mentioned, Riley wasn't friends with the girl. Maybe she just doesn't care." Alexo adjusts the collar of his jacket. "We are looking into her."

"No," Lady Em says simply. "There's no reason to delay anything. Take care of her now."

My breath catches in my throat. Beside me, Theo stiffens.

"She's a healthy lifeblood," Alexo objects. "We still haven't replaced Jayla, and removing another one would mean twice as much work. Russell is drinking the last of our stores to keep himself alive until he finds a replacement lifeblood."

"I don't care!" she hisses. "You have failed at your job and you will work extra hard to fix it. Go get the girl and end her."

"Of course," Alexo says, dipping his head toward her. He turns to leave, and I lose my composure.

I stand and throw myself over Theo, pushing off the vine wall until I'm out in the open. They don't see me at first. Alexo's hand takes the door handle and he pulls, but I won't let him leave this balcony. He won't kill my best friend.

He won't even get close to her.

Theo grabs for me but I'm too quick. I see red, and black, and the blue of that immortality stone. I know we're supposed to stay hidden, but I am too pissed off to care about that right now. This bastard will not take another life today.

"Over my dead fucking body!" I scream, launching myself at Alexo. "You will not touch my best friend!"

TWENTY-SEVEN

Everything goes black. I haven't passed out though—Theo has leaped in front of me. His black shirt blocks my vision and I try shoving him out of the way, but he's too strong. In just a few seconds, he's blocked me and pressed me against the wall, his arms outstretched to keep me from getting away. I pound on his chest, but he's not moving.

"Alexo," Lady Em says sweetly. I peer at her from around Theo's tightened bicep. "Do you understand why I questioned your ability to run this clan? Two members have been spying on us this entire time, and you had no idea."

Alexo's jaw tightens and he stares at Theo with a look that says he's truly betrayed right now. With all his scheming and spying, Alexo had no idea Theo wasn't loyal to him. "Please tell me this is your secret hookup location."

Theo hesitates. I can tell he's thinking about taking the easy way out, lie and say we were just up here making out. But even if that were true, it doesn't matter. I clearly heard everything they said. I've put a big red target on my chest by revealing that I'm here.

"Who is she?" Theo asks. "You have kept very important information away from me."

"That doesn't matter—" Alexo begins, but Theo cuts him off.

"I am a member of this clan now. You have not revealed this woman's existence to me, and that is a grievous mistake. You have betrayed the clan, Alexo."

"Don't talk to me about betrayal," Alexo hisses.

Lady Em steps forward. "So this is the Embrook refugee," she says, her eyes taking in Theo from head to toe. She gets so close I can smell her perfume, floral with a hint of cinnamon. The look in her eyes tells me she's not immune to Theo's good looks.

It makes my blood boil more than it already is.

"You speak of betrayal," she says to Theo. She really is stunningly beautiful which makes it even easier to hate her. Her crystal blue eyes focus on my boyfriend, who stands rigid, ready to fight. She tips her head to the side, then her lips stretch into a thin smile. "You speak of betrayal and yet I can see it in your eyes. You are not loyal to my clan."

"Who the hell are you?" he says through clenched teeth.

She stares at him for three seconds and then says. "I am your queen. I could have made your life wonderful," she says, running her hand down his cheek. It takes everything I have not to slap the bitch's hand away from my boyfriend. Her expression hardens. "But you cannot be trusted."

She whirls around, her piercing stare turning to Alexo. "You are more worthless than I even imagined," she hisses. Alexo visibly shrinks back, the pain of her insult slicing through him.

"He was vetted," Alexo says, trying to stick up for himself. "He passed every test. He has been a valuable asset to the clan."

"And yet you don't see the very truth that is in his eyes," she says, throwing a slender finger toward Theo. "This man is a traitor."

"There is no evidence—" Alexo says, his voice sounding more pleading with every second. For all his might and power, he's like a coward when faced with Lady Em.

"The evidence is right there!" Her voice seems to echo off the walls. Birds in a nearby tree scatter into the air, flying away from this vicious woman. "You do not see because you don't have the sight, Alexo."

He stutters out an objection. Lady Em swings her hand in his direction and he flies backward, his body landing with a crack against the balcony railing. My eyes widen. She was too far away to physically hit him, yet he reacted as if she did. There's no way...she can't be that strong.

It doesn't work like that.

Lady Em turns to Theo. "Move."

He stays where he is, shielding my body with his own. "Fuck. Off."

She quirks an eyebrow and then flicks her hand through the air. Theo's body launches to the left. He stumbles, but doesn't fall. Anger fills his gaze and he tries to come back to me, to put himself between us, but she holds out her hand, and although it is dainty and thin, he can't move. He is frozen on his feet. Lady Em stands between us. She looks at me and smiles. Her eyes trail down to the bracelet on my wrist.

"You're a lifeblood," she says evenly. "Pretty, no doubt. But how did you manage to make an immortal fall for you?" She casts a glance back toward her victim, my boyfriend, who she's still holding paralyzed with her hand. "Especially one so handsome as this one?"

I don't reply. I stand straight, and try to be strong.

Her eyebrow quirks. "You knew he was immortal." It's not a question, so I don't bother answering it. She steps closer to me, so close I can see the sparkles in each of the twelve immortality stones on her necklace. "What makes you so special?" she wonders aloud. "There is something in you." She glances back toward Theo and says, "You were absolutely right to choose her. She's special."

Theo drags in a ragged breath, which seems to surprise Lady Em. "What are you?" he says. It sounds like his vocal cords are about to burst, but he forces the words out. "Who are you?"

Lady Em gives him a scrutinizing glare. "I would love to answer that question if you weren't a filthy spy."

She flicks her other hand and Alexo is pulled from the floor. With another twist of her wrist, he is upright, standing on his feet again. He seems dazed for a few seconds but then fear flashes across his features. "I trust you with everything," she tells him, "And I come here and find you have an Embrook spy living in my mansion. Do you want to die now, or after I've finished killing these two?"

"My lady," Alexo says, his eyes filling with tears. "My lady, I never meant to harm you. I will make this right."

"No, *I* will make this right." She uses her powers to slam him against the wall again. He droops to the floor, his eyes fluttering open and closed. Satisfied with her treatment of her former clan leader, she looks back at me and then turns to Theo.

"What was your name? Theo?"

He doesn't say anything. She lowers her hand and his body softens as he regains control of it. He looks at me and there's a pain in his eyes that I've never seen before. *I feel it too*, I want to tell him. We are totally screwed. Instead, I stand strong for him. I won't show weakness. I won't make him feel guilty for my own fate.

"Theo," Lady Em says again. "As in Theodore Price."

He flinches. Lady Em laughs softly. "It *is* you. What a pleasure," she says, a coy smile playing on her lips. "You're even more handsome than the rumors say."

"Leave," Theo says, his voice hoarse. "Go now, or I'll kill you."

"Oh I'd *love* to see you try," she purrs. "You could wrap those hands around my neck anytime." She winks at him, then runs her fingers across her chest, where the massive necklace stretches from shoulder to shoulder. "Powerful as you are, Theodore Price, you only have one stone. I have a dozen. Now here's what we're going to do. You will bring me to the leader of the Embrook clan and I will spare your life. Do it without any attitude or objections, and I'll spare your girlfriend's life as well."

Theo doesn't hesitate to say, "No."

"No?" Lady Em pouts. "Aw, that's not the answer I want, sweetheart. Do my powers betray me, or do you actually love this girl? You might want to think twice about having to watch her die."

"You will not hurt her," Theo says. His hand clenches into a fist at his side and he glances at me for just a second. "You will leave, now."

"Why would I do that?" She lifts her chin a little bit and seems genuinely curious about how Theo can be so bold in the face of such a strong opponent. I want to think that he can move mountains and save us from any situation, but she was right. He has only one stone, and apparently, all of hers are strong enough to give her telekinetic powers.

Theo's stern expression morphs into a cocky smile. "You will leave now. Because if not, I will recite the *keímeno*."

Lady Em's eyes flash with fear. "There is not a soul on this planet who knows the *keímeno*."

Theo shrugs one shoulder. "Probably because I lost my soul when I became immortal."

A muscle in her jaw twitches. "You're lying."

"I will enjoy seeing the look in your eyes when I kill you with the most powerful immortality spell there is." He cracks his knuckles like he's getting ready to do it. I have no idea what he's talking about, but it seems to scare Lady Em enough to take a step backward. She's considering it.

Hope springs to my chest, filling my blood with warmth again. For the first time since I stepped out from behind the vines, there's hope that we won't die right here on the balcony. Theo has an ace up his sleeve.

This bitch is about to get what's coming to her.

"I believe you," she says after a long moment. She lifts her hand and flicks her wrist. "So you die first."

I expect Theo to fly backwards again, but he doesn't. Instead, his shirt rips open. The immortality stone on his chest flies through the air, ripping off his neck and landing straight into her hand.

Theo's shocked expression meets mine and then his skin turns blue and he crumples to the floor.

TWENTY-EIGHT

It's worse this time. When Theo collapsed in the parking lot that day his lifeblood died, he'd had a few minutes of consciousness. Now, as I drop to my knees in front of him, he goes pale, his breathing slows to a faint gasp every few seconds.

The sun is beginning to set now, the orange rays of light casting an eerie glow on this rooftop balcony. Just a few feet away from us, a gentle breeze ruffles the pine tree needles. It is a warm summer afternoon and below us, the whole house is going about their business, oblivious to the hell that's raging on this balcony.

The sound of laughter comes from a few feet away. Alexo is back on his feet, gripping his stomach as though this is the funniest thing he's ever seen. He might be a little delirious, but I'm not taking that as an excuse to laugh about Theo's quickly approaching death.

Anger like I've never felt before claws through my subconscious, embedding itself into every fiber of my being.

I hear a growl of rage and realize it's mine as I launch myself at Alexo, ready to punch the stupid smile right off his ancient face.

Then I get a better idea.

He's not wearing a tie with his suit today, and the top two buttons of his shirt are undone. His hair is a little messy too, worse now that Lady Em has thrown him around, but I remember it was also askew when he first walked out here, planning to make a phone call. Alexo made himself sexier for his call with Lady Em.

What a pathetic asshole.

Through the opening in the top of his shirt, I see a thick silver chain.

Behind me, Theo gasps for air. Blood pours out of his mouth, staining the painted concrete patio.

I don't have time to think about the consequences. I reach forward and yank the necklace right off his neck. Alexo snarls and reaches for me, but I step back and kick him, hard, right in the abdomen. He stumbles backward, his skin darkening as the life quickly drains from him. He's much older than Theo, because it happens even quicker. Theo once told me that the older the immortal, the quicker they die without a stone. I watch Alexo's eyes widen, then shrivel as he steps backward, thrusted by my kick. He crashes into the banister, then topples over it.

Alexo's immortality stone glows bright blue, warming my hand. I get an instant nausea feeling when I touch it. I run the short distance to my love and then I press it to his chest, putting the stone right over the blue marking where his last one was.

Theo's body convulses to life. He gasps for breath and his skin returns to its normal tanned shade. I hook the necklace around his neck so it won't fall off, and then I press a quick kiss to Theo's cheek. I need him with me. I can't fight these battles without him by my side.

"*Very* well done," Lady Em says. She claps her hands together, her eyes sparkling with joy. "You just killed a man to save your own."

My stomach rolls over. She's right. I'm a killer.

"*Amésos*," Theo utters as he pushes himself up to standing.

Lady Em's eyes narrow. With a flick of her wrist, I'm pulled right off my feet. My body feels like it's being sucked into a vacuum, as I hurl through the air until I come to a sudden and painful stop just in front of Lady Em. She flattens her palm against my back. I am still, unmoving. My nerves stand on end and every inch of me hurts like I've suffered a bad sunburn. I don't even try to move.

"Utter another word and I kill her," she says.

Theo closes his eyes. When he opens them, all the light has gone out. His beautiful amber eyes are now as black as the night sky. "Release her and I'll bring you to Embrook," he says, his voice a low growl.

"You want more than that," she says. "I can see it in your eyes."

He nods once. "Release her and safely remove her bracelet. I want her to stop being a lifeblood. Do this, and I'll bring you anyone you want."

Beside me, Lady Em seems amused. "That would be impossible."

Theo's jaw clenches. "If anyone can make her stop being a lifeblood, it'll be you. I've never seen power like yours."

She tisks. "That is true. I am more powerful than most immortals because I follow my own rules. I have cast off the orders of the clans and I have forged my own path. Soon, I will take over every clan and all of these men shall bow to *me*."

"So do it," Theo says. "Give me Cara back and remove her bracelet and I'll bring you to the Embrook leader."

My body aches and my eyes fill with tears. I want to be free, more than anything. But I can't let him compromise his clan now that I know the leader of this one is pure evil. I gasp for air, try to tell him to stop.

He doesn't even look at me. "Release her," he says again.

"You two must really love each other," Lady Em says as her beautiful pink lips dip into a pout. "You're willing to give up anything for this girl, and she's already given up everything for you."

"Do we have a deal?" Theo asks.

"We do not, Theodore Price."

It hurts to breathe, but my breath catches in my throat anyway. This doesn't make any sense. Theo is offering to give her what she wants. Why won't she take it?

Lady Em sighs. "When your precious girlfriend heroically killed my assistant to save your life, she solidified her own death. I *could* remove her bracelet, but I won't."

Theo's fists tighten as he tries to maintain control. "Why not?"

"Because," she purrs. "If I remove her bracelet, her lifeblood will die." Lady Em strokes my cheek with her free hand and I try to pull away, to no avail. My body hurts too much to move. She peers at me, her flawless skin radiant in the sunset. "This angel was Alexo's lifeblood. And now she's yours."

I can hear my own heartbeat in the silence that follows. Theo's face falls and he walks over to me, placing a hand on my cheek as tears fill his eyes.

Lady Em keeps her hand on my back, refusing to release me from her painful hold. "Your love is true, and I very much adore that, sweet child," she says to me. "When you killed Alexo, your bracelet was unlocked. You could have taken it off and lived a nice long life. But now you belong to Theodore. If I save you, he will die, and—" She exhales and shrugs. "I can't lose him. He is valuable to immortals everywhere."

"I will not help you if you don't save her," Theo says through clenched teeth. "I will never betray my clan."

Lady Em chuckles. "Sure you will. Eventually. I don't know about this doll," she says, smacking my cheek, "But you will live forever. And forever is a long time to deny my request."

She presses her hand to Theo's chest, her palm covering the new immortality stone. Theo's eyes go bloodshot and he sways on his feet. "Are you going to cooperate, sweet child?" she asks me.

I try to nod but I don't think it works very well. "I like you," she says, giving me a flirty smile. "And now that you're Theo's lifeblood, I think it's best that you both come with me."

Her hand leaves my back and the pain instantly disappears. It's replaced with a warm, woozy feeling as if I've suddenly drank too much alcohol. She nudges me in the arm. "Let's go."

I walk. I don't know why I listen to her and somewhere in the back of my mind I feel like I should be defiant, try to break free or leave. But I'm warm and fuzzy and my thoughts are mush. She's done something to my mind, but at least this time I feel floaty and happy instead of drenched in pain.

She leads both of us into the stairwell and then through another hidden door. We enter a concrete tunnel that smells like damp earth and we walk for what feels like miles. Eventually another door opens. I am tired now, woozy. Like I've stayed up for twenty four hours straight and all I'd like to do is sleep.

We are outside.

There's a van. It's shiny black. Windowless.

The door slides open and there's a man inside. He reaches for my hand and pulls me into the empty back area. Theo is beside me. I reach for him, and I think I hold his hand, but maybe it's just a dream.

The floor of the van rumbles and vibrates as we drive over a rocky terrain. Bluesy jazz music plays from somewhere far away.

I open my eyes and Theo is there. I can't really remember who he is, but I know that he makes me happy. I lean over and rest my head on his chest.

And I fall asleep.

THE IMMORTAL BOND

BOOK THREE

Copyright © 2017 Amy Sparling

All rights reserved.

First Edition April 11, 2017

Cover image from bookcoverscre8tive.com

Typography from FontSquirrel.com

All rights reserved. No part of this book may be reproduced in any form or by any electronic or mechanical means, including information storage and retrieval systems -except in the case of brief quotations embodied in critical articles or reviews-without permission in writing from the author at admin@amysparling.com.

This book is a work of fiction. The characters, events, and places portrayed in this book are products of the author's imagination and are either fictitious or are used fictitiously. Any similarity to real persons, living or dead, is purely coincidental and not intended by the author.

❦ Created with Vellum

ONE

I am awake.

I don't know when it happened, when I fell asleep or how I woke up just now, but I am here, covered in a thick blanket of foggy memories. Curious, I lie here with my eyes closed, feeling sleepier than I've ever felt. It's like an avalanche of melatonin fell on top of me and buried me into a coma-like sleep from which I never want to wake up. My joints ache, begging me to stay still. My head hurts a little, and my eyes are heavy with exhaustion.

But fear tickles at my insides until my heartbeat quickens. I remember now. A beautiful woman with wild short black hair and smoky eyeshadow, the bluest eyes I've ever seen. She is behind this.

I killed Alexo.

I tried to save Riley.

Did I save Riley?

What happened after? Theo. I saved Theo.

At least I think I did.

I squeeze my eyes shut and focus on keeping my breathing steady because you never know who might be watching you, waiting for you to wake up. Where am I? My face itches a little, and the air smells like ... new carpet?

Yes. I'm lying on the floor. There's a blanket on top of me, and the scent of new house in the air. Like that time Riley and I volunteered for Habitat for Humanity one weekend because Riley was crushing hard on this guy, Jack, who worked there. We painted bedrooms in the newly constructed houses. They had this new smell to them, like fresh lumber and drywall and paint. It smelled like the possibility of starting over, the birth of a new house untainted by drama or pain or poverty. It smelled like hope in there.

Yet somehow, the same smell here sends a shiver down my spine. This is not my bedroom. I've been taken against my will and put somewhere I don't want to be.

Slowly, my eyes crack open, trying to discern more details of my whereabouts without being noticed.

I'm in a room. It's small, like Uncle Will's bedroom at his old house. Square, with beige carpet and tan walls and white crown molding around the ceiling. A square table across the room has things on top of it. Bottles of water, snack foods. I can't see it all, but I can tell a little. There's not any more furniture in here, but there is a door in the corner. A shadow moves near my feet and I'm too scared to look down, so I close my eyes again, hoping for a few more minutes of solitude while I figure out what the hell is going on.

"Cara?"

I don't realize I'm on the verge of a panic attack, until hearing Theo's voice takes it all away and replaces the panic with joy, relief of unbelievable proportions.

I sit up on my elbow. "Theo?"

He closes the book he'd been reading, *Hideaway* by Dean Koontz, and puts a hand on my calf. With my eyes fully open, I take in the room again. I'm lying on the new carpet, my back pressed against the wall behind me. My feet are in Theo's lap, his back against the wall, his book in one hand.

I try to sit up, but dizziness washes over me, slowing my movements to a snail-like pace. "Take your time," Theo says. "You've been drugged."

I gasp, eyes wide. I am not a fan of drugs, especially if they're given to me against my will. "What kind of drug?"

Theo shrugs. "We were put to sleep. I don't think it was anything harmful, love. I've been checking on you and you seem fine."

"How long have you been awake?"

"A few hours." He looks at the book, where his thumb is holding his place about halfway through it. "However long it takes to read this much." He chuckles, the sound echoing off the walls of this small room. "This book is fucked up."

"Why did you wake up before me?" I ask, followed by, "And where are we?"

"Immortals heal faster, so I guess my body metabolized the sleeping drugs faster. As for where we are..." He sighs and glances around the windowless room. "No clue. Underground, probably."

He must see the fear in my eyes because he leans over and places a hand on my cheek. His amber eyes crinkle in the corners. "Cara, it'll be okay."

"Lady Em did this," I say, as that bitch's name comes back to me. Every moment I'm awake, I start to feel clarity again. The sleeping drug is wearing off and I'm remembering everything. Remembering *her*.

"What the hell did she do to us?"

I stand up, holding onto the wall for support. I expect Theo to jump up and try to keep me from moving, but he doesn't. He's calm, like always. I wonder if he's accepted the fact that we're prisoners, or if this is how he deals with knowing we're completely screwed—stoic calmness.

I walk across the room, toward the table. It's set up like some complimentary breakfast at a three star hotel. There's a coffee maker, paper cups and cream and sugar. Pastries, fruits, bags of chips and granola bars. Bottled drinks and Moon Pies.

I rush for the door in the corner and pull it open.

It's a small bathroom.

I turn back around to Theo, who is still sitting on the floor, but he's watching me with an expression I can't quite place. "Where'd you get the book?"

"It was on the table." He glances at the cover and curls his lip. "Not exactly my preferred genre."

"How do we get out of here?"

He motions behind him. It's hard to tell at first glance, but the solid tan wall has a rectangular line going through it, the outline of a door. There's no handle, no lock. No hinges. Just the faintest outline hinting that there might be something beyond the wall.

"It can only be opened from the outside," he says, as if reading my mind.

I say what I've been fearing since the moment I woke up. "So this is a fancy jail cell?"

He nods once.

"Lady Em is holding us hostage?"

"Looks like it."

I march across the room and put my hands on my hips. "Theo, what the hell is wrong with you?" Before, I'd kept my voice low, hoping that whoever is on the other side of these walls won't know I'm awake yet. Now, I'm yelling, unable to control it. "You're just sitting there! This is not okay! Stand the fuck up and help me find a way out of here!"

His eyes close, his lips forming a slight frown. When they open again, he's staring at the wall behind me. "Do you think I haven't already tried that, Cara?" His voice is gravely calm, and it sends chills down my spine. "I've checked every wall, every corner. There's concrete behind this new drywall. Concrete below the carpet. Concrete in the ceiling. The door is at least a foot thick and it's locked electronically from the outside. If Lady Em had made it easy to escape, I would have already done it."

I sink to the floor next to him, feeling like shit for having yelled at him just now. Of course Theo would try to get us out. Why did I doubt him?

My mind scrambles for a solution, no matter how impossible it might seem. "Theo, you're crazy strong. Why don't we just hurl that table at the door or something? See if we can't break out of here?" I tap the wall behind his head. "You said this is drywall. Let's rip it all off and see if there's a way to get out somewhere. This place smells like it was just remodeled, so maybe there's another door hidden somewhere."

"Yeah, that would probably work," Theo says. The way he says it though doesn't make sense. This is a good thing, yet he's acting like it's a bad idea.

"Well?" I grab his shoulders and put on a smile. "Let's get to work."

He takes my hands and pulls them down, putting them back in my lap. "I said brute force *would* probably work, love. This isn't a dungeon, it's just a room, probably a basement. But we can't attempt that."

I fold my arms over my chest. "Why not?"

He's silent for a long moment. Then he reaches for my hand, running his thumb over my palm. "Using that much energy would drain my lifeblood," he says, his voice solemn. Then he meets my eyes. "I can't do that to you."

TWO

I GUESS ALL OF MY MEMORIES HAVEN'T COME BACK YET, BECAUSE THEO'S words hit me hard. Alexo, Lady Em, being held prisoner. None of that matters as much as the bitter truth that I am now Theo's lifeblood. When Lady Em used her freaky telekinetic powers to rip Theo's necklace right off his neck, she was trying to kill him. Without the immortality stone the necklace contained, he would die quickly. I almost watched it happen just a few weeks before when his lifeblood died, leaving his stone useless.

So when she did that, I snapped. I did the only thing I could think of—kill Alexo and give his stone to Theo. What I didn't know was that the immortality stone on my bracelet was the matching stone to Alexo's. I was his lifeblood. The moment I ripped his necklace off and he began to die, I was free. I could have taken off my bracelet and turned back into a regular person, one who's not tied to a secret immortal world, my life slowly wasting away to give power to another.

But I didn't know that.

I thought only for Theo's sake, and I pressed Alexo's necklace to Theo's chest. I was once again connected via immortality stones, but this time, I was keeping him alive. The man I love.

Now, in the moments that follow, I relive the entire event over and over in my head. Lady Em's seemingly magical powers that allowed her to throw people across the room with just her hand. Alexo's cowardice when talking to her. The way his eyes looked when I stole his necklace and kicked him off the balcony.

I remember it all.

Theo sits against the wall, his head tipped back while he stares at the ceiling. I take his hand. "I don't regret it," I say. "Not a single bit of it."

"You should." His voice is cold. He turns to me, his eyes bloodshot. "I don't deserve to be alive at the cost of your life."

"Honey, it's okay." I pull his hand into my lap, hugging it to my chest. "We were always going to find a way to safely remove my bracelet. Now we just have to safely escape this place first." I put on a smile even though I've never been more doubtful or terrified in my life. "We'll be okay. You won't suck out too much life from me before we find a way to get this bracelet off."

"I don't deserve to be alive," he says in a low growl. "If I'm dead, you'll be free."

There's this resolute promise in his voice and it shakes me to the core. I grab his chin and make him look at me. "Theo, don't you dare say that. You're not making yourself die just to save me, okay? That's stupid."

"It's not stupid to save the one you love."

"Yes, it is," I say, knowing that if the tables were turned, I'd happily die for Theo. "You can't give up now. I have plenty of life left in me, and we'll find a way out of this."

He gives me this look like he doesn't believe me. And I guess I don't believe myself either. The truth is, this entire situation is so terrifying I don't know how to function, so I'm choosing to be positive. Otherwise, I might fall apart. It was bad enough knowing I was someone's lifeblood. But now I'm Theo's. Now it's personal. He can't live without a lifeblood and I can't live for long as one. This whole thing is screwed.

Theo leans forward and kisses me, his lips soft on mine. It's not romantic or steamy, more like a yearning for something to hold onto.

"You are so beautiful," he says, his voice softer now. He leans back against the wall and gazes up at the ceiling. "This world is made better with you in it. The same cannot be said for me."

"Shut up, Theo." I let out an exaggerated sigh. "I love you, but I'm not even going to entertain the idea of you dying right now, okay?"

His lips quirk and I am fully aware I just said I love him out loud. As my ears turn red, I keep talking. "Since we're stuck here for the time being, we should be productive."

"Sexually productive?" he says with a wiggle of his brow.

I punch him in the arm. "No way in hell. What if she walked in on us?"

Theo cracks a smile, and it takes away some of the chaos in my mind. He grabs my thigh and tugs me over a few inches until I'm sitting next to him. "This place could use a couch."

"And an exit," I say.

He laughs.

Now that the mood is a little lighter, I feel like chatting. Sitting here bored will only freak me out more than I am. I am worried about Riley. Worried about the other girls at the mansion. I'm worried about *me* and Lady Em and Theo's future. *My* future.

Hell, I am worried about everything.

"So you really don't know Lady Em?" I ask.

Theo picks up the paperback book and thumbs through the pages. The smell of old pages fills the air. "Nope. My Embrook clan was right; Alexo wasn't in charge of the Rosewater clan. But I never got to tell them that."

"You'll have a chance," I say, nudging him with my elbow. "We will get out of here."

Theo goes silent again. I keep talking. "How do you think that bitch got her powers?"

"I've thought about that all morning," he says, turning to me. He plants a kiss on my cheek before talking again. "One stone gives you immortality. Who knows what *several* stones do. I've never heard of anyone trying something like that. The stones are rare. You can't exactly make your own."

"I wonder what all she can do," I say, more to myself as I recall how she moved us around with just a flick of her hand. "Can she fly? Levitate? Control people with her mind?"

"God, I hope not," Theo says.

We eat a random assortment of food from the cart, and Theo and I take turns making up stupid games to play to pass the time. He reads me some of the book, but it's about a kid who kills his best friend by shoving him off a roller coaster, and I lose interest quickly, although I could listen to Theo talk forever. His voice is like honey, and the way his eyes peek up at me every few pages is really cute. Still, that book is gross.

I don't know how many hours have passed before I start getting sleepy. With only the recessed lighting in the ceiling, I have no idea what time it is. If the sun is up or down or somewhere in between. The bathroom has new toothbrushes and toothpaste, so I guess we're doing all right as far as being prisoners goes.

I sit back against the wall and snuggle the blanket into a ball in my lap.

Theo returns from brushing his teeth and sits next to me. "Come here," he says, holding out his arms. "I miss you."

I crawl into his lap, leaning against his chest while my legs hang off the side of his thighs. Theo's arms wrap around me, his head resting on my shoulder.

"Am I squishing you?" I ask.

"Not at all," he says, sighing softly as he holds me tightly. "Cara, at some point they will open this door. Whatever I say or do, I want you to just go with it, okay? Even if it's some off-the-wall crazy shit. Just go with it."

I nod. "What kind of crazy shit are you planning?"

Theo sighs. "I have no idea. Figured I'd make it up as I go along. I just need to know you'll back me up. No matter what I say, don't act surprised by it. Act like it's normal."

"I can do that," I say. My heart beats a little easier now that I'm so close to Theo. I can feel his own heart beating through his chest. Steady, soothing. We're both getting tired and it's been a very long day. But I still don't want to stop talking, if only to keep the silence away.

"So what was that weird spell you started reciting when we were in front of Lady Em?"

Theo laughs. A *real* laugh, which shakes me since I'm sitting on him. "It was total bullshit. The Embrook clan invented it a couple centuries ago. They claimed they'd found ancient documents that contain a ...*spell*... to immediately eradicate the immortal properties in the stone of the person you cast it on."

My mouth falls open. "What?"

Theo shrugs. "Immortality stones are science. They were created by an alchemist using scientific shit that's well beyond my mental capacity, but there's one thing they're not, and that's magic. For every action, there's a reaction. The stones are give and take. You can't just verbally say something and have it work."

"So it's a joke?"

"It's a scare tactic."

"Wow," I breathe.

"Only the members of Embrook know the truth about this made up spell. I forgot other immortals believe it. Apparently, even with her power, she's still afraid of a few Greek words."

"I wonder how she got that name," I say, pulling the blanket over both of us. "Is she royalty?"

"I've never heard of her." Theo kisses the top of my head.

"She seemed to know who you are," I say through a yawn.

"Everyone knows me," he says softly.

My eyes are heavy with sleep, my head resting softly on his chest, but I look up at him anyway. "Why's that?"

Theo smirks. "Because I'm a fucking badass."

"A badass who's currently trapped with no way out," I say, poking him in the chest.

He kisses my hair and tightens his hold around my waist. "A badass who will get us out of here. I promise you that, love."

THREE

For the first time in three days, I wake up to darkness. Total, pitch black, darkness. I blink a few times, push up on the carpeted floor and rub my eyes. There's no light switch in this prison room, and the lights never dim when it's dark outside. Is it really dark in here or did I go blind? The darkness swirls around my vision. Frantically, I press my back against the wall and look around. There's not a single shred of light in this room. I bring my hands up to my face, so close they touch my nose. I can't see them.

Am I blind?

How did this happen?

My breath hitches, and thoughts of spending the rest of my short life not being able to see flash across my vision. I savor the memories I have of my life, all of the things I used to see. This is not happening. Leaning to the side, I run my hand along the carpet, feeling for Theo's sleeping body. The last two days I've woken up in this bright room with him lying next to me, his arm draped over my side, his breathing steady and soft and reassuring. But now I feel nothing but the empty floor.

Reaching for my blanket, I pull it up over my knees and pull them to my chest. I drop my forehead to my knees and squeeze my eyes shut, praying that when I open them again, I'll see the room that has become my prison. The painted tan walls, the crisp white molding along the baseboards. The table that's slowly running out of snacks and bottled water. Minutes pass and I get the courage to open my eyes again.

Everything is still dark.

Tears well up and pour down my face. I whisper Theo's name but he doesn't reply.

In the darkness, I can hear the ragged hitches of my breathing, the *thump,*

thump of my heart. I hear my socks sliding across the carpet and the sound my head makes when it rests back against the wall. Being unable to see really does heighten your other senses.

For this reason, I know Theo is gone. The door opened while I was sleeping, and someone took him. Did Lady Em take him? Did she take away my vision, too? Is this a joke to her?

I press my lips together and breathe in slowly from my nose, willing myself to calm down. If Lady Em made me fall asleep, she could probably make me blind as well. I woke up from that, so there's a good chance my vision will come back. I grip the blanket to my chest and hope that my suspicions are right.

I close my eyes for a while, because leaving them open is pointless. The room feels colder now that I can't see anything. Almost breezy, like the air conditioning was left on too long. I wrap the blanket tighter around me and wait. That's all I can do lately—wait.

Only a few minutes have gone by when all of my senses light up like a bonfire. My breath catches in my throat. I hear something.

The overwhelming silence has broken. It's the sound of footsteps, careful and calculating, like someone is sneaking up on me. Weird, we've been in here three days and haven't heard anything from outside this room. I kind of figured it was soundproof.

My teeth dig into my bottom lip as the footsteps grow closer. I breathe very slowly. The footsteps stop when they sound just a few feet away from me. Shoes slide across the floor as the person shifts to face me.

I may be blind, but they can probably see. Do I look like a pathetic loser? All curled up in a blanket, my eyes wide and unfocused, my lip trembling?

I should have stayed on the floor, pretended to be asleep this whole time. Even evil villains have trouble kicking someone when they're down. Now I'm a sitting goose. A target. They can see me but I can't see them.

The footsteps shuffle closer to me, just a few feet away now. Instinct tells me to run, but with no vision, I can't go anywhere. I'd slam myself into a wall and that wouldn't help anything.

I hear the intruder draw in a breath. "It's just me," Theo whispers.

"Holy shit," I cry out as tears spring from my eyes. "Holy. Shit." I gasp for air because it feels like I've spent the last ten minutes holding my breath in fear. "It's you?" I whisper.

"It's me," he whispers back.

"Dammit, Theo." I put a hand to my chest, trying to steady my breathing. "Warn a girl next time."

He chuckles. "Sorry, I thought you were sleeping. I was about to bend down and scoop you up."

"Theo, I'm blind." My voice cracks and tears flow. "I can't see. What is going on?"

"Baby, you're not blind," he says, kneeling down to the floor. His hand reaches out and brushes against my arm as he feels his way up to my cheek. "It's dark as hell in here."

I breathe a sigh of relief. "Are you sure?"

"The power went out. There's a storm outside, and the power was flickering for half an hour." His hand leaves my cheek and then he takes my hands and pulls me up to standing. The world feels different when I can't see what I'm doing. Theo takes my hand and squeezes it. "Guess what doesn't work when the power is out?"

"No..." I say, unable to believe our luck.

"Yes. The door unlocked on its own. I found a way out of here, so let's go."

I don't say another word. I hold onto his hand and follow him as he feels our way to the door that used to be a crack in the wall. We walk through it and into someplace that smells old and is about ten degrees lower than it was in the room. Our shoes echo off the walls, so I think it must be a small hallway or something.

As we walk, a glorious thing happens.

I start to see.

Dim gray light appears ahead of us. It's so far away, but it's there and it's real. As we press on, the light grows bigger, illuminating the path before us. I can see now that we are in a hallway, or maybe more of a tunnel. The walls are made of big slabs of concrete, the mortar between them is all squished out of the sides like it was built a long time ago. The floor slowly angles upward and I realize Theo was right. We were underground. As the tunnel rises up to land, I hear the crash of thunder, see the quick flashes of light from lightning. It's daylight, but the sky is darkened from the storm. The air grows humid and cold, but I press on, walking even though my socks are wet and I forgot my shoes back in the room.

At the end of the tunnel, we reach an iron gate. I wrap my hands around the railing and peer outside. The land is green and stretches on for as far as I can see. In the distance, there's mountains, but it's nothing like I've ever seen in Texas. The storm blurs the landscape, and little drops of water splash on my face. I have this sudden appreciation for the outdoors, and for what it means to be free.

"It's locked," I say, turning to Theo. The look on his face tells me that we didn't come this far only to let a lock hinder us. My heart flushes with gratitude for Theo finding a way out of here. He's a man who keeps his promises, but I won't feel better until we're far away from here.

"I'll break it quickly," he says, grabbing onto the lock from the other side of the gate. "I'll use as little energy as I can."

"Just do it," I say, knowing that any extreme energy he uses is drained from me, his lifeblood. "I'd rather die out there than in here."

Theo's eyebrow quirks, like maybe he wants to say something about that, but then he turns his attention to the lock and twists it so hard the veins on his forearms pop out. I feel a little lightheaded, but I stand tall, not wanting him to see that.

There's a crash of thunder, and then the most glorious sound.

A lock breaking.

Theo shoves it off the gate and then swings it open wide, releasing us into the storm. I'm drenched within seconds, my feet muddy as we run across the little dirt trail that leads away from the tunnel entrance. All around us, the grass is up to our knees. It's hard to see beyond that because the world has been blurred by the torrential downpour. This is the kind of thunderstorm that gets warnings on the news for people to stay indoors and off the roads. It's dangerous out here.

But I don't care about the rain. We are finally free.

FOUR

"I don't think she's there," Theo says, his voice nearly drowned out by the loud thunder above. "The whole place seemed empty."

We've been running for a while, and I'm nearly out of breath. I'm also sick of inhaling rainwater. I turn around, my hand breaking free from Theo's. As much as I want to leave, I'm curious to see where we've been held prisoner. Lady Em's house is a castle.

It's small and made of stone, like a miniature version of the gorgeous castles in Europe. You could probably fit four of them into the clan's mansion in Austin. Speaking of Austin, I have no idea where we are right now, but it doesn't look like Texas.

"Let's hurry," Theo says, reaching for my hand again. "We have to get far away, and fast."

We reach an asphalt road, the kind of country road that probably stretches on for miles. Through the rain, I see nothing but green grass on both sides of the road. Theo goes left. I don't know why he chooses that way, but I jog along beside him, ignoring the ache in my side and the burning of my leg muscles. He's right. We need to get far away from here.

After a short while, the headlights of a truck approach. They slow down as it nears us, and Theo steps protectively in front of me. It's a white Ford that's seen better days. It rolls to a stop and the driver rolls down the passenger window just a crack so the rain won't ruin his truck.

"You two need a ride?" he calls out.

"Please," Theo says. "We can ride in the back so we don't get your truck wet."

The driver, a middle-aged man with red hair and a big, bustling beard, nods once. "Where you going?"

"Anywhere," Theo says.

"You," the guy says, pointing at me. "Come over here for a second."

I look up at Theo and he nods.

I jog over to the driver's window, hoping this guy isn't some kind of pervert. He studies me for a moment before he says, "Are you in trouble?"

Hell yes, I'm in trouble, I think. But he wouldn't know anything about that. He's talking about Theo and me being stranded on the road in the rain, not the immortality thing.

"Our jackass friends sent us on a scavenger hunt," I say, making up the lie as I go along. "We got lost and then it started raining."

He looks at me like he's trying to decide to believe me or not. He leans forward, his voice low. "This man isn't kidnapping you or anything?"

I smile. "No, sir. He's my boyfriend."

"Alright then," he says nodding toward Theo. "You two jump in back. Going anywhere in particular?"

"A gas station," Theo says. "As far away as you're driving."

THE RAIN HAS STOPPED by the time our driver drops us off at a gas station. It's still cloudy and the skies are dark and threatening, but at least it's not drenching us more than we already are. Theo helps me climb out of the back of the truck and he thanks the guy before he drives off. I shake out my hair, but it's no use. I'm soaked from head to toe.

Luckily, this is a nice gas station. It's more like a tourist rest stop than some hole in the wall, because there's two fast food restaurants connected to it and they have a gift shop in front. All of the T-shirts and novelty items say California.

"We are not even close to Texas," I say, looking up at Theo because anywhere else I look has someone staring at us. We probably look like shit, but come on. That's rude to stare.

"Let's get some clothes," he says, eyeing a rack of hot pink T-shirts. He reaches for his back pocket then curses under his breath.

"What is it?" I ask.

He exhales. "I forgot I don't have my wallet. The bitch took it from me."

My heart sinks. Not only are my current clothes soaking wet, they're filthy. I haven't had a shower or clean clothes in four days.

"Then let's just go outside and dry off," I say, curling my lip.

"Excuse me." The voice is scratchy, and it fits perfectly with the wrinkled woman behind the counter. She has tanned skin and plastic curlers in her hair. "You two pick an outfit and some sandals, on the house."

"Wow, really?" I say, feeling hopeful about something for the first time in a long time.

She nods. "You two look like you could use it."

"I appreciate it," Theo says. He chooses a black shirt and black swimsuit shorts that have the smallest possible California logo on them. I get the hot pink shirt because it's cute and a pair of short running shorts that make me yearn for a trip to the beach. The only shoes they have are flip-flops, but that's fine with me. After changing in the bathroom and thanking the woman profusely for the free stuff, Theo and I look halfway decent again. We could pass for a carefree couple going out surfing for the day.

And now that I'm not fearing for my life as much as before, I ask the woman if I can borrow her phone. She hands me a cell phone and then gives Theo some coupons for free food at the McDonald's next door.

I lean against the counter while I dial Riley's number, even though I'd rather have this talk in private, but I don't want this kind stranger to think I'm trying to bail with her phone.

Riley answers after a few rings. "Uh, hello?" she says, her voice curious.

"It's me," I say.

"Oh hey." The music in the background turns down a little. "What's up?"

"It's Cara," I say.

"Yeah, I got that part," she says with a laugh.

I frown. "You haven't seen me in four days and then I call from a new number and you're not freaking out?"

"Well you're with Theo, right?"

"Yes."

"Then you're fine!" She laughs. "Seriously, what's up with you? You sound kind of weird."

I sigh. "Here I am thinking you've been worried sick about me, and you don't even care."

"That's not true, Cara. I love you! But you're with Theo, so I figured you're fine. Like you went off on a ...mission or something. A love mission, I mean."

She's definitely in the mansion because she's talking in code. I put a hand on my hip. "What if I had been kidnapped and tortured and you didn't even care because you assumed I was fine?"

"Did you?" she asks, her voice slightly more serious now.

"Not exactly, but kind of," I say.

"Are you okay now?"

"I will be," I say. From across the gas station, Theo smiles at me while he waits in line at McDonald's.

"Good. Hurry home. I miss you."

"Is anything going on over there?" I ask. "Anything...suspicious?"

"Nah. I mean the girls are sad about Jayla, but everything is normal here."

"Wow." I take a deep breath. "No one's talking about Alexo?"

"I don't think so. Haven't seen him, though. He's probably on a trip."

"Yeah," I say. There's no reason to tell her everything now. I need to get with Theo to figure out what our plan is now that we're free from Lady Em's makeshift prison. "Well I'll see you soon, I hope. Stay safe."

267

"Will do. Love you!" she says all cheery and totally like herself. When she finds out what happened to us, she's going to feel bad about her lack of worrying.

"I love you too," I say, and then I hang up.

When I find Theo, he hands me the bag of food he got. He's talking on a pay phone near the restrooms. I didn't even know pay phones existed anymore. I wait until he finishes his call and then we walk back into the store as if we're normal people without a million secrets to hide.

Theo and I share lunch at a small booth in the eating area. There are kids everywhere, all running around and playing with each other. It's annoying. These kids, with their blissful lives, and these people working menial jobs and doing menial things. They have no idea how lucky they are.

"So what's our plan?" I ask.

"I'm still working on that," he says, reaching for a fry. "Kyle said things are fine there. He seemed to think me and you went off for a lover's vacation without telling anyone."

"Riley thought the same thing," I say, rolling my eyes.

Theo's dark hair falls in his eyes and he jerks his head to knock it back. He really is gorgeous even in situations like this. The black clothes look good on him.

"Some friends we've got."

I shrug. "So the guys don't know about Alexo?"

"Nope." Theo bites a fry.

"So... no one has gone outside and seen him there?"

"How often does anyone walk around that side of the house?" Theo shrugs. "Kyle did say something interesting, but it doesn't have to do with us. He said a member of Embrook called the house. Apparently one of their members was murdered recently and their stone was taken."

"Did you know who it was?" I ask, suddenly not feeling very hungry.

Theo shakes his head. "Kyle didn't know his name. Not that he would care, he's a member of Rosewater. Anyway, that's kind of unusual because murder is rare in the immortal world." Theo's brows pull together and then he looks at me, a small smile tugging at his lips.

"Your hair is cute when it's wavy."

I roll my eyes. "I prefer to straighten it."

"It's cute like that, too." Theo winks at me before going back to eating.

"So what's the plan?" I ask.

"I say we go back to the mansion. Lady Em kept herself a secret from everyone but Alexo. I don't know why she did, but it seems unusual for her to reveal herself now. Let's go back, pack up our stuff, and then get the hell out of there while we think of a way to destroy this bitch."

"Why can't we just run away?" I ask. "Grab Riley and just get the hell out?"

"Riley can't leave," Theo says. "We don't know who her lifeblood is, and she's bound by contract to stay at the mansion. Technically, you are too, but since Alexo is gone, the guys may not care. But whoever Riley is paired with will definitely want her around. He'd search for her if she left."

"Did you really not know whose necklace matched up with my bracelet?" I ask.

"I didn't know," Theo says. "I get my lifebloods from outside sources, so I wasn't privy to that information."

I nod and then think of a million other questions I'd like to have answered, though some of them might not have answers. "Theo...Why did she keep us there? What was the point? She didn't even talk to us."

"I have no idea, love. Immortals aren't in a hurry all the time like normal humans are. We live forever—we have time."

I take a sip of my drink. "It seems kind of odd that we broke out so easily...I keep thinking it was a trick or something. Or maybe I'm still asleep and dreaming this whole thing. I mean, when a crazy immortal chick kidnaps you, you probably can't break free the moment the power goes out."

Theo is quiet for a few moments. "I think it was fate giving us a bit of good luck. If my instincts are right, we have a hell of a lot more righting to do before we're free."

His words sting. I know he's right, but I've been refusing to believe it. Not only am I slowly dying from this bracelet, but now an immortal woman with powers is after us.

We eat a while in silence before I think of another question. "So how do we get home?"

"We don't have any money. So we'll have to hitchhike."

"All the way to Texas?" I groan. "This will suck."

"I'll keep you safe," he says, winking at me through his cocky smirk.

"I miss flying on a private jet," I say.

He laughs. Someone walks up to our table. I think he's going pass right on by, so I don't bother looking up at him. But then he stops.

"Theo?" he says curiously. "Is that you?"

FIVE

The man in front of us looks out of place in a gas station. He's wearing black pants and a white dress shirt, the sleeves rolled up neatly with a crease. His entire outfit is creased, crisp and seemingly impervious to wrinkles. He has a black tie but no sport coat. His watch is the size of my head and probably costs more than anything in this building. He has golden hair that's longer on top and shorter in the back. It's gelled, slicked over to the side. His beard is trimmed neatly, his smile crooked. A shiny gold ring sits on his left pinky and I wonder if he drinks tea with it sticking out. I'm not sure what it is about him, but he doesn't seem very trustworthy.

Theo clears his throat. "Michael."

He stands and the two men embrace in a quick but manly hug. Theo moves over to my side of the booth and gestures to his old seat. "Please, sit with us."

While Theo slides in next to me, the strange man sits opposite of us.

"Who's this lovely woman?" he asks, his dark eyes landing on mine. I stiffen. I'd bet my short, cursed life that this man is an immortal.

Theo's arm goes around my shoulders. "This is Cara. Cara, this is Michael. He's from Embrook."

The casual way he mentions another clan makes Michael's eyebrows rise up. I watch his gaze fall down to my wrist, to my bracelet.

"Tricky game you're playing, friend." Michael winks at me and then shifts his gaze to Theo. "I fell for a lifeblood once."

"I didn't know that," Theo says.

Michael's eyes meet mine again. "It didn't end well."

I look away.

"You're the last person I expected to see in a place like this," Theo says. His hand gives my shoulder a reassuring squeeze. "I didn't think you ever left the colonies."

Colonies?

Michael grins, the action warming his severe facial features and making him seem a little bit normal. "I never expected it either, brother. But business calls."

I guess that's all he's going to say on the matter because the silence that follows is more than a little awkward. Finally, Michael changes the subject.

"You look like shit."

"We hit a string of bad luck," Theo says, his brows pulling together. I've seen that look before. He's conjuring up lies to keep us safe. "Carjacker took everything, left us stranded on some country road." He runs a hand down his face like he's super embarrassed about it. "I didn't want to fight back, you know? If she gets hurt, I get hurt."

Michael nods. "Such is the fragile nature of lifebloods." He leans forward. "I'd love to know why you told her the truth."

"That's a long story, my friend." Theo sighs. "If you help us get back home, I'll make sure the elders credit you when I tell them of my discovery."

Michael's eyes narrow. "You completed the mission?"

"And then some," Theo says, his voice low.

Michael's face splits into a grin. He glances around to make sure we're alone, which we are because we're sitting in an odd shaped corner of the room. Michael reaches into his back pocket and pulls out several hundred dollar bills, sliding them over to Theo. "Here," he says, pulling something from his wallet. It's a shiny Visa card. "Prepaid. Five thousand dollars on it."

Theo pops the card and the cash into the zippered pocket of his swim shorts. "Thanks, man."

A blue beach ball rolls down the aisle, followed by a toddler who's chasing after it. We watch him until he's safely back with his mother. Theo's shoulders straighten. "I heard we lost someone."

Michael nods, his lips pressing into a thin line. "Clint Warwick."

Theo draws in a slow breath, then lets it out even slower. "He was a good guy."

Michael nods. "Yeah."

"And his stone is gone?"

"No fucking pawn shop in the country has seen it," Michael says, his lip curling. "When the murdering bastard does try to sell it, we'll be there. He'll realize he fucked with the wrong person."

"And the lifeblood?" Theo asks.

Michael shrugs. "Clint didn't leave any paperwork or records for us. We're still looking into it, but it should pop up soon. We always keep our lifebloods close, you know." He glances back at me. "Well, not *that* close."

"Speaking of falling in love with my lifeblood," Theo says, not falling for Michael's snide remark. He glances at me and smiles. "Cara was tricked into wearing the bracelet for another immortal from Rosewater. It wasn't until he—didn't need it anymore, that I ended up with his stone. Trust me, it was unintentional."

"Shit, man," Michael says. "That's harsh."

Theo nods once. "Is there a way to remove her bracelet and spare her life?"

"You could kill yourself, chap."

"Besides that," I say, my voice sounding foreign since it's the first time in a long time that I've spoken.

Michael doesn't even look at me. His forehead crinkles in the middle and he brings his fingers up to his lips while he thinks. "I don't know, Theo. Maybe."

"Who would know?"

Michael scratches behind his ear. "You really love this girl?"

Theo doesn't answer, and that seems like enough of an answer for him. "I'll ask around," he says.

"Thank you," Theo says. "And if you could get a note back to Embrook, tell them I'm close."

"Will do."

They shake hands before we part ways, and Theo waits until Michael has gotten into his Mercedes and driven away before he speaks again.

"There's a hotel two miles north of here. Do you feel up to walking?"

"Sure," I say, even though my feet already ache from that long run in the rain. But a hotel sounds glorious because hotels have showers and hot water and real beds.

We buy a couple bottles of water and Theo insists on paying back the woman for the free clothes now that we have some cash. We hit the road and walk hand in hand, the occasional car breezing by us as we walk in the grass off to the side.

"So Michael was a friend?" I say, peering up at him and wishing I'd gotten some sunglasses because now that the rain is gone, it's incredibly sunny.

"He's a member of Embrook," Theo says.

"But not a friend?"

"He's a brother. Not a friend."

"I noticed you lied a little bit to him."

"You can't trust everyone, unfortunately." Theo sighs and kicks a rock as he walks. "Michael was there when this country was founded. He was a mason. Friends with John freaking Hancock. He's a good guy, and he'll have my back when I need him to." Theo pats the pocket with the cash in it. "But I'd prefer to keep the details of some things to myself."

"He was here when America was founded?" I say, eyes wide. "That's insane. The things he's seen..."

Theo chuckles. "He helped a lot of slaves escape to the north back in the day. He even kept a few slave owners as lifebloods. He encouraged all of us to do it back then. Bad people make the best lifebloods."

"Did you do it?" I ask.

"Hell yeah. Rich slave owners who think it's okay to keep someone as property? Hell yes they were my lifebloods." He kicks that same rock again. "I only wish I could have gone through them quicker."

"I love you," I say, smiling up at him.

He watches me while we walk, and then he drops my hand and throws his arm around my shoulders, pulling me close to him. "I love you more," he says, kissing the top of my head.

SIX

"Um, Theo?" I say about half an hour later.

"Yes, love?"

We've stopped holding hands because now it's pretty hot outside and I'm already drenched in sweat and smell like someone who was formerly covered in rain and mud, then got all sweaty. I know Theo's in the same predicament, but I walk five feet away from him anyhow so he doesn't smell me.

I stop and peer at the building that's about two blocks away. "I thought you said there was a *hotel* here. The word hotel has certain connotations...you know, like being somewhat nice."

He chuckles. "Looks like a shit hole. The cashier should have told me it was a *motel*."

"It's better than nothing," I say, putting on a smile over my initial disgust.

The building is long and narrow, the word MOTEL flashing in a neon blue sign next to the highway. It looks vintage, like it's probably from the seventies, complete with shag carpet. Funny, how I spent my life in rundown foster homes and an outdated group home, and then Uncle Will's old house, and yet a couple of months of living in the mansion has spoiled me. My lip curls as we near the motel, and I find it a little funny how now I'm suddenly too good for a place like this.

I know I'm not. Deep down, I'm just a white trash girl from the bad part of Sterling. I am not above staying in a motel, no matter how much I might miss my oversized bathtub with jets and big fluffy bed at the mansion.

"Let's do this," I say, heading toward the motel's lobby door. "I am dying for a shower."

THEO SLIDES the key card into the lock—I'm surprised this place is updated enough for that—and we hold our breath while we open the door.

It's actually not bad at all. There's new beige carpet and black furniture that looks brand new as well. The walls have tacky artwork, but the bed looks comfortable.

"Oh *God*, I can't wait to sink into that bed," I say, staring longingly at it as I walk into the room. I stretch out my hands toward it, but I know I can't touch the crisp white sheets until I'm not as filthy as I am now.

"Let's wash the stink off us first," Theo says, locking the deadbolt on the door behind us. He heads to the window unit and turns on the air conditioning, then peers out the window. He looks both ways. I realize he's probably checking to see if we've been followed and that makes me a little frightened.

A shiver runs down my spine at the thought of Lady Em showing up on the other side of that door. Something tells me a simple deadbolt won't keep that woman out.

"Do you think we're okay?" I ask.

"Yes," he says without hesitation. "She wasn't home when we left." He closes the curtains tightly and then turns to me. "We're good."

His grin makes my toes tingle. He is so handsome, with his chiseled jaw and stubble on his chin. I'm in love with his messy hair, the way it always swoops over to the side. Even though it's probably sticky with sweat, I still want to run my fingers through it.

"I call the shower first," I say, making a run for the door.

"Oh, so not fair!" Theo calls out. "My showers are shorter than yours so I should go first!"

"I called it first, so I go first," I say, sticking out my tongue.

Theo makes a pouting face and I roll my eyes as I yank open the bathroom door. "I win, you lose."

I make this big show of walking inside the bathroom first, and then I stop short as soon as I see the shower. "Whoa."

"Whoa is right," Theo says, suddenly behind me. Though the outside of this place is shabby and run down, this bathroom has been remodeled. There's granite countertops, two sinks, and large framed mirrors above them, but that's not the fun part.

The shower is huge. It has clear glass doors and decorative tile work, with two shower heads hanging from the ceiling.

"You could fit, like ten people in here," I say, awed by the gorgeous tilework.

"Or two." Theo opens the door, leans in and turns on the shower. The one handle makes both showerheads pour out water, and soon, steam rises from them.

I forget all about our argument over who gets to go first. Theo steps forward, his neck bending down a little while he kisses me. His hands slide under the hem of my bright pink shirt, and I lift my arms so he can pull it off. He tosses it to the floor, then reaches for my shorts.

"Nope," I say, pressing my hand on his chest. "Your turn." I take off his shirt and try not to grin like an idiot when I see his chiseled abs. Even now, after seeing him shirtless several times, he still makes my heart race. Above it, his new immortality stone rests on his chest, in the center of his sternum. We both like to pretend these pieces of us don't exist, so I look away from it and focus on anything else.

I slide my thumbs in my waistband and push off my shorts, keeping my panties on. Theo grins and unsnaps his swim shorts. They fall to the floor and he steps out of them, wearing only a tight pair of blue boxer briefs.

My heart pounds in my chest as the steam rises all around us, fogging the mirrors. "I'll meet you in there," I say, taking a deep breath to calm my nerves. I'm afraid he'll object, but instead, he strips totally naked as if he has no reservations on earth—although with a body like that, I can't blame him—and he steps into the shower.

"This feels amazing," he says, his back to the water as he tips his head backward and the water washes over his face.

I take a deep breath and pull off my underwear, kicking it, along with my clothes, in a pile to the side. I don't even want to touch those clothes later because they're so filthy. I take one look behind me in the mirror, see my blonde hair all matted and messy, framing the dark circles under my eyes. The last few days have been total hell.

I glance back at the glass shower and see Theo's shoulders ripple as he stretches out his arms under the water. My life may be totally screwed up at the moment, but I deserve a little fun.

The hot water envelopes me the moment I step into the shower. I close my eyes and forget all my reservations from before. Right now all I care about is feeling the water in my hair, and the soap cleansing my skin.

"Feels amazing, huh?" Theo says, grinning at me while he stands under one showerhead and I move under the other.

"This is what heaven feels like," I say, holding out my arms so I can get completely covered in the warm, clean water. This is so much better than cold rainwater.

Theo reaches for a bar of soap off the shelf in the shower. "Turn around," he says, walking closer. He takes my hair and pulls it over my shoulder, then runs the soap along my back, massaging it in with his hands. I close my eyes and let him soap up my arms and shoulders. He steps closer and his erection presses against my back. I can't help but giggle.

"Sorry about that," he says, his hands running down to my hips. "He can't help himself."

His arms slide around my waist, bringing the bar of soap up and around my breasts. I turn back around and he soaps up my legs, his hands moving dangerously slow up my thighs. My cheeks burn red hot, but I don't ask him to stop. There's something so romantic about him caressing my body with the soap, and then the shampoo in my hair. When he's finished, I take the bar and wash him, too.

My hands run over his chest, up his arms and down his back. I take time to enjoy every inch of him, take in how unbelievably hot Theo is. When we're both clean, the smell of shampoo in the air, I lean my head into the water and close my eyes.

"It feels so good to be clean," I murmur as the hot water splashes down my body.

Theo's lips find mine as he steps right up against me, pressing my back to the wall. "It feels good to be dirty, too," he says against my lips. I grin and lean forward, running my tongue along his neck.

"You're absolutely right about that," I whisper as I press my hips into his.

His arms are around me in an instant, and I'm lifted off the floor until I'm eye level with him. His mouth crushes into mine, and I kiss him hard, thinking of all the times I've wanted him in the last few days but was too scared to make a move in that little room.

I feel his hand slide down my thigh and then he pulls my leg up and around his waist. I do the same with my other leg, holding onto his shoulders for support. When he presses into me, I shudder with bliss and hold on to him tightly, like the only thing that matters in this world is him. We make love until the water runs cold.

SEVEN

Theo is all business in the morning. While I'm lying in bed, snuggled up in the motel's soft bathrobe, he's up, pacing the floor and making a plan. We'd slept pretty well last night, all things considering. There's something about knowing you're in a room with a door you can open anytime you want that really puts the mind at ease. I'm not sure if these beds are amazing, or if I was just sick of sleeping on the floor in that underground room, but I feel like I slept on a cloud last night. All the aches and pains in my body evaporated over the last few hours.

The phone on the nightstand rings and Theo answers it quickly. I turn around to watch him.

"Yes," he says to the person on the other line. "Perfect, thank you."

"Who was that?" I ask when he hangs up.

"Good, you're awake." Theo smiles, then leans over me and goes for a kiss. I slap my hand over my mouth and he kisses my knuckles instead.

"Morning breath," I say under my hand. "Get away from me."

"I never want to get away from you," he says, but he does lean back and lets me get up and push off the covers.

"Trust me, morning breath kissing is not something we should do this early into our relationship."

"But me being alive solely because I'm sucking the life from you is okay?"

I give him a look.

"Sorry, love." He sits on the bed and leans his head back, looking at the ceiling. "Not something to joke about. As soon as we get home, I'll be calling every immortal on the planet to find a way to save you."

"Who was on the phone?" I ask again.

"Room service. They're bringing breakfast."

"There's room service in a place like this?" I say, remembering the little seating area off of the lobby and the sign that advertised complimentary breakfast. Usually free breakfast is something you have to get yourself.

"There is when you offer the sixteen-year-old kid at the front desk a hundred bucks to run some errands for you." Theo winks. "Are you going to brush your teeth or just leave me here longing for a kiss from my girlfriend?"

I throw a pillow at him as I stand up. "You are such a nerd."

He grips the pillow to his chest. "A nerd that's in love."

I roll my eyes as I make my way to the bathroom. The motel-provided toothbrushes kind of suck and the toothpaste is so not the quality kind I have back at the mansion, but it works.

As I'm rinsing my mouth, there's a knock at the door. Theo answers it. "Thank you, thank you," he says.

"Anytime, man," says the voice on the other side of the door. "You're my favorite guest."

When I step out of the bathroom a short while later, Theo is standing stark naked at the foot of the bed. I choke on my own spit and then try to compose myself. I shouldn't be so blown away every time I see this gorgeous guy, but I am.

"Breakfast first, sex later," Theo says, his smile brighter than the sun. Damn, he's in a good mood today. I can see why.

The kid from the lobby brought us a huge tray of assorted breakfast items from the breakfast bar. There's also two brown paper bags on the floor in front of the TV.

"What's that?" I ask.

"It's what a huge tip will get you," he says, tossing his wadded up bathrobe at me. He reaches into the bag and pulls out two cell phone boxes. "I had him run to the electronics store down the road and get us prepaid cell phones. The numbers are untraceable. I almost went out this morning to get them while you slept, but then I remembered there's a psycho immortal bitch after us, so I thought it would be better if I didn't leave you alone."

"I like that plan," I say, swallowing back the fear of being separated from Theo. Knowing he won't leave me in a time like this is pretty damn comforting. "Please tell me there's clothes in the other bag?"

Theo grins, putting his hands on his hips, his manhood on full display. "Why? You're not a fan of walking around nude all day?"

I give him a look. "You're free to show off your junk, babe, but I'd like some clothes."

"Your wish is my command."

He reaches into the bag and pulls out a package of men's boxers, which he tosses on the bed. There's a pair of men's shorts, a shirt, and some shoes in there for Theo, all brand new with tags. Underneath that, the kid from the lobby has chosen a pair of Converse, Roxy brand shorts, and a matching purple T-shirt for me.

"I guessed your size," Theo says, holding up the shorts to my bathrobe. "Do they fit?"

"You guessed right," I say, blushing a little. "There's no underwear in there for me?" I feel stupid asking, but come on. I need them.

"Hell no," Theo says as he puts on his clothes. "I wasn't paying some teenage kid to pick out panties for my girlfriend."

I put a hand on my hip. Theo grins. "But I did pay the housekeeper, who is a woman, so she'll be here soon."

My worry melts away. I'm not exactly a fan of hitchhiking back to Texas in short shorts with no underwear. Yuck. "When did you do all of this?" I ask. The last thing I remember was Theo and I falling asleep together on the bed.

"While you were sleeping. You were pretty knocked out, which I guess is from a few days of not sleeping."

"You're not tired?" I ask.

He shakes his head. "I'm focused." Now fully clothed, he walks up to me, his hands cupping my cheeks. "We're going to make it through this. I know we will."

I try to smile, but the fear of failing is hard to shove back. I mean, we're just two people and Lady Em has the power of twelve immortality stones. Plus, no one seems to know how to separate me from the bracelet without killing myself in the process. All that hope I'd had when we first learned about the stones is quickly fading away.

"How do we know she's after us?" I ask. "We haven't seen any signs."

"She's probably not." Theo leans down for a kiss and then brushes my hair out of my face. "At least not right now. Immortals don't see time the way we do. She might not come back to check on us for a while, so we need to use that to our advantage."

The housekeeper drops off a Victoria's Secret bag for us and Theo tips her a hundred dollars. She's chosen a beautiful pink lace bra that makes me feel prettier than I've felt in ages, and a variety of underwear. She also included a backpack so we can put our stuff in it, which wasn't on Theo's list, but it's very useful.

After I'm dressed, I feel like a normal person again. We take out the cell phones and save each other's new number into our phones while they charge.

Then I call Riley and Theo walks to the other side of the hotel room to call Kyle.

"This better be Cara," Riley says as she answers the phone, her voice sounding raspy with sleep.

"It is. Are you still sleeping?" I ask, looking at the clock on the nightstand. "It's ten-thirty California time, which means it's past noon in Texas."

"I had a long night," she says, yawning.

I'm instantly irritated. "You've been out partying all night and I'm stuck here with my life in chaos? Ugh, Riley."

THE IMMORTAL BOND

"Hey now," she says, sounding hurt. "I was not partying all night. I miss you a ton."

The pain in her voice makes me feel bad for my outburst. "I'll be home soon, I hope. I think we'll be hitchhiking back to Texas."

"Oh, gross."

"I know," I say with a sigh. I glance back at Theo and he's deep in conversation. He doesn't even notice me looking at him. "Try to be fully rested when we get home, okay? I have a lot to tell you. How's everything going there?"

"Same as usual. You sure you're okay?" she asks.

"Yeah. I'll explain later. Just—don't do anything suspicious."

"Now that's impossible," she says, and I can picture her sly grin.

"Riley!"

"No worries," she says. "I'll be patiently waiting for your return."

"Good. Call me on this number if anything weird happens."

When I hang up the phone, Theo ends his call too. He saunters over to me, his eyes filled with desire. "Did I hear you say the word hitchhiking?" he asks, his hands sliding around my waist and pulling me close.

"Yes you did, you big eavesdropper." I poke him playfully in the chest.

His thumbs tuck into the waistband of my shorts, the sensation of his hands sending a warm tingle down to my toes. "You'll be happy to know we aren't hitchhiking, love."

I lift an eyebrow, and focus on keeping my breathing steady which is hard to do because I can feel his erection pressing into my belly. "We're not?"

"I rented a car that will be dropped off in half an hour," he says. His tongue flicks across his bottom lip and then he kisses me quickly. "I used the fake name Brian Smith, so when they call me that don't look surprised."

"Could you have picked a more generic name?" I ask, laughing.

He tightens his hold around my waist and I slide my hands up his neck, pulling him close to me. "I tried John Doe, but that asshole already rented a car today. I had to pick another fake name."

His eyes crinkle in the corners and I lean up on my toes to kiss him. "I am so glad we have a car now," I say, running my tongue along his bottom lip.

"Thought you'd like that," he whispers. "We have twenty seven minutes until it gets here."

"Oh? Whatever shall we do to pass the time?" I say as I run my hand down the crotch of his shorts.

Theo's playful grin turns sultry. "Let me show you."

EIGHT

It's a beautiful California day. The sun is shining, and the grass is green. Even the people seem friendly as we check out of the hotel and walk to our rental car. It's warm, and the air feels great on my face. California summers aren't anything like the humid, awful summers in Texas. Maybe after all of this is over, and if I survive of course, maybe Theo and I could move to California one day. We could get a beach house or live somewhere more secluded. Just the two of us.

"You look very introspective." Theo nudges my elbow as we put our stuff in the trunk of the rented Ford Focus. "What are you thinking about?"

I shrug. "The future, I guess." Or one that I'm imagining because the way things are right now doesn't seem like I'll ever get to live happily with Theo on some beach house. At this point, I'm not even sure I'll see my next birthday.

"The future," he says, closing the trunk. "The only thing no one knows."

We get into the car and crank the air conditioning. It smells like cleaning chemicals and the fake pineapple scent of the air freshener hanging from the rearview mirror. As Theo pulls out of the motel's parking lot, I feel a surge of excitement. We're finally on the road, in a car. Finally going somewhere. We're no longer at the mercy of kind strangers, or pushing our bodies to run through rain and mud.

We are no longer trapped and helpless.

"I feel very free right now," I say, rolling down my window. I let my fingers fly along through the air as we pick up speed on the highway. The light catches my bracelet and I frown. "Well...mostly free."

Theo squeezes my thigh. "Mind if we stop for a snack? You wore me out back there."

Memories of our love-making just a short while ago make me blush from head to toe. We are getting very good at showing our feelings for each other.

Theo pulls into a gas station and we load up on sugary soft drinks and salty snack foods. It's totally not healthy in any way, but it feels good not to care about that right now.

The car has a GPS, so we set it to Texas and then cruise on the interstate. Theo and I talk occasionally, but mostly we just jam out to pop music on the radio and share a bag of M&Ms.

It feels good to be a normal person, if only for a little while. We pull over at stores to take pee breaks, and around three in the afternoon, we find a little Mexican restaurant off the highway and we stop for a late lunch.

The waitress treats us like everyone else. It feels good to order food and eat it and just chill out for a while. The enchiladas are incredible and their homemade sweet tea is the best drink on earth. I soak up these feelings and hold onto them, because as soon as we get back to the mansion, who knows what'll happen.

When we're back on the road after lunch, Theo tells me a little about the clans. He knows the most about Embrook, since that's his true clan. They were founded at the same time America declared its independence, and most of the elders of the clan were masons, and the very founders of the whole USA. He tells me they don't have any famous people like George Washington in the clan. The names everyone knows from the history books were just regular humans. It's the immortals who controlled them behind the scenes.

The Embrook clan was founded on the basis of hope and prosperity, and as Theo points out, independence. Their clan comes together for meetings and to help one another, like how Michael did for us by giving us cash. But the Embrook clan doesn't live together, or even near each other. They keep to themselves, each choosing to live their life the way they want. Theo says most of the Embrook clan still lives in America, but some travel around from time to time, like his friend Damien who lives in Greece.

Then there's the Dover clan, which Theo explains is the original clan. They're from Europe and were founded in the year 1200 by a man who was a direct descendant from the alchemist who invented the original two hundred stones. Back then, the stones were kept for only the elite, a few men of power or clergy of whom the creator felt was worthy. After he had been dead several centuries, his heir decided to form the original clan.

Dover clan is headquartered out of the Dover Castle in Kent, which is in the United Kingdom. Theo tells me the castle is a tourist spot right now, but what the tourists don't see is the clan members who live there in secret. Apparently, they're all pretty ancient, having been transformed into immortals once they were already middle-aged or older. According to the Embrook clan, the Dover castle is home to several immortality stones and their lifeblood stone mates. They've been hoarding them for centuries because Dover doesn't like the idea of expanding the number of immortals on the planet. It's because of this that the Dover Castle is heavily guarded from intruders.

As for the Rosewater clan, I already know a lot about it. It popped up recently, only a few decades ago. There's only a handful of members, one of which I killed. And now, thanks to Theo and me spying on the library's balcony, we know who's actually in charge of Rosewater.

A woman called Lady Em.

"Now it makes sense why Embrook wanted you to spy on Rosewater," I say. The sun is starting to set and we've crossed state borders into Nevada. "Rosewater just doesn't make sense. Especially since there have only been two clans for so long."

"Since the beginning of everything," Theo says, his hand on the wheel. "There's been two clans forever, until Rosewater. No one knows how they got the stones, or how they rose up into a clan. Obviously, the first thought was that they stole them from Dover Castle, but the Dover clan swears all of their stones are accounted for. They're quite pissed about the Rosewater clan as well."

"Did she make her own?" I ask.

Theo's eyes shoot to me. "That's impossible."

"How do you know?"

"I just do."

"So we know who runs Rosewater now," I say, looking out my window at the desert terrain outside. "But we don't know exactly why she does what she does."

"That's what's so worrisome. The guys at the mansion all seem like good guys. You know—for the most part. We need to get back home and I'll poke around and see if they know about her. Now that Alexo is gone, we could go through his room as well."

"That'll be pointless," I say with a snort. "His room is empty."

Theo gives me a disapproving look, probably because of how I stupidly went through his room without telling Theo about it. But it wasn't my fault Theo was gone for days on end doing immortal stuff with Alexo. I saw my opportunity to dive into Alexo's personal life, and I took it. And that's exactly what led me to watching Jayla get murdered.

I smile a little. It's kind of morbid to think like this, but Alexo killed Jayla and I killed Alexo. *You've been avenged*, I think. *Alexo won't be killing any more girls.*

A commercial comes on the radio station and Theo turns it off, filling the car with silence and the steady hum of the tires on the road.

"We'll get home and we'll act normal. Give it a couple of days, and I'll start prying around. We need to know where the guys' loyalty lies. If they know Lady Em, then we'll be screwed the second we walk onto the property."

"And if not?" I ask.

"They'll probably be pissed that they were led into the clan by Alexo under false pretenses. I was recruited, and I wasn't told a damn thing about her. I'm guessing the other guys don't know either."

"And if they don't...?" I say.

Theo grins. "Maybe they'll be on our side."

"The more people we have, the quicker we can defeat this bitch."

Theo grabs my hand. "My thoughts exactly."

NINE

We cross over the Texas border at two in the morning. My heart leaps at the Welcome to Texas sign, but then I see we're still eight hours away from Austin. This state is freaking huge. We've been driving two days, but we're taking our time, stopping at fun places and picking up more clothes along the way. On one hand, I'm tired of all the driving and want to be back home with Riley, but on the other hand, we have no idea what will happen when we get there. Lady Em could be waiting and all hell could break loose.

Theo suggests that we get a hotel for the night, and I'm happy to sleep in a real bed instead of dozing off and on in the rental car. The drive was exhausting, so we fall fast asleep and before I know it, the sun is peering in through the hotel's windows, signaling the start of another day.

"Babe?" Theo calls out. He's leaning over the bathroom sink brushing his teeth.

"What's up?" I lean against the door frame. I brushed my teeth before him, and now I'm fully dressed while he's still in his boxers. It's a pretty nice view.

"I need to take a quick detour." He rinses out his mouth and tosses the hotel's free toothbrush into the trashcan. "Is that okay with you?"

I shrug. "I don't mind."

"You might," he says, his face twisted in indecision. "I mean..." He exhales sharply. "It's not fun, but I need to do it and I'd rather do it now, than later."

"Does it have anything to do with me?" I ask.

His smile is a little sad. "No."

"Then let's go."

Theo sets the GPS for some town I've never heard of. It routes us off the main interstate and toward the east, just past Waco. We drive in silence, and I can tell whatever this side trip is about is bothering him. I'm curious for details, but I also feel like I should just keep quiet and not force him about it. When Theo wants to talk, he's good at talking. Right now he's doing his silent contemplation thing.

I lean back in the car seat and reach for his hand. He squeezes it. Our hands stay like that, lightly holding onto each other for the next hour.

We drive into an older neighborhood, where the houses are small and run down. The driveways are only wide enough for one car. Theo parks on the side of the road. "Would you like to come with me?" he asks. His expression is blank...maybe a little sad. I can't tell if he wants me to come or if he's hoping I'll say no.

"It's up to you," I say, offering him a small smile.

"Please come."

We walk up to the front door. It used to be blue, but now it's as faded as the white wooden siding on the house. Overgrown rose bushes line the porch, and the welcome mat has flowers printed on it. Theo knocks twice.

A little girl answers. She's probably five or six years old, with long brown hair and big dark eyes. "Hello," she says.

"Hi there. I'm a friend of your brother. Is he here?"

"He's always here," she says, stepping backward to let us in. "He's in his room."

"Thank you," Theo says.

The home is older, but it looks well-loved. The decorations remind me of old people, and the small flat screen TV in the center of the living room looks a little out of place. The girl bounces over to it and plops onto the rug, her attention once again absorbed into her cartoon.

I follow Theo down a narrow hallway and to a bedroom on the left. He knocks on the door, which is halfway open. "Julian?"

"Theo," a guy says in a Spanish accent. "Is anything wrong?"

"Nothing to worry about," Theo says, walking into the room. He turns to look at me, but I wave him away.

I stand behind, not wanting to intrude into someone's bedroom when they weren't expecting company.

"Who's with you?" the guy asks.

"My girlfriend." Theo waves for me to join him. "She's shy."

"Come in!" the guy calls out. It sends him into a coughing fit. "I want to meet you!"

With shaky knees, I venture into the room, a polite smile on my face, even though I feel incredibly awkward. I have a pretty good feeling I know who this guy is just by looking at him.

He looks like a teenager, and his room is filled with basketball posters and sports trophies. He's lying in his bed, looking pallid and, well, like he's on the verge of death. There's a dozen prescription bottles on his nightstand and an oxygen tank next to the bed.

"Hello," I say.

"Julian, this is Cara," Theo says, putting a hand on my back.

"Nice to meet you," he says, waving at me. "You're too pretty for a guy like Theo."

I blush even though I feel incredibly awkward right now.

"Julian is my lifeblood," Theo explains. "He has stage four lung cancer."

"Good ol' genetics," Julian says, tapping his chest. "I had a scholarship to college and everything, but no. Fuck you, Julian. Fate stepped in and said I hate you."

"I'm really sorry," I say. Seeing someone so young on their deathbed really puts things into perspective. Like the clan and their fake job postings to get girls to be lifebloods without their knowing about it. These things need to be stopped. The world has enough pain and suffering as it is.

"It's okay," Julian says. "Well...it's not, but it is. Your man here gave us a lot of money, a trust fund for my little sister and money for my grandma to keep paying the bills that aren't covered by her social security check."

His eyes are bloodshot but they sparkle when he looks at Theo. "Your man is my hero."

"I'm not a hero," Theo says as he sits at the foot of Julian's bed. "But I'm glad I could help."

"So what's going on, man?" Julian asks.

Theo's eyes darken. "I need the bracelet back." Julian's jaw drops in fear but Theo holds up his hands. "You'll be fine. I'm not wearing the matching stone anymore. Someone stole mine, so your bracelet doesn't work anymore. You can remove it safely now, and live out your remaining days a little longer than before."

Julian's brows pull together and he lifts his left hand out from under his blanket. He's wearing the stone as a bracelet, only his band is leather instead of silver like mine. It's the manlier version, I guess. He reaches over and unhooks the clasp, biting his lip while the bracelet slides right off, landing on his bed.

"Well, look at that."

Theo smiles. "You'll still get everything I've promised," he says, putting his hand on top of Julian's. "I will forever be grateful for the sacrifice you made for me. Thank you, Julian."

"Thank you, man," Julian says, his eyes filling with tears. "I was gonna die anyway, but now you've saved my sister's future and made my grandma's life less stressful. You're an angel."

"It's a small price to pay for your help, Julian." Theo takes a pen and pad of paper from the nightstand and writes down a number. I recognize it as the number to his new prepaid phone. "You call me if you need anything, okay? Pass it along to your sister as well. I know she's just a kid now, but should she need anything when she's older, she can always call me. I'm indebted to you for eternity."

Julian's eyes flood with tears and he nods quickly, wiping at his eyes with the edge of his blanket. "Thank you," he says, his voice barely a whisper.

Theo bends down to hug him and say goodbye. I wave awkwardly from the doorway. I don't even know the guy, but it's taking everything I have not to cry.

Julian winks at me. "Take care of my boy," he calls out to me.

"Don't worry," I say. "I will."

There's a lump in my throat as we walk back through the small house. Julian's little sister waves at us as we leave, and Theo tells her to make sure she locks the front door behind us.

When we get to the car, Theo rests his hands on the hood of it, dropping his head on top of them. He lets out a sigh. I walk over to him and run my hand down his back.

"Are you okay?"

"Yeah," he says with a slow nod. He draws in a deep breath. "It's just hard. Every. Single. Time."

He lifts his head and looks over at me, his eyes bloodshot. "Why do people like me get to live forever and kids like Julian die before they get into college?"

I look down at my feet. "Life can be shitty, Theo. But you're not a bad person for living."

He reaches into his pocket and lifts out the bracelet. The stone is dull now that it's not in contact with skin. "I figured she's not wearing mine," he says. "Lady Em," I mean. She didn't know who my lifeblood was and wearing a stone without a lifeblood attached to the other end is very bad news for an immortal. Looks like I was right."

"What if she was wearing it?" I ask.

Theo's lips press into a thin line. "Julian would have been in pain when he tried to remove his stone."

Seeing my startled expression, Theo smiles. "Don't worry, I was watching, ready to put it back on him if necessary. But I was pretty sure she wouldn't risk wearing my necklace. I was right." He grips the bracelet in his hand. "Now it won't work at all, so long as I keep this away from a living person."

"I bet that'll piss off that stone-hoarding bitch."

Theo chuckles, and it's the first time he's looked even remotely happy since setting the GPS for this location hours ago. "I love your insults, especially the ones for Lady Em."

I shrug. "I can get way more creative. I love picturing her walking around her stupid castle, pissed that we're gone, and pissed that she can't add another stone to that god-awful necklace of hers." I crinkle up my nose. "How the hell did she get so many stones in the first place if she didn't steal them from the Dover Clan's secret hiding place?"

Theo lifts his shoulders. "I've been wondering that. Dover wouldn't lie. They've been overly protective of that castle ever since—"

Theo freezes.

"Ever since...?" I poke him in the arm. "Hello? Did your motherboard malfunction?"

He doesn't laugh at my robot joke. His eyes are wide and filled with something I can't quite place.

"Oh shit," he breaths, turning toward me. "I know where she got the stones. And I know exactly what she's here for."

TEN

Theo doesn't want to talk about it until we're on the road. He says driving calms him and helps him think. So I buckle up and hang out while we weave back through the old neighborhood and cross through the town back to the interstate. This part of the state is hilly, and the roads scare me a little. Luckily, Theo is a great driver.

Half an hour passes and I've almost forgotten his revelation back at Julian's house. "It was around eighty years ago," he says, catching my attention immediately. I look over at him, studying the way his jaw tightens at the memory.

"I had only been immortal a couple of years, and one of the elders needed me to deliver some correspondence to an elder in the Dover Clan. Being in New England at the time, it took seventeen days to travel to Europe by ship."

He turns to me. "There wasn't internet back then, and no overnight postal service, either. I had to hand deliver the letter, which was written on thick parchment and sealed with the Embrook wax seal. I remember thinking it was pretty damn official looking."

"Wow, you're old," I say with a smirk.

"It's a shame they don't give me the senior discount everywhere I go," he says, his lips quirking up in the corner.

Some idiot in a red truck pulls out in front of us and Theo has to press hard on the brakes to avoid hitting him. Normally, he'd let out a curse at the inconvenience, but now he's so deep in thought it doesn't faze him.

"I still felt twenty one. I felt human. I wasn't entirely used to the fact that I was immortal. Honestly, not until you hit your fiftieth birthday and realize you're not getting any older, does it really sink in. Anyhow, I was terrified to visit the Dover clan. I'd only heard horrible stories about them and the idea of meeting an immortal that's a millennia old is kind of terrifying."

The GPS's female computer voice interrupts us, telling us to get in the right lane for an upcoming exit. Theo glances behind us and then switches lanes. "It's still a little terrifying meeting someone that old."

"I can imagine," I say. Theo was born in 1920, which makes him young by immortal standards, but it kind of freaks me out every time I think of it. When Theo was a kid, cell phones didn't exist. Television wasn't a thing, and cars were a luxury that couldn't even go fast. Most homes didn't have air conditioning. Women had only just been granted the right to vote.

I can't even fathom how many changes the immortals from the Dover clan have witnessed in their long lives. Nations rising and falling. Technology swarming by faster than you can blink. I wonder if it seems to go by quickly for them, the way time flew from when I was a kid until now, or do the ancient immortals see things slower than we do?

"So what happened?" I ask as I try to picture Theo being a new immortal back in the Depression era.

"Well, the boat ride sucked like hell. The whole ship was filthy and reeked like death. You eat fish constantly. I thought I'd never get back on land, and once I did, I fell to the shore and puked. I must have looked awful, too, because the guards at the Dover castle didn't want shit to do with me. They tried kicking me out until I fished out the letter from my bag and showed them the Embrook seal."

As we drive, the streetlights start to click on, and I realize it's already eight in the evening. Another whole day has gone by and we're still free, without a single sighting of Lady Em. I'm still worried about it all, but the tightness in my shoulders has lessened with each day.

"What did the letter say?" I ask.

"I wasn't important enough back then to know the contents and I'm probably still not," he says with a chuckle. "All I did was deliver it, and then I had to wait there two days for a reply. They gave me a guest room in the castle. Back then, it was a real functioning castle, not just a tourist spot. It was a fortress, impenetrable by enemy forces. I was just a poor kid from the States, so this was all insanely awesome to me. They had servants and ladies in waiting."

He snorts. "America has never been much like England. Anyway, they set me up in the guest chambers in the castle. I kept to myself that first day, but a servant was sent to invite me to dinner. They had me dress up all nice and stuff, and then we sat at this long wooden table that must have had a hundred people at it. It was a feast almost exactly like what you see in the movies."

He gazes off as he drives, shaking his head slightly. "I was such an idiot back then. I probably had no manners at all. I was just blown away by how amazing and ornate the castle looked, how fancy all the people were. And part of me just wanted to get home to the shack I lived in on the back of Damien's farm and get back to our milk delivery. That night, during dinner, there was a woman sitting a few places down from me. No one ever really said it, but she was clearly the mistress of Lord Timothy, one of the elders of Dover clan. I'm pretty sure he was *the* elder, now that I think about it. She was young and pale with long, dark hair. Like, down to her knees almost. She spent the entire dinner and then the party afterward fawning over Lord Timothy, even right in front of his wife, Lady Elizabeth."

I open my mouth to say something, but Theo's so lost in his story he doesn't even notice it. His brows pull together.

"That night, she snuck into my chambers while I was almost asleep. She crawled into the bed with me and tried kissing me. I shot up fast and jumped out, totally freaked out. I mean, she was the Lord's freaking mistress, and I was pretty sure they chopped off guy's hands or dick or something when they slept with a Lord's girl."

I can't hide my scowl. Theo grins. "No worries, love. I didn't want anything to do with her, mistress or not. She seemed a little off her rocker at the party. But it became clear that she was fascinated with my immortality. I remember her pouting that I wouldn't kiss her and then she sat on my bed and crossed her arms and said, 'You're one of *them,* aren't you?' I tried playing dumb because although we were in the castle of an immortal, it was still a secret and we couldn't go around talking about it to regular humans, which she was. But she wouldn't let it go. She wanted to see my necklace. She wouldn't stop talking about it. I walked her to my door and tried getting her to leave, but then she barricaded it and demanded that I make her immortal or she'd tell the Lord that I'd slept with her. That's when I had to drop my innocent act and confess that I was in fact immortal, but that I couldn't change her."

He looks over at me. "I was scared out of my mind. I thought I'd be fucking hanged after only a few years of immortality. But she believed me, and she left, only to come back the next night asking me to help her. She wanted to steal an immortality stone for herself. Not from the vault but..."

He swallows. I realize I'm gripping the edge of my seat now, the dark road and the passing of cars beside us a blur. I can picture the scene Theo has laid out, see him as a more innocent version of himself, way back in the day.

Theo continues, "She wanted to kill Lord Timothy and steal his stone. She was pissed that he'd recently chosen to spend the nights with his wife instead of with her because they were trying to conceive a son."

"What'd you do?" I ask.

"I left. Well, I told her the stone would do nothing without the lifeblood and then I left. As soon as the sun rose, I marched to the servant's quarters and checked the letter pile, found the Lord's reply and took it before breakfast. I hopped on the next ship and went straight home. I think that was a huge mistake now. If I'd known then..."

He shakes his head. "But I couldn't have known. I was young. Stupid. I was saving myself first."

"What should you have known?" I ask.

"The woman did take Lord Timothy's stone," he says, his voice somber.

"She killed him with a poisoned drink while he played a game of poker with members of the clan."

"Wow," I say.

Theo shakes his head. "That's not all. Eighteen men were slain that day, all immortals. The Dover clan stepped up their security from that point and no one was allowed into the castle who wasn't a member of the royal family or the clan."

"Does this mean what I think it means?" I ask.

Theo nods once. "That woman was Lady Em. Her name was Meredith. She envied the Lord's wife. She killed him and his men and stole the stones. Back then the lifebloods were held in the dungeon, and they were all slain as well. Dover clan claims they recovered the stones, but that has to be a lie. If Lady Em has twelve on her neck, the rest of the guys in Rosewater make up the other six."

I stare at the bracelet on my hand. Was it once worn in a dungeon by a lifeblood from a hundred years ago? Was this very bracelet one of Lady Em's stolen treasures?

"She cut her hair and took what she wanted," I say, chills running down my arms. "She calls herself a Lady even though she could never be one in real life."

Theo nods. "That's how she knew my name. We've met before, and I refused to help her. Something tells me she hasn't forgiven me for it."

ELEVEN

We make a temporary home at the Houston Holiday Inn. After the revelation that Lady Em is a scorned mistress from a century ago, Theo called his friend and sire, Damien, saying he wanted his advice before we do anything else. Since he lives on the literal other side of the world in Greece, it's taken him three days to wrap up whatever work he was doing and travel here.

I make a cup of coffee from the hotel's breakfast bar, adding two sugars on top of my creamer, until the drink is almost all cream and sugar. It's almost noon, but I've woken up to coffee the last three days with Theo, so now I'm starting to crave it. I take a sip and then walk over to where Theo is sitting near a large waterfall in the middle of the lobby. Despite being one of the biggest cities in the world, this hotel is nearly empty. There's not a single person hanging out in the lobby except for us. Last night, we'd spent hours in the hotel's rooftop swimming pool and only saw one other person, a guy who didn't speak English and preferred to hang out in the hot tub.

"I just got an email from Kyle," Theo says, looking at his phone. "He says Alexo hasn't checked in for a few days and he's wondering what he's up to."

"Well that's good, right?"

Theo shrugs. "I think so. But if Kyle wanted to lie to me to see what I know, email would be easier, right? On the phone or in person, it's harder to hide when you're lying."

I swirl the cream around in my coffee with a little red straw. "Did he ask when we're coming back home? If he starts getting pushy about making us return, then I'd worry."

Theo shakes his head. "No, he hasn't."

Ever since we woke up this morning, Theo hasn't let his phone leave his side because Damien should be here any minute now. We take a walk outside, roaming the streets of downtown like tourists. There are cute shops sprinkled in between the skyscrapers, but neither one of us actually wants to go inside of them. We've been on edge ever since Theo discovered who actually runs the Rosewater clan. Everything feels so out of sync right now. We're stuck waiting, wondering what to do and guessing what might happen.

Theo's been so out of it, he didn't even wake up when I pulled his arm off me so that I could go pee this morning. And then, when he finally did wake up, he got dressed from the dirty clothes pile. I made him change clothes into a new pair of jeans and a white T-shirt. He doesn't seem scared or upset, just weird. Like maybe he's been thinking too much.

Around one in the afternoon, he gets a call. It's so brief, I expect him to say it was a wrong number. Instead, Theo shoves the phone in his back pocket and looks toward the left. "There's a pool hall three blocks away. That's where we're meeting him."

"A pool hall?" I ask curiously. "In the daylight?"

Theo laughs. "What's wrong with that?"

I shrug as we start walking toward the left. "I guess I figured pool halls are more of a night time thing."

"Damien is a big fan of pool." Theo reaches for my hand and flashes me a smile that makes me remember the real him, not the guy he's been lately, weighed down with immortal drama. "He used to make good money in one night of hustling drunk idiots."

The pool hall is more family friendly than I'd imagined. I guess I pictured it more like a bar, but this place reminds me of a bowling alley. Long and narrow, with dozens of pool tables and loud music playing. There's a food bar and seating area, and large screen televisions hang from the ceiling, playing sports games.

My attention is immediately drawn to the man standing at a table in the middle of the room. He's wearing black pants and a plaid button up shirt, the sleeves rolled midway up his forearm. He has short copper hair but a decent beard, and he reminds me one of one of those lumberjack male models that are popular on Instagram. He's holding his cue stick and staring right at us.

"Damien," Theo says as we approach. They shake hands. I try to picture them back in the Depression era, when Damien owned a farm and Theo worked for him as a delivery boy. Damien's shiny black shoes and anchor tattoo on his arm make that image very hard to conjure up in my mind.

"This must be Cara," he says, reaching out his hand. I go to shake his hand, but he takes my fingers and brings them to his lips, where he kisses my knuckles like a true gentleman.

"Nice to meet you," I say, resisting the urge to curtsey.

"The pleasure is all mine." Damien winks, his bright blue eyes sparkling under the neon beer signs on the wall. "Would you like a drink?" he asks me.

"No, thanks," I say.

He looks at Theo. "Beer?"

Theo nods and Damien waves to a waitress who's been waiting just a few feet away, her tray already holding two frozen glasses of beer.

Damien racks the balls and Theo finds a cue stick from the shelf on the wall. I sit on a barstool next to the pool table, wondering how we'll get him up to date on all that's happened without looking like we're doing a secret drug deal or something. I watch an older man amble over to the jukebox and drop in some quarters. A few seconds later, Garth Brooks plays over the speakers.

Damien leans over the table, aims his pool stick, and breaks. Theo and I watch the table as the balls roll around, some of them sinking into pockets. He looks up, his expression casual. "Looks like I'm solids. You called me here for an emergency meeting," he says, like it's not a question, but a statement.

"I know who runs Rosewater," Theo says, just as plainly. I have to hide my smile because these men are so different than Riley and I. We'd be talking a mile a minute with information this serious. I would have grabbed her arms and she would have said *holy shit* about ten times by now.

Damien nods once, and then aims at the blue ball, sinking it into a corner pocket. "And Alexo?"

"Dead." Theo walks around the table, tapping his pool stick on the floor. "Her name is Lady Em, and she's the mistress who gave me trouble that time I traveled to Dover to deliver a letter."

Damien's eyebrows cocks and he misses his next shot. He holds his stick up and tilts his head. "The woman who supposedly slaughtered Lord Timothy?"

"The very same." Theo hits the green stripe ball and sinks it. "Dover's reserve of stones were taken. Lady Em killed all those men and took their stones. Remember the rumors that their lifebloods had been slaughtered, too? Dover tried hiding it, but it has to be true. It's the only thing that makes sense."

"How many stones was that? Twenty or so?" Damien's brows pull together as he surveys the pool table for his next shot. "Rosewater has only five members and you have your own stone."

"She has twelve," Theo says, meeting his gaze. "And the rest of the members have the others."

"Twelve stones?" Damien stands straight. "What does that mean?"

"She wears them all."

Damien tilts his head. "Why?"

"They give her powers," I say, stepping off the barstool. "She can move things with her freaking mind."

He cocks an eyebrow. "Did you see her do this?"

"I saw it, and I felt it," I say. "She held me down with just a flick of her wrist. My whole body seized up and couldn't move. The stones give her power."

Damien turns to Theo. "Why the hell haven't we heard of this before?"

"Because Dover clan keeps the stones and their power locked up. They've had stones for centuries and they're picky on who gets them, probably for this very reason. Too many stones gives you too much power." Theo sighs and scratches the back of his neck. "I'm guessing the only reason Dover allowed Embrook to remain a clan this whole time is because we abide by the rules they originally set forth. One stone per person, total secrecy on everything immortal. It's exactly why we can't figure out how to remove Cara's bracelet—we're kept in the dark about the extent of these things."

Damien sets his pool stick down, leaning it against the side of the table. "There's something more, Theo. Five elders of Embrook have been killed in the last week."

The whole room seems to go silent. The booming country music, the clashing of pool balls and the cheers of other people playing their games. It all fades into the distance as I watch the blood drain from Theo's face.

He swallows. "Five?"

Damien nods. "Dover has lost three men this week as well. They haven't been found, but they believe they might be dead and have asked Embrook to stay aware of our surroundings. I only just heard of the news this morning."

"Someone is killing us off," Theo says, his knuckles turning white on his pool stick. "It's her. She did it before and now she's doing it again. Killing and hoarding the stones for herself."

"The evidence would suggest so," Damien says in his level voice. "It would also explain why you two escaped her prison and she hasn't been looking for you. She's on a mission."

"She has stones and her own clan," I say. "What more could she possibly want?"

Theo grabs the square of blue chalk from the pool table and tosses it in the air, catching it in his palm. "Everything. She wants everything."

"Brother," Damien says, leveling his gaze at Theo. "You know more about her than anyone else at Embrook. We will warn them and Dover as well, but this woman must be stopped immediately."

"Then let's go stop the bitch," I say. My hands squeeze into fists.

The guys turn to me, and Theo smiles. "I love your enthusiasm, but we should think this one through."

"I will tell Embrook to go on high alert," Damien says. "We've lost five men, we can't lose any more. As for Rosewater... you're sure the other members are unaware of their true leader?"

Theo shakes his head. "I can't be sure, but I'm going to find out. If they've been lied to like I was, there's a good chance they'll agree to join me."

"Dover will have them killed," Damien says. "The Rosewater clan is no friend to the true immortals."

"They are good men," Theo says. "Let's have faith they will choose the right path."

Damien shakes his head. "Good or not, there's no way Dover will allow this clan to continue after its head leader has been severed."

I think about Riley, about Kyle, sweet innocent Kyle. The bracelets that were forced upon us. I agree that Lady Em should be taken out, and the clan uses innocent lifebloods and that's not okay. But no more Rosewater means no more Riley. We've spent all of our time at the mansion trying to discover a way to remove our bracelets and live. We've been doomed to die slowly from the moment we put those bracelets on.

But now, the timer has been shifted up. The end will be here before we know it, and we still aren't ready.

TWELVE

The familiar road stretches into the distance. I look out the window, squinting to see the outline of the mansion on the horizon. We're only a few minutes away now. My heart is racing, but Theo is calm. At least on the outside. I study him while he drives, admiring the outline of his jaw, the soft hint of stubble on his chin. His eyes are fixed on the road in front of us, but his lips curve up in a smirk the longer I'm staring at him.

"Looking at something interesting?" he says. His hand slips off the steering wheel and grabs my thigh.

"Not really," I say with a shrug.

"Ha!" He sticks out his tongue at me.

"You're being very cool about this," I say, exhaling slowly. "I'm over here freaking out."

"I'm trying to manifest good vibes. I'm pretty confident the guys don't know anything about Alexo, which means they won't be hostile when we get there."

"And if they are?" I ask.

He winks at me. "I'll leave the car running."

"Oh ha, ha," I say, turning to look out the window. "My best friend is there. I'm not leaving her."

Speaking of Riley, I send her a text telling her we're almost home.

YAYYY!!!!!!!! she replies back a few seconds later.

The gate code still works. We drive our rented car straight down the long winding driveway, and halfway to the house I realize I'm holding my breath. I tell myself to calm down. It's not like the car will suddenly explode if Lady Em is here. Still, I hold onto the seatbelt around my chest, and I don't feel at ease, even as we park in front of the garage.

The house is quiet on the outside. There's no splashing sounds coming from the swimming pool, no loud music indicating a party. It's noon on a Wednesday, but that doesn't exactly mean anything because this mansion has parties all the time.

"Ready?" Theo says, closing my car door behind me. It's taken me a while to step out of the car.

"Ready."

"First thing's first." Theo walks around the side of the garage. I follow him, more out of curiosity than worry. He walks halfway down the side of the house to where a metal box is mounted on the wall. He opens it up and rips out a couple of cables. "No internet, no spying on us," he says with a sly grin. "Only Alexo monitored what was going on in the house. Now he's gone, but we don't need his computer listening in."

"I wish we could have done that a long time ago," I say. It's so simple—the way to stop the surveillance doesn't require crazy computer hacking skills, but just the simple pull of a cord from the wall. I feel like laughing, or crying. Or maybe both.

We enter into the garage door because there's a keypad on the outside, so we can get in even without a garage door opener. Again, everything looks normal in here. The house is just the same, although I'm not sure what I was expecting. To be greeted by Lady Em in the living room like a pissed off mother who stayed up late because her kid missed curfew?

That hardly seems like Lady Em's style.

"I could use a snack," Theo says absentmindedly when we pass by the service kitchen.

My stomach is empty too, but there are more important things right now. "I need to see Riley."

"I'll take you."

Theo walks me upstairs, where things still look just like the day we left them. My name tag is still next to my bedroom door, but I skip right past it and go to Riley's room.

"Riley?" I say, knocking. "It's me!"

She swings open the door and greets me with a huge smile. "CARA!"

I throw my arms around her and we hug like we haven't seen each other in decades. And yeah, it's just been a few days, but I spent every minute of them worrying that Lady Em was going to kidnap her or something. Seeing her alive and whole and looking totally normal unties that final knot of anxiety in my stomach.

"I'm really glad you're okay," I say into her hair.

"Why wouldn't I be okay? I've just been here the whole time." She smacks my arm. "You're the one off traveling around mysteriously!" She tugs me into her room.

"Whoa," I say under my breath. Riley's room is in shambles. It's not close to as bad as Jayla's room, but it's definitely out of the norm for my best friend. There's dirty clothes on the floor, opened bags of candy and chips on the desk.

Her bed is unmade and the pillows are on the floor. It reminds me of how she used to get at the group home when we'd be buried in school work and she would drop everything to focus on one important class project. But we're out of school now, so there's really no excuse, especially when we have maids who are happy to clean up and make beds.

Riley glances behind me, noticing Theo for the first time. "I'm glad you took care of my girl," she says, using her Mom voice. "Shall we go get some ice cream and *talk?*"

"No need for ice cream," Theo stays, stepping inside and closing the door behind him. "I cut the internet cable that monitors the wall tablets. We can talk freely."

"Whoa," Riley says, eyes wide. "Won't they just turn it back on?"

"Alexo was the only person who monitored that account, and no. He won't turn it back on."

Riley lifts an eyebrow. "Why's that?"

Theo glances at me, his hand warm on my lower back. He raises his eyebrows as if asking if I want to tell her or if I should let him do it. There is so much she doesn't know yet. So many things have happened since that night Theo and I sat out on the balcony and spied on Alexo's talk with Lady Em. I don't even know where to begin. So I start with the most insane part.

"Alexo is dead. I killed him."

"What the *hell?*" Riley steps backward. "You *what?*"

"It was pretty badass," Theo says, cracking a grin. "She saved my life."

Riley crosses her arms over her chest. "Spill it."

Before I can talk, Theo gets a phone call. When he answers it, Kyle's voice is so loud on the other end that we can all hear it.

"Dude!" Kyle says. "Malina said you're home! Where the fuck are you, man? I checked your room and the kitchen and the garage."

Theo's tongue slides across his lips before he replies. "I'll meet you in the game room."

"Cool, cool. I missed you, man! Henry and Russell take the fun out of everything, ya know? I'm glad you're back. I've been bored as hell without any work assignments from Alexo."

The mention of our former clan leader makes us all look up. I'm just hearing him from the phone, but he sure sounds genuine to me. He can't possibly know that Alexo is gone.

"Yeah," Theo says with a fake chuckle. "See you in a minute."

"Well...that sounded good." I say, but it sounds like a question. "He seemed normal?"

"Kyle can be such a baby when I don't want to hang out with him," Riley says with a laugh. "We hung out a little while you guys were gone, but I've been busy so I keep blowing him off. I think Henry gets sick of him too, because Henry is more of the quiet silent type, ya know? Kyle just has so much energy all the time."

"Why have you been busy?" I ask, once again being reminded of exactly how much we need to catch up on from the last few days.

"Dude..." Riley holds up her hands. "I've been translating the book. But that can wait—I still need the deets on what the hell you two have been doing, besides killing people. I mean, seriously! What the hell?"

Theo leans down and kisses me on the temple. "Get her all caught up, and I'll go talk to Kyle."

"Bye," I say, unable to hide my smile.

Riley gives us a big eye roll, but as soon as the door closes behind Theo, she's back to business. "Start from the beginning."

The door swings back open, startling me. Theo runs a hand through his hair and I notice a vein on his forehead. "We can talk later. You're coming with me."

"What? Why?"

Theo glances behind him and then steps inside, closing the door again. "I can't leave you alone, not right now. I can't let you leave my sight. I've seen movies, okay? The bad guy always kidnaps the girl when the good guy's not looking."

He sounds a little crazy, but I can tell he's serious. His hand slides down my arm. "I'm not leaving you. Come with me to meet Kyle."

"Wait—Alexo is dead." Riley holds out her hands at her sides. "*Who* is the bad guy in this situation?"

I turn to Theo, giving him a serious look. "I can't leave her now. She needs to know everything, especially if that bitch might show up any second and we have to run. I'm not going anywhere without Riley."

"That bitch?" Riley says. "What bitch?" She's standing all rigid now, clearly aware that something is seriously wrong. This is how I expected her to act the first time I called her after breaking out of Lady Em's castle.

"You're right," Theo says, exhaling. He sits on the armrest of a nearby chair. "Kyle can wait. Riley, you might want to sit down for this."

IT TAKES an entire hour to explain everything to Riley. From the balcony, to Lady Em, to me being Theo's new lifeblood. The prison that was actually a nice room, and how we broke out and met two members of Embrook along the way home. Theo explains who Damien is to him, and that he's currently here in Austin, staying at a nearby hotel until we figure out what to do with Lady Em.

We all decide that at some point soon, we should tell the guys about Lady Em and how Dover clan will want their stones back when they discover that they've been stolen. Theo wants to be the one to do it himself, still keeping us girls in the dark as if we don't know about it. Riley agrees.

I think we should all come forward. Riley and I are a part of this now. Our lives are keeping these guys alive, so I think we should get a say in how we end this war, how we find a way to claim our lives back.

"I really don't think Kyle knows anything about this," she says after a long stretch of silence. "He's just so genuine and kind, you know? He looks up to Alexo."

I look at my hands. "You should have seen how sad he was when Alexo ordered Jayla to be killed."

"Poor Kyle. He's too nice for a life like that."

"He's terrified of doing wrong by the clan," Theo says. "Kyle was only made an immortal a few years ago. Before that, he was some ivy league college student with severe asthma. Immortality cured him of his allergies and breathing issues and now he lives a happy life. He's told me before that he'll do whatever it takes to stay on Alexo's good side."

"If we tell him the truth, do you think he'd help us?" I ask.

Theo makes a noncommittal shrug. "I hope so."

"Wait..." Riley holds up a finger. "Alexo is dead. Where's his body?"

I can't believe that never crossed my mind. A sudden image of a mangled dead body on the ground below the library's balcony makes me shiver. Shouldn't it be smelling by now? Surely the gardener would have seen it and reported it to the authorities. Oh shit.

Theo wraps an arm around me. "Alexo was old enough that his body would have decayed to the age it would have been if he died instead of turning immortal."

"What does that mean?" Riley asks.

"Dust to dust," Theo says, making his hands explode out like a firework. "Alexo is a pile of ashes by now."

I don't know why, but the idea of not having a body makes me feel like less of a killer. Alexo was ancient and he deserved to die. His body was mostly dead anyway, only being kept alive at the expense of my own flesh and blood.

THIRTEEN

I'M REALLY GOING TO MISS MY OWN PERSONAL SHOWER WHEN THEO AND I finally leave the mansion. We haven't exactly spoken about it, but since we're secretly planning to take down Lady Em, it's obvious we won't get to stay in the mansion since it's for the Rosewater clan. And that's a real shame because my shower is the most magical shower in the world. I know it's nothing but drywall and tile and plumbing and glass, but I can't imagine a contractor ever being good enough to replicate something like this in another house.

I lean my head back and let the hot water rinse out my shampoo. When I'm in this oversized bathroom, my feet warm on the tile floor, the shower scented with lavender, I can forget all about my worries.

Like how once Lady Em is taken care of, Theo will return to Embrook. I don't want to join another clan, especially as a lifeblood. And that's a completely different worry that plagues me every second of every day.

I am a lifeblood.

Still.

I grit my teeth as I stare at the bracelet on my wrist. The water splashes over it, oblivious to its power. I hated it before, and I hate it even more now, knowing that neither Theo nor I can remain alive if I'm not wearing it.

With a sigh, I turn the water hotter and lean into it, letting it wash away my every thought. For now, I'm safe in here. Showering is the one time each day that I can completely let go of everything that's sitting on my shoulders. I even sing a little, that's how restful and stress free I feel in this room.

By the time I reach up with a wrinkled hand and turn off the water, all of those problems settle back onto my shoulders, and that knot in my chest tightens. There is no escaping my uncertain future. It hangs over me like a cloud.

I step out of the shower and reach for my towel from a nearby rack.

"Damn," Theo says.

I jump, clutching my towel to my chest. I spin around and see him there, sitting on the stool I use to put on my makeup, a magazine in his hand.

"What the hell are you doing?" I say, my chest heaving from how badly he scared me.

"Just keeping an eye on you."

I roll my eyes and wrap the towel around myself, reaching for another one for my hair. "You are getting really extreme," I say, flicking drops of water on him as I walk to my closet.

We've been back at the mansion for a week now, and Theo still refuses to leave my side. He and Damien have hired private investigators to keep an eye on Lady Em, and Damien called in a few immortals from Embrook to beef up security on the mansion. They're stationed outside, around the property lines and at the two places where underground tunnels lead to secret rooms in the mansion. The Rosewater guys have no idea, of course, and it's been a constant debate between me and Theo on if we should tell them or not.

Now that Lady Em's identity has been revealed, Theo has pulled out all the stops. Seems like everyone has something to do now except for me and Riley. Actually no—Riley has been translating the book. I keep asking to help her but she has a system now, and it's quicker if she does it herself. She'll probably be pretty fluent in Greek by the time she's done.

"What happened to sitting outside the door while I showered?" I say, frowning at Theo as I get dressed. I pull on a pair of black yoga pants and a tank top with a sports bra. Theo closes his magazine and looks up at me. "I didn't sleep at all last night. Kept having these nightmares of you being taken away right from under my nose."

"Well, you could have told me that your neurosis has gotten worse," I say, tossing my hair towel at him. "I wouldn't have sang in the stupid shower if I knew you were in here."

Theo's smile softens. "It was really cute."

"Shut up, no it wasn't."

"You're a cute shower singer."

I turn away so he doesn't see me blush, and then I tousle my hair, deciding if I have the energy to blow dry it or not.

"You've been so annoyingly protective," I say as I towel dry my hair, deciding that yes, I'm too lazy to blow dry it. "I'm good at taking care of myself, you know. I grew up on the streets practically."

He stands and moves behind me, his hands resting on my hips while he stares at me in the reflection of the mirror. "I love you, Cara. That means I worry."

There's a crease in his forehead, a line of worry that's been there several days. Ever since—

"Wait," I say, spinning around to look at him face to face. "Are you being so protective because you love me, or because I'm your lifeblood?"

His eyes widen in surprise. "Cara..." He reaches for me but I step backward.

"You left me alone before. You'd leave me for *days* and not think twice about it. Then suddenly I'm your lifeblood and now you can't risk letting me get so much as a papercut. Because, God forbid, if I get killed, then you die, too."

The surprise on his face is replaced with hurt, and immediately I feel like an asshole for what I said.

A muscle flexes in his jaw. "If that's how you feel," he says, turning to leave.

But I can't let him go, not like this.

"Theo," I say, the word sounding like an apology in my stressed out voice. I reach for his arm. "Theo, don't go. I'm sorry."

It takes him a second to turn back to me. In that split fraction of time, I worry he'll keep walking and this will be our first fight. It claws my insides apart, until, finally, he turns back to face me.

"I wouldn't want to live without you."

I crush myself against him, wrapping him in the biggest hug my arms can make. "How are we going to get out of this?" I ask, my lips pressed against his chest.

His hands slide up and down my back, comforting me. "Think positive, love. It'll work out."

"Does thinking positive ever actually work?" I ask, gazing up at him.

He grins. "Well, it doesn't hurt."

FOURTEEN

Theo and I are the only people in the kitchen right now, because most people eat dinner before eight-thirty at night. We'd accidentally got caught up in bed and missed dinner with everyone else. I don't regret a thing, but I am starving. Lately I've been so stressed I forget to eat, and I'm not the kind of person who can just skip meals without getting grouchy.

Two seconds after the chef sets our plates down for dinner, Damien walks up, Malina trailing behind him, her brows pulled together in anger.

"Sir, I tried keeping him in the foyer," she says. "He pushed past me."

"It's okay," Theo assures her with a smile. "He's a friend. Thank you."

She gives an annoyed look at our new visitor and then turns to leave. I stare longingly at my food: homemade lasagna and garlic bread. When Damien arrives, it usually means we have to leave, or have some long ass meeting. I really, really wanted to eat.

I stab my fork into my food anyway, not bothering to say hello to our new guest. Damien looks extra hipster today, in dark wash skinny jeans with the cuffs rolled up at the bottom. His shoes are fake vegan leather and extra shiny, his shirt still plaid. The man loves plaid.

The chef has already disappeared behind the door, and Malina is gone, but Theo looks around anyway before saying, "Must be something big for you to barge in here. What's going on?"

Damien grabs a piece of my garlic bread and I scowl at him. "I got a pretty solid report from our investigators. Shall we go somewhere more private?"

"Hell no," I say, pulling my plate closer to me. "I'm hungry," I add innocently when the guys look at me like I've lost my mind.

Theo chuckles. "We can talk here. The guys are all out at the pool anyway."

It's another one of those nights where beautiful women come over to hang out and drink our free wine and catered appetizers. Damien pulls out a barstool and sits next to us.

"Lady Em works alone. Lives alone. Keeps to herself. They think that castle is her primary residence, though she has a few aliases and owns several properties."

"Where?" Theo asks.

He taps the wooden bar we're sitting on. "Here."

"I thought this was a rental?" I ask, my mouth full of food.

"It was built in 1999 by an oil tycoon named Jonathan Frances," he says. "When he died of mercury poisoning, he left the property and everything he owned to his half-his-age wife, Meredith Frances. I'm guessing the clan thinks it's rented because the name on the deed isn't Alexo's."

I shudder a little, knowing that this mansion I love so much belongs to that bitch. But in a way, it's a little funny to be living off her fortune. Take that, Lady Em.

Then I remember something that makes my heart skip a beat. The ornate tile work at the front door of the house. Right in the middle of the marble floor is a mosaic; it's the first thing you see when you walk inside.

A castle for my love. Established 1999.

A knot forms in my throat. She was immortal long before that. Lady Em made a man fall in love with her and give her everything, then she killed him. I wonder how many times she's done this, how many hearts she's broken all because the man she used to love broke her heart by choosing his wife over her.

When I look up, I realize I've missed out on the rest of Theo and Damien's conversation. I pretend that I've been listening all along as I catch onto the tail of their conversation.

"She has a lot of newspapers delivered to her," Damien is saying. "She spends hours in that castle pouring over newspapers and the internet, researching something. My investigators could only look through her windows with scopes, they couldn't get close enough to see details. But she's making a plan. She'll disappear for days at a time…probably trying to kill off other immortals, is my guess."

"If she wants more stones, why not kill off the Rosewater guys?" I ask with a shrug. "I mean, they're right here and she knows how to get to them."

"They're her clan," Theo says, and Damien nods. "She's making her own clan, one of which is all men and she's the only woman."

"She wants to be in control, is my guess," Damien says. "The other two clans are controlled by men. She's never been a fan of that, even back in the day when Theo first met her. She wanted power. Control. That's why Lord Timothy liked her so much, apparently."

"I don't want their dirty sex life details," I say, curling my lip in disgust.

My food is now cold, but I dig into it anyway, the emptiness in my stomach overpowering the quality of the food. Plus, since our chef made it, it's still pretty good. Damien steals another piece of garlic bread, but this time I ignore it.

"We need to be notified the next time she leaves," Theo says, pressing his fingers to the table while he thinks. He's completely ignored his chicken parm and I want to heat it up and eat it for him. I guess I'm the only hungry one here.

"When she leaves, we'll go and see what we can find in her little castle home."

Damien nods. "The investigators didn't see a single person come or go this week except for her. When she's gone, it'll be empty."

Theo's eyes sparkle. "We'll take every fucking stone she has."

"And then we'll have the full support and backing of the Dover clan. They'll handle it from there."

"Wait..." I say as an idea springs into my mind. "If Dover clan wants their stolen stones back so badly, do you think we could bargain for them?"

"I don't like where this is going," Damien tells Theo, and it kind of pisses me off because his voice has that *get your girl in line* tone to it.

I clear my throat. "If anyone can save me and Riley from these bracelets, it'll be the oldest clan in existence. We should offer them the stones in exchange for our freedom from being lifebloods."

Damien snorts. "Dover doesn't bargain. And they sure as hell don't care about lifebloods."

"It doesn't matter, if they care about their stupid stones, they'll do what it takes," I say.

Damien's jaw tightens. "And cause a war with Embrook in the process? I don't think so."

"I don't know," Theo says, flashing me a smile. "I think it's worth a shot."

FIFTEEN

On Friday afternoon, Riley walks into my room looking like someone who just pulled a twenty four hour shift at the world's busiest restaurant. Her hair is in a disheveled ponytail, and she's still wearing the shorts and shirt she had on yesterday.

"Hey," she says, letting herself into my room where Theo and I are watching a movie on my huge television. We're cuddled up at the head of my bed, our backs against a wall of pillows. Riley plops down at the bottom, below our feet.

"What is it with you and Jennifer Lopez movies?" she asks. She sounds more alive than she looks, which is good, I guess.

"I like them," I say, ignoring the look she gives me while I turn my attention back to Maid in Manhattan. It's probably my favorite JLo movie of all time. I mean, who doesn't love a rags to riches story?

"Don't look at me," Theo says when Riley turns an accusing gaze on him. "I tried to talk her into watching something that hasn't been in perpetual reruns on cable television for the last decade."

"It's a good movie," I say, turning up the volume on the remote.

Riley sits up, purposely blocking my view. "Let's go do something tonight. I think I've reached my limit on how long I can stay indoors."

There are dark circles under her eyes and she looks like she could use a good nap, but it doesn't seem to bother her. "What do you want to do?" I ask. I quickly follow it up with, "It can't be anything fun like mani/pedis because Theo will insist on coming with us."

"Hey, I can hang out while you go to the salon," Theo says. "Just pretend I'm not there."

Riley shakes her head. "No, I want to go out and have fun. Like see a movie. Get some dinner."

"Sounds like you want to go on a date with me," I say, placing a hand to my chest. "I accept."

"Sweet!" Riley grins. "Let's go somewhere with fried pickles, and let's see a movie with kickass fight scenes." She rubs her hands together, and even though her eyes are bloodshot and she kind of smells like stale coffee, she's getting more excited by the moment. "Since Theo is coming, I'll invite Kyle. Is that cool with you?" she asks him.

"Sure," he says.

"So it's a double date?" I say, giving Riley a knowing wiggle of my eyebrows.

"Oh, please," she says. She pulls a strand of my long blonde hair off my comforter and tosses it on the floor. "Kyle is my buddy, and that's all. We don't think of each other like that."

"Okay, maybe you don't, but does he like you? You shouldn't lead him on."

"I'm not leading him on," she says, standing. She smacks my thigh as she walks back to my bedroom door. "Let's meet up in an hour?"

"Is that enough time for you to shower and fix that rat's nest you call a ponytail?" I ask. Theo covers his smile with his hand.

Riley pretends to pop her collar. "Baby, you know it."

THE LOCAL MOVIE theater is packed, and I can tell it puts Theo on high alert. Kyle is being his usual normal self though, and I feel relieved when I see him talking a mile a minute about something he found hilarious on a TV show. We're waiting in line to buy tickets behind some girl and her boyfriend. The girl won't stop bitching to the guy about how if they'd bought tickets online, they wouldn't be in this mess of waiting in line. He keeps glancing off, particularly to stare at other women, and I want to grab the girl by the shirt and tell her to shut up and also that she's most definitely going to be single soon.

I don't mind waiting in line. It's something normal people do, and if only for a little while, it makes me feel normal, too. But Theo is unable to relax. He holds my hand tightly, pretending to nod along to Kyle's story, but really, he's surveying the area. There's nothing but teens on dates and old people on dates, and pretty much a lot of people on dates here at the movies.

Occasionally you'll see a group of friends walking in together, but there's so many couples here tonight, you'd think it was Valentine's day.

I'm on high alert too, but for a different reason. I keep checking Kyle for signs that he might be crushing on Riley. After all, they spend a lot of time together when Riley's not with me, and she's been known to break a heart or two in the past because she didn't like a guy who likes her back.

In our case, I guess it doesn't really matter if he is crushing on her—we'll probably all be gone soon anyhow. But I'm nosey, and a little protective over Kyle. He did try to save Jayla's life after all. I don't want him to be hurt.

Luckily, he's not acting like he thinks this might be a double date. When we step forward to buy our movie tickets, Kyle and Riley pay separately. Theo buys my ticket, but he uses his clan credit card that Alexo gave to him because it still works, and any way to screw over Lady Em makes us happy.

Since Riley wanted action, we get stuck watching a superhero movie that's a little too gory for my taste. I spend most of the two hours snuggling against Theo's arm and eating popcorn. It's not as romantic as I want it to be, because Theo is so rigid and uptight all night. He keeps glancing around like he expects Lady Em to jump out of the aisle and stab us all to death. His cell phone is on vibrate, and tucked in his jacket pocket and I swear he must reach down to feel for it at least fifty times during the movie.

"Chill out," I whisper to him during a loud fight scene. "We have security guards keeping track of her."

"I know," he says with a nod. "Sorry."

I slide my hand into his and rest my head on his shoulder for the remainder of the movie.

When the movie is over, Kyle and Riley immediately work together to find the nearest restaurant with fried pickles on the menu. Apparently, it's an inside joke between them, and they've had the chef try out several recipes for the perfect fried pickle, but he just hasn't nailed it yet.

"Okay, you've changed," I tell her as we walk back to Kyle's Camaro. "The Riley I know would never eat fried pickles."

She shrugs. "Kyle sold me on them. Now we need to find the perfect pickle. I'm thinking Red's Burger Shack. They have a four star rating on Google." She looks up at the boys. "Sound good?"

"I'm down," Theo says, throwing an arm around my shoulders. We climb into the backseat of the Camaro, which is the kind of seat that only lovers should ever share since it puts you right on top of each other. There's hardly any leg room and I'd hate to be back here with a guy I didn't like. Luckily, I'm with Theo and I don't mind the close quarters at all.

"I have a feeling this might be the place," Kyle says as he starts up his car. "Red's Burger Shack sounds like the kind of joint that would have the perfect crispy fried pickle with just a hint of seasoning."

"And homemade ranch dip, not that bottled shit," Riley says.

They grin knowingly at each other. Who would have thought two people could bond over freaking pickles?

"Red's?" Theo says. "Isn't that the Hooters wanna be restaurant that Russell loves because the waitresses dress like sluts?"

"I think so, now that you mention it," Riley says.

"Yeah, it is," Kyle says with a laugh. "Slutty waitresses and fried pickles. What could be better?"

"Slutty *waiters* and fried pickles," Riley says. "That would be better."

Theo and I exchange a glance, and then we look back at our friends who are now deep into the fried pickle conversation again.

Well, damn. I guess they are just friends after all.

SIXTEEN

When I wake up in Theo's bedroom, I'm a little disoriented at first. Sunlight filters in from the east window, casting a glow on the walls. I'm so used to my own bed in my own room that for a split second, I get panicky as thoughts of being trapped in Lady Em's underground prison haunt me. Then I open my eyes fully and realize exactly where I am.

I am safe in Theo's bed. He's sleeping beside me, his steady breathing a comforting sound. Usually he'll stay over in my room, not the other way around, but we'd been watching a movie in his room last night and I guess I fell asleep. I roll onto my back and stare up at the wrought iron candelabra hanging from the ceiling. Last night was a lot of fun. We had dinner and saw a movie and hung out with friends. I close my eyes and dream of a life where every Friday night is like that. Then the bracelet on my wrist gives me a gentle reminder that a dream like that can't ever happen.

Even if we find the stones Lady Em has stolen from immortals and bring them back to the Dover clan, they might not give me the way to remove the bracelet. And even if they did, Theo is still an immortal and there's definitely no way to make him stop being one. He'd die, and I'd be no better off than I am right now.

The only other solution is for me to become an immortal.

My heart aches as I think the words, but it's true. I've been trying to ignore it, shove aside the very idea every time it pops into my brain. Although the idea of living forever and having money, my love, and a life doing whatever we want sounds like heaven...the reality is hell.

I can't take someone else's life away from them quicker just to keep me alive. Theo has been doing it for decades, and he's honorable about the whole thing by finding people who are already dying. I admire him for that, but I can't see myself doing the same thing. I don't think I could take someone's life, especially when I have nothing to offer this world in return. Theo is fighting the good fight, sacrificing his lifebloods for the sake of his mission to defeat the leader of Rosewater.

What would be my mission? Nothing.

Just like all the other times I think of the future, I try to shove it all out of my mind and focus on the *right now*. But it's not working today. All I know is that eventually I will die with this bracelet.

And without it, I'll die too, it'll just take longer.

And despite it all, Theo will live forever.

Now my anxiety is so high I climb out of bed and walk to Theo's bathroom where I turn on the shower. The hot water feels good, but it doesn't erase my thoughts. Every day that goes by is another day I can't stand to think about what the future holds for us. It's hard to live in the moment when everything that comes after is a total nightmare.

After my shower, I grab a towel and dry off as much as I can because Theo keeps his room very cold. I'll have to cross the room to his closet to steal some of his clothes to wear and I'm not in the mood for being freezing and wet.

There's a hard knock on the door and I startle, my hands holding a towel over my hair. Then I realize the knock wasn't on the bathroom door, but the door to Theo's room.

"Give me a minute," Theo calls out.

I open the bathroom door a crack. He sees me and smiles, then holds a finger to his lips, signaling for me to be quiet. I leave the door cracked open, knowing I can't be seen from the bedroom door because it's around the corner.

"Morning, Henry," Theo says.

"Do you have a minute to talk?" Henry says, forgoing his usual friendly small talk.

"Sure, man. What's going on?" I can tell Theo is as concerned as I am by the tone of his voice.

Henry sighs. "I can't get ahold of Alexo. This is highly unusual because he always keeps in touch. It's been a week, now."

"Why are you coming to me?" Theo asks.

"Have you heard from him? Do you know where he might be?"

Theo pauses. I grip the door, my ear pressed to the crack so I can hear everything. "How much do you trust Alexo?" Theo says finally.

"Of course I trust him," Henry says, sounding a little offended.

"I know, but how much?" Theo asks again. "If I told you Alexo made me privy to a certain...benefactor of the clan...would you know who I'm talking about?"

"I don't understand," Henry says. "Alexo has told me everything."

"Except about the benefactor?"

"Who are you talking about? There is no one else." Henry sounds defensive now.

"I'm not trying to rile feathers," Theo says calmly. "I'm just wondering if your loyalties are solidly with the man who kept information from you, or if you'd choose the right path, if given an option."

"Theo, I don't know what the hell you're talking about," Henry says, his voice low. "But Alexo gave me the stone that saved my life. I owe him everything and I will always be loyal to him."

"Okay," Theo says. "To answer your question, no I haven't heard from him." There's a click of the door closing and then Theo exhales. I poke my head out the door and see him run his hands down his face. "This might be harder than I thought."

AT LUNCH, Bethany sends out an invite to the girls to try the new chicken tacos she's been perfecting from her own secret recipe. Riley and I figure we should probably go since we've stayed away from everyone lately. Theo comes too, because he's still refusing to leave my side even though we're only going to be in the kitchen downstairs, and not at a wild party full of threatening strangers.

Riley is already there when Theo and I arrive, and she's saving us two seats. I guess she knows by now to expect Theo wherever I go. At least until Lady Em is taken care of.

"Wow, Bethany, this looks amazing," I say as I settle onto the barstool Riley saved for me.

"Thank you," she beams. She's wearing a pale yellow dress with white sandals, and her golden hair is pulled back in a bun. Her face is dewy with sweat, her cheeks pink and excited.

The kitchen table is a bar-height wooden area that fits about ten bar stools. She's covered it with a colorful tablecloth in reds and blues. It's a make your own taco set up, with a huge tray of shredded seasoned chicken and bowls of several toppings.

Olivia and Nia walk in last, still wearing their pajamas. After Jayla died, these two girls seemed to find comfort in each other. It does feel weird, even after a couple of weeks, to be missing one girl. It makes me remember how the guys had to get a new girl to wear Jayla's stone. I wonder who it is, and why they don't live here yet.

Bethany puts some Spanish music on the radio and it really sets the mood for lunch. Her food is really good and it feels like we're at a cool bistro instead of in our house.

I make a couple of tacos and pile some chips and salsa on my plate. Even though it was a girl's only thing, Kyle stops by and makes a plate as well.

Riley handles the small talk way better than I do, and although I try to join in with talking about TV shows, and fashion, and what malls have the best food courts, I'm just really not feeling it. Every time I look at Bethany, Nia, or Olivia, all I can see is that they're going to die. Soon. The world may see three pretty girls, but I see three caskets about to be nailed shut.

We're nearly finished eating when Malina walks in, her lips pursed into a frown. "Theo," she says, like it's a sentence.

He sets down his Coke and looks back at her. "Your friend is here. He agreed to wait in the parlor for once."

Theo smiles. "Thanks, Malina. I'll go see him."

I drop the chip in my hand and turn to Riley. "Don't let anyone throw away my plate. I'm not done yet."

She laughs. "Like there's not *tons* of food left."

In the parlor, Damien sits on a black leather chair. He stands when he sees us. "Can we talk here?" he asks.

"Quietly," Theo replies.

"I'll get right to the point," Damien says, pausing to acknowledge me with a tip of his head. "She bought a plane ticket to Europe. A private car is on its way to take her to the airport."

"Perfect."

"I'll set up a perimeter with some of the guys, you go inside and find the stones," Damien says. "I brought the equipment that sends out sound pulses into walls to see where the hidden rooms are. If she's got the stones locked way, we'll find them. We need to act fast. It could take days to scour that place and we don't know when she's returning."

"We'll go now," Theo says. He looks at me. "Unless you're not done eating?"

"Screw eating," I say as hope floods into my chest, and happiness fills me like never before. "Let's take back what isn't hers."

SEVENTEEN

Damien secures a private jet for us at the local airport. It belongs to the Embrook clan and ironically, it's parked right next to the Rosewater jet in the hangar. It's not as nice as the other one, but when it comes to private jets, they're all pretty amazing, and anything beats sitting coach with a hundred strangers. We're all pretty quiet on the flight to northern California where Lady Em's private castle home is currently empty. I'd thought I would be nervous, maybe even a little scared when it came time to go back.

But as we land on a runway in sunny California and pile into a rented Chevrolet truck, I realize I am not scared at all. I'm also not nervous. Maybe it's because she's not there and we won't be locked up again. Or maybe I'm just getting used to the fact that I'll probably die by the end of this anyway.

I should leave a note for Uncle Will, thanking him once again for all that he's done for me over the years.

The castle looks different now that it's not raining and the sky isn't darkened by clouds. It doesn't look as majestic or castle-like. It almost seems like it was built maybe fifty years ago, out of bricks like a normal house, but someone fancied up the outside to make it seem more like a castle. I'm not sure how to describe it, but it's not really that cool at all. It seems below Lady Em's style, especially knowing that she owns the mansion in Austin. Why not live there full time?

Theo drives down the winding gravel driveway, parking to the left of the garage. There are two other guys here, dressed in all black. The security guards Damien hired. They nod at us as we get out of the truck.

"You two go ahead," Damien says as he walks to the bed of the truck where he's laid out all of his equipment. "I'll be searching the perimeter for hidden rooms and underground bunkers."

"You ready?" Theo asks me. He holds out his hand.

I take it. "Let's go."

Theo uses a crowbar to bust open the front door, which is a heavy wooden slab of a thing that goes with the castle-like exterior. Once we're inside, the whole place smells like roses and it also looks a lot like a real house and not a castle. I'd been picturing stone floors and walls, giant sweeping murals and metal candlesticks—pretty much like what the castles look like in movies and TV shows.

Instead, the walls are drywall instead of stone, painted in deep rich colors like burgundy and hunter green. There's a sitting room to the left filled with stuffy old people furniture, floral print everything, and an antique coffee table. It's so not what I'd picture being Lady Em's style, but if she was raised in a different time period, maybe she never grew out of it.

There are dozens of paintings on the walls. Half-melted candles in the sconces that line the hallways. I let Theo lead the way through the house, opening doors every so often. The rooms are lavishly decorated in antique furniture and artwork, but it looks as though no one has lived in this house for centuries. Lady Em is a strange woman, that's for sure.

We make it to the back of the house having seen nothing out of the ordinary, and certainly no stash of immortality stones. The last room at the end of a long hallway is locked. Theo bends down and peers through the hole. The door is made of dark wood, and a rusted brass lock has a large keyhole that you can see right through. He grabs the doorknob with both hands and shakes it, then pushes in hard.

The sound of wood splintering finally gives way and the door opens, the lock broken. The air floods my senses with the smell of rose perfume and there's no mistaking that this is Lady Em's bedroom. There's a large four-poster bed in the center of the room, a plush burgundy rug underneath it. Sheer curtains drape over the headboard and rise up into the ceiling. The bedspread is red satin and it's decorated with dozens of throw pillows.

There's a writing desk off to the side, stationary and wax seals waiting to be made into letters. Her antique wardrobe is tall and long, and I pop open the door to find dozens of beautiful gowns hanging inside.

"I found something," Theo says.

He's standing over the nightstand next to her bed. The little drawer on the front of it is open, his fingers still resting on the handle. I rush over there and see a single immortality stone set in a necklace.

"Is that yours?" I ask, recognizing the silver chain.

Theo nods. "It's useless to her without the lifeblood." He reaches down and takes it, sliding it his pocket. "Let's search the rest of the room."

Several minutes go by and we tear the place apart looking for the other stones she's stolen. The search is useless though, and after I've personally kicked and pried at every single floorboard to make sure none of them are secret hiding places, I stand up and wipe my hands on the front of my jeans. "They must be somewhere else."

Theo's forehead creases. The sudden change in his expression makes me nervous. He looks at me quickly, then turns toward the bedroom door.

A man appears. He's probably seven feet tall, and he's so muscular he might have trouble fitting through the doorway. "You're not allowed to be here," he says, his voice deep.

"And who are you?" Theo asks as casually as if he'd just walked into a bakery and wants to order a cupcake.

"I am Lady Em's personal security," he says. A vein pops out in his forehead. "Who are you? Why are you here?"

Theo tisks. "You're a terrible security guard, dude. We just walked right in the place."

"Impossible!" he says, his wide face twisting into a scowl. "The doors are locked."

Theo chuckles. "Where the hell did she get you? The warehouse of idiots?"

It's right about now that the guard realizes we're not some of Lady Em's friends just coming over to hang out. He looks at me, and then back at Theo. "You need to leave."

I'm a little scared of the guy, even if he is kind of stupid. He's nothing but huge bulging muscles, after all, and those things can be used to hurt us. Theo doesn't seem too concerned.

He takes the necklace out of his pocket and holds it up. "Where does she keep these?"

The guy's face flashes with recognition, and maybe even a little fear. "You need to leave, or I will make you leave."

"You won't make me do anything," Theo says, sliding the stone back into his pocket. "Where does she keep them?"

The hulking giant in the doorway grits his teeth. "Leave or I will kill you."

"Well, now you just pissed me off," Theo says. There's a hunger in his eyes that I've never seen before. He cracks his neck to the side and then tosses a wink my way before he charges forward.

The guy launches as well, his meaty fist raised and ready to punch Theo right in the face. Theo ducks, then grabs the guy's wrist as he throws the punch. Theo pulls the guy's weight forward and throws him to the ground. Then he swipes a curtain right off the freaking wall.

It only takes a second, but the curtain is now wrapped around the guy's neck, and his face is turning bluer by the second. He kicks and struggles, but soon he stops, the only energy he has left he uses in an attempt to breathe.

"You don't have a stone," Theo says through gritted teeth. "That means she hasn't made you immortal." He kneels down, digging his knee into the guy's abdomen. Judging by the guy's gurgle of pain, it doesn't feel very good.

"She doesn't care about you," Theo says, tugging the curtain a little tighter around his neck. "So why remain loyal to her? Help me and you'll be helping all of society."

His eyes are bloodshot, his face a picture of agony. But it only takes a few more seconds before he makes what resembles a nod. Theo loosens his makeshift noose a little. "Where does she keep the stones?"

"Fuck you," he spits out.

I cringe, because the guy is only going to piss off Theo more. "Don't worry," Theo says, turning to me. "I'll just kill him and we can find the stones the old fashion way."

"Fine!" the guy says. Panic seems to light up his whole face.

"Oh now you're cooperating?" Theo says, tightening the curtain around his neck. "Seems like it's a little too late now, buddy."

The guy thrashes and groans, begging for Theo to give him another chance. I'm pretty sure it's all just an act on Theo's part, but he's doing a damn good job of being convincing.

"The...safe," he says.

"Where?" Theo asks. His forearm muscles are taut as he grips the curtain.

"Attic," he says again. "Where I sleep."

"That explains why my men never knew you were here," Theo says, seeming to take his sweet time talking. "They looked for people inside the house, but not in the attic. So there's a safe up there?"

He nods. Well, he does what can only be considered a nod.

"What's the combination?"

"His birthday," the guys says.

"Who's birthday?"

His expression darkens. He doesn't know whose birthday is the combination, and now he's terrified to die.

"It's Lord Timothy," I say. I don't know for sure, but who else could it be? Plus this guy is cooperating with us, so I don't want him to suffer any more than necessary.

Theo releases him, then stands up. He holds out his hand, palm toward the guy just like Lady Em did before she blasted us with power. The guy cowers like a scared dog. Just as Theo must have suspected, this guy is used to her torture with the power she's obtained.

Now all Theo has to do is pretend he has the same power. "Leave," he says. "Walk out the front door and leave and never come back."

"Y-yes—yes sir," the guy mumbles.

With one hand facing the guy, Theo gets his phone with the other hand and calls Damien. "A man is leaving," he says into the phone. "Let him go. If he tries coming back, kill him."

"Thank you," the guy says as he scrambles to his feet.

"Lady Em is no friend of yours," Theo tells him. "If you want to remain alive, you'll never seek her out again. And you will never speak a word of this to anyone."

EIGHTEEN

Damien calls Theo's name from somewhere in the castle. The guard that Theo had let go has been gone a few minutes now, and we're still in Lady Em's bedroom, looking for anything that might be of importance before we head to the attic.

Theo walks to the door. "I'm down here," he calls back. "The long ass creepy hallway."

Footsteps jog down the length of the creepy hallway and Damien appears, his brows pulled together. "*Who* was that?"

Theo straightens his shirt which had gotten rumpled while he fought with the guy. "Lady Em's secret guard who lives in the attic."

"The attic?" Damien scoffs, running a hand down his beard. "The one place we didn't scout out before we came over. Who lives in an attic?"

"That guy, apparently." I look up at the ceiling, even though I know the attic door won't be in here. "He said the stones were in a safe in the attic. Let's get them and get the hell out of here." I shudder, glancing at the statue of a crying woman in the corner. "This place is creeping me out.

Damien and Theo chuckle, even though I wasn't being funny. Together, we search through the house again until we find a narrow metal staircase that spirals up into the ceiling. It's tucked away in the utility room that looks like a modern add-on to the old house. The door at the top of the stairs is open.

"I'll go first," Theo says, stepping in front of me. He puts a hand on the metal railing and begins scaling up the tiny steps, the metallic sound echoing off the walls in this small room. I'm behind him, with Damien behind me. It feels safer to be sandwiched between these two immortals, but the truth is that anything could be up here and none of us are prepared for it.

I watch Theo's body disappear into the hole at the top of the stairs, and briefly wonder how that massive man was able to fit through it at all. Theo's quiet for a minute, and then he calls out to us. "It's safe to come up."

It's awkward because the stairs end at the top of the ceiling, which is the bottom of the floor in this room. There's no handrail in the attic, just a square hole I have to step into. Theo holds out a hand for me, but I still feel uneasy. I don't say anything though, because Theo is already being protective of me. I don't want him to suggest that I sit this one out.

Once I'm inside, I look around. The walls are slanted inward with the roofline, but the attic spans nearly the entire house. It's mostly empty, cobwebs in the corners, dusty footprints on the wooden floors. One corner of the room has a bed, a minifridge, and a television on the floor. There's a laundry basket full of clothes at the foot of the bed, and an open Coke bottle next to the TV.

"What a sad life," I say, suddenly feeling sorry for the guy Theo banished from here. "We should have let him take his clothes or something."

"He'll be fine," Theo says.

Damien enters the attic space and makes pretty much the same face I did as he looks around. "So what are we looking for?"

"A safe," Theo says, walking hunched over through at attic so he won't hit his head on the low roof. "There's some stuff over there," he says, pointing toward a stack of boxes.

I turn the other way, still trying to free myself of thoughts about that guard. Lady Em has this huge home all to herself, yet she keeps her guard in the attic? That's just weird. Plus, as it's already proven, it makes for a crappy guard when he's not in the house ready to defend it.

Sunlight peers in from a vent in the roof, illuminating something shiny in the far corner of the attic. I venture toward it. An old sheet is draped over something square. I think it's furniture at first, but the shiny golden corner that's sticking out from the sheet looks like a picture frame. Only it's as tall as I am.

I pull the sheet back to reveal a golden framed painting. It's at least five feet tall, and ancient by the looks of it. Curious, I pull the sheet all the way back until it falls to the floor. Then I stand back, eyes wide as I take in what I can only assume is supposed to be a piece of art.

It's a portrait if a man with dark red hair and pale skin. His eyes are severely green, and I wonder if they're true to real life or if this was the artist's flattering exaggeration. The man is wearing a black cloak with a coat of arms on the breast pocket. His hands are folded in his lap. He looks regal. And bored.

"What's going on over there?" Theo calls out. He drops a box back on the stack he and Damien had been searching through and pats his hands on the front of his jeans.

"It's a painting of some guy," I say, stepping back so they can see.

"That's Lord Timothy," Damien says.

I look back at the painting. The man has an sharply angular face with a long nose and a stern expression. He's not exactly handsome, and it makes me question Lady Em even more. I mean, if you're going to fall crazy in love with someone and become a mass murderer because of it...shouldn't the guy at least be hot?

As the guys walk over, I step to the side and notice that the painting is leaned against something. I peer behind it and my heartbeat quickens. "I found the safe!" I call out.

That makes them walk a little faster. Theo pulls the painting off the safe and leans it against a nearby wall. And there, exactly as the guard had said, is a safe. It's black and shiny, not covered in dust like everything else in this attic. The dial in the center is lined up with the number zero. "What's his birthday?" I ask.

Theo looks questioningly at Damien.

Damien shrugs. "Hell, I don't know. You've met the guy."

"I didn't ask for his date of birth," Theo says sarcastically. Damien curses under his breath.

"You guys are so old," I say with a laugh as I take out my cell phone. I Google *Lord Timothy Dover Castle birthday* and then turn my phone to face the guys.

"How did you two survive in the days before handheld smartphones and Google?"

Theo grins and then leans over, kissing me on the cheek. "Thank you, love."

The birthday combination works and the safe pops open. It is completely empty besides ten blue velvet jewelry bags sitting on a shelf. Theo takes one and pours the contents into his hand. One immortality stone bracelet, and the matching necklace. "That wasn't so hard," he says.

Damien's finger touches each one and then he looks up, his forehead crinkling in the center. "Ten. Where did ten come from? I figured she had eight from the eight recent murders."

Theo sighs, shaking his head. "This bitch is on a murder streak." Regret flashes across his eyes. "I've been in this clan for months. I should have figured this out ages ago."

"It's okay, brother." Damien claps Theo on the shoulder. "We found it now. We'll put an end to this."

I want to say something, especially a gleeful shout about how these stones mean I will get my life back when we bargain them to the Dover clan, but the moment is too serious right now. The former owners of these stones were all immortals, many of them from Damien and Theo's clan. They were friends, and now they're gone because of one woman's desire for power.

"Let's get the hell out of here," Theo says, his eyes flitting to me. He makes this half smile and I can tell he's trying to pull himself out of the funk of knowing how many people died recently. I give him a half smile back.

"So what's next?" I ask. "We fly to Dover?"

"We fly back home," Theo says, shoving some of the jewelry bags into his pockets. Damien does the same with the other half. "Then we figure out a solid plan going forward."

I press the safe closed and make the number line back up with zero. I get a little thrill when I picture Lady Em returning here to find her home broken into, only to rush up to the safe and sigh in relief when it looks how she left it. She'll think we couldn't get in.

Joke's on her.

I want to argue about going home to make plans, but I hold my tongue. Plans are what make things successful, not barging around doing whatever you want. Right? I've made it this far, I can wait a little longer.

As we turn to leave, it almost sounds like…well…no, it can't be. But then I hear it again. I look up and see Theo and Damien walking toward the stairs, totally oblivious to the sound coming from behind the safe.

"Hello?" I call out.

Theo's footsteps stop. "Cara?" he says. I don't look at him. I'm looking toward the safe. Or rather—what's beyond it.

"Hello?" I say again. "Is someone there?"

"Yes," a soft voice calls back. "We're here. Who are you?"

NINETEEN

Theo whirls around, his eyes wide. Damien stands rigid. Both men look like they're preparing to fight, but they must not have heard what I did, because that voice was a child's.

"Where are you?" I call out. For a moment, I wonder if it's a ghost trapped in this attic. Normally I wouldn't believe in things like that, but that was before I discovered that immortality was a thing. Now, I'm likely to believe anything.

"We're in here," the voice calls back. It's so soft and tiny that I can't tell if it's a boy or a girl, or even how old they are. Just that they're very small, and probably weak.

"Cara," Theo calls out. "Wait." He rushes over to me, then puts a hand on the safe, looking for something that isn't there. Maybe he's thinking the ghost thing, too.

I pull out my phone and turn on the flashlight. The roof comes to a peak just behind the safe, and right there against the wall is another door. It's only about four feet tall, but there's a padlock on it and soft sunlight shining in through the crack on the floor.

"Who are you?" I call out.

"Who are you?" the voice says back.

"Do you work for Lady Em?" Theo says.

The voice is quiet for a while. Finally, it says, "Is that her name?"

"Open the damn door, Theo." I fix a glare on him. "It's a kid! Just open it."

"Be careful," Damien says, having suddenly appeared to my right. His jaw is clenched, a curious look in his eyes.

I roll my eyes and lift up my hands in surrender. "Fine, fine. I'll back up," I say, taking a huge step backward. The guys are trying so hard to protect me without making it look like they're protecting me. But I can take a hint.

They both seem relieved to have me step back out of harm's way, and I know I should be happy that Theo cares about me, but damn. Now is not a time for that.

Theo grabs the padlock and yanks it sideways, ripping the metal plate it's attached to right out of the wall. If it was that easy, I wonder why the kid didn't just kick their way out.

Of course, with the hulking giant of a guard up here, I guess I can understand.

Theo opens the door and sunlight floods into the dark attic. Damien steps up right behind him so I can't see inside, but the foul smell of something hits me so hard I almost choke. I pull my shirt up over my nose, covering it with my hand. Whoa. That is a bad, bad smell.

Theo and Damien step into the room. Their silence speaks volumes. I creep forward, curiosity digging into me. The room is very bright, thanks to a wall of dust-covered windows. It's about the size of a classroom, and the ceilings are all low.

The smell is so rank it makes my eyes water, but I can't stop walking toward it. I hear Theo curse. Damien gags. I keep my hand covered over my nose and step into the door frame, expecting something awful.

But it's so much worse than my imagination prepares me for.

A dozen children sit on the floor, wearing filthy clothes, their doe-eyed expressions staring at us in fear and wonder. Their skin is dirty, their hair matted, and in some cases, bloody. One corner of the room has a single toilet with no privacy walls. There's a table with loaves of bread and peanut butter, but that's all. Moth-eaten blankets cover the floor.

The stench is so bad it makes tears fill my eyes. My stomach tightens and if I had eaten anything in the last few hours, I'd surely be puking it up right now.

As I look around the room in horror, I see where the main source of smell is coming from. A dead body.

"What the hell is this?" I say, but my words aren't nearly enough for what I'm thinking.

Theo turns to Damien, who looks like he's going to pass out any second now.

"Why are you here?" I ask the group of kids. Most of them look around the age of ten or twelve, but they're all skin and bones, so maybe they're older. It's hard to tell. A girl with matted blonde hair and a ripped dress pushes herself up on her knees, but the very act looks painful to her. "We can't leave," she says, holding up her arm.

The sight of her bracelet sends a weight straight to the bottom of my stomach. A quick count tells me there's twelve kids in here.

"These are her lifebloods," Theo says, his voice soft, filled with disbelief. "She keeps children as lifebloods."

"We last longer," one of the boys says. He has dark skin and a big cut on his face.

"How did she find you?" I say. "Don't you have families? Are you missing children?"

He shakes his head. "We're all orphans. But we're from different places. She says she's going to adopt us and then she takes us here."

"Can I ask about the dead body?" Damien says, his voice muffled because he's talking under his hand. He hasn't stopped looking in that direction since I walked in here.

"It's an example," the boy explains. "If you take off your bracelet you die and she leaves your body here to remind us that we belong to her. So we don't take off the bracelets."

"Sometimes people take them off anyway," the first girl says. "Because it's better than being here. I want to, but I don't."

"Why's that?" Theo asks.

She shrugs, her bony shoulders shaking. "Because then she'll go find another kid to replace me."

My hands tighten into fists at my sides. Rage like I've never felt before bursts forth from somewhere in my heart, and it fills me from head to toe. Lady Em has been evil her entire life, but this is a new low. This is abhorrent, unfathomable. And it won't be left unpunished.

"They're coming with us," I say.

Theo and Damien don't even try to argue. A door on the other side of the room leads to an outside staircase. The fresh air helps clear out the rancid stench of rotting flesh, but soon we realize that some of the kids are too weak to walk themselves down the stairs. They're the ones who have been here the longest, and they probably won't make it much longer with the bracelet siphoning out their energy.

I drop to my knees and pick up a little girl, who wraps her bony arms around my neck. She stinks like body odor and mildew, but I let her hold on tightly as I carry her down to the grass below. The kids all perk up once they're outside, but it's clear that many of them are malnourished and sick.

Damien and Theo work silently, each taking down one kid at a time. Once they're all freed from their attic prison, Theo closes the door back and stares down at me from the top of the stairs. He doesn't have to say anything. I know what he feels. I feel it, too.

Damien calls the two men he'd brought with us to leave their posts. Between all of us, we have three extended cab trucks. Nine of the kids sit in the backseats and the three oldest boys who are the strongest sit in the bed of our truck. I tell them we're taking them to safety, but that they can't remove their bracelets.

"Not yet," Theo says, giving them what is supposed to be a smile. He doesn't look so sure of himself. "We're going to take you somewhere safe."

As we drive to the airport, I'm thinking all the questions I can't say out loud because there's kids in here who don't need to know how worried I am. We drive with the windows down and the air conditioning cranked. They all smell absolutely horrible, but I try not to let it affect me because it's not their fault.

Theo grips the steering wheel, his eyes focused on the road that leads to the airport and our private jet. I've already done the math in my head, and there's room for everyone to fit aboard, if only just barely.

"We can't just take them to social services," I say absentmindedly as I stare out the window. Having grown up in the system, I've seen kids get adopted out and then come back because their parents decided they didn't want them anymore. This isn't that kind of situation, though. We can't just take them back. They have bracelets. They'll die without them, and that will cause a huge issue since the normal world knows nothing about immortality.

"What do you think we should do?" Theo asks. "I mean, besides the obvious." He puts a hand on my arm. "We're going to get them cleaned up and fed and clothed." He smiles at me and it warms my heart to see the tender caring side of him. He's always been kind to me, but being kind to these children makes me warm inside. He could easily say it's not his problem and leave them to fend for themselves. But he's not. And that's just another reason why I love him.

"Thank you for saving us," a girl says from the backseat. She's the girl who talked to me in the attic. The one who is too brave to succumb to taking off her bracelet because she wants to save someone else from her same fate.

"What's your name?" I ask her.

"Ashlee."

"How old are you?"

"Twelve."

I remember being that age. It's when Uncle Will adopted me. I was struggling in school and I didn't fit in because I didn't have fancy clothes or the latest gadgets. But I had Riley. Being twelve sucked though.

"Well, Ashlee," I say, giving her a smile. "You are welcome. I'm sorry we didn't get to rescue you sooner, but you're safe now."

"When we go back," she says as she bites her lip, "Can you tell them to let us stay in the group home? We don't want to be adopted again."

Tears fill my eyes. The group home sucks. It was always better to be adopted. This poor girl and all the other kids deserve real homes with loving parents. And now they might be too scared to ever try to love someone again.

In this moment, I know exactly what I want to do. It hits me like a freight train, taking over every other goal in my life. I want this more than I want freedom from my own bracelet. More than I want to find a way to be with Theo forever without taking lives from an immortality stone. I don't just want this. I need it. I look over at Theo. "You have a lot of money, right?"

He makes a weird face. "Yeah."

"I want to keep them," I say, my decision resolute. All the noise in the backseat quiets, and I'm keenly aware of three sets of eyes on me, plus Theo's. "I want to give them a home. All twelve of them."

Theo glances back at the girls, who stare at him with expressions of wonder and fright. They don't know us at all, but I hope they can sense that we're better than Lady Em. We're the good guys.

"Of course, love," he says, giving me a soft smile.

"When can we take the bracelets off?" the girl asks.

"Soon," I say, turning to face them. They watch me intently, their dirty faces eager and slightly hopeful. "Your bracelets are attached to Lady Em's necklace, which you probably already know."

They nod. "So as long as she's alive, you can't take them off. But you don't need to worry for long, because I'm going to find her. And I promise you," I say, gritting my teeth. "I will kill her."

TWENTY

For a group of children, these kids are pretty quiet on the entire flight back to Texas. A few of them ask to use the restroom, but the rest of them either sleep or stare off into space. I feel so awful and I don't have the first clue what I should do besides feeding them and giving them new clothes and a shower. And even then, I'm not sure how to go about doing that when the only home I have at the moment is occupied by several other people who absolutely cannot know about this.

When we land, I call Malina and ask where everyone is. She tells me the girls are in their rooms and Henry is also in his room. Russell and Kyle are in the gym. I guess I couldn't get lucky and hear the response I was hoping for, which is that everyone suddenly decided to fly to Jamaica for the next month.

"Can you have the chef prepare some food for me?" I ask her as our motorcade of three trucks gets close to the house. "I need about two dozen sandwiches, some chips and two dozen water bottles. Have them all spread out on the tables in the gardens."

"Okay, I'll get right on it," she says.

"Thanks," I say, lowering my voice. "Could we have your discretion as well? I don't want anyone knowing about my new visitors just yet."

"Not a problem, Cara."

"Oh, and ask Chef to make the sandwiches have meat and stuff in them. No peanut butter and jelly." Having seen what Lady Em served the kids, I think they'll all be happy to eat something besides peanut butter.

"Great idea," Theo says when I hang up the phone. "Food should be first, then we can get let them take showers and get new clothes. There's boxes of new clothing in the basement so we should find something for everyone."

"I didn't even know we had a basement," I say, lifting an eyebrow.

"It's connected to the underground hallway you used when you spied on Alexo."

"Ah..." I say, wishing I hadn't just remembered that day. "So what are we going to say if one of the guys sees us?"

"I've got it worked out, I think," Theo says. He slows the truck at the gate and leans out of the window to punch in the gate code. "We'll tell them this is a business operation, orders of Alexo. It'll keep them quiet for a while so we can figure out what to do."

"You're a genius," I say.

Theo smirks.

"Whoa!" Ashlee says as we drive toward the house. "You live here?"

"Yep," I say, flashing her a smile. "We're going to hang out here a bit until we figure out how to take care of you guys."

"Cool," she says, her eyes bright and excited as she peers out the window.

Theo drives the truck off the main brick driveway and toward the gardens. I've seen catering trucks do the same thing, so I know the ground is solid. He parks under a shade tree at the far end of the gardens, which is probably hidden by enough greenery that no one can see us from the mansion. Damien and the other member of the Embrook clan park their trucks next to ours.

All of the kids pile out and we help the sick ones to the tables in the gardens. The flowers and plants are thick and lush, making a winding pathway into the center where a courtyard is set up with several tables that have built in shade canopies on top. It's the perfect spot for entertaining because the floral gardens smell amazing and there's enough shade trees to keep it mildly cool in the summer. Right now it's also the perfect place to hide twelve ratty kids.

Chef worked quickly, and there's already a full spread of food on a long table near a garden wall of peonies. Theo tells the kids to dig in, and they excitedly fill their plates with sandwiches, olives, cheese, veggie sticks, and fruit. There's juice boxes and soda, but I encourage the kids to drink water since I'm positive they haven't had enough of it lately.

Once everyone is settled, I text Riley.

ME: come to the gardens immediately. Come alone.

Riley: on my way

I walk to the outer edge of the gardens and wait for her there. She waves at me as she crosses the mansion's large lawn. "What's up?" she says. "Did it work?"

"We got the stones," I say, nearly forgetting what she was asking in the first place because so much has happened since then. "But we got something else, too."

Riley lifts an eyebrow. "Is it bad?"

"Well...it's not good." I motion for her to follow me. "We found Lady Em's lifebloods."

"Oh." Riley sounds relieved. "Well that's to be expected, right? I mean she has to have them somewhere."

I stop just at the edge of the last row of greenery, where the children are eating just a few feet beyond our sight. "Riley." I swallow the lump in my throat. "They're children."

Riley's face goes pale. "Orphans," I say, feeling my insides twist with revulsion at the very thought.

"No," Riley says.

I nod, then step out of the way so she can turn the corner and see for herself. "Oh shit," she breathes. "No. No way. This is..." Her eyes scan the group of children who are sitting close together, each of them hunched over their food as if they're afraid it'll be taken away at any minute. "This is pure evil."

"Yeah." I look up and see Ashlee watching me. She waves, her dirty face curving into a smile. I wave back.

Theo and Damien talk quietly to each other as they stand guard over the children. Both of them look like they're not exactly sure what they should be doing.

"I'm going to take care of them," I tell Riley. "Theo has money—I don't know what exactly I'll do, but I'm thinking we can buy a house and let them live with us. They're all orphans anyway, and until I kill this bitch and deactivate their bracelets—" I stop and shake my head. "No, forever. I want to take care of them forever, Riley."

She nods quickly and wraps her arms around me in a quick hug. "Me too. We'll give them a good life, at least as long as we can."

"What do you mean by that?" I ask.

Her gaze meets mine and my heart sinks. "Our bracelets," I say. "We'll get rid of them, Riley. We got the stones back from Lady Em and we'll return them to Dover and they'll tell us how to remove our bracelets."

"And then what?" she says, her voice breaking. "Is your boyfriend going to give you enough money to raise twelve kids while you grow old and he lives forever?"

"Riley," I say, taking a step back. "That was horrible."

Her face falls. "I know. It was mean. I'm just...I'm freaking out here, Cara. I've been translating that book for days and it's just getting to me. I'm learning everything about immortality and yet I'm sitting here slowly dying. If we do manage to get out of these bracelets, what then? We have nothing and no one. We'll be back to living on the street, even if the clan does decide to give us a hundred thousand dollars as a paycheck. That's not much on the whole scale of things."

"What are you saying, Riley?" It's so weird hearing her speak so candidly about this. Normally we keep it quiet, both of us hoping it'll all work out somehow.

She glances at the kids, her eyes flitting to Theo and Damien, and then back to me. "I want to be immortal."

Her words hang in the air for a long moment. "Riley..." I say finally. "You'd have to kill people to do that."

"I know. And I don't like that idea, but Theo...he does it humanely."

"How could we do that though? We don't have riches to bribe terminally ill people."

"We could borrow from him until we did get riches?" she suggests. Then she crosses her arms. "Wait. You just said *we*. I thought you were against the idea."

"I am," I say quickly. "I mean..." I exhale and gaze up at the blue sky. "I can't kill others to stay alive. But I also can't live and die as a human without Theo by my side."

"Well, I'm doing what you're doing," Riley says. "Whatever you decide, I'll be there with you." She makes this little smile but it doesn't reach her eyes.

I stare at Theo across the gardens. He is so handsome and kind and good to me. And yet he is so far out of reach. "I just wish there was a way."

"Me too," Riley says softly.

"Well, hello there," Henry says from behind me. I whip around, coming face to face with the man. His long dark hair is in a low ponytail that the breeze is tossing around. Henry may have said hello to me, but his eyes are focused behind me.

"What do we have here?"

TWENTY-ONE

"Just uh..." I blink, cursing myself for suddenly losing my ability to form coherent sentences. "Just feeding some kids," I say, slapping on a haphazard smile. I mean, that's a coherent sentence. It may leave more questions than answers, but at least I managed to say something.

Holy crap, what is wrong with me? Obviously, that stupid sentence doesn't do anything. Henry brushes right past me, Olivia and Nia on his heels. They both toss me scornful looks, and it's like I'm right back in high school with the popular bitches judgmentally smirking at me as they walk by. I scowl right back at them, then stand tall like I have nothing to hide. What are they even doing here?

"What is this?" Henry asks, his voice sounding more angry than curious each time he speaks.

Theo comes over, the picture of calmness as usual. "Henry, hello."

"What is this?" he says again. "Who are those children and why do they look like they've been pulled from a tornado?"

"If you'll lower your voice, I'll be happy to explain," Theo says. He notices the girls behind Henry and lifts an eyebrow. Nia and Olivia can't pull the stupid smug looks off their faces. Makes me want to slap it off.

"She's hiding something," Nia says, pulling all the attention to herself. She points at me. "I overheard her on the phone with Malina. She was telling her to keep quiet."

"That's not—" I begin, but it is true, so I can't exactly say much. "What the hell is your problem?" I say instead. "We're in the same clan here. You're acting like you're trying to get me in trouble when I've done nothing wrong." That's also a lie, but it sounds convincing and Nia flinches. Good, maybe she feels bad for ratting me out.

Olivia shrugs. Her black dyed hair and heavily applied eye makeup don't scare me. Underneath the scary goth look, she's just a tiny girl who couldn't beat up a fly. "It sounded like you were up to something bad, so we told Henry."

"Because obviously jumping to conclusions is the right thing to do," I snap.

"Ladies, you can go now," Theo says to Nia and Olivia. They don't even try arguing with him before they turn around and leave. I breathe a sigh of relief as I watch them go, their metaphorical tails between their legs. I know we weren't the best of friends or anything, but if I heard them tell Malina to keep quiet, I wouldn't go tattle on them the very next second.

The children haven't even noticed this exchange, and I'm happy to see they've opened up a little since they started eating. Now some kids are talking to each other, some are even laughing. Ashlee has taken to passing out juice boxes and water bottles to the kids who've already drank their first round.

"Let's talk around the corner," Theo says to Henry. Then he turns back to Damien, giving him a questioning look that can only mean *will you watch the kids?* Damien nods. I wonder how many time this centuries-old immortal has been asked to babysit.

Theo and I walk Henry around the corner of the gardens and I wait for Theo to talk first. Now that the initial confrontation has worn off, Henry doesn't look so pissed. Now he's more contemplative. "Did you kidnap children?" he asks, his voice quiet.

"Yeah, actually," Theo says with a smirk. "That's kind of exactly what we did. But as you can tell, they've been neglected and abused so we're taking care of them for the time being. We'd prefer to say we rescued them over kidnapping them."

"We are not a clan of child rescuers or humanitarians," Henry says through clenched teeth. "We have to keep a low profile. What you're doing here—it's unacceptable. What if the police show up here? If you want to do good, do it somewhere else."

"Listen," Theo says. He drags his hand down his mouth, like he's struggling with whatever he's thinking. We haven't exactly thought this plan through very well, and I knew we'd have to do something eventually, but I didn't think our lunch would be crashed this early by a member of the clan. I still want to get the kids cleaned up and dressed in new clothes. We can't do that if Henry is going to get pissed about it.

I start mentally thinking up nearby hotels that might not notice if we bring a bunch of dirty kids there, but I come up empty. It's hard to go unnoticed with a group like that. One or two kids I could hide, but not a whole caravan.

"I'm not going to lie to you, Henry," Theo says after a moment of contemplation. "You've become a close friend to me over the months, and I just can't do it. You're a good guy."

Henry crosses his arms over his chest. "So don't lie to me. What is going on?"

"We need all the guys here. I'll explain it to everyone and then we can see where to go from there."

My eyes widen and Theo just puts a hand on the small of my back. He nods as if he's just convinced himself that he's doing the right thing. "Yeah. This is happening. Get all the guys together. Tell them to meet me in the den and I'll explain it all. I have quite a lot to talk about."

"We can't get all the guys together," Henry says. "Alexo is still gone and he's not responding to my messages."

"Yeah, well that can be addressed at the meeting."

Henry shakes his head. "I won't have a clandestine meeting of the clan without our leader there. You need to explain yourself, but you can do it to me and then I'll tell Alexo."

"That's not going to work," Theo says, rocking back on the balls of his feet. "I admire your loyalty to Alexo, but your plan won't work. We need to gather the guys now and have a crucial meeting. Then you can reassess where your loyalties lie."

Henry's brow dips inward. "I don't like where you're going with this, Theo. Alexo needs to be at the meeting."

"Well, that's not going to happen." Theo's shoulders lift, his head tilting to the side.

"And why not?" Henry says.

"Because Alexo is dead."

TWENTY-TWO

Malina and Damien help me round up the children and bring them into the mansion's gym while Theo and Henry call a meeting together. The gym has a locker room with plenty of showers and towels, as well as a big area for the kids to play and hang out. The two oldest girls and boys are all fifteen, and they agree to help the younger ones shower and get dressed. Malina brings a bunch of shirts and shorts from the basement. I can tell she's concerned about the kids, and she promises me she'll take care of them while we're in the meeting.

"Everyone?" I call out, waving my hand in the air to get their attention. The kids are standing near the entrance to the locker rooms. Our oldest boys and girls have lined them up like they're in school. Everyone seems to be doing much better now that they have a belly full of nutritious food and water. They all turn to me at the sound of my voice. I am suddenly brought back to the memories of being in the group home, and how the adults in charge would round us up to yell at us about behavior and manners and rules. I shake away the thought.

"In case you don't remember, my name is Cara," I say to the crowd of eager and curious children. I try to smile, but they're so pitiful looking it breaks my heart. "This is Malina," I say, gesturing to her. She waves. "She's here to help you get settled in, okay? I have to go to a meeting but I want you to all shower and get clean and then put on some new clothes. Then you can hang out here in the gym until I come get you. Malina will show you the bathrooms and get some first aid supplies if you have any cuts or scrapes, okay?"

They nod in unison. These kids are nothing like the unruly jerks I used to live with in the group home. Months of fear caused by Lady Em must have turned them into model kids who don't act out. It makes me sick just to think about.

"You all have to stay in the gym area, okay? I'll come get you soon and we'll find a place for you to sleep and stuff. It's all going to be okay. Just bear with me for now."

"Thank you!" Ashlee calls out, motioning for the other kids to do the same. Soon, they're all shouting thanks to me, and one boy around eight years old runs up and hugs me. It feels really good to be helping someone out for the first time in my life.

I start getting nervous as I make my way through the house and to the den, where everyone is already waiting. Nia, Bethany, and Olivia are the only members of the house who aren't here. The guys are standing facing Theo. Kyle looks a little confused, but the rest of them seem to know something seriously epic is about to happen. I'm still not sure what Theo has in mind until he starts talking.

"Let me start by saying that I have nothing but respect for every one of you," Theo begins. "You're all decent men and make a good immortal, in my opinion."

There's an instant shift in the air, a panic caused by Theo saying the I-word in front of me, a *lifeblood*. He draws in a breath. "Yes, I said it. Immortal. Cara knows what's going on."

Kyle's eyes go wide, his cheeks turning pink. Russell and Henry stare at me like I've grown an extra head, but I try to remain impassive.

"I figured it out on my own," I say, just in case they're about to attack my boyfriend. "Theo didn't tell me."

"She knows," Theo says. "So does Riley."

Now Kyle's cheeks are extra pink, and he looks like he might throw up. The other two guys are handling it well, all things considered.

Henry clears his throat, giving Theo a look. "Ah, yeah, the other thing," Theo says. "Alexo is dead."

Russell shifts on his feet. "What in the hell?"

Theo holds up a hand. "Please, brother. Allow me to explain."

The next several minutes are the most awkward of my life. Theo starts from the beginning—which I worried would be the worst place to start. Luckily, the guys listen as he tells them about his true clan and how Embrook sent him to discover who was really the brain behind the new clan of Rosewater. Theo stays calm and explains how there's no way Alexo could have been running the show, and that's why he had his mission.

He fudges the story a little bit, leaving out the part of me removing my bracelet being the reason I discovered immortality. Instead, he tells them I discovered the book in the library and put two and two together, and that Theo confirmed my suspicions. It's better this way, because if they know how weak he was with me, a lifeblood, then it'll look bad on him as an immortal. The true reason I'm alive today is because Theo put my bracelet back on before I died.

He shouldn't have done it, but his love for me overpowered what clans consider to be the right thing to do.

He then explains about how Jayla left behind the video, and we then spied on Alexo on the balcony. Theo really lets it all out—he holds no secrets back from the guys, despite how we've been lying and going behind their backs for weeks now.

When he explains the exact way Alexo died, I worry the backlash will finally come. But something else happens.

"Cara." Henry says my name. "What you did was a selfless act of bravery."

I don't know what to say, so I just watch him. He turns to Russell. "I will not stand behind a man who lied to us about the very origins of our clan. Alexo is a traitor."

"I agree," Russell says, his jaw clenched. "He led us to believe he was in charge, that he was the sire of this entire clan. But he never truly let us know the reasoning behind all the business transactions we did for him."

"He was keeping secrets for Lady Em," Theo says. "He was being pushed around and controlled by her, and she's proven to be manipulative and evil."

"Our entire clan is a lie," Kyle says, speaking for the first time since Theo began this long story. His forehead is wrinkled and he looks about ten years older from the stress of hearing all this.

"I want to meet this woman." Henry's lips press into a thin line.

"Wait," Kyle says, holding up a hand. "Where did the kids come from?"

"They are Lady Em's lifebloods. She kept them imprisoned in a filthy attic room above her house. Cara took them home with us."

"Probably a good move," Kyle says.

"I want to meet this woman," Henry says again. "She will explain herself."

"I haven't even gotten to the best part," Theo says, running his hands down his jeans. He then explains about the missing stones and the murdered Embrook and Dover clan members. It's pretty obvious that Alexo has never informed the guys of the other clans and their very long history of order and honor. It's now that Theo explains the way things work in the immortal world, and the understanding between the Dover clan and Embrook. All three of the men look petrified, and I can't say I blame them. They're finding out for the first time that their clan is rule-breaking and immoral, and hated by the other two.

"She was building her own clan for her own selfish reasons," Theo says. "And now she's murdering other immortals to obtain new stones since she can't get them from Dover's secure location. If we don't kill her first, the Dover clan will."

"Then let's be first," Kyle says, his eyebrows lifting in excitement. "Let's throw her in a hot attic with no food or water, see how she likes it."

"I'm loving the way you think," I say. "But she has to die as soon as possible. It's the only way those kids will be free. Who knows how long they've been trapped in there. They might not have much time left."

"Do you plan to care for them?" Henry asks me. I see admiration in his eyes, though his tone was a little judgmental.

"Yes," I say. "After Dover frees me from being a lifeblood. I will take care of them for as long as they need."

"What makes you think you'll be freed from being a lifeblood?" Russell says. He's the only member of the group who seems the most gobsmacked by the revelation that Alexo was lying to them.

I explain about stealing the stones back from Lady Em, and how if anyone can fix me, it'll be Dover. They're the oldest immortals and they'll know all the inner workings of how immortality works.

"What about Theo's lifeblood?" Russell asks. "What will he do if you're freed from the bracelet?"

"He'll find a replacement and we'll swap places." Just saying the words makes me feel sick to my stomach, but I have to trust that the terminally ill lifebloods Theo chooses are happy with their decision.

"And Riley?" Kyle says. There's a look in his eyes that says he knows more than he lets on.

"She'll do the same, I guess. We're not staying lifebloods anymore. I refuse." I fix a look on the three men in front of me. "And you should all reconsider your lifestyle, by the way. Just because your lifebloods are treated well doesn't mean it's okay. They should know what they're getting into. You should give the girls here the opportunity to free themselves instead of slowly killing them."

Kyle looks ashamed, and for a brief second, so does Russell and Henry.

"Alexo said we had no other choice," Henry says after a moment. "But if there is another way, I will happily take it."

Damien had been silent this whole time, standing in the corner of the room, but now he speaks up. "She knows not what she says." He glances at me, and I scowl. "She only hopes for freedom from the Dover clan, but I don't think giving them back the stones that are rightfully theirs will make them feel favorable to her at all. She'll be lucky if they even entertain the request before they kick her out."

"Well, I have to try," I say, standing my ground. "There has to be a way out of these bracelets without killing me or Theo. Once I discover how, I will share it with the other girls."

"I think that's about all there is," Theo says, breaking up the tiff that was starting to form between me and Damien, Theo's oldest friend. "You now know everything I know. If you choose to remain a clan, I will try to vouch for you, but Damien is right. Dover clan is brutal and ruthless when they're betrayed, and I fear they will demand your stones back. They will most likely want you dead before they'd recognize Rosewater as a real clan."

"Then what do we do?" Henry says, his voice level even though there's fear in his eyes.

Theo exhales. "You can leave now and live a life of secrecy, staying one step ahead of your enemies. Or you can stay with me, and I'll do what I can to make Dover recognize you."

"With your cooperation, the Embrook clan will back your legitimacy," Damien says. "You all seem like decent men, and Embrook doesn't care where you get your lifebloods."

"I care," I say in a huff, but no one notices.

Theo's Adam's apple bobs. "You are with me, or you are not. Make the choice now."

I listen to my own rapid heartbeat in the silence that follows. But it doesn't take long. The former men who were loyal to Alexo all decide to take Theo's side.

"We will fight with you to take down Lady Em," Henry says. "And then you will fight with us to prove our legitimacy as a clan. The Rosewater Clan deserves to stay. I'm not a coward, and I'm not going anywhere."

"Agreed," Russell says. "We're not running and hiding. We will stay together and fight."

TWENTY-THREE

"I'm not sure it's such a good idea," Riley says. She fixes me with a serious look that is so unlike my best friend. We're in the gym surrounded by twelve clean kids, all wearing brand new T-shirts and pants, some of which are a little too baggy on the smaller kids.

"Look, they're going to be here a while," I explain in a low voice. "The guys in the house have agreed to it, and so it's not like we can keep them a secret from the other girls. We should just ask her."

Riley lets out a huff of air, but then she agrees. She calls Bethany on her cell phone. "Can you come down to the gym real fast? I need your help."

She puts the phone back in her pocket and looks at me. "Bethany is on her way."

"Cool," I say, turning to the kids. "Okay guys, we're about to get a tour of this big house. Does that sound fun?"

They all eagerly agree. Though too skinny, the kids look much better having taken a shower. The dark T-shirts hide some of the bony frames that look malnourished and sad. In all, we have seven girls and five boys, ranging from ten to fifteen years old. Ashlee has been here the longest, which means she's the wisest of the group, but she's also seen eleven other kids die and be replaced. She says she was adopted just before Christmas, which means she's been a lifeblood for around seven months. Theo and the guys think that because she's so young, she'll probably survive two years with a bracelet, so that's good news. It means she hasn't been drained of too much of her life force yet.

The rest of them are in good shape, too. As soon as I murder Lady Em, they'll be free. And then, if they want to stay with me and Theo, I will promise to take care of them no matter what. We'll build our own mansion and we'll take care of them. My eyes sting with tears as I think about the love and care and food I'll make sure they have. They'll all get the best clothes and the trendy cell phones and they won't be treated like scum by the other kids in school. This will be a good thing. Even if Theo stays an immortal while I become mortal again without my bracelet, at least I'll have the kids to keep me occupied until I grow old. Maybe after they grow up, I'll become a foster parent, and I can try to rescue as many kids as possible from the system. That can help me cope with losing Theo. Although it probably won't help much.

Bethany arrives, her eyes wide as she takes in our visitors. I take it Nia and Olivia didn't rush off and tell her about the kids after Theo told them to go back to their rooms. Good. I hope they feel stupid that their little plan to rat us out didn't work.

"Hi Bethany," I say cheerfully, waving her over. "We have some houseguests."

I know she sees their bracelets because it's impossible not to notice the shining beautiful jewelry on the wrists of kids wearing plain clothes, so I say, "They're from another clan and need a place to stay. I was hoping you could work your magic and give us all a tour of the mansion."

She brightens. "Of course! That would be fun!"

Although Riley and I know the mansion better than even Bethany does by now, I like the way she gives the tour. She's sweet with the kids and she shows them all the exciting parts first, like the pantry full of food and the swimming pool and movie theater room. The kids slowly come out of their shell as we go from room to room, and when a pair of girls ask if we have any Disney movies, they don't want to leave the theater until I promise them we'll come back to watch a movie after the tour.

Since Theo and the guys are now huddled together in one of their rooms discussing plans of taking down Lady Em, Riley and I take care of the kids. When we get to the upstairs, Bethany and I go into the five empty bedrooms on the girl's end of the hall. There are no more empty rooms on the guy's side, so that means the kids have to share rooms.

When I start asking the kids who they'd like to share a room with, I'm surprised to see them clam up and look at each other nervously. "What's wrong?" I ask. "We could put the older kids together in a couple of rooms, and the younger kids can be together in another room. Does that sound good?"

Ashlee and another fifteen-year-old boy named Jaden look at each other. She leans over and whispers into his ear and he nods. "We'd like to stay together, if that's okay."

I look at Riley. She seems to catch on before I do. "It's safer that way," she says, leaning down to put her hands on her knees as she looks at the kids. She winks at them. "I totally get it. How about this: You guys look in each of these five rooms and then pick your favorite. Then we'll bring a bunch of mattresses in and you can all have a big sleepover! Sound fun?"

They cheer and rush off to look through the five open doors. Most of the bedrooms are set up like mine and Riley's, though some of them have better views of the lake because of where they're located.

"They'll probably want their own rooms eventually," Riley says as we watch the kids run from one room to the next. Jaden holds onto a girl who can't walk well, helping her get around. "They just feel safer together right now."

"Yeah, that makes sense," I say with a sigh. I hope these kids haven't been so emotionally scarred that they'll never be able to have a happy life again. My heart breaks for them, but I vow to do all I can to make them happy again.

After we've made good on our promise to drag all the mattresses over, Malina comes up and tells us she could have had the help do that instead. She gets another maid and they put clean sheets on the mattresses and make sure there's enough places to sleep for each kid in the room they've chosen, which is right across the hallway from Riley's room.

As promised, we all go back to the movie theater room and put on Frozen for the kids to watch. I get them all popcorn and candy even though Malina gives me a look and says it'll ruin their appetite for dinner, which is spaghetti and meatballs because Chef says the kids will love it. I don't care. Let them spoil their appetite with candy. They deserve it.

WHEN THE CREDITS appear on my TV screen, I look down at my phone.

Me: Still in the meeting?

Theo: Not much longer, love.

It's ten thirty at night and I've just finished watching The Wedding Planner with Jennifer Lopez. Riley is on the floor over by the window in my bedroom, working on the computer translation. There's a half-eaten pint of ice cream next to her. My ice cream is fully eaten, the empty carton on my nightstand.

After watching the movie, the kids scarfed down the spaghetti and meatballs as if they hadn't just eaten a ton of candy. The whole house came together for the meal—the guys, Nia, Olivia, Bethany, and me and Riley. It was fun, to say the least. We ate at the large dining table, with Theo at one end and Henry at the other. Afterward, the kids went to their room and all promptly fell asleep. I've checked on them three times.

Each time I get up, Riley sighs and rolls her eyes and tells me I'm being overprotective. The kids know where my door is and they've been told to come get me if they need anything. Still, I can't help but check on them. Each time I have though, they've all been passed out, sleeping blissfully on clean sheets in a clean room.

The same thing happens now, as I poke my head into their door for the fourth time tonight. Everyone is asleep. I smile and gently close the door, then go back to my room.

Riley is pacing the floor. I lift an eyebrow as I go back to my place on the bed.

"What's going on with you?"

She takes a deep breath, stops her pacing right in front of my bed and lets it out slowly, her lips forming an O shape. She wrings out her hands. "It's done."

"What's done?"

"The book," she says, sitting on the foot of my bed. "The whole book. It's done. I translated it from Greek to English."

I sit up straighter. "And?"

While her short hair is a mess around her face, her face is expressionless. "It doesn't say a word about removing a lifeblood bracelet."

I groan and toss my head back. "Dammit."

"There was one thing," she says, pinching the bridge of her nose. "It didn't really make sense though, but it had a word that meant *perpetual,* which took me forever to translate. It was used like, *perpetual lifeblood.*"

"What does that mean?" I say.

She shrugs. "It had a drawing—let me get it."

She grabs the book and opens it to a bookmarked page. The drawing is more like a scribble, and it's hard to decipher what it's even supposed to be. "Perpetual lifeblood..." she says, pointing to the Greek words at the bottom. "It looks like two broken stones to me. Right? Like if you have two stones and break them then your two lifebloods might be...perpetual?" she says the last word like she's confused. She screws up her face and shakes her head. "Nah. It doesn't make sense. Anyhow, it doesn't tell us how to take off the bracelet, just how to stay perpetually a lifeblood and that doesn't help."

I study the page, the words all foreign to me. I'm about to ask for the English version she translated so I can read it, but I know it's no use. Not only are the translated sentences weird and hard to understand, but the whole book is about being immortal, not about freeing your lifebloods. It makes sense that our answer wouldn't be in here, but still—it hurts like a slap in the face to know that the book I've put so much faith in has let us down.

"I'm sorry," Riley says with a sigh. "Have you put any more thought into becoming an immortal?"

I shoot her a look. "Even if I got over the fact that we have to take people's lives to be immortal, how—besides murder—would we get our own set of immortality stones?"

Riley flinches. "I guess I hadn't thought of that. I guess if Dover is happy we brought back the stolen stones, maybe they'll..."

"They're not going to give us two of them," I say, unable to hold back the frustration in my voice. "They're very picky about who they allow to become immortal and two teenaged girls are the last people they'd consider."

She turns around and then falls to her back on my bed, tucking her hands under her head while she stares out the window. "I guess it as just wishful thinking on my part. I mean, I'm happy to go back to a normal human who ages and dies, but I can't stop daydreaming about wanting to be an immortal. How amazing life could be."

Her words hit me hard because I've been thinking about it, too. I try not to, and I try to focus on the here and now. I tell myself I can't in good conscience take someone else's life to let myself live, but it doesn't stop me from daydreaming about an eternity with Theo.

There's a knock on my door and we both sit up. "Come in!" I call out, assuming it's Theo.

It is Theo, but he has Henry with him. I sit up straighter, then hop off the bed entirely. It's very awkward having him in my bedroom. "What's going on?" I ask.

Henry dips his head toward me in a hello. "We have discussed it. We want to tell Nia, Olivia, and Bethany the truth about the bracelets."

"Wow." Riley's surprise mirrors my own.

"But we probably can't save them," I say, feeling like shit but knowing Dover might give me and Riley our lives back, but not them. "What if they freak out?"

"It's a risk we have to take. I can't continue like this," he says, his lips pressing together. "We have all agreed. We want them to know."

I open my mouth to comfort him, but there's really nothing I could say to make this easier. "Good luck."

TWENTY-FOUR

The house is eerily quiet, considering what's going on outside of this room. After Henry and the guys decided to tell the secret of immortality and lifebloods to the other girls, Theo and I stayed back. I thought for sure Theo would go with them, but he said the girls are *their* lifebloods, not his. It was their problem and their call with what they wanted to do. I'm guessing the real reason he didn't want to be there was because it will be insanely awkward and even more sad. Finding out your life is ending soon is a hard pill to swallow.

Riley went back to her room a while ago, taking the laptop with her. She claimed she was exhausted and wanted to get some sleep, but if I know her at all, she's probably up right now, pouring over the translation trying to find something she missed. That book has become her sole reason for existing lately. When we're not doing something, she's working on it. I'm surprised she's not completely fluent in Greek now.

For now, it's nearly midnight and Theo and I are lying in my bed on top of the blankets. There's some stupid reality TV show on, but I don't bother changing the channel because I'm not really paying attention to it anyhow. My eyes are on the screen, but my mind is far away. So many things have happened in the last few days, and they all seem to be a bunch of new problems, not answers to the old ones.

Theo runs a hand down my hair and I tuck in closer, cuddling up against his chest. His body seems like it was made exactly for mine. The way we fit together, whether standing or lying down or even when I'm sitting on his lap—it's like he's been fashioned from a mold where I'm the other half.

"I need a shower," he says with a heavy sigh while he keeps stroking my hair. "This has been a long day."

"Don't leave," I say, grabbing his shirt. "Just fall asleep dirty with me."

He chuckles. "I feel nasty though. Let's both shower."

He takes my chin and tilts my head up so we can kiss. I close my eyes, reveling in the feeling of his lips on mine, even if it only lasts for a quick moment. In those few seconds, everything is perfect. Once I'm back to reality, the weight of the world crushes back on top of me.

I sit up on my elbow. "Okay," I say, glancing toward the bathroom and gauging how much energy I have for this. "A quick shower."

The water is hot and steamy and it feels great on my back. I tip my head backward, letting it wash over me. Theo's hands massage shampoo into my scalp and it feels amazing. I let him wash my hair, and then he slides the soap down my back. The first time we showered it was sexual, full of desire. Now, maybe we're both exhausted, or life is too crazy, but Theo runs his hands over me with a new type of love and affection. Neither one of us are feeling up to doing anything more tonight, but being together and sharing our time with each other feels like the greatest stress relief ever.

When we're both clean and dried off, I slip into a big T-shirt and crawl into bed next to Theo. He smells amazing, a mix of my green apple body wash and his deodorant. I kiss his neck, breathing him in, and then cuddle up close, pulling the sheets over my shoulder. With his arm wrapped around me and the sound of his steady heartbeat while I lay on his chest, I feel perfect for the first time in days.

But I'm not tired anymore.

"Why can't I sleep?" I say with a groan. "I was exhausted a few minutes ago."

"I can't seem to turn my brain off," Theo says. "This was an intense day."

"I'm happy we have the kids," I tell him. "They're the craziest thing that happened today, but that's not what's bothering me, really. They're easy to take care of and we have Malina helping us. What I can't stop thinking about is what comes next."

"Same here, love." Theo kisses the top of my head. "Damien's people haven't found a trace of Lady Em in Europe. They couldn't even find her leaving the airport once she arrived. She's clever and she's staying hidden."

"She has to turn up at some point," I say. "She wouldn't abandon her stones at her California house. And as soon as she gets there, I'll be waiting."

"You don't have to be the one to kill her, you know."

Theo's hand gently draws circles on my back, and it's the funniest thing because we're laying here talking about murder and he's stroking my back with love an tenderness. I laugh. "Oh, yes I do. I can't wait to kill her."

"It'll be dangerous, love. We should take her out from far away. Maybe get a sniper rifle."

"Screw that. I want to see her die. I want it to be at my hands."

His lips slide into a crooked grin. "Okay, that was kind of sexy, and that's also weird that I feel that way."

I laugh and some of my anger melts away. "Baby, I'll kill our enemies for the rest of our lives."

"Mmm, talk dirty to me," he says, chuckling. "Seriously though..." Theo pauses to kiss me, and I can see the hesitation in his eyes. "This is dangerous. We don't know how it'll play out, but we both agree she should die to save those children and as revenge for all the innocent people she's killed. Not to mention, if we don't kill her then Dover will. But whatever happens, we have to be smart about it. I can't lose you in the process."

"I know," I say, trying to hide my annoyance. "I'll be safe. I won't go charging head first into killing her or anything. It's just—she tried to kill you. That really pisses me off."

Theo's phone rings and he makes this annoyed expression. I nudge him. "You should answer it."

He leans over and looks at this phone on the nightstand. "It's Kyle," he says, answering it. "Hey man. Yeah, I'm awake. What's up?"

I watch Theo while he's on the phone, but I can't hear what Kyle's saying. After a few seconds, Theo puts him on speakerphone. "Say it again. Cara is listening."

"Hi Cara," Kyle says, his voice filling the quiet of my bedroom. "So...tonight was interesting. They told Nia, Olivia, and Bethany about the stones and...well, their first question was why weren't you and Riley there. When they found out you two knew about it and they didn't, they were more pissed about being kept in the dark than the fact that immortality exists and they were being used as human batteries."

"These girls have some weird priorities," I say sarcastically. "What else happened?"

"Well...like I was telling Theo just now, Henry thinks we can secure the ownership of the mansion after Lady Em is gone. They want to ask the other clans to recognize us as our own clan and then we just keep this place as our home base."

"That's a good idea," I say, looking up at Theo. I can't read his expression though, so I don't know what he thinks. I know he wants to go back to Embrook, but I want to stay here. "And the girls?" I ask.

"After their initial shock, they were crying and stuff. I felt bad and told them that you're working on finding a way to remove the stones safely and we told them the guys are all on board with getting terminally ill lifebloods like Theo does. So... now they're all happy thinking they'll find a way out of the bracelets."

Theo sighs. My chest aches because yes, I am trying to save us all, but with Damien's constant negativity, and how little I actually know about the Dover clan, my hope that this will work out is dwindling.

"I guess it's better for them to stay hopeful," I say. I remember all the emotions I went through when I discovered my status as a lifeblood. I'm still going through these feelings on a daily basis, and they're never good. It's just the start for the other girls. I want to call Bethany and hug her and tell her it'll be okay. I'm not even friends with the other two girls, but I kind of want to hug them, too.

"Theo, there's another thing," Kyle says. "Man, we really want you to stay with Rosewater."

"What do you mean?" Theo asks. He leans forward on his elbow, his phone on the bed in between us.

"We mean you should stay here, leave Embrook. You feel like a part of the family now, and with Alexo gone, we need someone knowledgeable to help us find our place as immortals."

"That's assuming Dover lets you guys stay a clan," he says, his eyes flitting to me. Something tells me the chances of that are slim to none.

"Yeah I know..." Kyle sighs into the phone. "But if it works out. We'd like you to stay. Just think it over, okay?"

"I'd want to stay," I say. It's something we should discuss in private, but now the words just fell out of my mouth in front of Kyle. Theo watches me intently. I shrug. "I'm not a member of Embrook. I'm a member of Rosewater. I love this house more than anything, and it has room for the kids, and if Alexo and Lady Em are gone, then who cares if we take over the clan?"

"I like your way of thinking," Kyle says, his smile evident in his voice.

Theo doesn't budge though. He's still looking at me with curiosity. "I guess we'll talk with you tomorrow," Theo says into the phone. "We have a lot to think about now. And breakfast is going to be weird as hell when the other girls are there."

"Everything about life is weird right now," Kyle says. "Cara, can I talk to you for a minute?"

My eyebrows narrow. He didn't exactly say it, but it sounds like he wants to talk in private. I pick up the phone and take it off speaker. "I'm here," I say. Theo rolls over onto his back, tucking his hands behind his head.

"Yeah so...I don't know how to say this." Kyle's voice is low, just a fraction above a whisper. "I...I want you and Theo to stay with us after this situation is over. But, I also want Riley to stay, too. Do you think she will?"

"She does what I do," I say, confident in my best friend's loyalties. "We'll decide what we're doing together, but I want to stay, so she will too." I look over at Theo, who's staring at the ceiling. "If we get to stay here at all, I mean."

"Cara. Do you think she'll forgive me?"

Chills prickle over my arms at the emotion in his voice. Kyle, sweet Kyle, who can't do anything wrong. "Why would you need to be forgiven?" I ask.

He's silent for a long while. "Because she's my lifeblood," he says softly. "She's like a sister to me now, Cara. I would have never asked you two to interview for the job that day had I known how great you are. How great Riley is. She's—" he sighs. "She has no reason to forgive me after this, but I don't want to lose her. I don't want to lose you and Theo. You guys are all the family I have."

"Does she know she's your lifeblood?" I ask.

"No."

I feel a smile tugging at my lips even though this situation is nothing but tragic. "I think she'll be happy to know that, Kyle. You're her favorite. If we have to be slowly dying for someone here, she'll be happy it's you."

"Will she forgive me though?" His voice is so hopeful, so on the verge of breaking with bad news.

Now I really am smiling, because Riley was right about one thing. He's a good guy. "She'll forgive you, Kyle. Of all the shit we have to worry about, you shouldn't waste your time worrying about that."

TWENTY-FIVE

"I kind of thought I might be Kyle's lifeblood," Riley says the next morning. We're eating breakfast, but I can't seem to eat much because I'm too excited that today might finally be the day we go to the Dover Clan.

"Why's that?" I ask. Last night Kyle must have told her right after he talked to me.

She shrugs and fishes out the marshmallows from her cereal with her spoon. "Right from day one, he seemed to be protective of me. Always making sure I was okay. We're both not attracted to each other in *that* way, so it was like...what's the deal? Then we found out about immortality, and I guess I just assumed that's why."

"He was afraid you'd be mad at him," I say, taking a bite of my apple turnover.

She shakes her head. "Nah. I'm mad at myself for getting into this situation, but not mad at him. Especially since they were all brainwashed by Alexo that this was how they were supposed to have lifebloods."

I smile at her as I pick at my breakfast. My coffee is untouched, and as delicious as this pastry is, I'm just not feeling it. I wish I could be as calm as she is about everything. Theo walks into the kitchen with Damien on his heels. They've been strategizing all morning, and I look up expectedly. "Well?""

Theo holds up a printed piece of paper. "Just booked the next flight to the UK."

I squeal and jump up, nearly knocking over my barstool. "Finally!"

"I wouldn't get your hopes up, kiddo," Damien says.

"Shut it, hipster." I don't even bother looking his way as I throw my arms around Theo. I know Damien will be dressed like he just got off his barista shift at Starbucks. "Pack light. We're only staying for one day," Theo says. "We leave in an hour."

I turn to Riley. "Take care of my kids, okay?"

"*Your* kids?" she says, her gaze narrowing. "I care about those orphans too, ya know."

"Good, that means you'll take care of them!" I leave my breakfast on the table, knowing Riley will probably finish my pastry for me, and I rush back to my room to get ready for my first international flight. I'd gotten my passport back when I first started living here since they promised opportunities for travel. Funny, how back then I thought the travel I'd be doing would be for vacations, not begging a centuries-old immortal clan for my life back.

To avoid suspicion, Theo and I pack the immortality stones into jewelry cases and put little price stickers on them. That way when we go through the airport lines, we can show our fake business cards that say we're jewelry makers on our way to sell to some of Europe's finest shops.

The international flight takes forever, and although I try to sleep, I spend most of the flight laying against Theo's arm watching movies on my cell phone. But now we're here, in Kent. The air is crisp and the tourists are everywhere. I'm trying really hard to play it off like I'm not a tourist too, but it's hard. I'm on the other side of the freaking planet, after all.

Theo knows right where to go, and we don't waste any time getting there. You can see the castle from a long ways away, and even though the surrounding land has been stacked with modern buildings and amenities, I can still picture how this castle looked centuries ago. It's set on top of a hill with a grand brick wall encircling it. The castle itself is square, rising up several stories tall. It's a tourist spot now, so there's signs and walkways and a place to buy a ticket for the castle tour. The tours close at four in the afternoon, and now it's six so the castle is empty.

Or at least, people think it is.

Theo gives a password to the guard at the front entrance and we're taken into the castle, guards flanking us on all sides. I hold tightly to Theo's hand, the leather briefcase of immortality stones in my other hand.

The castle is absolutely stunning, but we only see it for a second and then we're taken to the side, through a set of doors, and down to an underground tunnel. We walk for several minutes, and then come to a set of wooden doors with guards standing on either side.

They let us inside. The room is pretty large for being underground, and dimly lit by torches mounted to the walls. A roaring fireplace fills the back wall, lighting the room in flashes and shadows. There's a large table facing us with four people sitting behind it.

Four immortals.

They're adorned in velvet cloaks and golden jewelry. They look just like royalty from the eighteenth century. In the middle sits an older man with salt and pepper hair. Next to him, wearing the same coat of arms embroidered on her cloak, is a woman with long brown hair and fine wrinkles on her face. She looks to have been about forty years old when she became immortal. There's an elegance about her, the way she sits and presents herself, the way her hands are folded in her lap. It makes me straighten my shoulders a little bit.

Two men sit on either side of the couple in the middle, and they're dressed in black. They're both older too, probably turned in their fifties. They stare straight at me, their expressions hard as stone.

"Theodore Price," the man in the middle says. "What a pleasure to see you again."

Theo bows slightly. "Thank you, Lord Marcus."

I panic a little because no one told me how to behave here. Do I bow too? Do I curtsey? What the hell do I do?

Theo extends an arm toward me. "This is Cara Blackwell. She is my lifeblood and my lover, though the two titles were not intentional."

"How does this happen?" Lord Marcus asks with a slight tilt of his head.

"She became my lover first when she was unaware of immortality, and was then tricked into wearing the bracelet by another member of the Rosewater Clan."

The lord lifts an eyebrow. Theo continues, "That member has been killed. I have come to you today with two requests."

Lord Marcus nods. "I'll hear them."

"The first is that, on behalf of the Rosewater Clan, I'd like to petition to have the three remaining immortal members of the clan recognized as a legitimate clan who means no harm to the elders or the sake of immortality."

"Has the woman been eliminated?" he asks. So he knows about Lady Em, and he wants her gone. That makes both of us.

Theo takes a breath. "Not yet, sir. But soon."

"Very well. With her gone, the Rosewater clan may live in peace."

Theo dips his head in a bow again. "Thank you."

"What is your second request?"

Before Theo can speak. I do. "I would like to have my bracelet removed safely so that I can live out my life as a normal human again."

The silence that follows my request awakens butterflies in my stomach. When I'm nervous, I talk too much. "And also for my best friend," I add. "Actually...just tell me how to do it myself and that will be great."

"What makes you think such a thing is possible?" he says.

I swallow. "I thought if anyone knew how, it would be you, sir."

Lord Marcus chuckles and turns to look at the woman next to him, who is probably his wife. Her lips curve upward in a demure grin. I notice her immortality stone is laid into her necklace pendant differently than the ones I've seen before. Hers has a solid band of silver running horizontally across the middle. It wraps around the stone and then curves and lines the outside before curling over at the top to make a loop for the necklace chain to go through. I think it's weird to put a band of silver across the middle of the stone—it hides all the beauty of the stone itself. Maybe she's scared of it falling out of the setting.

"I'm afraid I cannot offer you such a thing," Lord Marcus says, pulling my attention away from his wife's chest.

"So there's not a way?" I ask. My heart hasn't quite caught up with my brain yet, so I don't feel as much pain as I will in a minute.

He stares at me. "I didn't say there isn't a way. I said I won't do it. If I tell one human how to reverse a lifeblood, how will I know she won't run and release all of them?"

"I won't," I say quickly. "Just myself and my best friend." *And the other girls of Rosewater,* I think. Still, that's not as bad as wanting to release all of them worldwide.

Beside me, Theo's shoulders fall. I shift on my feet, suddenly remembering what I'm holding in my hand. "What if I offer something in return?" I ask.

The Lord's chin stiffens. "What could you possibly offer me?"

I hold up my briefcase. Before I can even say anything, a guard rips it from my hands and brings it to the table.

"Hey!" I yell. Theo grabs my arm and gives me a warning look. I grit my teeth and stay put even though I'd like to run up and punch that asshole in the face for taking my stuff.

"That's my offer," I say, trying to keep my voice level. "Tell me how to remove my bracelet safely and I'll give you those as a thank you."

Lord Marcus opens the briefcase. His eyes widen when he sees the contents. The other people at the table all seem as confused as he does, and then he narrows his eyes at me. "How did you get these?"

"Lady Em had them put away," I explain. "Theo and I broke in and stole them back for you."

He closes the briefcase and looks me over from head to toe. "The Embrook clan is pleased with your efforts."

My heart brightens a little. "I'm sorry you lost good people. We will be killing Lady Em as soon as we find her. She won't do this to anymore of your people."

"No, I don't believe she will," Lord Marcus says.

Beside me, Theo watches me with a pained expression. Doesn't he see this is looking up for us? I turn back to the elders, holding up my wrist.

"May I please have the secret to removing this thing?"

His wife looks at him. She frowns slightly and then looks away.

"No," Lord Marcus says quickly. "Goodbye."

The guards beside us move to usher us back through the door we came from, but I don't listen. I am a blur of anger as I charge toward the table.

"I sacrificed my life for you!" I scream. "The least you can do is help me!"

I make it halfway across the room when a hand grabs my arm so hard it

357

probably breaks the bone. My eyes lock onto Lord Marcus and he simply shrugs his shoulders at my pain. "Give me my life back or I'll fucking destroy these stones!" I roar, breaking free of the guard's grasp of my hand. I charge toward the briefcase.

There's a loud sound, a shock of unimaginable pain, and then everything goes black.

TWENTY-SIX

THE HUSHED SOUND OF VOICES IS THE FIRST THING I HEAR. THEN IT'S the gentle hum of the road, the vibration of the tires on asphalt a familiar sensation under my body. I blink slowly, and find that I'm in a car, laid across the backseat. The voices are Theo and Damien's, from the front of the car. Relief pours over me that it's only them, and not some of Lord Marcus's henchmen. Theo is driving. I watch him silently, trying to make out the words he says.

My head is pounding like my skull was cracked open and filled with hot lava. I reach up and touch my forehead, feeling the bruised skin. What happened to me? Where am I?

"Now that she's back, it's only a matter of time before she finds out what we did," Theo says.

Damien's face glows from the bright screen of the phone in his hand. I realize now that it's after dark, the only light coming from occasional street lights and the neon green lighting on the radio in the car.

"She's only been to her room," Damien says, reading his phone. "We have guys watching through the windows and she hasn't been to the attic yet."

"She might not realize her attic security guard is gone," Theo says.

"This could be an easy attack," Damien adds. "Get a sniper, one shot to the head."

"Absolutely not!" I say with a dry mouth. I push myself up in the backseat, but my head throbs so much it overpowers me and I fall back down.

"How do you feel?" Theo asks, sneaking glances at me between driving.

"Like my head is going to explode."

"You took a pretty good hit," Damien says. "Straight to the stone floor."

"What happened?" My memories are foggy wisps that don't stay put in my mind.

"You threatened the leader of the Dover clan, Cara." Theo rolls to a stop at a red light and looks back at me, his lips creased in a frown. "They could have killed you."

"They almost did," Damien says. "Luckily, they have enough respect for Theo that they spared his lifeblood. If you weren't connected to him, you'd be toast."

I swallow the bile in my throat and slowly push myself up into a sitting position. Shame pours over me, bringing heat to my cheeks. I kind of remember that. I remember being really mad when they wouldn't tell me how to remove my bracelet.

"I'm sorry," I mumble.

"It's over now," Theo says. "I promised Dover we would never return and they spared your life. We're headed to the airport now, and we'll be home by morning."

My mouth is dry and tastes stale. I haven't had anything to eat since we left the plane but I'm not hungry. My stomach is filled with regret, and my head hurts so bad I'm on the verge of crying. I blink away the tears though. This isn't the time for that kind of weakness.

"I should have kept two sets of stones." I stare at my hands. "Those bastards don't deserve them. We did all the hard work and they don't even care. No thanks. No appreciation."

"Why would you have kept stones?" Theo says. "It's clear they won't bargain with you."

Damien snorts. "A fact I've been saying from day one, I'd like to add."

I ignore Damien's sarcastic comment. "I should have kept them for me and Riley."

The moment I say it I feel like a snake. Like some lesser life form that just sunk as low as you can possibly go.

Theo twists around in the driver's seat. "You want to be immortal?"

I shrug. "It's better than dying, which is all I can do now."

"I won't let you die," Theo says. A muscle in his jaw twitches. "There has to be a way, and I'll find it."

"You won't," I say. "You haven't. We'll go months and months looking for something we'll never find and then I'll drop dead and you'll get a new lifeblood." I fold my arms across my chest and stare out of the window. "If I'd been smart enough to keep two sets of stones then Riley and I would be fine. I'd use convicted rapists as lifebloods. It'd be great."

"Cara..." Theo says, his voice strained. "I had no idea you wanted to be immortal. I thought you loathed the very idea of it."

"This sounds like something you two should talk about in private," Damien says. "It's getting entirely too awkward up in here."

"There's nothing to talk about," I say.

Theo looks like he disagrees, but he just keeps driving.

The international airport is just as busy in the middle of the night as it was in the daytime. I don't know why I find this interesting, but I do. I guess you assume people are home with loved ones sleeping late at night, but some of them are out traveling. Maybe traveling to loved ones, or rushing to get away from them.

As we step up to the ticket counter, Theo asks the woman about flights back to Texas.

"No," I say, stepping up to the desk. "California, please."

The woman looks old enough to be my grandmother, and the fine lines in her cheeks tell me she's not one for putting up with nonsense. She raises a brow and looks at Theo, who looks at me.

"Why California?" he says.

"You know why," I say back. "We don't need to plan, we just need to act."

"Sounds alright to me," Damien says, drumming his fingers on the edge of the counter. "I am so ready to be done with this shit and get back home away from you guys."

"He makes another great point," I say, giving him an annoyed look. To the woman, I say, "California, please."

"There's a flight leaving in forty five minutes, but only first class seating is available."

"We'll take it."

She looks at Theo again, as if to get permission. It really annoys me that she assumes the woman here has no say in the matter. "Three tickets please," I say in my rudest voice.

Theo nods slightly, which annoys me, but apparently, the woman can't buy a fucking plane ticket without the man's approval.

Everything is kind of annoying me right now. From the kids running around being too loud in the waiting area, to the Starbucks being out of coffee at two in the morning. I let the annoyance build up inside of me instead of shoving it away, all in an effort to be as pissed as possible when I come face to face with Lady Em.

No one takes me seriously. From immortal clan members who are older than dirt, to a stupid old woman at the airport. I'm sick of being underestimated and tossed aside. I'm not some worthless loser from the ghetto who will never amount to anything.

I am worthy. I won't cower down and beg for anything to be given to me anymore. I will make good on the promise I made to those twelve kids waiting on me at home. I might have to die eventually, but they will live long happy lives.

Because I have decided to stand up for myself and take what I want.

And the only thing I want right now is to see the life leave Lady Em's piercing blue eyes.

TWENTY-SEVEN

When the plane lands in California, my veins start pumping with adrenaline. I am fearless, and I am ready to free those kids and put an end to Lady Em's reign of terror. Unfortunately, all of my excitement has to wait an hour while we rent a car and drive to the castle that she calls a home. After having visited the real Dover castle, her place is nothing more than a pile of bricks and arrogance. But I can see the similarities from the way Lady Em decorates her place to the way the real castle looked. She's still holding on to her past, dreaming of a life with a man who didn't really love her.

She's so beautiful, she could have had anyone she wanted, I think as I sit in the back seat of our rented Suburban. She *did* have many lovers over the years, it would seem. Like the guy who built her the house in Austin, who probably loved her like crazy as evidenced by the stone mosaic in the foyer. She only used him though, just like Lord Timothy used her.

In the car ride, Theo calls the clan back at home and tells them the good news. They're all excited to be officially recognized as a real clan, and I'm happy for them, too. But my happiness is overshadowed by the impending doom of being tethered to my bracelet. The pain sinks into me now. The Dover clan didn't help me. They didn't confirm or deny that there is a way to help me, either. I can choose to spend my remaining months searching for a way or just try to live happily until I die. No matter what, one thing is certain.

I won't have Theo forever.

I'll have him until I die, so I guess I'll have him for the rest of my life, but he will go on, choosing new lifebloods and living a long—impossibly long—life.

When we're a few miles away from Lady Em's house, we pull over to get gas. Theo thinks we should have a full tank in case we have to rush out of there in a hurry.

As Theo pulls the Suburban up to the gas tank, I lean forward. "Hey, Damien? Could you pump the gas?"

"What am I, a bus boy?" he says.

I give him a pleading look. "Please?"

He glances from me to Theo and back. "Fine," he says, unbuckling his seatbelt.

As soon as the door is closed behind him, Theo takes my hand. There are dark circles under his eyes from the lack of sleep he got on our flight home. His hair is wilder than usual. The black button up shirt he's wearing is all wrinkled and I realize I probably look just as bad in my jeans and shirt. We haven't showered in twenty four hours, after all.

"Theo," I say, looking down at our intertwined hands. "When I die—" I pause to gather my thoughts. The very idea of dying makes my heart rip to pieces, but this needs to be said and since we're about to meet Lady Em, this might be the last time I can say it. "When I die, I'm afraid you'll try to do something stupid like let yourself die and not get a new lifeblood right away."

Theo frowns, and that expression alone tells me I'm probably right in my theory. I look him in the eyes. "Don't. I want you to live. I want you to take care of the kids until they're grown and don't need you anymore. And only then can you think about dying, but even then..." My chest aches with the idea of Theo living long enough to find another lover. Someone he loves more than me. "Even then... consider living."

Theo reaches for me, wrapping his arm around my neck and pulling me across the car's console. I'm still sitting in the back seat, but my face is pressed against his chest. "Cara, I love you. I didn't know love before I met you." He squeezes me tightly, his hair smelling like the airplane's air freshener, but I hold on tightly. "I'll take care of the kids," he says, pulling back to look at me. "But I'll never give up on finding a way to save you."

He smiles, his thumb running across my cheek. "I already have an idea. What if we get you an immortality stone, and get you a lifeblood. You'll still be my lifeblood, but you should be immortal, too, right?"

I shake my head. "It says that won't work in the book Riley translated."

Theo's face falls so quickly it feels like I've been punched. "I'm sorry," I say, pulling him into a hug. "If my bracelet can't come off, then I die. And that's going to happen. I'm accepting it more every day."

"Or I can die," he says. "You deserve your life more than I deserve mine."

I grit my teeth. "You will not kill yourself to free me from this thing."

Tears spring to my eyes. I grab onto his shoulders and force him to look at me. "You can't do that to me. You might think you're saving me, but I can't live without you, Theo. Promise me you won't do it."

Tears fill his amber eyes. His hands are warm on my cheeks as he brings me in for a kiss. "I promise," he whispers against my lips.

His words fill me with relief.

Outside, the gas pump makes a thump sound when the tank is full. Damien hooks the handle back on the pump and then walks over to the passenger side of the car. If he was watching our exchange in the car just now, he doesn't say anything. He takes out his phone and calls someone.

"We're almost there," he says. "Okay. Thanks."

He hangs up the phone. "The guys say she hasn't left her room in an hour. She's sitting at her desk, reviewing something. She's literally a sitting duck right now. They're going to call me if she moves."

"We need to drive fast," I say, tapping the center console with my palm. "Let's go."

We park on the side of the road at the end of the long winding driveway that goes to Lady Em's fake castle. There's a calm over my body, despite my every nerve ready to spring into action. I am ready for this. In a few minutes, it'll all be over.

We make our way down the driveway, knowing that Theo and Damien's friends from the Embrook clan are hidden outside of the house, watching Lady Em as we approach. So far, so good. She's still at her desk.

When we get to the front door, Damien reaches into the waistband of his bands, pulling out a small pistol.

"Dude!" I hiss. "Put that away."

He gives me this condescending look. "Guns kill people faster than anything," he says. "*I'm* doing this," I snap. "Put it away."

"You can take the lead, but it's a good idea," Theo says, his hand gentle on my back. "If it comes down to a you or her thing, we're going to pick you."

I grit my teeth, knowing he's right. I just really want to do this for myself. I nod and let out a breath. "Okay, but stay back. I want a chance to do this my way."

"Deal," Damien says. He doesn't put the gun away, but he does lower it. He curls his hand toward the door in a gentlemanly fashion. "Ladies first."

I enter her home for the second time. The front door is unlocked, showing Lady Em's profound arrogance. The Embrook guys said she never even bothered to check on her guard, so she probably assumes he's still here, still watching over her house from the attic.

Stupid.

I make my way through the oddly-decorated house, to the long hallway that leads to Lady Em's bedroom. My heart thumps in my chest, a mixture of elation and nerves. She's just beyond that door at the end of the hall. I picture her, sitting at the desk, doing whatever research she think will help in her task of taking over her little piece of immortality. Up until now, I had no idea what I'd do when I faced her. I'd been hoping the perfect idea would come to me.

And now it does.

I glance back and see Theo and Damien about ten feet behind me. They kept their promise to hang back. I throw them a wink and then put my finger to my lips. I turn back and walk straight up to Lady Em's bedroom door. I remember from the first time I was here that her desk is to the right.

THE IMMORTAL BOND

I grab the doorknob and twist, then push open the door quickly.

The curtain Theo used as a noose is still on the floor, crumpled into a pile. She hasn't even touched it. Has she noticed it?

Lady Em sits at her desk, her short black hair wispy around her face. Her chin rests in her elbow as she looks over a spiral notebook and a newspaper. She doesn't even look up.

I have come to kill her, and she's not looking up.

"Do you treat all your visitors with such apathy?" I ask. My voice rings out through the quiet room. I am fully aware that Lady Em's powers could throw my body across the room at any moment, but I'm hoping to catch her by surprise.

She looks up slowly, almost as if she's bored. Her eyes meet mine and there's a slight hint of recognition behind them. I realize now that the dark circles under her eyes weren't there last time I saw her.

"Did you come to kill me?" she says plainly, as if my threat of death is simply a slight annoyance to her day.

I swallow, and the right words come to me. "I know where the Dover stones are hidden."

She looks up suddenly, her eyes narrowing. "I know what you're doing," I say, standing strong and confident. "And I want to join you."

TWENTY-EIGHT

Lady Em closes her notebook and shoves it away. "Why would I trust you?" her voice is measured, calculating.

I think on my feet. "Because I just walked in here alone, with nothing." I hold up my hands. "I don't even have a cell phone."

"That hardly means anything," she says, still sitting at her desk. "I kept you locked in a room and you broke free. Why would you come back to work with me?" I'm standing just inside the doorway, knowing the guys are somewhere back in the hallway listening in.

"Because of *him*," I say, making the last word sound like a piece of gum stuck to the bottom of my shoe. "He broke us out, he made me go with him." Her eyebrow quirks and I can see her getting drawn into my story. I make up more of it as I go along.

"He forced me to do whatever he wanted," I say. "I thought you were remarkable when I learned of your power, but all he did was talk bad about you. I thought I loved him but—" The lie sits heavy on my tongue and I don't want to say it, but I can tell I have her full attention now. "But he didn't love me," I reply.

Lady Em sits straighter in her chair. Her eyes never leave mine. "He certainly seemed like he loved you."

I shake my head. "It was all an act. He didn't care about me." I think about her history with Lord Timothy and choose my words carefully. "He has other lovers, women he cares about more than me. He just used me to do his dirty work. I was nothing more than a toy."

Lady Em swallows. There's a flash of pain across her eyes. I remember what Theo told me about her making a pass at him all those years ago. Even she wasn't immune to his gorgeous looks. She hasn't forgotten that he rebuked her, that he turned away all of her advances no matter how beautiful she was.

I take this thread and run with it. "He has a real lover in the Dover clan," I say, twisting my face into a fake agony that she totally falls for. "He loves her, not me. But when I became his lifeblood up on that balcony—" I choke up as if I'm in true pain. I cover my mouth with my hand and then look at her. "I guess he realized he better keep me alive so that I keep him alive. So he pretended to care about me but he didn't. It was all an act so he could make sure I stayed his lifeblood."

I hold up my wrist, turning the bracelet over. The stone sparkles in response. "I got away from him, but not before I heard them talking about your plans."

"And what plans do you think you know?" she asks, leaning forward.

"The whole Rosewater clan knows it," I say. "They've been talking and scheming, saying they want to kill you and take over the clan themselves." This part isn't a lie, of course, and it really gets her attention.

"They know nothing," she says with an indignant huff.

"They know you've been killing immortals and taking their stones."

She stiffens and then her eyes narrow into slits. "You have no proof."

"There's twelve sets of immortality stones in the safe in your attic."

She's silent for several seconds, her expression blank. Then her lips flatten and she rises from her chair. "How did you know that?"

"Because I'm on your side," I say, holding out an innocent hand to stop her from doing anything. She's still behind her desk, but now that she's standing, my heart beats a little faster. This is going well, I just need to convince her a little more.

"While you were gone, they had people spying on you in England. I came here to see for myself if you were really gone. I met that meathead guy who lives in the attic and he told me about the stones."

"I will kill him," she says through clenched teeth.

I try to smile but I don't think it works. If she'd only taken five seconds to walk around her own house, she'd know this is all a lie. "It's okay. Please let me join you. I know where Dover has hidden their stones. We can take them. We can start our own clan. I don't need someone like Theo. I get that now. I just need to do my own thing."

"Why would you want to join me?"

"Because you're smart enough to work on your own. I should have never trusted a stupid man."

"No, you shouldn't have," she says, her voice softening.

I'm not sure if she thinks she can trust me yet, but she relaxes a bit. "Where are the stones?"

"They're in a room under the castle." I make it up as I go along, using my memories of the castle's layout. Lady Em knows that castle better than I do, because she actually lived in it for years, so I shouldn't get too detailed. I keep my voice level and hide any trace that I'm lying by looking her right in the eye. "I was there. We met Lord Marcus, and they had a meeting in the very room where the stones are held. They have them all in a display case."

"Guarded heavily by security," Lady Em says.

I nod. "Yes, but, Lord Marcus liked me. He invited me back to his chambers. He offered to make me immortal."

"This means nothing," Lady Em snaps.

"I told him I would only do it if he'd let me pick the stone myself." I put on a sly grin and take a step forward. Lady Em doesn't move, meaning she's not preparing herself for an attack from me. Another stupid move on her part. "He agreed. He's been sending me love letters, asking me to join him and become immortal."

"He is a snake," she says, her lip curling. "He and his dead brother are both snakes."

I wonder if the dead brother she's referring to is Timothy, but the way her demeanor turns to pure hatred tells me it probably is. I nod quickly. "I was thinking I could get him to take me down there, tell him I want some private time alone with him while I pick out my stone."

Her eyes fill with delight. I smile. "Little does he know, you could be right behind me, waiting for him to be off guard." I shrug helplessly. "None of the guys in the Dover clan have powers like you do. I think you could easily get rid of him and then the stones would be ours for the taking."

Lady Em puts her hands on her hips. "Why should I trust you?"

"You shouldn't," I say, and it's the truest thing I've ever told her. I hold my chin up. "I don't trust anyone, not anymore. I only trust myself. You should only trust yourself, too. I almost ruined my life by trusting a stupid man, and I won't make that mistake again. What I'm asking from you is for a partnership."

"Tell me where the stones are hidden," she says. "I want an exact description so I know you aren't lying."

Shit.

She is so close, and yet I can't take her down yet. Her necklace, the large thing that spreads across her chest, sparkles in the dim lighting. It keeps her alive, keeps her powerful, and takes away the life of those sweet children back in Texas. If I could only get ahold of it. Only find a way...

"Well, it's kind of complicated," I say, trying to remember every detail from when I visited the castle. I should have paid better attention to my surroundings. "You know that place where the ticket booth is now?" I ask.

Her brows pull together. "I haven't been there in decades, child."

"Oh. Well it's like a tourist spot now. There's a ticket booth, and if you walk past it and go up to the castle walls, there's a door..." I'm rambling now, desperately trying to think up a way for this to work. I don't know how long I've got before Damien jumps in with his stupid gun pointing at Lady Em. I don't know if he's a good shot, or if he'll fumble and she'll use her powers against us.

THE IMMORTAL BOND

I notice the notebook on her desk and take another step forward. "Actually, could I just draw it for you?"

She sits at her desk and takes a pencil from the drawer. I walk over slowly. She holds out the pencil and I take it.

She opens her notebook to a blank page in the back and then slides it over to me.

I get closer, trying not to show my excitement. I am now just a few inches away from her as she sits at her desk. I put my hand to the paper and swallow back my fear. "Okay so, here's the castle," I say, drawing a square. The tunnels that run under the castle can be reached by entrances that are outside of the main wall. "Here's the wall thing that goes around it," I say, sketching a wall. Lady Em watches my hands intently as I draw. Now that I've labeled the front and side of the castle, marking where the ticket booth is, I'm completely out of details to use so I have to make them up.

I lean over the desk, the pencil in my hand as I pretend to think about my drawing. "I don't know how many tunnels run under the castle," I say, biding for time. "I only know the one I went in. Do you?"

"There are a few," she says, her eyes on my drawing.

From this close, I can't stop staring at her necklace. The elders of the Dover clan had seemed so powerful and royal with their single stone necklace. Lady Em has twelve, all spread across her chest in an ornate brocade necklace. "Your necklace is so beautiful," I say, unable to stop myself. "I wonder why no one else thought to use more than one stone."

"Because everyone else believes what they've been told," she says. Her fingers slide across a few of the stones and then she looks back at my drawing. "I dared to think deeper than anyone else in the clan, and I tried new things. I found something they never thought to look for. Immortality...plus more."

"You're so smart," I say, letting my voice transform into star-struck excitement. "I'm so thrilled to partner with you."

It's funny how well these lies come to me. Every time she believes me, I feel more of my nerves float away. Now she looks up at me, a smile on her lips, and I know I've got her, hook, line, and sinker. She believes me.

She trusts me.

"It's this tunnel here," I say, scratching my pencil across the paper. As I draw a circle around it, I glance back at Lady Em's neck. The ornate necklace clasps at the back, just like every other necklace I've ever seen. There's nothing fancy to it.

"Well? Where do you go once you're in the tunnel?" she asks.

"Hell," I say softly.

She points to the door on my drawing. "What did you say?"

I stand. This is my chance. "I said you go to hell. At least that's where I assume you'll go."

In a flash, I grab her necklace with both hands, twisting the snap until it breaks. Lady Em jumps, but she's not fast enough. The white gold jewelry is soft, malleable, and meant for beauty, not durability.

I hold on tightly and pull my hands back. The necklace rips off her chest. Lady Em's face contorts in anger. Half a second later, her face erupts into dust.

I'm holding onto a necklace in an empty room. Dust and ashes are all that's left of Lady Em. They coat the chair, the floor, and some of it floats up into the air. I hold my breath and step backward to avoid inhaling her.

"It's done," I call out to the guys waiting in the hallway. Theo and Damien walk into the room, bewilderment on their faces. Damien's gun hangs limply in his hand.

I hold up the necklace like a trophy. "The wicked witch is dead."

TWENTY-NINE

It's hard to explain what I'm feeling. Lady Em was the ultimate bad guy of the clan, the person responsible for countless murders and the abuse of children as lifebloods. She created the Rosewater clan out of the blood of other immortals, and she deserved to die. Killing her has been my mission pretty much since the day I met her.

And now she's dead, and the world is right again. My kids at home are freed, Jayla's death is avenged. The promise we made to the Dover clan has been fulfilled.

I should be happy.

But instead of feeling joy, I walk around in a daze as Theo, Damien and I clear out Lady Em's house. We find the paperwork for the properties she owns, as well as the social security cards and adoption papers for the children back at home. I hold back the urge to vomit when we find boxes of adoption papers for other kids she's used as lifebloods over the years. I do shed a tear though, for the souls of those innocent children whose lives ended too soon.

After we've ransacked her place, which is our place now I guess, we take what we need and head back to the airport and our private jet. Lady Em owned that too. Henry says he can get all of her properties transferred to the clan, so that we'll legally own everything. I'm not sure it matters though, when you're immortal you can get away with anything.

Damien says we could probably get a lot of money selling Lady Em's castle house because of the high price of California real estate. I think I'd rather burn it to the ground and dance on top of the ashes.

As we settle into the jet, I lean over and take Theo's hand. We have six boxes of gold bars loaded into the cargo area. Those things were so heavy the guys needed a dolly to move them. We also have paperwork and precious jewels, some of which I know date back a century or two, all stuff we took from Lady Em's house. I wonder where she got it all. Or where she stole it.

Theo's thumb runs across my palm. "How are you doing?" he asks.

"Fine." I say it quickly. An impulse response to a question you hear all the time.

He leans closer, his shoulder pressing to mine. "You don't look fine."

I give a little shrug and look out the tiny window to the cloudy sky below. "I guess...this was a huge victory for us today."

"It was," he agrees, a smirk appearing on his lips. "You were particularly amazing."

"I just—" I exhale. I feel selfish as hell saying this, but it is what it is. "We killed her. We saved the kids and we saved the clan. But we didn't save me." I swallow the lump in my throat. "We didn't save Riley or Bethany or Olivia or Nia. We're all still doomed."

"Don't say that, love." Theo's eyes meet mine and then he looks away. "We're all looking for a solution now. The guys have had a change of heart about their lifebloods, so they're researching, too. We'll find something."

"They don't know shit," I say, rolling my eyes. "Those guys didn't even know other clans exist, Theo. How are they going to help us?"

Small lines appear in his forehead as he watches me. Theo is too considerate to tell me what I know to be true: that the situation is hopeless. "We'll find something," he says, leaning against me and resting his head on top of mine. "I love you."

"I love you too," I say softly. I close my eyes and let the gentle hum of the jet engines lull me to sleep. There will be time to fret tomorrow. For now, I'm exhausted.

A FEW DAYS after our return, I'm still not used to how the house is now. Everyone is like an entirely different person. The guys aren't quiet and aloof anymore because there are no more secrets. I try to avoid the other girls as much as I can, but I see them every now and then. The three of them have formed a closer friendship now that they're going to die soon. I don't know why Riley and I are on the outside of it, but I feel like we should join them soon. We're all in this fucked up fate together, after all.

I spend my time with the kids, learning their names and ages and where they're from. Most of them aren't really kids anymore, since they're teenagers or nearing their teens. They feel like kids though, and I have this fierce desire to protect them from all that is bad in the world. We take them shopping and I go crazy with Lady Em's credit cards, buying Air Jordan's and Sketchers, among other shoes, American Eagle for the girls, and whatever the boys think is cool. It's like therapy, giving these orphans anything they want. It makes me feel really good about the world, at least my little part of it.

Damien still hasn't gone home to Greece, and he's been spending a lot of time with Theo and the other guys while they work out the mysteries of the immortal world. Damien won't exactly admit it, but I think he doesn't want to see me die. And I'm 99% sure he has a crush on Riley, which is kind of hilarious because she's so not into hipsters.

On Friday when the weather is particularly nice, one of the kids suggests that we have a Mexican dinner night. Julio is from Mexico, and was put into foster care after both of his parents died. He's been missing his culture and I think this might be the perfect way to cheer him up. Julio and I spend the morning with our chef, going over all the Mexican dishes he'd like to serve. My mouth is watering by the end of the conversation, and Julio is so excited his cheeks are pink from all the smiling.

We go to the store and pick out colorful tablecloths, decorations, and some piñatas just for fun. Kyle rents a margarita machine and Olivia and Nia string up colorful lights around the patio by the pool, which is where we'll be eating dinner tonight.

The whole area is set up with delicious Mexican foods and we play Spanish pop music over the speakers. The other kids shower Julio with questions and words they want him to translate into Spanish. I've never seen them so happy.

As the foods are brought out and everyone digs in, piling their plates high with tamales and tacos and quesadillas, I lean against the concrete railing on the porch, so overwhelmed with love for my new, diverse, crazy, fun family.

Theo walks up wearing a sombrero. They're not very good quality because we got them cheap at the party store, but he looks cute anyway. He's holding a plate filled with corn husked tamales. "These are the best tamales I've ever eaten," he says, his mouth full.

"Julio gave Chef the recipe parts he could remember from his mom's cooking. Chef filled in the rest and they came out pretty good. Julio was excited."

"I love that we're doing this," he says, taking another bite. "We should let all of the kids explore their culture and do something for each of them. Make them feel like an individual and not just one of many orphan kids."

"I love you so much," I say, my heart feeling like it's going to explode.

He grins and puckers up to kiss me, but I shove him away. "Ew, tamale breath."

"The tamales are amazing though," he says, pointing one of them at me. "You should be delighted to get a tamale kiss."

I roll my eyes. In the distance, Henry emerges from the house, wearing his glasses. He only wears them when he's doing paperwork, which means he's probably still working on Lady Em's documents that we gave him. He knows a lawyer who is both very good and also a con artist. Last I heard, they were going to forge her signature on all of the deeds, transferring them to the clan. I think they were going to call us a business and get some kind of business license so that we'd all equally own the assets. I like that plan, even though I won't be here very long.

Henry nods at us and then walks over to talk to Russell, who is giving three boys a piggyback ride around the pool.

"Hey, Theo?" I say as a question comes to me. "I'm your lifeblood. Riley is Kyle's. There's only Russell and Henry left, but we have Nia, Olivia, and Bethany, and they replaced Jayla with someone. Who are the other two immortals?"

"Our pilot and Chef," Theo says, still eating his tamales. "The pilot's name is Sean but he lives alone. He's kind of a loner. He was friends with Russell, they both fought in World War One. Chef chose Jayla's replacement...a terminally ill person. He took that suggestion from me."

"I guess that makes sense," I say. "So have you guys discussed what you'll do once we're all gone? You might want to become really good friends with a hospice center or something."

Theo's expression darkens. "Babe, this is so not the time to talk about this. You're not going anywhere."

I shrug. "I will someday. Even if the bracelets come off, I won't get to stick around. I'll age and grow old and die."

"If we take your bracelet off, I'll beg you to become immortal," he says. "I'm not ready to give you up."

"We'd never find another set of immortality stones," I say as I gaze off at the distance. This is the kind of conversation that is very hard to have while looking in someone's eyes. "You know the Dover clan won't give us one of theirs."

"There are other ways," he says. "Find an immortal who is ready to leave the world and has no use for their stones. We'd have to beat everyone else in line to get one, but it can be done."

"I'm not leaving Riley," I say. As if reading my mind, she looks up from her chair at the dinner table. She's wearing a sombrero too, but it dwarfs her tiny head, making her look like one of the kids around her. She grins and waves at me. I wave back.

"We should join the party," I say, taking Theo's hand and squeezing it. "There's plenty of time to talk about how I'm going to die later. Right now, let's just have fun."

Theo smiles and the knot in my chest tightens. I push it back as we join the table. The kids need love and family right now. That's what I'll be for them, as long as I can.

Dinner flies by with laughter and jokes and delicious food. The girls start begging to jump in the pool, but I make them wait thirty minutes so their food can digest. Kyle and Riley become the margarita machine's biggest fans. Soon, they're singing along with the Spanish music they don't even know the words to. The sun is setting on another beautiful Texas summer evening. In all, the night has been perfect.

THE IMMORTAL BOND

"Cara!" Maddie, a little girl with long black hair and the world's biggest pout on her face calls my name. "Are there more cookies inside?"

"I don't think there's any more of these," I say, looking at the empty tray. "Chef baked them special for tonight."

"I can ask him to make more," Theo offers.

"It's okay," she says, crossing her hands over her chest. "I just wanted one sugar cookie and one chocolate chip but there's only one of each one left."

There's a sugar cookie on her plate, and a chocolate chip cookie in Ashlee's hand next to her. "Here," Ashlee says, putting the cookie on her plate. "You can have mine, it's okay."

"No, I don't want to take yours," she says, putting it back on Ashlee's plate. "I just wanted to taste both of them."

Riley walks over, pushing her sombrero up so it stays out of her eyes. "I have an idea, kids." She breaks both cookies in half and then presses the halves together to form two cookies that are half sugar, half chocolate chip. "Perfect!" she says, giving each kid one of the double cookies.

"Thank you!" the girls shout in unison.

Kyle says something and Riley laughs. Conversations flutter to life and everyone's going on with their night, but I can't stop looking at those cookies.

"Theo," I say, my voice shaky. I reach for his arm and grip it tightly, my fingers digging into his skin. My vision fades out around the sides, until the only thing I can see is his face. My heart is pounding and sweat breaks out across my forehead, and now that I've had this idea, it's all I can think of.

"Oh my God," I say in a voice that doesn't even feel like mine.

Theo's brows wrinkle in concern. "What is it babe? Are you okay?"

"Perpetual lifeblood," I say. Riley stops talking mid-sentence and looks over at me. I stand up. "I know how to save us."

THIRTY

It takes every ounce of energy I have to wait until the dinner is over. Theo and Riley practically attach themselves to me, hovering over me like I might disappear at any moment. I told him we have to wait until dinner is over and the kids are in bed before I tell them about my idea.

If this works, it'll be the best day of my life.

If it doesn't, it'll be the last.

For now, I want to enjoy my new family for a just a little while longer. When dinner is over, and the kids are shuttled off to their rooms to shower and get ready for bed, I tell Malina to start reading a bedtime story to the younger kids if I'm not there by nine. I send up a prayer that I will be here to read to the kids tonight, and that more than that, I will no longer be mortal.

I tell Riley and Kyle to meet us in the library. It seems only fitting to try it out here, in the room with the book that taught us everything we know about immortality. Theo is quiet, a little ruffled around the edges. I think he hoped I'd tell him my theory back at dinner, but I've kept it to myself. Part of me likes the suspense, but the other part of me is hoping this will work. I'm pretty sure it will. So much, that I'm about to risk my life with it.

I stand with Theo in the middle of the library while we wait on Riley and Kyle. He watches me, his golden eyes never leaving me as I pace the length of the carpet in the middle of the room. "Babe, I love you," I say, stopping in front of him.

"What are we doing?" he says, gripping my arms tightly.

"We're testing out a theory."

The door opens. Riley and Kyle enter. Kyle's looking a little green with worry, but Riley's face lights up when she sees me.

"Spill it," she says, scampering up to me with delight in her eyes. "How are you going to save us?"

"Perpetual lifeblood," I say. Theo and Kyle exchange a glance, but Riley nods.

"Did you figure out what that means?"

"I think so." Riley's grin is contagious, so now I'm smiling even though I'm still a little nervous. "Theo, you said you knew of an immortal who fell in love with this lifeblood a long time ago, but you never knew what happened to her."

"We still don't know," he says.

"I think I do. She didn't become an immortal, but she didn't have to die either. When we were in the Dover castle, I noticed the necklace Lord Marcus's wife was wearing was kind of odd. It had a big band through the middle of it, and I didn't know why you'd cover up such a beautiful stone. Lord Marcus had the same thing." I look at my bracelet. "Then it hit me. She doesn't have one stone. She has two."

The room goes as silent as the pages of the books around us. I reach into my pocket and pull out a dagger that I'd stolen from Lady Em's jewelry box. The blade is short and sharp, the handle encrusted with precious gems.

I turn my wrist over and press the point of the dagger into the center of my immortality stone. Theo inhales sharply as I press it down, the blade cutting into the stone easier than I'd imagined. The stone breaks in half, a perfect cut. All eyes are on me as I twist and slide off one half of the stone. I pull it off the bracelet and hold my breath.

Nothing happens.

I place the loose half of my stone into Theo's hand and then lean up on my toes and kiss him. I reach inside his shirt and take his necklace, cupping it in the palm of my hand. "It can't be away from my skin for very long," he says softly.

"I'll only be a second," say, smiling up at him before I pierce the dagger into his stone, breaking it perfectly in half again. It's almost as if the stones were created to be split like this, I think as I slide out the top half of his stone. I take mine from his hand and place it back into the setting. The two halves pull together as if magnetized. I press the pendant back to Theo's chest, then place his half of the stone onto my bracelet. The same thing happens—both stones press together in the center.

I take a deep breath and look into his eyes. "I feel fine," I say.

He nods. "Me too."

"Perpetual lifeblood," Riley breathes. "Oh my God, you did it."

"What does this mean?" Kyle says, his own hand touching his necklace on top of his shirt.

"I think it means we'll both live forever," I say. "I'm giving him life while he's giving me life. It goes on forever."

Theo scoops me into his arms, lifting me off my feet. "You are amazing," he says, holding me tightly. When he pulls away, there are tears in his eyes. "I never have to lose you," he says.

I grab his shoulders and kiss him with all that I have. "I hope you're okay with that."

"Are you kidding?" he says, grinning from ear to ear. "This is a dream come true."

"Okay lovebirds," Riley says, yanking the dagger out of my pocket. "Kyle, are you with me?"

He rips the button right off his shirt, pulling open the fabric to reveal his necklace. "There's no one else I'd rather be bonded to for life," he says with a playful grin. "Let's do this."

We split their stones and the process goes perfectly. After a little while of jumping up and down and crying in my best friend's arms, we realize that this is the start of a new life. A life of happiness and family and love. An immortal life, forever bonded with the people we care about.

It's getting late, and I still owe a bedtime story to the younger kids, but we call an emergency meeting with the other adults. I explain it all to them, and everyone eagerly agrees to be bonded to their immortal or lifeblood. Since our pilot is several hours away, we agree to wait until the morning to complete everyone else's perpetual lifeblood transformation. Everything goes smoothly, and for the first time in a long time, I can breathe easily. There is hope for the future, and I've never felt so alive.

"What is this about?" I ask Theo as we make our way through the mansion.

"No clue, but for once, I'm not internally freaking out at the idea of a meeting," Theo says, tossing me a grin.

It's been a week since we all became immortal, and Henry just called a meeting. I'm living in Theo's room permanently now, so it feels weird always being on this side of the mansion. After the kids got used to the place, they started wanting more space so we gave them my old room in addition to the other empty rooms. Now they sleep three kids to a room, and they all seem very happy.

Bethany, Nia, and Olivia are doing well, too. Now that we're all immortals, it feels like we can take things slowly, figure out what we want to do with life. Nia has enrolled in art school and wants to pursue a career as a tattoo artist and Olivia has started cosmetology school. Bethany has been spending a lot of time with the kids, saying she'd love to homeschool them and help out in the future if we ever adopt more orphans. As for me, I've just been taking it easy. I spend the nights with Theo in our bed, and in the mornings, I sleep late curled up next to him. I'm allowing myself to enjoy every little part of the man I love, knowing that nothing will take him away from me any time soon. Eventually, I'd like to find my place in this life. Find a cause I can work on, a way to make the world a little better. For now, I'm hanging out with the kids, redecorating the room I share with Theo, and getting to know my new immortal family on a deeper level.

When we get to the den, everyone is already there. Bethany is sitting weirdly close to Russell on the couch. They're bonded forever now, and although I never pictured them as a couple, I can kind of see it now. I think they like each other. It's an unusual pairing, but it's cute anyway.

"Theo, Henry says, dipping his head toward him. "I'll get right to the point."

Nerves fly around in my stomach because Henry is being so formal. It almost feels like how a meeting with Alexo used to feel. Theo must sense it too, because his shoulder stiffen.

Henry's stoic expression turns to a smile. "Every immortal clan has a leader. It's usually the eldest of the group, or so we've seen with our research. But we have chosen you."

Henry gestures to me. "And Cara. You two have saved our clan and helped reshape it into what it is now. We want to keep the tradition going. We want to be a clan that goes down in the history books for good, not evil. We will swear an oath to protect each other for the rest of our days."

Everyone in the room stands, even Riley, who winks at me. It all feels so formal. Henry holds out a hand to Theo. "Brother, do you accept?"

Theo looks at me. I nod and he shakes Henry's hand. "I accept."

Henry pulls him into a hug and then steps in front of me. "I would be honored to call you sister," he says. "Do you accept?"

I take his hand and shake it. I only say one word, but it's filled with the promise of all of the good things to come.

"Yes."

The End

Thank you for reading The Immortal Bond! If you enjoyed the book, please consider leaving a review on Amazon or Goodreads. It doesn't even have to be long; just one sentence helps out a lot!
Click here to leave a review

Want to be the first to know about new books, exclusive giveaways, and more? Join my monthly newsletter! Each month is packed with at least one book giveaway, gift card giveaways, eBook deals, and news in the book world. You can unsubscribe at any time.
Click here to sign up.

AMY SPARLING

♡ Amy

ALSO BY AMY SPARLING

Believe in Me
He's got fame. She's got nothing. Jett and Keanna's epic love story unfolds over this 8 book series.

The Team Loco Series
Three famous dirt bike racers and the girls who win their heart. A sweet YA romance series.

Ella's Twisted Senior Year
When a tornado takes her home, Ella is forced to move in with the boy who broke her heart.

Sweets High Romance Series
A contemporary teen romance series based on three couples that go to the same school. These books can be read in any order.

ABOUT THE AUTHOR

Amy Sparling is the bestselling author of books for teens and the teens at heart. She lives on the coast of Texas with her family, her spoiled rotten pets, and a huge pile of books. She graduated with a degree in English and has worked at a bookstore, coffee shop, and a fashion boutique. Her fashion skills aren't the best, but luckily she turned her love of coffee and books into a writing career that means she can work in her pajamas. Her favorite things are coffee, book boyfriends, and Netflix binges.

She's always loved reading books from R. L. Stine's Fear Street series, to The Baby Sitter's Club series by Ann, Martin, and of course, Twilight. She started writing her own books in 2010 and now publishes several books a year. Amy loves getting messages from her readers and responds to every single one! Connect with her on one of the links below.

Printed by Amazon Italia Logistica S.r.l.
Torrazza Piemonte (TO), Italy